"So just who is going to be my bodyguard?"

O'Halloran's gaze locked with hers. Her heart slammed against her chest as he held the door and stepped inside the elevator. As one big hand cupped her jaw, she acknowledged that somehow she had managed to completely misread the situation.

His head dipped. She had a fractured moment to log the masculine scents of soap and skin, the heat blasting off his body. His mouth brushed hers once, twice, then settled more firmly.

Heat and sensation shot through her as he angled her jaw to deepen the kiss. A split second later, O'Halloran released her and stepped back out into the hall.

He hit the close button. "Honey, who do you think is guarding you? I am."

O'HALLORAN'S LADY

LADY

BY
FIONA BRAND

First published in Great Britain 2013
by Mills & Boon, an imprint of Harlequin (UK) Limited,
Eton House, 18-24 Paradise Road, Richmond, Surrey TW9 1SR

© Fiona Gillibrand 2012

ISBN: 978 0 263 90350 8
ebook ISBN: 978 1 472 00703 2

46-0313

Harlequin (UK) policy is to use papers that are natural, renewable and recyclable products and made from wood grown in sustainable forests. The logging and manufacturing processes conform to the legal environmental regulations of the country of origin.

Printed and bound in Spain
by Blackprint CPI, Barcelona

Fiona Brand lives in the sunny Bay of Islands, New Zealand. Now that both her sons are grown, she continues to love writing books and gardening. After a life-changing time in which she met Christ, she has undertaken study for a bachelor of theology and has become a member of The Order of St Luke, Christ's healing ministry.

To The Lord, who really did renew my strength while I was writing this book.

"Guard me as the apple of your eye; hide me in the shadow of your wings."
—Psalm 17

Acknowledgments:
Huge thanks to Stacy Boyd, my editor,
for her patience, expertise, encouragement and grace.
Thank you!

Prologue

Disbelief and cold fury gripped Branden Tell as he sat in the echoing solitude of a cavernous warehouse. Motes of dust lit by beams of late afternoon sun drifted through the air as he read Jenna Whitmore's latest romantic suspense novel.

The words on the page seemed to swim and shimmer before his eyes. But no matter how hard or how long he looked, the truth he thought had been lost in the smoke and fire and confusion of the past kept stubbornly reforming.

Six ugly letters spelling out *m-u-r-d-e-r*. Black ink on a pulp page: pointing the finger at him.

He broke out in a sweat; his heart was pounding as if he had just run a race. He wondered how much Whitmore actually knew. Given that she had not gone to the police but instead had included the details of his past crime in a novel, he had to assume she probably didn't know much. He was willing to bet she had stumbled on her conclusions by pure, dumb luck.

He blinked rapidly and tried to think. Would anyone else notice the connections Jenna Whitmore had unwittingly made and link them to her cousin's death in a house fire six years ago?

The answer swam up out of the acid burn in his stomach. Marc O'Halloran, the hotshot police detective who had been hunting him with a dogged, relentless focus for the past six years. He would.

Two months ago, almost to the day, O'Halloran had walked into a security firm Branden supplied with alarms while he had been there delivering a consignment. The second he had recognised O'Halloran, he had turned on his heel and left, but he had felt O'Halloran's gaze drilling into his back as he walked.

The close shave had almost given him a heart attack. There was no way O'Halloran could have recognised him, because he had been wearing overalls and a ball cap pulled low over his forehead. He would have looked like a hundred other tradesmen or casual labourers. He had found out later that O'Halloran had been following up on a lead on the fire that had killed his wife and child, checking on who had installed the alarm in his house.

Six years and O'Halloran was still hunting him.

The fear that gripped Branden for long, dizzying moments almost spiralled out of control. He had to think.

No. He had to *do* something.

Snapping the book closed, he found himself staring at the photograph of Jenna Whitmore on the back cover.

She was nothing like her cousin, "The Goddess."

Natalie had been blond, leggy, tanned and gorgeous. Jenna was her polar opposite; dark-haired and pale-skinned with a firm chin and the kind of high, moulded cheekbones that invested her dark eyes with an incisive quality he had always found unsettling.

In that instant, a crude solution formed. After years of wondering when he would appear in one of Jenna's books as a hero, or maybe as some interesting second-ary character who could become a hero, he had finally made an appearance, as the villain.

He had mostly read all ten books now, even though he hated reading, because he needed to know if Jenna had written about their shared past. He had found out, just before everything had come to pieces, that Natalie had confided to Jenna that she had a secret friend. For years he had been certain that any evidence that he was linked with Natalie had burned along with everything else in the house, but now he had to assume that Whit-more, who had been close to Natalie, could be sitting on some hard evidence. Since Natalie had been crazy about social networking, it would probably be in the form of emails on Jenna's computer.

His fingers tightened on the novel. In all of the books, the hero had never changed. Whitmore had called him Cutler, Smith, James, Sullivan and a whole host of other names, but the name changes didn't disguise the fact that she was really writing about O'Halloran. The same hard-ass, hero type who had made a habit of ruining Branden's life through the years.

His jaw clenched. O'Halloran had even dated then married The Goddess, the girl *he* should have had.

The distant sound of sirens jerked his head up. For a split second, he thought that it was too late, that the cops were coming for him. He stared a little wildly at the familiar, ordered gloom of the warehouse, and his desk with its neat piles of forms, installation orders and packing notes.

Clamping down on the burst of fear, he strained to listen.

The sirens were receding.

He remembered the fire that, by now, would be a raging inferno. The chemical warehouse would burn for days, soaking up police hours with roadblocks and evacuation procedures. He was safe, for now.

But that didn't change the fact that it was past time he left the country. After the scare two months ago, he had systematically put plans in place: a new identity complete with passport and bank accounts. He had even bought a condo on Australia's Gold Coast. He just needed a little more time to liquidate assets.

He stared at Jenna's face, which, after years of being pretty but slightly plump, had metamorphosed into something approaching beauty. Turning the book over, he studied the cover, his jaw locking. Just to tick him off, the guy they'd put on the cover even looked a little like O'Halloran.

Old rage, fuelled by his intense annoyance that cutting and running was going to cost him big-time, gave birth to a stunning idea. He didn't know why he hadn't thought of it before.

If he was going to lose his business and his expensive, commercial property, which he hadn't been able to offload, damned if he would leave Whitmore and O'Halloran feeling like winners. Instead of venting his temper by flinging the book at a wall of boxes filled with the latest generation of security systems and automated gates, he placed it carefully on his desk, checked his wristwatch and sat down at his computer.

He had almost forgotten that tomorrow was the anniversary of Natalie's death.

Once again it was time to prove that he was a lot more intelligent and creative than anyone had ever given him credit for, past or present.

Including Jenna Whitmore and Marc O'Halloran.

Chapter 1

Pleasurable anticipation hummed through Jenna as she slit open a box stamped with the familiar logo of her publisher. Setting the knife she'd used to cut the packaging tape down on her desk, she extracted a glossy, trade-sized paperback: her latest novel. Glancing at the back cover copy, she flipped the book over to check out the cover...and for long seconds her mind went utterly blank.

Swamping shadows flowed over broad, sleek shoulders and a lean, muscled torso. Moonlight glimmered across sculpted cheekbones, a blade-straight nose and a rock-solid jaw. By some trick of the light, for a heart-pounding moment, the dark, molten gaze of the man depicted on the cover, shaded by inky lashes, appeared to stare directly into hers.

Her breath hitched in her throat as her sunny office

faded and she was spun back nine years, to the stifling heat of a darkened, moonlight-dappled apartment, Marc O'Halloran and a fatal attraction she thought she had controlled.

Memories flooded back, some bittersweet, others hot and edged and earthy. The clean scent of his skin as he had shrugged out of his shirt, the sensual shock of his kiss. Heart-stopping moments later, the weight of his body pressing down on hers...

Groping blindly for her chair, Jenna sat down. Her heart was hammering and her legs felt as limp as noodles, which was crazy. After nine years, the few weeks during which she had dated O'Halloran—and the one out-of-control night after they had broken up when she had made love with him—shouldn't have still registered. Especially since she had spent more time avoiding him than she had ever spent mooning over him.

More to the point, she had gotten over him. It had taken time, the process had been a lot more difficult than she had expected, but she had moved on with her life.

Taking a steadying breath, she forced herself to dispassionately study the masculine image that decorated the front cover of the novel.

It wasn't O'Halloran. Plain common sense dictated that fact. Like her, O'Halloran lived in Auckland, and the book had been published and printed in New York. The cover model would have been someone picked from an agency list in Manhattan.

By some freak chance, whoever had designed the cover had just somehow managed to choose a model who looked like O'Halloran.

At a second glance, the differences were clear. The

model's nose was thinner, longer, and his mouth was fuller. As broodingly handsome as he was, overall he was just a little too perfect. He lacked the masculine toughness to his features that was a defining character-istic of O'Halloran, the remote quality to his gaze that spelled out that O'Halloran was neither gym-pumped nor cosmetically enhanced. He was that breed apart: a cop.

Frowning, she replaced the book back in the open carton, closed the flaps and stowed the box under the desk, out of sight.

Feeling distinctly unsettled, she strolled out to the kitchen and made herself a cup of tea, using the calming routine of selecting a fragrant fruit variety and a pretty mug to put herself back into work mode. The distant sound of a siren almost made her spill hot tea over her fingers and shoved another memory back at her.

The last time she had seen O'Halloran had been from a distance, four years ago, when she had narrowly avoided running into him in town. Dressed in a suit and wearing a shoulder holster, he had been on police business. The grim remoteness of his expression and the presence of the weapon had underlined the reason she couldn't afford him in her life. Maybe her reaction had been a little over-the-top, but after losing both her father and her fiancé to military front lines, the last thing she had needed was to fall for a police detective. Like soldiers, cops bled. More to the point, in the line of duty, they died.

She had seen what being married to a soldier had done to her mother; the separations and the constant fear, the shock when the bad news finally came fol-lowed by intense, bone-deep grief.

Less than a year later, her mother had died of cancer. Jenna had read the specialists' reports and listened to the medical experts but that hadn't shifted her inner certainty that what her mother had really died of had been a broken heart.

The final kicker had been when, even knowing the risk, straight out of high school she had gotten engaged to a soldier. Dane had also been her best friend, which was probably why he had slipped beneath her defences. But that hadn't changed the fact that he had died in a hot, sun-blasted foreign country on some covert mission.

A week after it had happened she had finally been informed. In the midst of her grief, somehow the fact that Dane had been lying cold and dead in a hospital morgue for seven days, while she had spent that time shopping and planning for a wedding, had added to her disorientation. She had loved Dane. She should have known something was wrong. Instead, she had been choosing invitations and having fittings for a dress she would never wear. Her own lack of connection to a man she had been prepared to marry had been subtly shocking. It had underlined a distance, a separation, from Dane that she had witnessed in her parents' marriage, and in that moment she had understood something basic about herself. She couldn't live that life.

She needed to be loved. And not only loved, but also to be the cherished focus of the man she chose.

Fingers shaking slightly, a ridiculous overreaction, she placed the mug on a coaster and seated herself in front of her computer.

Maybe her need for a deep, committed love was unrealistic and overly romantic, but she knew her nature.

As much as she had wanted to share her life with Dane, she knew now that it would never have worked. She couldn't compete with the adrenaline and danger of combat and undercover missions.

She couldn't afford to fall for anyone who was going to place themselves on the front lines, either militarily or as a civilian.

She refreshed the screen and found herself staring at a manuscript page from the book she was currently editing. A love scene.

Jamming the lid of the laptop down, she strode out of her office and grabbed a jacket. She needed air, lots of it. Stepping out onto her porch, she closed the front door of her house and locked it behind her.

But slamming the lid on the Pandora's Box of her past was more difficult. As she walked, more memories flickered in a series of freeze frames. The undertow of fascination she had felt the first time she had seen O'Halloran. The bone-melting excitement of their first kiss, as his big hand had curled around her nape and his mouth had settled on hers.

Her stomach clenched. Emotions and sensations she had thought long dead flared to life. She felt like a sleeper waking up, her pulse too fast, her skin ultra-sensitive; she could smell more, hear more, feel more. It had been years since she had felt so alive and, with a jolt, she realised that it had been years since she had felt anything much at all.

As a professional writer, her life was necessarily ordered and quiet. She worked long hours to meet her deadlines, and most evenings she went online to chat with fans or reply to emails. A couple of times a year she travelled to conferences and did promotional tours, coinciding with the release of her books. Apart from socialising for business, *cloistered* was the term that came to mind.

At the age of twenty-nine, thanks to her solitary career, and the pressure of work created by the success of her books, she had a gap the size of a yawning abyss in her social and sexual life.

Thanks to an inconvenient perfectionist streak that had seemed to become more pronounced with every year, she had trouble meeting anyone with whom she could visualise having an intimate, meaningful relationship.

As in sex.

Another hot flashback to the night in O'Halloran's apartment made her stomach clench and her breasts tighten. She definitely wasn't a nun, but for nine years she had lived like one. She hadn't set out to be so isolated and alone—lacking almost any semblance of human warmth in her life, lacking the mate she wanted—it was just the way things had worked out.

Or was it?

The feeling of constriction in her chest increased as she examined the extremity of her reaction to the cover of her new book.

She had gotten over the loss of both of her parents; and she had gotten over Dane. The fact that they had never slept together, because he had surprised her by proposing literally minutes before he had shipped out, had meant they had never had the chance at a full, intimate relationship. As much as she'd loved him, in her mind, he would forever remain a part of her childhood and teen years, not a part of her adult life.

For the past few years, as much as she had wanted to

find someone she could fall for, marry and have babies with, she hadn't come even remotely close.

As outwardly attractive as her dates had been, there had always been something wrong. They had been either too short, or too tall, or their personalities just hadn't appealed. She had been picky to the point that most of her friends had long since given up introducing her to eligible bachelors.

Now she had to consider that the reason she had never been able to move on to the healthy, normal relationship she craved was because at some deep, instinctual level, O'Halloran still mattered. That in the weeks they had dated—and maybe because he was the first and only man she had ever made love with—in a primitive, purely masculine way, he had somehow managed to imprint himself on her so deeply that she had never been able to open up to another relationship.

She stopped dead, barely noticing the trees that dappled the sidewalk with chilly shade, or the young mother with a stroller who walked past her. It was even possible that in some sneaky, undermining way, she had fallen for O'Halloran because of his dangerous occupation; that the reason she wasn't attracted to a "normal" nine-to-five guy was because her years on military bases had hardwired her to be attracted to edgy alpha types.

She forced herself back into motion again, automatically turning down the street that led to a small park. The sick feeling in her stomach increased as she strolled, along with the desire to bang her head against the nearest wall she could find in the hope that that salutary action might jolt some sense into her.

She felt like she was staring down a long tunnel inscribed with the words *obvious reason for multiple relationship failures.*

Now was not a good time to realise that as hard as she'd tried to bury her past and the attraction to O'Halloran, like the heroine in her book, she hadn't succeeded.

And now it had come back to bite her.

Two hours before midnight, and the clock was ticking....

On edge and gripped by a tense air of expectation, *haunted by a past that had teeth*, Marc O'Halloran, clad in a pair of grey interlock track pants that hung low on his hips, closed the door on his private gym. A towel from the shower he'd just taken slung over one muscled shoulder, he padded through the darkened luxury of his Auckland waterfront apartment, not bothering to turn on lights.

Stepping out on his terrace, he allowed the damp chill to settle around him like a shroud as he stared broodingly out at the spectacular view of the Waitemata Harbour. To one side, the graceful arch of the Harbour Bridge was almost obscured by a wraithlike veil of mist, and the headland that was Devonport, with its naval base and steep streets crammed with houses, glittered quietly.

Below, street-lighting from the busy viaduct glowed through the wrought-iron railing that edged his terrace. The pulse of neon lighting from the busy restaurants and bars flickered garishly in time with the beat of a jazz band, adding a strident, unsettling rhythm to the night.

As Marc stepped back into his lounge, the glass of

the bi-fold doors threw his reflection back at him. The scars that marred his right shoulder and his forearms were an unwelcome reminder of the house fire that had taken the lives of his wife and small son six years ago. Luckily, the broken neck, courtesy of the falling beam that had also damaged his shoulder, hadn't required surgery or scars, just months in a neck brace.

Nothing too major, he thought grimly. He had lived.

Walking through to the laundry, he tossed the towel in a basket, grabbed a fresh T-shirt out of the dryer and pulled it on. Minutes later, after collecting a glass of ice water from the kitchen, he entered his study. The view of the port, and the shimmer of city lights, winked out as he switched on a lamp and unlocked his briefcase.

Bypassing the correspondence file from the security business in which he was a partner, he searched out the bookstore bag that contained the novel he had bought during his lunch break.

Hot off the presses, the latest Jenna Whitmore.

With an effort of will, he shook off the miasma of guilt that went with the impending anniversary of his wife's and child's deaths, and the hot burn of frustration that the only crime he had never been able to solve had been the murder of his own family. Dropping the paper bag on the gleaming surface of his desk, he studied the cover with its tense, dark backdrop.

The book was a suspense, but also a romance, not something he normally read, but he had once dated Jenna so, out of curiosity, he had bought her first book.

To his surprise he had been hooked from the first page. Despite her link to his past—one of the links that he had systematically eradicated from his life—Jenna's books had become a guilty pleasure and a deep, dark secret. If the detectives he had used to work with at Auckland Central or his business partner in the security business he now part-owned, Ben McCabe, ever found out that he read romances, he would never live it down.

Automatically, he turned the book over and examined the publicity photo on the back cover. Despite the tension that coursed through him, he found himself gradually relaxing. Jenna, who also happened to be his dead wife's cousin, frequently changed her hair. The constant process of reinvention never failed to fascinate Marc.

This time she had opted for caramel streaks to complement her natural dark colour and a long, layered cut. As modern as the cut was, the overall effect was oddly elegant.

When they had dated, even though it had only been for a short time, he had liked Jenna's hair exactly how it had been, long and soft and completely natural. Although he was willing to be converted by the lighter streaks and the sexy cut, which highlighted the delicate curve of her cheekbones and made her dark eyes look long and unexpectedly smoky.

Settling into a black leather armchair set to one side of the desk, he propped his bare feet on an ottoman and flipped open the book.

The vice-like grip of guilt and frustration, the knowledge that approximately an hour from now, the man who had murdered his family would contact him, slowly eased as he forced himself to turn pages.

Reluctantly engrossed by words that flowed with a neat, no-nonsense economy, Marc ceased to notice the silence of his Auckland apartment and the inner tension that sawed at his nerves.

As the minutes flowed past, he sank deeper into the story, noting that it was her best yet. The hero, Cutler, a detective, had a lot of grit and texture, and the procedural details were right on the button.

The plot reached a crescendo as Cutler and the heroine, Sara, after a series of tantalising near misses, finally, electrifyingly, made it to Cutler's apartment.

Unexpected tension burned through Marc as he was drawn through the passionate interlude. By the time he had reached the end of the love scene, he had ceased to visualise the damp chill of a rainy afternoon, and instead his mind had shifted to another season, another room, filled with heated shadows and moonlight....

The sound of distant sirens brought his head up, an automatic reaction that, after two years out of the force, he hadn't been able to kick.

His jaw tightened. Thinking about Jenna was crazy. Since his wife, Natalie, and their baby had died in a house fire, Marc had had no interest in another committed relationship. He had enough guilt to process.

Added to that, he hadn't seen Jenna in years and, apart from one unplanned episode *after* they had broken up and following a near accident with a car, they had never made it anywhere near a bedroom.

A vivid memory of Jenna scrambling off the couch they'd ended up sprawled across nine years ago, moonlight flowing over the pale curves of her body, jolted him out of the story altogether. A new tension coursing through him, he put the book down.

Broodingly, he recalled flickering images of her fastening the low back of her dress. The tense expression on her face as she'd searched for shoes and her handbag. She had refused a lift and waved her cell at him, indicating she had already called a cab.

Marc hadn't pushed it. The fact that they had slept together after they had broken up had underpinned the awkward minutes until the cab she'd ordered had slid into his drive.

The blinding fact that it had been Jenna's first time had added to the tension, although Jenna had brushed it off. He could still remember her quiet assertion that if it hadn't been for the adrenaline-charged moments when Marc had stepped in and saved her from being hit by an obviously drunk driver, what had just taken place on his couch would never have happened.

Marc had had to accept her self-contained approach. He'd been aware that she hadn't liked the fact that he was a police detective or that he commanded an armed first response team, the Special Tactics Squad.

When he'd started dating Jenna's cousin, Natalie had held a similar view. She hadn't liked the long work hours, the seaminess or the danger, and she hadn't liked being closed out of that part of his life.

After the first year of marriage, Natalie had wanted him to quit the force and go back to law, in which he had a degree. His parents, both lawyers, had their own successful law firm, and she hadn't been able to understand why he didn't want to be a part of it.

The argument had been the start of a wedge in their relationship he hadn't been able to mend. When it came down to it he preferred the practical, hands-on approach to justice that police work offered him, rather than the intricacies of negotiating the legal system.

The whoosh of incoming mail on his computer brought his head up. Tension slammed into Marc as he noted the time: eleven o'clock, exactly. He had been so engrossed by the book, and the window into the past it had opened, that he had forgotten the time.

Jaw taut, he strolled to his desk and read the email.

The message was simple. The same message he had received every year for the past five years on the anniversary of the house fire. A fire he had been certain had been started deliberately, an act of revenge by the notorious criminal family he had been investigating at the time.

Catch me if you can.

Cold anger edged with frustration burned through Marc. Although, there was a certain relief in the fact that the waiting was over. Punching the print button, he waited for the hard copy of the taunting message to feed out.

He had never been able to trace the message to an actual person, or prove the message was connected to the crime. Each time he had traced the email to the server, the name and physical address hadn't panned out. The trail had been predictable, a string of stolen identities, mostly deceased persons, through which cash payments via fake bank accounts had been made. Non-existent people and random addresses, all added up to a wild-goose chase.

Despite his contention that the house fire that had killed his family and put him in hospital had been a copycat crime committed by someone other than the serial arsonist the police had been hunting at the time, no one had bought into his theory. Since the arsonist had died during a shootout just after he had tried to set a police station on fire, there was no one to question. The supposed perpetrator was dead, the fires had stopped, end of story.

Grimly, Marc filed the message with the others in a heavy manila folder that contained every police or fire department report and newspaper article relating to the fire and the death of his wife and small son.

Maybe he was being obsessive about his hunt for a shadowy criminal. Maybe he had been wrong all along, and the investigative team who had sifted through what was left of his house were right. The psychological reports that had finished his police career were adamant on that point.

Even so, Marc couldn't let go. The two people he had cared about most had died of smoke inhalation when he should have been at home, protecting them. Instead, he had used his free time—the quality time he should have been spending with his family—working surveillance on a powerful criminal family who had slipped the net on his last operation.

Courtesy of the injuries he had sustained getting Natalie and tiny Jared out of the house, he had ended up flat on his back in hospital for weeks. Further months on sick leave while he had waited for his neck and shoulder to heal, followed by reconstructive surgery for his shoulder, had added to his frustration. By the time he had been fit for duty again, the case had been closed.

He was no longer a detective, but he had not dropped the case. Thanks to bequests from his grandparents and a talent for investment, Marc was independently wealthy. Enough so that he had been able to buy in to the security business he presently co-owned and could afford to fund an ongoing private investigation into the case.

When he had finally woken up from sedation in hospital to find that both Natalie and Jared had died, grief and cold fury hit him like a blow. Despite the gloomy prognosis on his fractured neck, he had made a vow.

It was too late to save his family, but he would use his talent for solving crime, which had resulted in their deaths, to bring the man he was certain had murdered them to justice.

He hadn't made a significant breakthrough in the six years he had chased leads and walked down investigative dead alleys. But the murderer who was taunting him would make a mistake, and when he did Marc would be waiting.

It was just a matter of time.

Chapter 2

An hour before midnight, *and the anniversary of Natalie's death.*

Jenna walked through the darkened parking lot of the shopping mall in central Auckland, glad for the casual warmth of jeans and boots and the cashmere coat belted around her waist to push back the chill.

Overhead, thick clouds hid any hint of moon or stars. On the ground, streamers of cold mist rose off damp concrete and wreathed ranks of wet, glistening cars, adding a dismal air to a chilly winter's night.

Behind her, footsteps echoed, the tread uncannily mirroring her own so that at first she had thought the step was just an echo.

Adjusting her grip on the carrier bags, which thumped against her legs with every step, she walked a little faster, although speeding up was an effort. She was tired from a string of late nights and too many hours spent at her computer. From the scratchiness at the back of her throat and the sensitivity of her eyes, she suspected she was also coming down with a virus. The diagnosis was further confirmed by the chills that periodically swept her and the aches and pains that seemed to have sunk into her bones.

She strained to listen behind her and logged the moment the change in her pace put whoever was following her out of sync with her step.

Automatically, her too-fertile writer's brain analysed the tread. There was no sharp tap of heels. The sound was more deliberate, solid, so it was likely the person wasn't female. He was probably one of the young guys she had seen hanging at the entrance to the mall on her way out.

Now that she knew there was definitely someone behind her, the fact that he hadn't either veered off, or walked briskly past, but had chosen to remain approximately the same distance behind and maintain her snail's pace sent a chill shooting down her spine. The farther she walked away from the lights of the mall, the more sinister the trailing footsteps had become.

As she approached an SUV, in an effort to catch a glimpse of whoever was behind her, she slowed and glanced in the wing mirror.

Apart from wet cars and dark, thin air wreathed with mist, as far back as she could see, the parking lot appeared to be empty.

In that same instant, she registered that the footsteps had stopped. Somehow that was more frightening than if she had actually caught a glimpse of whoever had been following her.

Heart pounding, she swung around and skimmed the rows of cars. The background hum of city traffic, the distant blare of a car horn, seemed to increase the sense of isolation in the misty parking lot, the muffling, encapsulating silence.

Somewhere off to the left a car engine coughed to life. She let out a relieved breath. Mystery solved. Whoever had been behind her must have stopped to unlock their car just seconds before she had gotten up the courage to check on him.

Castigating herself for the paranoia that had leaped at her from nowhere, she adjusted her grip on the carrier bags, and continued on toward her car.

She had parked on the far side of the lot, next to the clothing department stores, because when she'd made the decision to do some late night shopping, she hadn't originally counted on buying groceries. Her goal had simply been to get out of her house, away from her office and the memories that, at this time of year, always seemed to press in on her.

Normally a dedicated shopper, happy to price and compare until she found exactly what she wanted, she'd found the items she'd needed too quickly. Unwilling to leave the bright cheerfulness of the mall and the simple human comfort of being amongst people, even if no one bothered to speak to her unless she handed money over a counter, she'd strolled on into the supermarket.

Shopping this late was ridiculous; the task could have waited until morning. But tomorrow was the anniversary of her cousin Natalie's death and she hadn't wanted to do anything as frivolous as buy pretty clothes. Especially since her aunt and uncle, who still struggled with their grief, expected her over for dinner.

Behind her, she could hear the car her "stalker" had climbed into accelerating toward the exit, going too fast. She caught a glimpse of a glossy, black sedan, pumped up at the back, and the flare of taillights as he braked. It occurred to her that the car, an Audi, looked like the same model the villain had used in her latest book, which seemed appropriate.

Annoyance at the casual cruelty of the man, if he really had been trying to scare her, replaced the last wimpy remnants of fear. She didn't normally wish bad things on people, but a sudden, vivid fantasy of the Audi being pulled over and the driver being issued with an offence notice was warming.

Feeling a whole lot more cheerful, she angled across the lot toward her car.

Ahead, a noisy group of young people exited the mall and stopped right next to the shiny new Porsche she had bought to celebrate the release of her book. She saw with relief that they were trailed by a uniformed mall security guard who was keeping an eye on them.

Simultaneously she registered that the obnoxious Audi, which had apparently missed the exit ramp, was now doing another circuit of the lot. Distracted by the kids milling around her car, she sped up. As she did so, she automatically hitched the carrier bags higher and in that instant one of the handles broke and the contents of the bag cascaded onto the pavement.

Staggering a little at the sudden release of weight on one side and muttering beneath her breath, Jenna set the bags down. Luckily the bag that had broken had been filled with packets and cans, not fruits and vegetables. One eye on the kids, who were still grouped around her

Porsche, she started retrieving cans, some of which had skittered across the lane.

As she bent to pick up a packet of rice, the throaty sound of an engine caused her to jerk her head up. Twin headlights pinned her. Adrenaline shoved through her veins, momentarily freezing her in place. The black car, which she had momentarily forgotten, was roaring straight for her.

Dropping the rice and cans, she flung herself into a gap between two cars, hitting the wet concrete of the parking lot a split second before the car accelerated past, so close the vibration shimmered up through pavement and hot exhaust filled her nostrils.

Loose hair tangled around her face, Jenna pushed into a sitting position, logging grazed palms that burned, and a knee that seemed temporarily frozen and which would hurt like blazes in a minute or two. Thankfully, her handbag, which had been slung over one shoulder, was on the ground next to her, although the contents, including her car keys and phone, had spilled across the concrete.

"Are you all right?"

The calm male voice jerked her head up. For a split second, heart still pounding with an overload of adrenaline, she saw O'Halloran. The illusion winked out almost immediately since, apart from hair color and a lean, muscular build, the security officer didn't look anything like her long-ago ex.

Although, she could be forgiven the error, she thought a little grimly, as she allowed him to help her to her feet.

The last time she'd had a run-in with a car, nine

years ago to be exact, it *had* been O'Halloran who had come to her rescue.

She noted the name on a badge pinned to the pocket of the security officer's shirt and dredged up a thin smile for Mathews. "I'm fine, thank you. Just a few bruises."

And a whole lot of mangled shopping.

While Mathews asked her questions about the near miss and made some notes, Jenna tested out her knee. It hurt and was already stiffening, but at least she could put weight on it. Although, it would be black and blue by morning.

Limping, she began gathering up her things, starting with the contents of her handbag. The rice was history, grains were scattered all over the concrete, but she found the broken plastic bag and stuffed it into another carrier bag, along with other grocery items that had rolled loose.

Mathews collected the bags containing her dress and shoes and insisted on carrying everything to her car and stowing them for her.

As he closed the passenger side door he cast a steely look at the kids, who had drifted farther down the mall and were now grouped outside a café.

"Are you sure you're okay? If you need medical attention we've got a first-aid station in the mall."

Ignoring the burning pain from the scrapes on her palms, Jenna checked in her handbag, found a business card and handed it to him. "I'm okay. The only thing I'd like is the registration of the vehicle, if you can get it."

He tucked her card in his shirt pocket. "No problem. I'll check out the security footage, but with the lights at this end of the lot knocked out by vandals and the mist, I can't guarantee anything."

Feeling increasingly stiff and sore, Jenna climbed into the leather-scented interior of the Porsche although, for once, she couldn't take pleasure in the car. With a convulsive movement, she locked the doors, fastened her seat belt then sat staring at her shaking hands and grazed palms.

No, she definitely wasn't *okay*.

The driver of the black Audi had to have seen her. She had been standing in the middle of the lane, caught in the glare of his headlights, and yet he hadn't so much as slowed down. If she hadn't gotten out of his way she would have been hit. At the speed he had been travelling, she would have been, at the very least, seriously injured.

Maybe she was going crazy, or she'd written one too many suspense stories, but she was almost certain that what had happened hadn't been either a joke or an accident.

Someone had just tried to kill her.

Lamplight pooled around Jenna as, too wired to sleep after the near miss in the mall parking lot, she set a mug of hot chocolate down on her desk and booted up her computer. Sliding her glasses onto the bridge of her nose, she vetoed any idea that she could work on her manuscript. Since she couldn't settle to sleep, it stood to reason that she was way too jittery to write.

Clicking on the mail icon, she decided to stick with the less brain-intensive task of answering emails until she got tired enough to actually sleep. Her laptop beeped as a small flood of emails filled her inbox.

Minutes later, she opened an email and froze. Fighting a cold sense of disorientation, she pushed her glasses a little higher on her nose and forced herself to reread the message that had just appeared in her fan mail account.

I hate your latest book in which you have portrayed ME as the villin. Besides the romance and the hero being unreel (no one looks that good) the villin is not as bad as you're making out, he deserves a medal for not trying to do away with Sara in the first chapter. Take "Deadly Valentine" off the market NOW. If you don't you will regret it.

Jenna drew a long, impeded breath. As chilling as the content was, and the veiled threat, the writer of the email, ekf235, had no particular literary aspirations. He had misspelt *villain* and *unreal* and had committed the cardinal sin of joining two independent clauses with a comma instead of a semicolon. If her editor, Rachel, saw it, she would have a fit.

Jenna sat back in her office chair, her normal determination to see the positive side of every fan letter she received, even if it was scathingly critical, absent. The misspellings and dreadful grammar, the sideswipe about her characterisation, didn't take away from the fact that whoever had written the letter was nutty enough to think she had patterned the villain on him.

Since Jenna had never heard of ekf235, let alone corresponded with him, that claim was highly unlikely.

For long seconds, Jenna stared at the screen of her laptop, and tried to catalogue all of the men she had known through her life, but her mind seemed to have frozen. It was mild shock, she realized.

For the second time in one night.

Hooking her glasses off the bridge of her nose, she sat back in her chair, and rubbed at the sharp little throb that had developed at her temples.

She was tired and sore, despite taking a couple of painkillers and rubbing arnica and liniment into her bruised knee. She shouldn't have started on emails this late. Buying in to the ramblings of an emotionally disturbed person, who didn't have the courage to reveal their real identity, was always a mistake.

Taking another deep breath, she let it out slowly and tapped the button that generated her auto-reply, thanking the fan. A small whooshing sound indicated that the reply had gone.

She glanced at her collage board, which was littered with all of the various materials she had used as inspiration for the highly successful series of novels that had shot her to the top of bestseller lists.

The only photos she had were those of various male and female models, which she'd cut out of magazines over the years to provide inspiration for her heroes and heroines.

Massaging the throb in her temple with fingers that still shook annoyingly, she wondered what O'Halloran would think about the cowardly, threatening email then pulled herself up short. After the episode with her new book cover, then the moment in the mall parking lot, she had decided that for her own emotional well-being, the sooner she managed to cut O'Halloran out of her life, past and present, the better.

Blinking away tiredness, she examined the rest of the board, which was littered with snapshots and pictures of houses, landscape settings and assorted weaponry.

She had not amassed anything much about a villain. As a rule of thumb, she had found that the less that was said about a villain the better. Mystery was far scarier than knowledge and, besides, fans of her stories responded to the hero, not the bad guy.

Picking up her hot chocolate, she sipped and let her mind go loose, a technique she used to help with memory, especially for allowing seemingly insignificant details to surface. She frowned when her mind remained a stubborn blank.

The person who had emailed had claimed that she had used him as the villain, which meant she must have met him at some stage. There was always the danger that, subliminally, she could have remembered and applied characteristics from someone she had known in her past. In *Deadly Valentine*, she had been influenced by a couple of incidents from the past, but she was also aware that those incidents—the delivery of a single rose and a secret online "lover"—were neither new nor unusual elements.

One thing was sure, no one she had ever met, or knew, came even close to the devious fictional criminal who had hunted Sara down in *Deadly Valentine*.

The only character she had ruthlessly drawn from real life was the heroine, Sara, a private investigator whom Jenna had based on herself. Somehow her own persona and single lifestyle had seemed to fit Sara Chisolm even better than they fitted Jenna.

In the fictional world Sara moved in, living alone was a bonus. Although maybe the fact that Sara was a little on the hard-boiled side and far more confident in the bedroom than Jenna could ever pretend to be had something to do with that.

Her finger hovered over the delete button, but in a moment of caution, she decided she couldn't afford to blot the email out of existence altogether. The meticulous filing habit she had nurtured over the past eight years of researching detective and police procedural material for her books was too ingrained. In eight years she had not deleted one piece of correspondence without first obtaining a hard copy, and she was not starting now.

She didn't expect to hear back from the poisonous fan. Her innocuous thank-you email was designed to neutralise unpleasantness, and it usually worked, but that didn't mean she shouldn't be cautious.

She pressed the print button and waited for the sheet to feed out.

The internet provided a forum for a lot of flaky people. Most of them were harmless. The thought that the vague threat in the email could eventuate into an actual problem was something she was determined she was not going to lose any sleep over, but she couldn't dismiss it altogether.

As a writer, she had lost count of the number of times an inconsequential document had proved pivotal in her fictional investigations. Perhaps that was why the email had felt so chilling.

Shoving the hard copy into the plain folder that contained her negative fan mail, and which she kept in the bottom drawer of her desk, she deleted the email.

On impulse, to balance out the unpleasantness, Jenna opened a folder in which she kept all of the mail she received from the technical experts who helped her with research. She selected the file containing all of the correspondence from Lydell88.

As she read through the last couple of emails, the tension that had gripped her faded. Lydell wasn't exactly a shoulder to cry on, but reading his no-nonsense prose was, in an odd way, steadying.

There was nothing to indicate where Lydell88 lived. All she knew was that he was an Auckland cop with considerable experience, and that he didn't mind answering her occasional questions. She had found him by emailing the Auckland District Office. One of the detectives had eventually responded by supplying her with Lydell88's email address.

Generally he supplied precise police procedural information, but over the years he had begun making incisive, relevant comments about her plots and characterisation, indicating that at some point, he had begun to read her books.

His compliments were sparing, but she valued them all the more for that. When he liked something, he was unequivocal about the matter and she basked in the glow for days.

Lately, he had even begun to suggest plot lines she could develop in future books. The ideas were well thought out and stemmed from an intimate knowledge of her characters and an even better understanding of the criminal mind.

However, she was aware that wasn't what gave her the warm glow of delight every time she opened one of his emails.

Over the years, talking with Lydell88 about the technicalities of developing the police procedural side to her stories had, in an odd way, become the closest thing she had gotten to a date that she could actually enjoy, which was strange considering that he was a cop.

She guessed it came down to mutual interests. They both enjoyed the books, she as the writer, he as a reader and researcher. Somehow, those two things had gelled along with a subtle, intangible quality she could only call chemistry, and they had become immersed, together, in that fictional world.

When her editor had holidayed with her last summer, Jenna had allowed her limited access to the file, keeping the more private exchanges to herself. It had seemed too personal to share the conversations they'd had about the romance of the postwar era, or that Lydell88 thought she should try her hand at writing in that period.

Rachel had been riveted, and they had spent the long summer evenings trying to profile Lydell88. And, more importantly, trying to decide what he looked like.

Jenna hadn't received anything from Lydell88 lately. He generally only ever instigated discussions about her latest book, a line in the sand of which she was sharply aware. Early on, she had considered the fact that he could be either elderly or married, but had rejected both ideas. The tone and style of Lydell88's emails suggested he was younger rather than older, and at no time during their discussions had he ever mentioned a partner, or children, so she assumed he was single.

Respecting his desire for privacy, and relieved that there was no pressure for their discussions to be anything more than they were, she limited her contacts by only initiating correspondence when she started a new book and needed to check facts.

She was waiting with anticipation to see what he thought of *Deadly Valentine*, although it was early days since it had only just been released into stores.

Closing down the program and the laptop, she

hooked her glasses off the bridge of her nose and set them beside the keyboard. The pleasant glow she had received from rereading Lydell88's last email faded as she noticed her bottom drawer, which contained her negative fan mail, wasn't quite closed.

Nudging the drawer shut with her foot, she collected her empty mug and switched out the lights, but the damage was done. As hard as she tried to dismiss it, the unpleasant threat delivered by ekf235 had rocked her.

Feeling abruptly exhausted, Jenna stepped into her warmly lit hallway and closed her study door. Limping through to the kitchen, she rinsed the mug and placed it in the dishwasher then began her nightly routine of checking locks.

She had bought the roomy old Victorian house a couple of years ago with the royalties from her first six books, and as wonderful as it was, it had a lot of doors. Despite her attempt to remain upbeat, the silence seemed to ring as she walked through the house. For the first time, instead of taking pleasure in the elegant ranks of French doors and tall sash windows, she couldn't help noticing the large amount of glass through which she could, conceivably, be watched.

Despite the luxurious kilim rugs she had strewn on the glossy, kauri wood floors, her footsteps echoed eerily. As she switched out lamps, shadows seemed to flood the large, rambling rooms, sending a preternatural chill down her spine and making her vividly aware that she was very much alone.

Security wasn't an issue, she reminded herself. The property was alarmed and gated and her fence was high and in good repair. A brief glance at the blinking light of the alarm system she'd had installed shortly after she had moved in assured her that the house was secure.

Jenna carried a glass of water up the long, sweeping staircase lined with, admittedly, gloomy Whitmore family portraits. She avoided the dark stares of ranks of long-dead relatives. Lately the sepia-toned record of the past and her lack of current family portraits had become a depressing reminder of the emptiness of her personal life.

It was one o'clock before she finally climbed into the elegant French provincial-style bed she had bought in response to an article she'd read on curing insomnia.

Apparently, there were two keys to getting a good night's sleep: forming a routine and setting the scene for a restful night.

She was hopeless at the first, so she'd decided she could at least make her bedroom look as serene and inviting as impossible. With dark teak wood and white-on-white bed linen and furnishings, her bedroom could have been lifted straight out of a movie set. Unfortunately, that fact didn't seem to make any difference to her sleep pattern, which was erratic.

As she switched off the light she became aware of sirens somewhere in the distance and recalled the current story in the news. Apparently there was a serial arsonist on the loose, a creepy coincidence since six years ago a serial arsonist had been responsible for Natalie's and her baby's deaths.

She stared at a bright sliver of moonlight beaming through a gap in the heavy cream drapes and found herself fixated on the possible identity of her poisonous fan.

She had not been callous enough to use Natalie's mysterious death in her story, but she *had* drawn on the fact that Natalie had had a secret online friend who had sent her Valentine's-style gifts: single long-stemmed white roses and chocolates.

Although the idea that the person who had sent the threatening email could be Natalie's long-ago secret admirer was definitely pushing theory into the realms of fantasy.

It had to be a coincidence that she had received the email on the anniversary of Natalie's death.

Chapter 3

The next afternoon, Jenna drove to the cemetery. The cars occupying almost every space and the large numbers of well-dressed people walking through the grounds signalled that a funeral was in progress.

Gathering the bunch of flowers she had placed on the backseat, she slipped dark glasses on the bridge of her nose and strolled through the grounds. The sun was warm, the air crisp, the sky a clear, dazzling blue. Large oaks cast cooling shade on row after row of well-tended plots.

As she neared the vicinity of Natalie's grave, she noted the lone figure of a man. For a split second she thought it could be O'Halloran. Her heart slammed against her chest then she dismissed the idea. The man was tall, but not tall enough, and on the lean side rather than muscular. He was also wearing a ball cap, something that she had never seen O'Halloran wear.

A large group of mourners moving toward the parking lot obscured her view. The next time Jenna got a clear view of the gravesite, that part of the cemetery was deserted.

She strolled the rest of the distance to the grave, which was already decorated with a wreath of pink roses and a tiny blue teddy bear, which Aunt Mary would have placed there first thing that morning. Blinking back the automatic rush of tears at her aunt and uncle's pain, which, after all the years, showed no sign of abating, she unwrapped the bunch of bright yellow and pink chrysanthemums she'd bought from the local florist, and placed them in a stone vase set to one side of the headstone.

Extracting a bottle of water from her purse, she topped up the vase. Straightening, she stepped back to admire her handiwork, and became aware that she was no longer alone. She spun a little too quickly, wincing as her knee, still stiff and sore, twinged. The plastic bottle bounced on the grass as a large hand briefly cupped her elbow.

A small shock ran through her as she processed dark, cool eyes beneath black brows, clean-cut cheekbones and a tough jaw made even edgier by a five o'clock shadow.

For a split second, even though she knew it was O'Halloran, she had trouble accepting that fact. Six years had passed since she had last seen him up close, and in that time he had changed. His hair was still the same, dark and close-cut, his skin olive and tanned, but his face was leaner than she remembered, his gaze more remote. A scar decorated the bridge of his nose, and his chest and shoulders were broader, as if he worked out regularly, which, given the rehab he'd had to do following his operation, was probably the case.

The rough jaw, oddly in keeping with his long-sleeved T-shirt and black pants, added a wolfish quality that signalled that whatever else O'Halloran had been doing, he hadn't taken the time to shave. A small quiver shot down her spine when she realized that O'Halloran was studying her just as intently as she was studying him, and suddenly, the notion that the large, fierce male looming over her had anything remotely in common with the model who had posed for the cover of her latest book was ludicrous. "I didn't expect to find you here."

Instantly, Jenna regretted the bluntness of the comment, even though it was true. Since Natalie's and Jared's deaths, O'Halloran had almost completely distanced himself from the family, politely declining all invitations. According to her aunt and uncle he seemed to have no interest in visiting the grave. She had certainly never seen him here any other time she had visited, or seen any evidence that he left flowers.

O'Halloran retrieved the empty water bottle and handed it to her. "I visit. I just try to keep out of Mary's way. The stuffed toys are hard to take."

The blankness of O'Halloran's gaze made her chest squeeze tight. For the first time, she saw it for what it was, grasped just how deeply O'Halloran had been affected by the loss of his family. It was etched in his face, in the muscle pulsing along the side of his jaw.

He had not attended the funeral because he had been flat on his back in hospital at the time.

While he was injured, she had worried about him to

the point that she had tried ringing him and, once, had even gone looking for him. She hadn't found him. Like a wounded animal, O'Halloran had gone to ground. Months later, he had surfaced but had continued to keep his distance.

Crouching down, she retrieved the cellophane wrap for the flowers and stuffed it in her purse along with the bottle. "I'm sorry, I should know better than to make assumptions."

His gaze touched on hers as she straightened, before shifting to a group of mourners drifting past, sweeping the cemetery, with a mechanical precision, as if he was looking for someone. "You've had your own grief to deal with. The military is hard on families."

She frowned. "How did you know that I came from a military family?"

His gaze was suddenly way too percipient, reminding her of just how seductively dangerous O'Halloran could be. The last thing she needed was a reminder that aside from possessing the kind of dark, dangerous good looks that made women go weak at the knees, O'Halloran had another set of traits that had always threatened to melt her on the spot. He liked women. He was solicitous of and ultra-protective of them, and he didn't seem to have a built-in fear of emotional reactions. Nine years ago, after the near miss with the drunk driver, O'Halloran's offer of a shoulder had proved to be her breaking point.

He shrugged. "Your family didn't tell me, they closed ranks. I checked newspaper records and paid a visit to the military base."

"Why?" The question was blunt and just a little rude. She didn't care. Years ago, O'Halloran's failure to find out the most basic facts about her life, his easy defection, had hurt. In that moment, she realized how much she had deceived herself about him. In her heart of hearts, she had wanted him to come after her, to insist that what they had was worth the risk.

"I was worried about you. You were too closed-off, too self-contained. I couldn't figure out why you should be that way. I needed to make sure you were all right."

And suddenly, that night nine years ago was between them; the stifling heat, the edgy emotions, her shattering vulnerability. On the heels of the discovery that, like it or not, she had been carrying some kind of a torch for O'Halloran for nine years, the conversation was abruptly too much.

Glancing at her watch, she picked up her bag and hitched the strap over one shoulder. "I need to go. I'm late for an appointment." She aimed a blank smile somewhere in the direction of his shoulder. "It was good to see you."

And she wished that she hadn't. After her moment with the cover yesterday, she wasn't sure what she felt for O'Halloran. All she knew was that his memory was a lot more manageable than the man himself.

O'Halloran fell into step beside her, making her tense. "I'll walk you to your car." His fingers slid around her wrist, sending a hot, tingling shock down the length of her arm. He turned her palm up, so that the grazing was exposed. "How did that happen?"

Jerking free, she quickened her pace, wincing again as the movement put just a little too much pressure on her knee. Annoyed, Jenna resisted the temptation to rub the knee. The last thing she needed was to invoke O'Halloran's protective instincts.

Although, grimly, she noted that if she had thought

O'Halloran hadn't seen the elastic bandage beneath her leggings, she would be wrong. "Nothing much. As it happens, I had another run-in with a car."

O'Halloran threw her a sharp look, as if he was as surprised as she that she'd touched on a topic that was so closely connected to the hour they'd spent in his apartment making love. But that didn't stop him from firing a string of questions at her as they walked, his voice relaxed and low-key, almost casual, although by the time they reached her car he had mined every salient detail.

"Ticked anyone off lately?"

She found her key and depressed the lock. "Yeah, a fan."

O'Halloran opened the driver's side door, his arm brushing hers as he did so, sending another one of those small electrifying shocks through her. "Are you telling me," he said quietly, "that you think the driver aimed for you?"

Jenna tensed as a replay of the shiny black car heading straight for her at high speed flashed through her mind. "Not exactly, there was no room. If he had swerved he would have hit another car and damaged his own. That's what saved me. I dived between two cars. What bothers me is that he had a long time to see me and he never slowed down."

"It could have been some kid—"

"Playing chicken. I thought of that." Her fingers tightened on the strap of her handbag. "The only problem was it didn't feel like a game."

She took a deep breath. Here was the point where O'Halloran called the men in white coats with the interesting drugs and the padded cell. "Whoever it was, I got the impression he wanted to hit me. Even if he had braked seconds before, he still would have hit me, and he didn't brake."

Instead of dismissing her statement as emotional overreaction, O'Halloran crossed his arms over his chest and seemed content to listen. "And the disgruntled fan? Where does she come in?"

"He," she corrected. "When I got home I found a threatening email."

His expression altered very slightly. Jenna couldn't even say what it was, exactly, that had changed, just that the temperature seemed to drop by several degrees.

Briefly, she outlined the content of the email, omitting her own suspicion that the poisonous fan, aside from being someone from her past, could be somehow linked with Natalie. So far, that part was just a theory, and she didn't want to cause any unnecessary upset. She couldn't forget that O'Halloran had never believed the house fire that had killed Natalie and Jared had been a random arson. According to her aunt, he'd believed that his family had been targeted because he was a cop, and despite leaving the police force, it was an investigation he had never given up.

O'Halloran's gaze settled on her mouth for a pulse-pounding moment. "I'd like to see a copy of the email."

Digging into his pocket, he found his wallet and handed her a card. "You can scan it or fax, or alternatively, drop it by my office."

Battling the sudden warmth in her cheeks and a humming, deepening awareness that was definitely scrambling her brain, she took the card and slipped it into her handbag. The last thing she had expected was that O'Halloran would want any contact with her at all, and the fact that he seemed to want to help her increased the unsettling awareness. "I've deleted the email, but I did keep a print copy. I'll send it to you."

"Did you report the accident?"

"Not to the police. I talked to one of the mall security guys. He was going to check out the parking lot tapes and get back to me."

"What was his name?"

"Mathews."

Another string of questions about the security set-up at the mall and she found herself haemorrhaging more information, including her phone number and email address and eventually handing over Mathews's business card.

She drew a deep breath, feeling suddenly too aware and a whole lot confused. Giving her details to O'Halloran shouldn't have felt like part and parcel of a dating ritual, but suddenly it did. "You don't have to check up on it."

He tucked the card in the pocket of his jeans. "I drive past there on my way to work. It won't hurt to see if Mathews managed to record the licence plate."

O'Halloran held her door as she climbed into her car. The clean, masculine scent of his skin and the faint whiff of some resinous cologne made her stomach clench. Not good!

Stepping back, he lifted a hand as she pulled out of her parking space.

Heart still beating way too rapidly, Jenna couldn't help checking out her rearview mirror. O'Halloran was still studying the mourners gathered in knots and strolling toward cars and she suddenly knew what he was doing at the cemetery.

The dark casual clothes that made him fade into the shadows, the reason there were no flowers.

He wasn't there to mourn; he was surveilling Natalie's grave.

Frowning, Marc watched as Jenna's car merged with traffic.

He had come, as he did every year, to watch the gravesite from a distance and see who visited apart from Natalie's family. Although this year, with a big funeral in progress, the exercise had been a little pointless.

Grimly, he noted that, as with other years, the only bright spot of his vigil had been when Jenna came to place flowers. Now that she had gone, the vigil felt empty.

In point of fact, after blowing his cover so thoroughly, the whole exercise of watching the gravesite was now a waste of time. If the perp had been anywhere near, he would be miles away by now.

Sliding dark glasses onto the bridge of his nose, he turned back to study the cemetery, which was now emptying rapidly. After a few minutes Marc gave up searching for the lean guy wearing the ball cap who had stopped by Natalie's grave.

The man hadn't left anything at the gravesite, or taken anything away; Marc had established that much while he had talked to Jenna. It was possible the man had been seeking out another gravesite and had simply stopped to read the name on Natalie's headstone, but something about him had caught Marc's attention.

Marc was certain he had seen the man before somewhere. He didn't know where or when, but it would come to him.

The moment when Jenna had told him that she had received a threatening email replayed itself, shoving every instinct on high alert.

He didn't like coincidences, and he didn't believe in this one.

There was a connection. He didn't know how, or why, he just knew that in some serpentine way, and after six years, that Jenna held the key to the breakthrough he needed.

Frustration and disbelief held him immobile for long seconds. For years he had meticulously researched every piece of information and evidence connected to both the house fire and the police investigation he had been involved with at the time. He had assumed the motivation for the crime against his family was a revenge attack based on his police work. Now he had to revise that approach.

The thought that the killer had had another motivation entirely was a quantum shift. In his research and briefs to private detectives, he had kept the focus on the criminal family, who were, ironically, because of his personal investigation, now mostly behind bars for a series of other crimes.

He had made the basic error of discounting Natalie's life, and he hadn't factored Jenna in at all. Two mistakes he would now address. He should have examined every aspect of Natalie's life. Jenna, as her cousin and best friend, should have been at the top of his list.

One thing was certain, if Jenna was the key to unlocking the identity of the killer then from now on every part of her life was of interest to him.

The decision to refocus settled in, filling him with a tension that had nothing to do with the investigation and everything to do with Jenna and a past that still tugged at him.

Nine years ago Jenna had attracted, tantalised and frustrated him. When he had found out that she had been an army brat and that she had grown up on military bases here and overseas, she had fallen into context. The ease with which she'd walked away from him when he'd been certain she had wanted him had suddenly made sense. She was used to moving from base to base and never putting roots down. She was used to saying goodbye, and flat out "no." After she had lost a father then a fiancé, she was used to losing, period.

Digging his keys out of his pocket, he strolled toward his truck, which was parked at one end of the lot, out of sight from the main part of the cemetery.

Broodingly he went back over the few minutes he had spent with Jenna. She had been wearing leggings that clung to her slender legs, a hoodie and sneakers, as if she were on her way to the gym.

The clothing was sleek and mouth-wateringly sexy. Like the car she drove, it underlined the changes that had taken place in Jenna's life. Always intriguingly quiet and self-contained, she was now confident and successful, with a sophistication that packed a double punch.

Marc stopped dead as the extent of the attraction humming through him registered.

Damn, he thought mildly. That was something he was going to have to keep a lid on. He couldn't work effectively if he couldn't keep his mind on the job.

Maybe it had been the book he had read last night, and the steamy sex scene, which had shunted him back to the past. Maybe it was just that he was tired of being solitary and alone and his libido was doing the talking.

Whatever was to blame, like it or not, he wanted Jenna Whitmore and, to complicate matters, he was pretty certain she wanted him. He had to consider the likelihood that they would end up in bed, sooner or later.

But first, he had a killer to catch.

Chapter 4

Electrified by the unexpected meeting with O'Halloran, and the taut awareness that seemed to have settled into her bones, Jenna drove to the gym for her usual midafternoon workout. An hour's circuit of exercise machines and weights followed by a shower and she felt physically relaxed. Although the exercise had failed to dislodge the edgy knowledge that kept making her pulse shoot out of control: that, incredibly, despite O'Halloran's low-key manner and cool control, he had been just as aware of her as she had been of him.

When she had finished, Jenna retrieved her bag from her locker, showered, changed and headed for her car.

As she stepped out from beneath the awning that protected the front entrance, her mind still dazedly, sappily fixed on the minutes she'd spent talking to O'Halloran, a scraping sound jerked her head up. She jumped out of the way just as a pot plant came hurtling down from the terrace of one of the apartments over the gymnasium, exploding in a shower of potting mix and terracotta shards on the sidewalk.

One of the trainers, Amanda, a sleek blonde with a lean, toned body, rushed out from the gym. She stared at the splattered remains of what had once been a pretty, trailing geranium. "What happened? Are you okay?"

Jenna brushed soil off one of her shoes. "I'm fine. It missed me by a couple of feet."

Amanda shook her head. "I don't know how it could have fallen. I rent one of those apartments and there's a three-foot wall running along each terrace. The only way anything could fall down was if someone was silly enough to balance a plant on top of the wall."

Stomach tight, chills still running down her spine, Jenna stepped out from the shade into the warmth of the afternoon sunlight and peered upward. If there had been anyone on one of the several terraces directly above her, they were long gone now.

If she had been just a half second faster the pot would have hit her. "Looks like someone was silly enough."

Amanda nudged a terracotta shard with her foot. "What a mess. I'll have a word with Helen. She'll make sure that whoever owns the pot plant knows what happened." She frowned. "You look white as a sheet. You should come inside and sit down, maybe have something to drink."

Jenna backed away, more interested in scanning the apartments above than being soothed, but with the afternoon sun slanting across the windows they looked featureless. At a guess, most of the apartments were empty, since it wasn't quite five. The occupants would still be at work. "No, really, I'm fine and I need to get home." Aiming a blank smile in Amanda's direction, she walked quickly to the car and fumbled the key in the lock.

Glancing in the rearview mirror as she drove to the mall closest to her suburb, she noticed a black Audi following just a little too closely. A small unpleasant jolt almost made her miss the turn.

It was the same type of car that had nearly run her over the previous night. The same car her villain had driven in her latest book.

When the Audi didn't follow her into the parking lot, but instead merged with traffic flowing into the inner city, she let out a shaky breath. The Audi had to be an unnerving coincidence. In a city as large as Auckland, who knew how many of them were zapping around.

She found a space and parked then sat for long moments until her pulse rate returned to normal. She was still unsettled from running into O'Halloran, and on edge in a skittish, feminine way that was utterly at odds with her usual calm control. She was also stressed from the near miss with the pot plant.

When she realized that she was also unconsciously watching the entrance to the parking lot, waiting for the Audi to cruise in, she grabbed her handbag and exited the car.

Paranoia wasn't her favourite state of mind, and she'd already had enough of it in the past twenty-four hours to last her a lifetime.

Looping the strap of her handbag over her shoulder, she strolled into the mall, her stride almost back to her normal, fluid speed now that the workout had loosened up her knee.

Her first port of call was the information kiosk on the ground floor. She asked if Mathews was in and supplied her name. Minutes later, Mathews stepped out of a nearby door.

The conversation was short and to the point. O'Halloran had already called in and they had gone through the security tapes. Mathews handed her a blurred black-and-white print of the parking lot, capturing the Audi close in against the mall building itself. "That's the clearest shot of the car and the plate. Unfortunately, the quality of the cameras isn't great, and the mist further reduced visibility." He shrugged. "A couple of the letters of the plate are visible."

Jenna thanked Mathews and stowed the print in her bag, her pulse once more racing, because O'Halloran *had* come to check on the tapes, proving that he had been serious about helping her. Apparently she had just missed him.

Following her usual track, she called at a number of specialty stores and bought a baked cheesecake to take around to her aunt's for dinner that evening along with a fresh fruit salad and organic yoghurt.

The drive home was uneventful until she took a motorway off ramp and the black Audi cruised up close behind her again.

A horn blared, jerking her gaze back to the road and alerting her to the fact that she was veering into the next lane.

Heart pounding, Jenna corrected her steering then glanced in the mirror to try and see if it was the same car she had seen earlier.

Her stomach tightened at the black colour and the darkly tinted windows, which gave the Audi a menacing aura. Which was exactly what she had intended when she had written about the car in her book.

It looked like the same vehicle, but, unfortunately, she hadn't thought to take the registration number before, so she couldn't confirm that it was.

The car stayed behind her, too close for her to make out the licence plate. The tinted windows meant that beyond a vague, sinister shape she couldn't see the driver.

She changed lanes then glanced in the mirror again as she made the turn, but the Audi had already accelerated away.

Still on edge hours later after she had gotten home from the family dinner, Jenna decided that scanning a copy of the poisonous fan letter and emailing it to O'Halloran could wait until the morning. Spending time with her aunt and two cousins, both of whom were married with children, had been a welcome distraction, but the instant she had gotten in her car to drive home the fear that she would be followed had kicked in. She hadn't, but the possibility had made the drive unpleasant. The last thing she needed to do before bed was add to her tension by rereading the threat.

Walking quickly, she did her nightly round of the locks, checked the alarm was set, made herself a hot drink and climbed the stairs to bed.

Ensconced in the soft nest of duck-down pillows with her Aunt Mary's remedy for sleep, hot milk laced with malt, and the Bible open on her lap at the most comforting section, the Psalms, Jenna tried to relax.

She had a sudden flashback of the pot plant smashing on the pavement.

If she hadn't heard the faint scrape of terracotta

against stone, as if someone had pushed the heavy pot plant, and stopped to look up, she would have been either seriously injured or killed.

The series of unnerving incidents had to be pure coincidence. No one was trying to kill her. Clearly, she had let her imagination run away with her.

Jenna took a sip of hot milk and malt and focused on Psalm thirty-four, deliverance from trouble.

Midnight came and went. She set the empty mug down on her bedside table, replaced the Bible on her nightstand and switched out the light. Turning on her side, she forced her thoughts away from the incident with the pot plant and the malevolent Audi...and her growing conviction that the fan who had written the nasty email was making good on his threat.

Instead, she allowed herself to think about the chance meeting with O'Halloran, and the fact that he had gone to the mall and checked out the security tapes.

The change of focus was instantly soothing. O'Halloran had a rock-solid quality, a take-no-prisoners attitude, when it came to crime and injustice. She had always liked that about him. Somehow, without saying a word, he conveyed an impression of tough, no-holds-barred, protective strength. If he ever got hold of the guy driving the Audi—and she was abruptly certain that it had been a guy, not a woman—she wouldn't want to be in his shoes.

Yawning, she turned over in bed. Her head was swimming with tiredness. As her breathing finally slowed, her thoughts shifted irresistibly back to her first meeting with O'Halloran. Although, nine years ago, she hadn't called him O'Halloran, she had used his first name, Marc.

She had been in her final year at Auckland University and Marc had been taking the same criminal psychology paper she had been studying. They had ended up sitting side by side at a lecture then had gone out for coffee afterward.

The second she had found out he was a cop, she should have made her excuses and left. Instead she had let Marc buy her a second coffee, and introduce her to his friends, two other detectives doing the same course. Still raw and grieving after Dane's death, O'Halloran had somehow slipped beneath her defences. Aware of the dangerous undertow of fascination, she had kept him at arm's-length, promising herself that she would pull back before it was too late. Although, as she'd found out today, controlling O'Halloran and the attraction that had blindsided her hadn't exactly been her strong point.

Frowning, Jenna banished O'Halloran from her thoughts and concentrated on keeping her mind blank until mind-numbing oblivion finally sucked her under.

Aware that she was immersed in a recurring dream, Jenna almost surfaced from a fitful sleep.

She should make herself wake up properly, give herself a good talking to, but the compulsion to drift back into a past that included O'Halloran was unexpectedly powerful. Letting out a breath, she ceased to think. Instead she allowed herself to sink back into the dream, back into the past....

The summer evening was warm enough that she had folded up the gauzy turquoise stole that went with her gown and stuffed it into her evening bag as she hurried out of the hotel ballroom. Stepping into the ladies' room, she checked her reflection in the mirror. Her face was flushed and her hair was definitely mussed. Aside from those details, she looked composed enough, which was a surprise given that she had just won a minor tussle with a date who had suddenly turned from shy and harmless into a ravening octopus.

Jaw set, she hunted in her evening bag, found a spare hairpin and did her best to fix the elegant twist of hair on top of her head. Satisfied that she no longer looked like she'd been dragged backward through a haystack, she made her way to the hotel lobby.

There were no taxis outside the hotel, so she spoke to the concierge. He ordered a taxi but informed her that thanks to a high-profile football game and a rash of conferences, the wait time was half an hour, minimum.

Jenna thanked him. Unwilling to wait in one of the cozy private bars, in case her Jekyll-and-Hyde date came looking for her and added insult to injury by offering her a ride home, she strolled outside to wait.

Twenty minutes later, tired of kicking her heels, she walked back into the lobby to check on the arrival time of the taxi and stopped dead when she saw O'Halloran at the concierge desk.

His back was to her, but there was no mistaking his height, the sleek width of his shoulders or the tough line of his jaw. Heart slamming against her chest, because she was abruptly certain he was looking for her, she turned on her heel and stepped back outside.

Extracting her cell from her evening bag, she tried calling her aunt and uncle, something she had done at approximately five-minute intervals. The call went through to voice mail, signalling that they were still out to dinner with friends. Unfortunately, she hadn't thought to ask which set of friends so she didn't have an alternate number to try.

Slipping the phone back into her bag she glanced at the entrance doors of the hotel and caught another glimpse of O'Halloran as he strolled out of one of the small intimate bars and into another one. Looking for her.

Maybe it was an overreaction, and maybe she was wrong, but instead of waiting a little longer and risking O'Halloran finding her, she started walking. Leaving the hotel on foot wasn't smart, but after the wrench of breaking up with O'Halloran less than two weeks ago, she wasn't about to jeopardise the progress she had made by spending time alone with him.

Aside from the bone-melting attraction, she was acutely aware that despite her efforts to keep things casual they had been on the verge of becoming lovers. The knowledge that she had been a heartbeat away from sleeping with a man she had only known for a few weeks, when she had never come close to sharing that intimacy with Dane, had struck her forcibly.

It had taken courage to make the break with O'Halloran, but it was done, and she wasn't going to complicate the situation by being a wimp now. To cement the decision, she had made arrangements to go overseas. She was newly graduated and free as a bird. She had a friend she could stay with in Sydney and a series of job interviews lined up. She didn't have a clue what she would end up doing for a living, but she flew out in ten days' time.

The decision to leave had filled her with relief. She had read somewhere that one way to neutralise issues and problems—and fatal attractions—was to create geographical distance from them, and she could attest to that fact. Just buying the air ticket had been liberating.

Behind her, she registered footsteps, almost drowned out by the sound of an approaching vehicle. Ahead, warm light flowed from a restaurant. All she needed to do was reach the pooling light and she would be able to ring her uncle again and see if he could come out and pick her up.

She crossed the road, more worried by the footsteps and a potential mugging—or worse—than the car. She was now on a one-way street. The vehicle wouldn't come her way. It would have to veer off at the intersection and continue on downtown.

The sound of the vehicle increased to a roar as, instead of slowing for the intersection, the driver accelerated. Frowning, Jenna glanced over her shoulder. She caught the silhouette of a man as headlights blinded her. It occurred to her that it could be O'Halloran, but all of her attention was taken by the car, which had somehow missed the turn at the intersection and was careering down the one-way street in the wrong direction.

She stepped onto the narrow path that hugged the edge of a bridge. Adrenaline surged when she realized that the man behind her was much closer. She thought he said her name but at that moment the threat from the car became paramount, because the driver appeared to be aiming straight for her.

Dragging at the entangling layers of her skirts, she kicked off her high heels and began to run.

Panic squeezed the breath from her lungs. She needed to reach the end of the bridge and get off the footpath.

She heard her name called again. O'Halloran. Relief coursed through her.

The loud detonation of the vehicle hitting the curb

almost stopped her heart in her chest. Simultaneously an arm snaked around her waist and she found herself lifted up and propelled the last few feet off of the bridge. A split second later, they hit the grassy turf that bordered the stream and the car fish-tailed past, bare inches away, filling her nostrils with the smell of burning rubber and exhaust fumes.

With a second loud thump, the car veered off the path, back onto the road. Headlights glared and a horn sounded as it almost hit a vehicle accelerating down the one-way in the legitimate direction, then sped off into the night.

O'Halloran, who was sprawled over her, shielding her with his body, pushed to his feet and helped her up. "Are you all right?"

Still shaky from the near miss, but oddly elated, crazily, because O'Halloran had noticed that she had left the hotel and had come after her, Jenna found her evening purse, which had landed on the grass a few feet away. "Yes, thanks to you. If you hadn't followed me—"

The glow of a streetlight glanced across taut planes of his face as he handed her her shoes. "You should never have left the hotel on foot. Don't you read the newspapers?"

Jenna fitted one shoe then almost overbalanced as she stepped into the second. With a clipped word, O'Halloran steadied her, and the next minute she was in his arms, pressed hard against the muscled warmth of his chest. "I would have given you a lift," he muttered, then his mouth was on hers.

The passion was hot and instant, and it threw her even more off balance. She had been kissed before by O'Halloran, but it had never felt this needy, this visceral.

Mostly, in the weeks they had dated he had seemed content to let her dictate the pace. As much as she'd appreciated his gentlemanly approach, she had taken that as a sign that she was not in any way special to him. Now, for the first time, she registered that what they had shared had mattered to him, too.

When he would have pulled back, she cupped his neck and held him there, leaning into the hard planes and angles of his body. Long seconds passed, and eventually he lifted his head, his gaze narrowed and glittering. "Do you want me to take you home, or do you want to come with me?"

The question hung in the air, raw and edged. Her throat felt thick, her chest tight. She knew what he was offering. She could be with him now, for the night: no strings.

The thought that after tonight she would probably never see O'Halloran again, that this could be her last chance with him, touched a chord somewhere deep inside her. Fierceness and longing welled up, gripping her so tightly she could barely breathe.

The idea that they could be together was both hurtful and mesmerisingly, impossibly tempting. She wanted O'Halloran, that had never been at issue. And she was leaving soon, so there was no danger that she would be tempted to cling.

Before she could reason it out any further, and remember all of the factors that added up to a *no*, she said, "Yes, I want to come with you."

Half an hour later they reached his apartment. O'Halloran didn't bother to switch on a light. He simply tossed his car keys on a hall table, pulled her into his arms and kissed her for long, drugging minutes.

Shrugging out of his jacket, he pulled her into a sitting room lit by moonlight streaming through French doors.

Winding her arms around his neck, Jenna went up on her toes and angled her chin for his kiss. She could feel the ridge of his arousal against one hip, the rough glide of O'Halloran's palms on her naked back.

She jerked at his tie and unfastened buttons and felt the zipper on her gown give way, the soft slide of fabric as the halter-neck tie at her nape released and her dress puddled on the floor. With a stifled groan, O'Halloran dipped his head and took one breast into his mouth and the night turned molten.

Long seconds later the world tilted sideways as she found herself swung into O'Halloran's arms then set down on a couch, the leather cool against her back.

O'Halloran came down beside her and she pulled him close, loving the heat blasting off his big body, the flagrant sensuality of his skin against hers, the masculine weight and scent of him. Somewhere outside, music played in the distance, a slow, languorous beat that seemed to permeate the night as she ran her palms down the long, muscular line of his back.

She felt his fingers tugging at the waistband of her panties, then she was completely naked. Fumbling at the fastening of O'Halloran's pants, she dragged the zipper down and felt him hot and silky in her hands.

With a stifled sound, O'Halloran's hand stayed hers. Impatiently, he finished undressing. Moonlight gleamed on jet-black hair, the sleek muscularity of broad shoulders as he came down between her legs.

When O'Halloran finally sheathed himself and slid inside her, the moment was primal and extreme. She logged his flare of surprise at the difficulty of penetration, the question in his eyes, then his mouth came down on hers and she ceased to think as the night dissolved....

Jenna came out of sleep, her heart pounding, her skin drenched with perspiration. She blinked, for the briefest of moments unable to separate the dream from reality. She could still feel the touch of O'Halloran's hands, his mouth, the weight of his body pressing down on hers....

Taking a steadying breath, she studied the confines of her room—the dim outline of her bedroom dresser, the moulded rose on the ceiling—in an effort to reorient herself.

She hadn't dreamed about making love with O'Halloran in years, although she guessed after her emotional episode with the book cover, she should have expected her subconscious to throw her a curveball. That revelation reinforced by her sharply physical response to O'Halloran at the cemetery had reignited the inconvenient, simmering attraction.

It was there, a part of her, whether she liked it or not, and now she had to deal with it. Despite writing any number of agonising scenes dealing with the exact same romantic problem, she had no earthly clue how she could nullify it in herself. Theory was all very well, the only problem was her body didn't seem to respond to logic.

Climbing out of the entangling sheets, she walked to the window, drew back the curtain and stared out into her back garden. Cold seemed to press through the glass, making her shiver.

The accident had featured in her dream also.

Her too-creative mind had obviously resurrected the old incident, because of what had happened the previous night. As frightening as it had been at the time, she had never considered that the almost-accident nine years ago had been anything more than some drunk driver who had lost control of his, or her, vehicle.

She had certainly never thought that it might have been a deliberate attempt to kill her.

Although there was a curious symmetry to the events that kept popping into her mind. O'Halloran had featured in both. He had been there to save her nine years ago; now, suddenly, he was back in the picture again.

She had a brief flash of the moment in the cemetery when his gaze had dropped to her mouth.

Heat pooled low in her stomach when she considered the fact that, nine years on, she still wanted O'Halloran, and he wanted her.

She rubbed at the goose-flesh that decorated her arms and stared blindly at the moonlight-washed garden.

The thought made her stomach knot and her heart pound. She was twenty-nine, almost thirty, successful at what she did and calmly in control of her life. She shouldn't be so affected by a simple physical attraction— by chemistry. But it seemed that where O'Halloran was concerned nothing was simple.

For years, she had buried her head in the sand and lived a life devoid of emotional and physical intimacy. She hadn't questioned her refusal to sleep with any of the men she had dated, or her preference to remain single, she had simply put it down to her perfectionist streak and isolating career.

But in the space of little more than a day, that had all changed. After years of living alone, eating alone and sleeping alone, she wanted what other women took for granted. She wanted a husband who loved her, the closeness and the intimacy and the heart-pounding sex, and she wanted them with a fierceness that seemed to be growing by the minute.

To compound her madness, she didn't just want those things with some misty, as-yet-unidentified man. She wanted them with O'Halloran.

The following day, after getting more and more annoyed every time she thought about the encounters with the black Audi, and with the blurred mall photograph and the misspelt email tucked into her handbag, Jenna walked into the Auckland Central police station.

She had spent the past two hours doing radio interviews, so she was dressed for business in a charcoal-grey jacket and skirt, with red accessories, a sleek pair of heels and matching bag. Maybe what she was wearing shouldn't matter because she was there to report a crime, but she figured with the weirdness factor of being stalked by a fan, she needed every bit of credibility she could scrape up.

After waiting for a good twenty minutes, she took a seat opposite the detective she had been assigned.

Detective Farrell, a slim, attractive brunette, her desk swamped with files, was dismissive. Harassment in the form of a disgruntled email from a fan, which did not contain any concrete threat, and Jenna's suspicion that she was being followed by someone driving a black Audi, were not strong enough evidence to justify any further action. The reason she had seen the Audi on a number of occasions was probably because the person who drove the car lived nearby.

Keeping her cool, Jenna explained that the car was the same make and model she had used in her latest book and, to compound things, the same type of car that had almost run her over in the mall parking lot. Briefly, she related the incident with the pot plant outside her gym, and her conclusion that she was being stalked.

Farrell's gaze sharpened at that. She took details, asked Jenna to fill out an official complaint then promised to put a detective on the case, although they couldn't help with extra security for her upcoming book tour. "We'll certainly look into the allegation of stalking, but until we get something more concrete I can't commit man hours solely for protection. If we can trace this car or collect evidence of a crime like vandalism or a break-in then the picture changes. If you're worried, you should arrange security for your tour."

Farrell rose to her feet, indicating that the interview was over. She apologised that they couldn't do more up front, but with a mini crime wave on their hands in the form of a gang war and a manhunt for a serial arsonist, they were already short-handed.

Jenna thanked Farrell for her time as she packed away the email. The interview had gone as she had expected, but she'd had to try. With a publicity tour for *Deadly Valentine* beginning in just two days, she had hoped the police would at least provide her with protection for the signings. Most of them were in large department stores and were well-publicised. With crowds of shoppers milling around, they were obvious venues for a stalker.

As she stood up to leave, Farrell's gaze sharpened.

"You're Natalie O'Halloran's cousin, right? I used to be Marc's partner. How's he going with his new business?"

The mention of O'Halloran sent a small tingling shock through her. Jenna's cheeks warmed as she fielded the enquiry using the odd snippets of information that her aunt had let slip.

The yawning gap in her knowledge about O'Halloran added to her sense of disorientation. She wanted O'Halloran, and the intensity of the attraction and the sudden U-turn she had made were just a little bit scary. Especially when she considered that what she knew about his present life would fit on the back of a postage stamp.

Although, that would soon all change, since he was her next port of call.

O'Halloran's Lady

Chapter 5

Jenna strolled into the sleek offices of VIP Security and made an enquiry at the front desk. A short phone call later, the pretty redhead showed her through to O'Halloran's office.

Dressed in a suit with a crisp white shirt and blue tie, O'Halloran was standing in front of a large bank of windows, a cell to one ear, his back to the expansive view of the harbour. Jenna disguised a sudden attack of nerves by glancing around the large, cleanly furnished office.

Now that she was here, she couldn't help feeling a little pushy and intrusive. Worse, she was beginning to feel that she had imagined O'Halloran's interest, and that his protective behaviour was simply a knee-jerk reaction he would have toward any woman in trouble.

His gaze neutral, he terminated his conversation and

indicated she should sit in one of the comfortable leather armchairs grouped around a coffee table.

Dragging her gaze from the way his jacket fitted the broad width of his shoulders, Jenna sat down.

Instead of taking the chair opposite, he walked to his desk and picked up a file. "I checked out the numbers I could get off the plates of the Audi and came up with a list." He extracted a sheet of paper from the file and handed it to her. "Do you recognise any names?"

She studied the list, which included personal and company names, and shook her head. "Sorry, no."

She rummaged in her bag and extracted the folded email she had promised to give him. As she did so a small journal fell out, flipping open at a page of ideas she had jotted down for the book on which she was currently working.

O'Halloran retrieved the journal and seemed instantly riveted by the lines of neat print. He handed it back to her. "Notes for your next book?"

Jenna stuffed the journal back in her handbag. At least that answered any question about whether or not O'Halloran knew what she did for a living. "It's my current work in progress. It should be on the shelves in about eighteen months."

To cover the suddenly awkward silence, she handed O'Halloran the email. "I didn't know you knew I wrote."

O'Halloran, apparently absorbed by the printed email she'd given him, took the leather chair opposite. "Mary told me when you sold your first book."

Of course. The wild speculation that O'Halloran could have read one of her books died. She didn't know why she hadn't thought of that before. Aunt Mary was inordinately proud of the fact that she had gotten published.

O'Halloran frowned. "How many times has this guy written to you?"

Relieved, Jenna grabbed at the new direction of the conversation. "Just once, as far as I know. I did a check of all of my email files and I can't find anything else from that address."

O'Halloran frowned. "Have you taken this to the police?"

"I've just come from Auckland Central. A Detective Farrell's making enquiries."

His gaze sharpened. "Elaine Farrell's a good cop. If anyone can track this guy down, she can."

"But not you?"

"That wasn't what I said."

Relief washed through her—for a minute there she had thought O'Halloran was going to back away from helping her. Too wired to sit, Jenna rose to her feet and walked to the window. "Good, because someone's playing games with me, and I'm not entirely sure why. If it's the poisonous fan, then the motivation doesn't quite stack up. He says he wants me to take the book off the market, but the fact is I don't have the power to do that. Plus, there's one other thing."

A relevant fact she hadn't been able to elaborate on with Detective Farrell after her reaction to Jenna's statement that the stalker was using the same car as the villain in her book. "The fan who's stalking me is using details from my latest book."

"The Audi?"

She shot O'Halloran a startled look, surprised that he had made the connection with the Audi so quickly.

He looked neither incredulous nor disbelieving, which was a relief, because she badly needed someone to believe her.

Walking back to her seat, she sat down. "That's right. The villain in *Deadly Valentine* drove a black Audi. He used it to creep Sara out." She cleared her throat. "Sara is the name of my heroine."

Firming her jaw she decided there was no point in not revealing the entire embarrassing truth. "And that's not all." She was suddenly glad she was sitting, not standing. "I based Sara on myself."

"Her character?"

"And her schedule. Normally, Sara, as a private detective, is involved in investigations. In *Deadly Valentine* she tries to take time off from solving cases to write a book. I used my daily routine, including my writing hours and all of my weekly appointments, as a model for Sara's schedule."

"You could change your routine."

"I have, now. The problem is, I think he managed to track me down to the gym I use and followed me home from there, so I'm pretty sure he now knows where I live."

O'Halloran's head came up. "Have you noticed anyone suspicious near your house?"

Relief flooded her. O'Halloran's instant acceptance of her situation convinced her that she had done the right thing in approaching him. Farrell had been efficient, but Jenna knew for a fact that when O'Halloran had been a cop, his instincts and his reputation for capturing criminals had been second to none. "Not yet." And she had been looking. "An even bigger problem is that I have a book-signing tour planned in a couple of days. All of the venues are well-advertised. Whether I change my routine or not, it now doesn't matter, he can still find me."

There was no easy way to say it. All she could do was be blunt. "That's the reason I'm here, I need protection."

Marc gave himself a mental shake, and forced himself to concentrate on what Jenna was saying rather than the shadowy hint of cleavage in the vee of her jacket and the ultra-sexy red heels, which made her legs look even longer and more elegant. In point of fact, he never ogled women when they came into his office. Business was business and separate from his after-hours life. As both a cop and a bodyguard he occasionally had to offer comfort to women, which he was good for, but he had never been tempted to cross the line into the personal.

Until now.

Grimly, he ignored the tension that had gripped him the instant Jenna had walked into his office and the uncomfortable pressure of his semi-aroused state. If he hadn't been entirely convinced about Jenna's reasons for thinking she was being stalked, the look on her face would have been enough. She was genuinely concerned, and with some of the weirdos that were around—especially online weirdos—she should be. With the growing hype around Jenna's books, the signings would be packed out. "You look like you could use something to drink. What would you like, coffee? Tea? Or something cold?"

Jenna opted for coffee, with sugar, so he walked out to the dispenser in the hall and got two coffees. By the time he returned, she was out of her seat and investigating some of the books that lined one wall.

Against the plain cream decor, she stood out like an

exotic orchid in her dark suit and red shoes. The charcoal grey of the suit, which should have looked boring and a little nerdy, was somehow transformed by the sexy cut that clung to every delicate curve.

Jaw tightening at the sudden raft of memories, he set the coffee down.

Jenna slipped a book on criminal psychology she'd been examining back in the case. "I see you're still interested in detective work."

He saw the moment she registered that maybe the topic wasn't a happy one.

"I'm sorry," she said quietly. "You must miss detective work, you were passionate about it."

He shrugged. "I still am, but I've got other focuses now." Detective work had cost him his wife and child. From that point on, he had learned to temper the idealistic streak that had driven him so hard.

He was still black and white with his ideals. As far as he was concerned, justice was clear cut. If you did the crime then you deserved to do the time. Stepping out of the job had been a wrench, but overall it had been good for him. Leaving the force had also carried the bonus of allowing him to continue with his private investigation into the crime that had killed his family, a situation that had caused a lot of friction with his superior officer.

The edgy highs and lows were absent from his security work, but he didn't miss the seamier side of life, the drunks or the narcs. Overall he had learned to live with the challenge of co-owning the security business.

Strolling over to his desk, Marc picked up his phone. "Private protection is a good option. With the shortage of police staffing, Farrell would probably be stretched to provide protection unless you received a threat that involved physical harm."

Jenna crossed her arms over her chest and stared out of his window. "Can we not talk about Detective Farrell, please?"

O'Halloran was silent for a beat as he absorbed the subtext. Farrell was a good cop, but her bedside manner left something to be desired. He had never minded her abrasiveness. It had worked for him, because the last thing he had needed was a female partner who wanted more than just a professional relationship. Besides, he figured Farrell's manner was a coping mechanism. "VIP protection is expensive."

"I can afford it. I have a list of dates and the locations of the book signings." She dug in her handbag and handed him a sheet of paper. "We'll need to stay away, but that's no problem. Naturally, I'll pay all travel and hotel costs. Like I said, I can afford it."

Marc noted Jenna's use of *we* as if she assumed he was going to bodyguard her personally. The increased heat in his loins underlined the reason why that was not a good idea. "I'll have to check with my partner and see who we've got available."

Jenna's gaze locked with his, and the flash of hurt in her eyes made him feel like a heel. "Of course."

Marc stepped into Ben McCabe's office. McCabe, an ex-member of the New Zealand Special Forces, the Special Air Service, was on a call and looked harassed.

He finished the call and checked his watch. "I'm out of here. Gotta pick up the kids from school today."

Marc steeled himself against the subject of kids. He didn't often allow himself to think about the son he had lost in the house fire, but he couldn't ignore the small painful fact that if Jared had lived, he would have been a similar age to McCabe's small son. "I know we're committed with the art exhibition at the museum but I need a guy. Who's on standby?"

McCabe slipped his laptop into a briefcase and checked his watch again. Since his wife was a high-profile member of the mega-wealthy Lombard hotelier family, security for his family was always a burning issue. "For the next week, no one. Howard and Burke are on vacation, Kinsella's off sick. Why?"

"I've got Jenna Whitmore in my office."

McCabe frowned as he slipped his cell phone into his pocket. "The name's familiar."

"She's a novelist."

McCabe's expression cleared. "I saw her on TV a couple of weeks ago. She writes romance novels. My wife reads them."

"Romantic suspense, actually."

McCabe's blank expression informed Marc that he shouldn't have bothered to make the distinction. "She needs protection for her upcoming book tour."

McCabe looked distracted as he searched the surface of his desk. "Then you're going to have to do it, because there isn't anyone else."

Marc's jaw firmed. "What about you? I could take your place at the museum job."

McCabe found his car keys. "And art's a lot more straightforward than personal bodyguarding? Sorry." He sent Marc a rueful grin. "Jenna Whitmore is female. Even if I had the time, which I don't, Roma would have me hung, drawn and quartered if I even mentioned that

I was thinking about guarding a young, single woman. You'll have to do it."

Another flash of heat went through Marc at the thought of spending several days in close quarters with Jenna. He had decided he wanted Jenna, and it was a fact that he needed to stay close to her because he was certain that she was connected with the killer he was hunting. But the last thing he needed was the distraction of a sexual liaison, at least not yet. When they went to bed this time, he wanted to take things slow and easy. Nine years ago he had given in to adrenaline, and the jealousy that had seared him when he had found out, just days after their break-up, that Jenna was dating someone else. Not quite a cop, but close. A police recruit who had taken the same criminal psychology paper. Consequently, he had rushed her and for a woman like Jenna, it had been the wrong approach.

His jaw tightened. That sealed his decision. "I have priorities. Protecting Jenna Whitmore isn't one of them."

For one thing, with McCabe based at the museum for the next few days, supervising the security for the high-profile art exhibition, and every other able-bodied employee contracted out, he was more or less tied to the office. Problem solved. Jenna would have to approach another security firm.

Marc heard a whisper of sound behind him. Frowning, he checked the door. The corridor appeared to be empty.

McCabe snapped his fingers, as if he'd just had a light-bulb moment. He dropped his briefcase back on the desk. "There is a solution if you want it. Phillips can do office duty."

He opened a drawer and pulled out an address book. Flipping through, he found a number, scribbled it on the back of a business card and handed it to Marc. "He's staying at an apartment down on the viaduct, but he's not a happy camper. Give him a call, I guarantee he'll be in the office before you put the phone down."

Marc took the card. The option was viable. Phillips, an ultra-fit adrenaline junkie who had broken his arm rock-climbing, had been constantly wandering into the office like a lost soul, complaining that he hated the downtime. Another ex-cop, he was more than qualified to cover in the office over the next week.

McCabe grabbed his jacket and briefcase and headed for the door. He frowned. "Jenna Whitmore? Didn't you used to know her?"

"She's a cousin of my wife."

McCabe looked briefly arrested. "The woman you used to date?"

Marc's brows jerked together. "How did you know about that?"

McCabe lifted a brow. "This is a security firm."

With a sense of resignation, Marc slipped the card with Phillips's address into his pocket. He should have guessed. He had done a thorough background check on McCabe before he had bought into the business. It made sense that McCabe had been just as cautious. "We were just good friends."

McCabe's smile was enigmatic. "Sure. Don't break the company rule."

After McCabe's fall from grace when he had guarded Roma Lombard, who was now his wife, Marc figured there was only one hard and fast rule.

Be sure before you sleep with the client.

Chapter 6

I have priorities. Protecting Jenna Whitmore isn't one of them.

After using the facilities in the ladies' room, Jenna washed her hands and yanked a paper towel from the dispenser. In the process, the dispenser flopped open and a pile of towels cascaded onto the floor.

Muttering beneath her breath at the obviously faulty piece of equipment, she jammed the bunch of excess towels back into the top of the dispenser and closed the unit. It didn't look right, but there was nothing she could do about that.

Feeling increasingly irritable, hurt and mortified, she dried her hands on the one towel she had kept for herself then tossed it into the trash.

Balancing her handbag on the counter, she took time

out to apply fresh lip gloss and control the burst of anger and hurt. She didn't normally lose her temper.

Although that was because she was literally tied to her computer in her own home. No one else lived there, so of course there was no one to get mad at.

Feeling even more annoyed, with her life as well as with O'Halloran, she took another calming breath and strolled back to O'Halloran's office, bracing herself to be, at the very least, neutral.

There was no need. When she walked into his office, O'Halloran was talking on the phone again. The sun slanting through the window accentuated the clean lines of his profile, his rock-solid jaw. While she'd been in the bathroom, he had taken off his jacket and rolled up his sleeves. She dragged her gaze away from tanned, muscled biceps.

She couldn't help noticing that he looked fit and toned, as if he worked out. She guessed if he still personally took on VIP protection jobs for selected clients, a high level of fitness would be required.

Seconds later, he ended his conversation and strolled back to his desk. Too upset to sit, Jenna avoided his gaze and concentrated, instead, on a series of framed certificates on the wall. She remembered with a jolt that O'Halloran had qualified as a lawyer before he had applied for the police college.

O'Halloran's expression was remote as he produced a sheaf of papers. Jaw tight, she wondered who he had managed to get to protect her.

"We can offer you our VIP protection service for the period of your book-signing tour, but before we go ahead with the paperwork I'm going to have to ask you a few personal questions."

"Maybe I can shorten the process. I live alone, and I don't have any pets or lovers. I do not have a current relationship."

Come to that, she didn't have a recent-past one, either. Not that it was any of O'Halloran's business that the only man who had been on her personal horizon for the past few years was a man she had never met. She didn't even know what her number-one fan, Lydell88, looked like since he had never supplied a photograph.

With a shrug, he handed her the agreement. "You sound like you know your way around a protection contract."

Jenna took the sheets. "I had to research VIP protection for one of my books so I rang up a security firm. They were happy to tell me about their business and gave me a sample contract."

Dropping her handbag on the floor, she sat and examined the pages. The print was just a shade too small for comfort. Automatically, she reached for her spectacles, then froze.

It was a small thing, but there was no way she was going to allow O'Halloran to see her wearing spectacles. She had gone to a lot of trouble with her outfit and her make-up. She wasn't going to ruin it all now with a pair of nerdy glasses.

"If the print is too small, I can get Melanie to dig out a large-print version."

She pretended not to hear the question. "This looks complicated."

His rueful grin made her stomach tense.

"People are always complicated."

She lifted the sheets a fraction closer, trying to ignore the crazy hit of attraction. Men who didn't want you around, even when you were prepared to pay them, shouldn't be attractive. "As opposed to art. That's pretty straightforward."

O'Halloran's brows jerked together. "I knew it. You heard."

Jenna tried for a distracted look, which wasn't hard since she was trying to read the tiny print without squinting. "Heard what?"

"What I said in McCabe's office."

His narrowed gaze skewered hers. With an effort of will Jenna dragged her gaze free and tried to ignore her crazy, automatic response.

She turned a page. "McCabe. That would be the tall, good-looking one."

O'Halloran crossed his arms over his chest. "I don't tend to think of him that way, but we're probably talking about the same guy."

She gave up on trying to read a contract she could barely see and gave him the kind of steely glance she usually reserved for the marketing people when they messed with her covers. "All I need is a bodyguard for a few days. If you don't want to take on the job, fine. I'm sure you'll have someone who can."

"You're upset."

"Not in the least."

"Good. Then shall we get down to business?"

Minutes later, after O'Halloran had gone through the agreement clause by clause, underlining the disconcerting fact that even if he hadn't chosen law as a career he had all the attributes of a lawyer, Jenna signed.

She placed the pen beside the contract, folded her copy and tucked it into her handbag. "I'm sure, whoever this mystery bodyguard is, he'll be excellent at the job."

A knock on the door broke the simmering tension. A tanned, muscular man, who looked like he had just walked in off the beach or a ski slope, entered the room. Despite the fact that one arm was encased in plaster, he could have been a poster boy for a bodyguard movie.

O'Halloran introduced Troy Phillips.

Jenna shook Phillips's hand. When he smiled, he was even more dazzling. She couldn't help thinking that if he was her protection at her book signings, which were overrun with women of all ages, he was the one who was going to be mobbed.

Grimly, Marc propped himself against his desk and noted the interested gleam in Phillips's gaze and Jenna's response.

It was a watershed moment. Jenna was single, attractive, vulnerable and his.

Despite his reservations, he couldn't allow anyone else to protect her for the simple reason that he didn't want any other man that close to her.

If he'd had any doubts that he was involved with Jenna, they would have crashed and burned in that moment. If Phillips had been fit and ready for duty, instead of here to answer calls and shuffle through some paperwork, there would be no way he would let him near her.

Jenna sent him a coolly professional glance that grated, and agreed to be in touch about exact travel dates and times.

Aware that he had been expertly dismissed, Marc followed her out into the corridor then punched the call button on the elevator.

Jenna glanced at a colourful abstract painting, which decorated the wall opposite. "Phillips certainly looks fit."

Marc folded his arms across his chest. "He could probably handle just about anything with one arm tied behind his back, but he's not on active duty at the moment. It's not our policy to assign security personnel with broken limbs to a job."

He saw the wariness in Jenna's gaze and could have kicked himself. He had put that look there. She knew he had been looking for someone else to guard her, although not the reason why. If he could take back those moments he would.

The elevator doors slid open. She sent him a fierce glance as she stepped into the elevator. "Then who is?"

Marc muttered an imprecation beneath his breath, held the door before it closed and stepped inside the elevator. "Who do you think? I am."

"You said you didn't want to do the security."

"For good reasons. Personal reasons."

The flare of surprise in her eyes made his chest tighten. Cupping her jaw, he dipped his head, giving her time to pull back if she wanted. He was taking a risk in kissing Jenna. He couldn't rule out the fact that he had completely misread the situation; it had happened before.

He caught the startled moment of eye contact, the faint hitch in her breathing, then his mouth brushed hers once, twice, then settled more firmly.

Heat and sensation shot through him. Images of that long-ago night rose up to haunt him as she lifted up on her toes and angled her jaw to deepen the kiss. His phone vibrated, breaking the moment. Reluctantly lifting his head, Marc forced himself to release her and step back out into the hall.

As the doors slid closed on the elevator, he squashed

the urge to take the stairs and continue the conversation down in the lobby. Although it wasn't exactly a conversation that he wanted anymore, and now Jenna knew it.

Checking his phone and opting to leave the call, he strolled back to his office, although his mind was no longer on work.

It had been nine years since he had dated Jenna. A lot of water had passed under the proverbial bridge since then, but one thing was still true.

Whether she was dressed in jeans and oversized shirts, her long hair loose, or encased in a sexy, sophisticated suit with heels, the qualities that had originally drawn him were the same.

She had been funny, ultra-smart and sweet, with an intriguing bluntness that had been refreshing. She had also seemed to get his cop humour and she hadn't blinked an eye when he'd had to carry a weapon, something that actively frightened most women. He guessed that coming from a military family showed.

He had wanted more—a lot more—than the casual dating that had seemed to suit her, but the second he had pushed she had closed down. He had accepted the rejection. He hadn't wanted to let her go, but he had moved on. Almost ten years on she had developed some complex, fascinating layers that hooked him in even harder.

And the attraction wasn't all one way. The kiss, at least, had proved that.

Which was a relief because this time he wasn't prepared to cut his losses and step back.

Jenna drove to her local cinema to watch her usual five o'clock movie, but she could barely concentrate on traffic.

The kiss with O'Halloran replayed itself, making her toes curl and almost making her miss her turn.

The acute awareness that had held her in a vice-like grip as the elevator door had closed gripped her again, along with a dose of sheer, feminine panic. She had dreamed about making love with O'Halloran. She'd had trouble not thinking about him for most of the day, but in the space of a few seconds, the kiss had changed everything. It had been a statement of intent and a claim.

O'Halloran hadn't wanted to guard her because he had wanted to keep work and his personal life separate.

The thought that O'Halloran now considered her to be part of his personal life sent another wave of heat through her.

Whether she was ready or not, it was too late: they were involved.

She parked in the gloomy underground parking area at the mall, locked the car and remembered to make a note of anyone around her. She found her phone, which had a very good camera, and carried it in her hand as she walked into the building. If anything untoward happened, she was determined to at least take a photo of whoever she thought might be following her.

She bought her ticket then spent a few minutes sitting in the cinema lobby, observing people coming and going. Five minutes before her movie was scheduled to start, she walked into the now dim cinema and headed for *her* seat.

She liked to sit near the front, because the seats were less popular, so she usually always got the middle seat, and often no one else occupied the row. The front row also gave the illusion of almost being in the movie, which added to the experience.

As she walked toward her favourite seat, something white attracted her attention. At first she thought it was a piece of rubbish on the seat that the cinema staff had failed to clear away.

But the scent of roses hit her and suddenly her skin was crawling.

A single white rose was placed neatly on the seat that she usually occupied, if no one else had claimed it.

The scene could have been cut from *Deadly Valentine*.

A single white rose had been the calling card of the villain who had stalked Sara.

Chapter 7

Spine tingling, because whoever was stalking her had been here just minutes ago, and could still be in the theatre, *watching her*, Jenna walked quickly to the side aisle and forced herself to skim the ranks of seats and study faces.

The theatre wasn't packed. The movie was part of an arts festival program, so had limited appeal. Something about a balding head and the glint of spectacles sparked a memory. She lifted her camera to take a picture. At that moment the lights went out and sound thundered from the stereo system. Startled, she inadvertently pressed the shutter as the phone slipped from her fingers. The flash temporarily blinded her.

Someone uttered a short, uncomplimentary phrase. By the time she had found the phone and located where the balding man had been sitting, he was gone.

Her mouth was dry, her heart hammering. Tension zinged through her. She didn't know why she had singled him out, some detail had alerted her. She could have been wrong, but if so, why had he left?

Ignoring the incensed glances being sent her way, and the fact that a member of the cinema staff, with flashlight in hand, was heading straight for her, she walked quickly back to the seat that had the rose neatly placed on it. Crouching down, she took another photo. As she did so she noticed that the rose had a piece of clear cellophane wrapped around it at the base and a white ribbon.

Rising to her feet, she apologised to the teenage boy with the flashlight and agreed that she was leaving. Repressing a shudder, she picked the rose up by the flower head so that she wouldn't touch either the stem, cellophane or the ribbon.

As far as Jenna was concerned the rose was evidence. It was a long shot, but it was possible that a verifiable fingerprint might be found on the wrapping. In terms of getting a conviction, there would probably be no gain, but if she could identify the perpetrator then that would most likely stop him from stalking her.

Minutes later, she walked back out into daylight. Unlocking her car, she placed the rose carefully on the passenger seat. Reaching into her purse, she found the business card O'Halloran had given her.

Fingers a little unsteady, she pressed in his number and waited for him to pick up.

The calm timbre of his voice was reassuring. Taking a deep breath, she made an effort to speak slowly and deliberately. "He was here, at the movies. He left a rose on my seat."

The tension in her voice must have alerted him, because he didn't ask any questions about the rose. "Are you all right?"

"I'm fine." She drew an impeded breath. "I saw him."

There was a brief silence, although in no way did Jenna get the sense that O'Halloran was either still or contemplative. She got the impression that he was moving, fast. "Does he know that you saw him?"

"I think so, since my camera flash went off in his eyes."

There was another silence punctuated by a muffled thud as if a car door had just been pulled shut. "Where are you now?"

Jenna gave him directions to the mall. Satisfaction took the edge off the adrenaline rush as she heard the sound of O'Halloran's vehicle accelerating.

"Get in your car, lock the doors. I'll be there in ten minutes. If you see him again, get out of there and call me."

"I haven't seen him since I left the cinema."

"Good. Ten minutes."

Feeling shaky, mostly from the adrenaline that had been shooting through her system ever since she had spotted the rose, Jenna hung up and locked herself in her car.

As tempted as she was to watch the entrances to the parking lot for O'Halloran's arrival, she forced herself to watch the mall entrance. There were four entrances, so the chances that her stalker would come out of this one—if he was still in the mall—would be small. But if a bald man came out there was a possibility she could get another picture, maybe even a car registration.

That thought reminded her about the photos she had

taken in the cinema. Thumbing through the menu of her phone she brought up the two photos.

There was a clear shot of the white rose. The other, ruined by the odd angle caused by her losing her grip on the phone, showed a man with his hand up, as if he didn't want his photo taken.

The faint, sweet scent of the rose filled the interior of the car as she stared at the indistinct image. A creepy, tingling sensation swept the length of her spine.

It was him, she was certain of it. Although, who he was she had no idea, because his facial features were almost entirely obscured. All she had was an indication of age, somewhere in his thirties or forties, the fact that he was bald and wore glasses.

It wasn't a lot to go on, but it was *something*, even if the police wouldn't recognise it as concrete evidence.

A sleek, dark truck slid into the space next to her.

O'Halloran levered himself out from behind the wheel. Emotion, impulsive and almost overwhelming, swept through Jenna as she unlocked her car and climbed out. The irritations and disappointments of their earlier meeting—the searing moment when he had kissed her—dissolved in a rush. O'Halloran had turned up and he was forgiven.

Crazily, she felt like throwing herself into his arms. Her jaw clenched against the desire. After what had happened in the elevator that would be the equivalent of giving O'Halloran a green light and she hadn't had time to think that far ahead yet.

O'Halloran strode around the side of her car and gripped her shoulders. "Are you all right?"

"I'm fine, I managed to get the ro—"

The sentence was smothered against O'Halloran's

muscled shoulder as he pulled her close for a dizzying few seconds. Palms flattened against the hard wall of his chest, she registered the heat of his body, the clean, male scent of him, the faint resinous scent of cologne.

O'Halloran's gaze locked with hers, for a breathless moment she thought he was going to kiss her again, then she was free.

He dragged his fingers through his hair and avoided her gaze, as if he needed a few seconds. "Let's see the photo you took."

"He was sitting in the cinema. It was dark, so the shot is not great." She reached back into the car, found her phone and brought up the last two shots.

As O'Halloran studied both photos, it fleetingly registered once again that he hadn't questioned her panic over the rose, which struck Jenna as odd. After all, there were a number of innocent reasons for a rose to be left behind. The most obvious was that it had been a dating gift left behind by mistake. Although, Jenna was certain that if she was ever offered a rose on a date she wouldn't forget it.

O'Halloran frowned as he studied the indistinct shot of the man with his hand up, covering his face. "What makes you so sure it's him?"

She rubbed her arms. "I'm not sure. I just thought that the guy who left the rose might still be in the cinema, waiting to catch my reaction. When I looked up, *he* was watching me."

"Did he approach you?"

The remote quality of O'Halloran's gaze, the terse, incisive questions, made her stiffen. If she hadn't known that he had once been a cop, she would know now. "No. I was asked to leave by one of the cinema staff. The next time I checked back in his direction he was gone. But I got the rose."

She opened her car door, and indicated the white rose nestled on the passenger seat. O'Halloran's expression didn't change, but she felt like the temperature had just dropped by a couple of degrees.

"Have you touched the cellophane?"

"I picked it up by the flower head."

"Good girl. Was there a card?"

"No. Nothing." An automatic shudder went through her. The villain hadn't attached a card in *Deadly Valentine*, either, because the rose itself had been both message and threat, signalling that the villain had never forgotten Sara's rejection of him.

"Wait in the car. I'll be a few minutes."

"If you think I'm following that order you can forget it." Jenna grabbed her handbag and locked her car. She didn't want to stay behind in the car being creeped out by the rose for one more second. "I'm coming with you."

O'Halloran looked impatient. "There's no point. I'm just going to talk to mall security and see if I can't find this guy on one of their cameras."

"In that case, I'm definitely coming with you. I saw a whole lot more than the camera caught so there's a good chance I can make a positive ID."

O'Halloran looked like he wanted to argue, but Jenna didn't give him the chance. Tucking the strap of her handbag over her shoulder, she made a beeline for the mall entrance.

The security office was cramped, and the duty officer, a tall, impressively built Polynesian woman, wasn't happy about letting them in.

O'Halloran flashed his business card and ID.

Jenna started to explain that she had an upcoming book signing in the mall, when the security guard interrupted her with a grin. She knew exactly who Jenna was, because she was halfway through her latest book.

She pulled the book out of her desk drawer and introduced herself as Selene. After a short, animated conversation, Jenna obligingly signed the book.

Selene eyed O'Halloran curiously. "You look familiar, too."

Jenna felt her face warm. She quickly passed the book, front cover down, back to Selene. Now was not a great time for O'Halloran to know that by some weird coincidence, the male model her publisher had used looked uncannily like him.

O'Halloran closed the door on the small office. "You've probably seen me around. I used to be a detective down at Auckland Central."

Selene looked mildly interested. "That's probably it."

Relieved, Jenna let out a breath as Selene sat down at her computer and found the cinema complex cameras.

All six came up on the screen at once. "How far back do you want me to run them?"

O'Halloran checked his watch. "Try an hour, and fast-forward the disks. The guy is balding with glasses and could be carrying a white rose. If we spot him, or anyone carrying a white rose, we can always rewind and go frame by frame—"

"A white rose? Like the one in *Deadly Valentine*?" Selene gave Jenna an outraged look.

Jenna could have hugged her for making the instant connection. It made her own reaction to the rose seem low-key and utterly normal. It was also a warming feeling that someone else could instantly see what the stalker was doing.

O'Halloran's hand landed briefly on the small of Jenna's back, the warmth from his palm burning through the fabric of her suit jacket and distracting her from the conversation, as he moved her closer to the computer screen. He indicated which videos each of them would watch and Jenna tried to concentrate as her two screens began to replay, but her mind was still stubbornly focused on the electrifying moment when O'Halloran had touched her.

The hint had been distinctly possessive and laced with a touch of impatience, because this was all taking a lot longer than he had probably planned, but that didn't change what she had felt.

She recognized what it was, although she hadn't felt it in years—the same riveting, tingling awareness she'd experienced when O'Halloran had stepped into the elevator and said he would be guarding her.

The kind of heart-stopping, searing attraction that had once come close to ruining her life.

As dangerous as this stalker could be, O'Halloran was potentially even more dangerous on a whole other level because she now knew it had taken her years to get over him. In point of fact, she had never gotten over him, because if she had she would have been in another relationship by now.

O'Halloran glanced at her for a heart-pounding moment, making her aware that he had picked up on her restlessness. Mouth suddenly dry, Jenna was more than happy to concentrate on the screen.

Selene frowned as the videos flickered. "If this guy

is using details from your book, then he's got to be a reader, a *fan*."

Still acutely aware of O'Halloran, she kept her gaze glued to the screen. "Men do read my books. I have one male fan who reads every book then emails me."

"Maybe it's him."

"Different email address—"

Selene rolled her eyes. "Don't be fooled by that. He probably has one address to romance you, the other to scare you, know what I mean? You should take this to the police."

Jenna blinked at the connection Selene had made. A connection she hadn't considered, but now realized she should. Although it made her feel faintly sick to think that her favourite fan could be just one side of a psychotic personality. "I've already spoken to the police."

"Huh. In that case I bet they weren't helpful."

O'Halloran's expression was impatient. "Police have to follow procedure. Cyber bullying and internet offences are rife. They can't commit man hours on the strength of an email that contains no specific threat."

Jenna peered at a man who appeared to be skulking behind a group of Japanese tourists. "Apparently you have to be hurt before they take that kind of thing seriously."

"Sounds like exactly what happened with my ex." Selene cast a dark look at the banks of monitors. "That's why I took this job. This way I get to sit and watch the entrances all day. If I see anyone even remotely *resembling* Dean I call ground security. Honey, you should get the cops to run a check on your—" she sketched quotation marks in the air "—*good* fan. Sounds to me like a definite case of Jekyll and Hyde."

She stopped one of the videos, hit a series of keys to zoom in on a bald man, then abandoned the inspection when the zoom revealed that the man was elderly with a moustache. "What's this fan's name?"

"He just calls himself Lydell88."

"That settles it. If he genuinely likes your books, why doesn't he use his full name? Or, for that matter," she muttered darkly, "his *real* name. You don't seriously think anyone today is called Lydell?"

O'Halloran indicated the screen closest to him. "There's our man."

Selene froze the image and zoomed in on a man wearing a brown jacket and a ball cap. Jenna's stomach tightened. The ball cap, aside from hiding any sign of baldness, obscured most of the man's face. He wasn't carrying a rose, but he did have a shopping bag.

Selene started the video playing again. While she and O'Halloran watched the man progress through the mall, she worked with two other screens. The result was that they were able to watch Ball Cap practically until he stepped into the movie theatre.

Selene played the last video through again. All the hairs at Jenna's nape lifted as she watched the calm, methodical progress of the figure, the occasional glint of glasses as his face always angled away from the cameras.

If she hadn't been sure before, she was now. The glasses fit, as did his size and the brown jacket. He seemed younger than she had expected, but maybe that had more to do with her perception that bald men were older, which absolutely was not the case. The clincher was that he had gone to the same movie she had, and arrived there early. It was him.

O'Halloran's expression was remote. "Whoever he is, he seems to know exactly where the cameras are."

Selene nodded. "He keeps his head down, his face away from the camera. I'd say he's done his homework."

Jenna studied the blurred image, which supplied approximate height and build, but little else to add to what they already had. "A shame we can't see the rose, that would have been conclusive."

O'Halloran shrugged. "Farrell wouldn't jump through any hoops even if we could see the rose. The fact is, you can't prove he left it there for you in the first place, because there was no card. Anyone could have gone and sat in the front row and found the rose."

As much as she hated to admit it, Jenna had to agree.

Every piece of "evidence" she had was frustratingly without substance. All she had were a gut feeling and a few details from a fictional book that seemed to be coming true in her own life, none of them particularly menacing or life-threatening. Yet.

O'Halloran produced another business card, scribbled on the back of it and handed it to Selene. "Can you email me a copy of that footage?"

Selene took the card. "No problem. Hey!" She laughed and shook her head. "I know why you're so familiar."

Jenna groaned inwardly as Selene dragged out her copy of *Deadly Valentine* and turned it over on the desk, so the vibrant cover with its larger-than-life, half-naked hero was displayed.

Selene stared at O'Halloran. "You look like Cutler." She looked at the cover then back at O'Halloran again. "Man, that's freaky. You could *be* Cutler."

Chapter 8

O'Halloran insisted they pay a visit to Auckland Central, and take the rose in for fingerprinting.

Jenna slid into the front passenger seat of his truck, which was black and sleek and upholstered with leather. She had decided to leave her little Porsche in the parking lot, since the mall was so close to home. At this time of night it wouldn't be easy finding parking near Auckland Central Police Station.

Farrell wasn't in, but one of O'Halloran's old colleagues took Jenna's statement, and packaged and booked the rose for fingerprinting. A couple of days, max, and they would have a result, provided the perpetrator had a fingerprint record.

By the time they walked back to O'Halloran's car, the sun was setting, and the streets were filled with couples strolling to one of the many restaurants located along Ponsonby Road.

O'Halloran unlocked and held her door. When he climbed behind the wheel, he didn't immediately start the engine. "I don't know about you, but I'm hungry."

Jenna, still on edge since those moments in Selene's office, and the woman's blunt comment that he looked like the hero of *Deadly Valentine*, was so hungry she felt faint. "I could eat something."

"Take-out, or do you want to go to a restaurant?"

"Take-out, please." Then she wouldn't have to look at O'Halloran across a table while they ate and face the unpalatable truth that had hit her in Selene's office. That one of the reasons she had never been able to forget O'Halloran was that she had been unconsciously patterning all of her heroes on him.

He started the car and merged with traffic while they debated what to eat. Because her workday was so sedentary, she needed to watch her weight so, in the end, she opted for Chinese.

After collecting the food, O'Halloran placed the paper sack of containers on the backseat. "We'll pick up your car first."

Minutes later, he turned into the mall parking lot. After checking that no one was lurking around, he waited for her to get in the car then leaned down and spoke through the open window. "I'll follow you."

Her fingers tightened on the wheel. "Where are we going?" Although she had a sneaking suspicion.

"Your place. I was going to check out your house tomorrow, but it's a better idea to have a look around now."

A small chill went down her spine. Until that point

she hadn't known how seriously O'Halloran was taking her allegation of being stalked.

She didn't voice the other thought that had been dominating her mind ever since O'Halloran had asked if the guy in the cinema had approached her.

She had taken his photo. It wasn't a good one, but he didn't know that. She had also taken the rose, which quite possibly had his fingerprints on the wrapping.

Whoever he was, he was more calculating and methodical than the misspelt email he had sent would seem to suggest, which told Jenna that the mistakes in the email had probably been deliberate. A smokescreen created by someone who understood the process of criminal profiling.

And he now had to assume she was in a position to identify him, that she could be a threat to him.

Wearing a pair of overalls branded with the city council logo, and carrying an official-looking clipboard, Branden Tell walked through the block of flats adjacent to Jenna's old mausoleum of a house.

She had taken his photo. He couldn't believe it. *And* she had taken the rose, something else he hadn't anticipated. He didn't know what she had done with it. He had left the mall immediately, just in case she called security, but he had to assume that she had taken the rose to the police.

His fingerprints had to be all over the cellophane, although that wouldn't do Whitmore any good because he didn't have a criminal record.

However, if he did ever get caught on one of the little night excursions he indulged in just to break the boredom, that would change things. The minute the police ran his prints through their computers they would connect him to a whole raft of crimes. They would lock him up and throw away the key. By the time he got out, he would be an old man.

All he had wanted to do was frighten her into withdrawing the book from stores and cancelling the book signings. And if one of the "accidents" he had planned for her worked out, he would send a whole bunch of white roses to the funeral. The last thing he needed was a whole lot of publicity about the book, and people lining up to read *Deadly Valentine*. He didn't think that cops, most of them men, would read Whitmore's books, but *he* had read them so he had to assume that some other men would, too.

After the near miss with the pot plant, he was pretty sure he had her spooked, but she was proving oddly stubborn and resourceful, the complete opposite of the soft, vulnerable Jenna he remembered.

He skimmed the windows of the apartment block, checking for movement or evidence that he was being watched. Although, he expected that at this time of night most residents would be either eating dinner or watching the news on TV.

Jenna living next door to the apartments was a gift because it meant he didn't have to expose himself to an entire street of nosy neighbours by entering through her front gate. Even pretending to repair the gate, he would still attract notice. Most tenants of large apartment blocks were happy to accept the presence of anyone in workman's overalls on the property, automatically assuming they were there on behalf of the landlord.

With a raking glance at the end apartment, which appeared to be empty, he disappeared under the dark overhang of a tree. Tossing the clipboard into the long grass, he levered himself over the wooden fence, landing in the middle of a shaggy green shrub that smelled like insecticide.

Muttering beneath his breath, he worked his way free and emerged from the heavy undergrowth directly opposite a room lined with bookshelves that looked like her office. Walking around to the kitchen, he extracted a set of picks from his pocket. Within seconds, he had the door open.

Taking a penknife from his pocket he released the blade and walked quickly through to Jenna's alarm system, one that a firm he supplied had installed. Accessing the panel, he used the master code to disarm the alarm. He checked his watch. He didn't have much time to find what he needed.

The afternoon light was dimming as he walked through the house. Suppressing his irritation that Jenna had actually gotten wealthy writing those ridiculous books, he found her office and began a systematic search.

Streetlights glowed, illuminating the murky twilight as Marc turned into Jenna's driveway. Her sleek little Porsche disappeared into a garage, so he parked on the broad sweep of gravel fronting an old Victorian house that had had a distinctly modern makeover. The lines of the villa were colonial, but the biscotti paint job with aubergine accents was cutting-edge.

He checked the automatic wrought-iron security gate, frowning a little at the slow-motion action. Someone could easily step through and hide in the shrubbery in the time it took for the gate to close. He would get one of their techs out to reprogram the system. If he had to, he would replace the gate himself.

As he exited the truck, he checked out the front garden, a stretch of smooth lawn edged by a tangle of heavy, dark undergrowth. The border of shrubs was thick enough that it mostly hid the house from the road, but it also provided a convenient hiding place for anyone breaking into the property.

Dark clouds massed overhead. A droplet of rain splashed the bonnet of the truck. The scent of ozone, the quick flight of a bird as if something had disturbed it, combined to set him subtly on edge.

Frowning, he skimmed the street, which was empty. He put his unease down to the incoming electrical storm, which seemed to charge the atmosphere, the cool rush of damp air heightening his senses and making his skin prickle.

He grabbed the sack of take-aways and found his briefcase as Jenna strolled toward him.

The murky light made her creamy skin look magnolia-pale and her eyes even darker. She had unbuttoned her charcoal-grey jacket, revealing the mint-green camisole she was wearing underneath. Silky and utterly feminine, it was a startling contrast to the long grey skirt and red accessories, somehow creating the effect of an edgy, retro elegance that matched the house and garden.

In that moment, Jenna came into sharp focus for Marc.

Her delicate features and stylish haircut aside, there was a strength in her firmly moulded cheekbones, the set of her jaw and the clear direct way she met his gaze. Nine years ago, Jenna hadn't been overtly sexy; the main word that had always sprung to mind had been *nice.* Now her cool, underlying sensuality, which had nothing to do with any descriptive as innocuous as *nice*, hit him like a kick in the chest.

Forcing himself to suppress the kind of reaction he hadn't felt since he was a teenager, he turned his attention back to the garden. "Nice property."

She shrugged. "It's too big, but I've always loved it. I used to walk past it every day on the way to university, and the privacy suits me."

He handed her the paper sack of take-out containers. "Take these inside. I need to do a quick walk around the grounds before it gets too dark. I won't be long."

Her expression tightened fractionally, informing him that she wasn't quite as composed as she seemed. Out of nowhere, like the unscripted moment in the mall parking lot that afternoon, a fierce surge of protectiveness hit him. He had known that the run-in with the stalker had shaken her. He just hadn't realized how much.

Grimly, he clamped down on the impulse to pull her into his arms. He had already pushed the boundaries with the kiss in the elevator; he didn't want to scare Jenna off by pushing for too much, too fast.

He watched the slim, graceful line of Jenna's back as she walked up the steps to the front door, the satiny fall of dark hair shot through with lighter streaks. The attraction that had flared to life when he had met Jenna at the gravesite was showing no signs of fading, and now he didn't expect it to.

He knew his nature. When it came to women, for him the situation had always been black and white. He either felt something or he didn't; there had never been any middle ground.

That was one of the reasons it had been so easy for

him to remain single since Natalie had died. He simply
hadn't felt anything strong enough to tempt him into
an actual relationship. He'd had occasional casual liaisons, but as convenient as it would have been for those
liaisons to grow into something more, a part of him had
remained remote and uninvolved.

Until now.

Grimly he registered the growing tension in his body,
his utter masculine focus on Jenna.

Jenna turned and shot him a veiled look as she unlocked the door, letting him know in a subtle, entirely
feminine way that she had noted his interest but that the
jury was still out. "I'll get you a flashlight."

Marc's gaze shuttered. "There's no need, I have one
in the truck." And the last thing he wanted was for
Jenna to insist on coming with him, just in case he
found evidence that someone *had* been on the property.

He checked to make sure Jenna had disappeared inside then collected the flashlight and the other piece
of equipment he wanted: a Glock 17 handgun with a
shoulder holster.

Shrugging out of his jacket, he pulled on the shoulder
holster, fastened the webbing then unlocked the metal
storage case, which held the gun. With swift, practiced
movements, he slotted the magazine into its casing,
holstered the gun and shrugged back into his jacket.

Picking up the flashlight, he locked the truck and
began a systematic examination of the fence and garden.

In the thickening twilight, the powerful beam had the
effect of making the evening seem darker than it was.
Sounds seemed more distinct, the scents of city and garden intensified. He waded through foliage, checking the

fenceline, and looking for areas of crushed foliage. A few steps farther on and he discovered a dilapidated shed.

Directing the beam of the flashlight into the shed, which was filled with a jumble of old tools and firewood, he kept moving. Another few steps and he found a damaged shrub and trampled ground directly across from a room with a large bay window and a desk. At a guess, Jenna's office.

From the kitchen window, Jenna glimpsed the flickering beam of the flashlight and the pale flash of O'Halloran's shirt as she placed the take-out containers in the oven. O'Halloran had taken a good five minutes to work his way around one side of the house, she guessed it would take him the same to check out the other side, and in the meantime she didn't want their food to go cold.

Tiny droplets of rain speckled the window. She flicked on a light to brighten up the kitchen, and frowned when nothing happened. She tried a second light switch with no better luck. Power outages weren't uncommon, especially in her suburb with its old plantings of graceful but tall trees. Every time they got a strong wind, branches swayed and hit lines, or came down altogether.

Shrugging, she hunted out candles and a lighter and laid them on the table where they'd be easy to find then strolled toward the stairs, intending to change into some warmer clothing before O'Halloran came in.

She flicked on another light switch, just in case the problem in the kitchen was a blown fuse and the rest of the house still had power. When the hall remained dim, she frowned. The weather was definitely deteriorating, but as yet the wind was hardly strong enough to cause a problem.

A small trickle of unease, courtesy of the creepy episode in the mall, inched down her spine. Although it was ridiculous to think that anyone could have been in the house. The power had been on when she'd walked into her home, because she had turned off the alarm when she'd walked into the hall.

Added to that, the alarm included a wireless connection to her broadband modem. If anyone tried to interfere with the alarm in any way, aside from the ear-splitting siren and instant call to the security company, it was programmed to text her phone with a message. If anyone had broken into the house, she would have known about it before she had gotten home.

Still feeling vaguely unsettled but putting it down to the crazy day and the fact that she was hungry, she walked through the shadowy interior of the house, her heels echoing on polished floorboards. Movement caught her eye. Her pulse jumped, but it was only O'Halloran glimpsed through one of the French doors in the sitting room, checking the fence.

Letting out a breath, she forced herself to relax. O'Halloran was large, muscled and an ex-cop who had been a decorated member of the Special Tactics Squad, an elite frontline squad of armed police. If her poisonous fan was anywhere near the property, then he was the one who had the problem.

On impulse, she walked through to her office and checked her laptop. The battery should have kept it going, and she had a surge protector, but sometimes freak occurrences like lightning strikes could fry the electrics anyway.

She glimpsed O'Halloran again. He lifted a hand. Reassured by his presence, but still on edge, she disconnected the laptop from the power source and, on impulse, decided to take it upstairs. It had about four hours of battery, so if she wasn't too tired later on, she could work at the small portable desk in her bedroom.

Still feeling oddly tense, she walked upstairs, deposited the laptop on the portable desk positioned in one corner of her room and kicked off her heels. She quickly changed into slim-fitting jeans and a polo-necked midnight-blue sweater that clung softly to her hips.

With the light almost completely gone now, she searched in her bedside table and found a penlight.

She glimpsed O'Halloran out of her bedroom window as she slipped into more comfortable flats and her breath lodged in her throat as she recalled the tension that had gripped her as she had unlocked the front door.

O'Halloran's gaze had been focused and intent. In her various dating forays she had glimpsed desire, and quite often liking, but none of her dates had ever looked at her in quite *that* way.

Somewhere downstairs a floorboard creaked, pulling her out of her reverie. She could no longer see O'Halloran outside. Frowning, she walked out onto the landing and stared into the deep well of shadow cast by the staircase.

The house was old. It creaked when the timbers warmed up during the day, then again when it cooled down at night. There was nothing to be alarmed about, but with the fading light, and without her cheerful array of lamps glowing, the atmosphere was definitely creepy.

She should flick on the penlight and walk down the

stairs, but some preternatural instinct kept her frozen in place in the dark, her gaze glued to the hall below. Despite O'Halloran's presence, she kept getting an unnerving tingling sensation down her spine.

It was stress, she reassured herself. With the unpleasant incident at the cinema and two interviews at Auckland Central, it had not been an easy day.

Another creak, as if someone was stepping lightly, sent adrenaline shooting through her veins.

Someone was there. "O'Halloran?"

Chapter 9

Mood grim, O'Halloran completed the circuit of the house, ending up back by the area of trampled shrubbery. The weather was closing in, with heavy, dark clouds massing. Fat droplets of rain splashed down as he passed the beam of the flashlight over the trampled area.

Something pale gleamed in amongst the shrubbery.

All the small hairs at Marc's nape lifted. A piece of cloth, or paper, that hadn't been there five minutes ago. He said something short and hard beneath his breath. He must be losing his edge.

The cold itch down his spine now made sense, because whoever had broken the shrub had been on the property while he searched it.

Flicking the flashlight off, he levered himself up and smoothly over the fence.

Bare minutes later, as he checked the vehicles parked

out on the street, the niggling sense that something was wrong coalesced into cold knowledge.

He flicked a glance at the still darkened house and began to run, cutting back through the property with its ranks of apartments. When they had driven in to Jenna's drive, the electronically controlled front gate had worked and he had noticed a porch light glowing. In the past few minutes, with the fading sun, Jenna should have switched on lights. The big old house should be clearly visible from the street. Instead it was shrouded in darkness.

When he had done his last circuit of the house, he hadn't noticed the porch light glowing. Either Jenna had switched it off, which didn't make sense, or in the minutes since they had arrived, the power to the house had been cut.

The intruder hadn't left, and he wasn't outside.

He was *in* the house.

Chills running down her spine, Jenna padded out onto the landing.

In the time she had been upstairs, the last light had gone. The glow of sodium streetlamps flowed in the front windows, hammering home the fact that her power outage was an isolated event.

She didn't know how it had happened, but she had to assume that someone had gotten inside the house and switched the power off. Her jaw tightened. The first thing she should have done was walk out to the front hall and check the fuse box, but she had been so distracted by O'Halloran's presence that she hadn't thought to check.

She paused, holding her breath for long seconds as

she listened and allowed her eyes to adjust to the heavy gloom.

A scraping sound from the direction of her office made her stiffen.

It couldn't be O'Halloran, he was still outside. She had seen him just minutes ago strolling toward the left side of the house. If he had entered by the front door, with its steps and hardwood verandah, regardless of how light he was on his feet, she would have heard him.

The flicker of a shadow made her heart slam in her chest. A flowing solid shape, darker than the pooling shadows below, emerged from her office and paused at the base of the stairs.

Suddenly the tension that had hit her when she had collected her laptop made sense. The intruder hadn't just been in the house, *he had been in her office when she had collected her laptop*.

If he was in her office, it also followed that he had probably been after her laptop, because there wasn't much else of value in there.

She sensed more than saw him looking up the staircase, and froze. She was not directly in his line of sight. She was standing off to one side. With most of the bedroom doors shut, closing out any ambient light flowing through windows, this part of the house was now in almost complete darkness. As exposed as she felt, the odds were that he couldn't see her.

Another creak sent another small nervy shock of adrenaline through her. That was the second-to-bottom tread, which meant he was now on the staircase, and climbing.

If it was the guy who had been stalking her, she had to assume it was because he wanted the laptop.

Although she wasn't sure what he thought he would achieve by stealing her computer. The only possible reason would be to hurt her by depriving her of her work and sabotaging the publication of her next two books.

She considered her options. She could yell for O'Halloran and hope that would scare away the intruder. But given that he had to know O'Halloran was on the property, and that he had chosen to remain in the house despite the danger, she couldn't bank on that option.

He also wanted her laptop badly enough to come upstairs, knowing that she was here. Possibly the only thing she could do was stop him from taking her computer.

She had done a self-defence course, and she kept in good shape jogging and working out. He no doubt thought that taking the laptop off her was going to be easy, but after the day she'd had, if he wanted it, she decided grimly, he was going to have to rip it out of her cold, dead hands.

Easing her feet out of her shoes, Jenna backed away from the landing rail and the slow, gliding advance of the intruder. The back of one hand brushed against the wall.

Swallowing the sudden tightening panic that gripped her chest, her throat, she followed the wall until she hit the frame of her door. Her room was lighter than the landing, although just enough that she could make out the silvery gleam of her laptop.

Sliding the penlight into her jeans pocket, she picked up the computer and shoved it under her mattress then looked around a little wildly. In the end, out of time, she picked up a heavy earthenware vase that was sitting on one of her dressers and positioned herself to one side of the door. If she could hit him hard on the head, with any luck, he would go down. Then she could run. It wasn't much of a plan, but it was all she had.

Holding the vase above her head, she stared hard at the opening. The quality of light in the doorway altered. She hadn't heard anything and, eerily, she still couldn't see anything until he turned his head and the frail light flowing through the window gleamed on pale irises. It was then she realized the reason she couldn't see him was that he was dressed entirely in black, and he was wearing a balaclava.

The urn came down with a thud that sent a shock-wave up both her arms. He grunted, but in the instant before the vase hit his head, he had shifted sideways and it had bounced off his shoulder.

The sound of the vase shattering split the air. "Bitch."

A gloved hand clamped her throat and she was shoved back against the wall with force. The back of her head connected sharply. Convulsively, she reached for breath, but his fingers squeezed, cutting off air.

Above the pounding of blood in her ears, the la-boured rasp of his breathing, dimly, Jenna registered a thundering sound. Not the approaching storm. O'Halloran was coming up the stairs.

The explosive sound of something shattering, followed by a sharp crack had sent a kick of adrenaline through Marc that almost stopped his heart.

Grimly castigating himself for not considering that Jenna's stalker could still be on the property after he'd noted the crushed foliage, he lunged up the last two stairs. The Glock clasped in his hands, he crossed the

landing and stepped into a room filled with cold swirl-
ing air.

For a split second he thought he was too late, then
his eyes, by now adjusted to the darkness, easily picked
out Jenna sitting on the floor, gasping for breath, and a
curtain flapping in the breeze.

Before he could ask if she was all right, her gaze
sliced to his, steady and oddly fierce. She stabbed a finger at the window. "I'm okay. He went off the balcony."

Marc didn't stop to ask why her voice was so raspy.
By the sounds he had heard it was a given that she had
been hurt. From the shards of crockery crunching un-
derfoot, he savagely hoped she had given as good as
she'd got.

Jaw tight, he holstered the Glock and flowed out onto
the balcony and over the side. As he climbed down the
gnarled limbs of wisteria that clung to the house and
festooned the balcony, he made a mental note that the
ornamental shrub had to go. If it could be climbed down,
that meant someone could also use it to gain entrance
to the house.

A crashing sound below, at a guess the plastic waste
disposal bin he'd seen tucked discreetly outside the
laundry being knocked over, signalled that the intruder
was down.

Marc hit the ground running. He glimpsed a flickering movement and registered that the reason he was
finding it so hard to pinpoint the intruder was because
he was dressed entirely in black, including a balaclava.

Cursing himself for not having a pair of night-vision
goggles on hand, he waded through undergrowth. From
now on he would make sure he had the full kit for night
surveillance stored in the trunk of his car at all times.

Flinging aside whippy branches, he boosted himself up and over the fence, but, from the sound of pounding footsteps, he knew he was going to be too late. He ran out on the road in time to see a pair of taillights winking as a van turned and accelerated away.

Sucking in a deep breath, he turned to study the property he had just run through. The intruder had been unexpectedly smart. He had bypassed the expensive properties on the other two boundaries, and the street entrance, in favor of using one that had multiple tenants. Judging from the bikes stacked against walls, the old sofas and boxes of empty beer cans, most of them were students. World War Three could break out in their front yard and they wouldn't notice.

He wouldn't underestimate the stalker again. Although he hadn't been caught entirely flatfooted. He had bagged the clipboard and pen he had found lying in the grass.

More importantly, he had gotten the registration number for the van.

Chills running up and down her spine, Jenna stared out into the storm-tossed night and watched as O'Halloran climbed over her fence with fluid ease.

That was too easy, she thought starkly. She was going to have to build the fence higher. Stepping back inside her bedroom, she remembered the penlight in her pocket, extracted it and flicked on the reassuring beam of light.

Hands shaking with an overload of adrenaline and reaction, she closed the French doors and locked them then turned to survey the mess. Pottery shards littered the floor and somehow the dresser nearest the door had been overturned, probably when the intruder had stumbled off balance after she'd hit him. A set of elegant glass perfume bottles were scattered amongst the pottery shards, some of them also smashed.

Stepping out onto the landing, she made her way gingerly downstairs. Her head was throbbing from the crack she'd received when the back of her head had hit the wall, and her throat felt tender. She hadn't looked, but she was guessing she would have a necklace of interesting bruises by morning. She also felt a little weird, unsettled and shaky, her pulse pounding way too fast. Mild shock, she realized.

A shudder went through her when she remembered the moment her assailant had gripped her throat. The hold had been tight, and more than a little personal. In that moment, with his eyes glittering into hers, she had gotten the distinct impression that whoever he was, he hated her.

If he hated her, it followed he had to know her.

Swallowing painfully, she reached the hall just as O'Halloran strode in the front door.

His gaze locked on hers, and she drew a swift breath.

His expression was remote, implacable, his eyes shooting cold fire.

"Are you all right?"

"Yes."

"You don't look it."

"Thanks," she said shakily.

A split second later, she was in his arms, his hold firm enough that she could feel the unmistakable bulge of a shoulder holster.

She remembered O'Halloran stepping through her bedroom door, a large black gun held in both hands, his toneless voice, the efficient way he had checked on her before ghosting out onto the balcony and over the side. She had heard the intruder clambering down her wisteria vine; O'Halloran had made almost no noise, he'd seemed to move in a bubble of silence.

As if sensing her tension, O'Halloran eased her a little closer, and wrapped her tighter, cradling her against his chest. His warm palm cupped her nape, urging her to rest her head on his shoulder.

"Ouch."

His fingers probed and found the bump forming at the back of her head. "He hit you."

She blinked at the utter lack of emotion in his voice and then, like a bolt out of the blue, she finally got it, she finally got *him*. O'Halloran wasn't either emotionless or disconnected; he was blazing mad.

Some people got emotional in stressful situations. From what she knew of O'Halloran, he never did, which was what had made him such a good cop and the perfect bodyguard.

She couldn't remember one single occasion, even counting the tragic house fire, when he had lost control. Nine years ago, when she had broken up with him, had been a case in point. His calm, measured response had convinced her she had done the right thing.

She had always thought his lack of response had signalled a basic inability to feel, but she was suddenly, stunningly aware that the opposite was the case. O'Halloran cared; the measured response and flat voice was just his way of coping.

"He didn't exactly hit me," she said cautiously. "My head bounced off the wall."

There was a moment of tense silence. "What else?"

For a brief moment, she simply soaked in the careful way he was cradling her, the knowledge that O'Halloran cared that she had been hurt. "Just the bruising on my throat."

O'Halloran swore softly. "I need some light."

Releasing her, he gently prised the tiny penlight from her hand, walked the few steps to the fuse box and beamed the light into the cavity while he turned the power back on.

He flicked a switch and the hall flooded with light. Peeling back the polo-neck of her sweater, he gently touched the tender area, sending streamers of tingling heat radiating out from that one small point of contact. "I'm going to kill him."

The soft flat statement was subtly claiming and wholly electrifying. Although, Jenna knew she shouldn't build too much into it. She had just been threatened and attacked, and O'Halloran was with her in the role of protector. He was male, powerful and in control in the kind of take-charge, alpha way that was hard to resist, but she also knew that he would fiercely guard whoever was in his care.

He handed her the flashlight then insisted on examining the bump on the back of her head.

She winced as he probed, but when he asked if she wanted a doctor, she refused. "I'm not concussed. I had concussion when I was a kid and I know what that feels like. That's just sissy bruising."

O'Halloran's mouth kicked up at the corners. The glint of humour, the moment of uncomplicated intimacy, filled her with a crazy, giddy warmth.

After everything she had been through that day, Jenna reflected, the most important thing shouldn't be that somehow, despite all of the bad things that had happened, she and O'Halloran were in it together.

O'Halloran insisted that she walk through to the kitchen and sit down while he got ice for her head. He turned on lights, found a bag of frozen peas, wrapped a kitchen towel around it and made her hold it against the bump.

He opened cupboards. "Where do you keep your first-aid supplies?"

She directed him to the pantry then obediently swallowed the painkillers he gave her along with a glass of water.

She insisted he also hand her a second ice pack for her neck, this one frozen beans. When he frowned at the request, she gave him a level look. "If ice can take down the bruising on my head, it can do the same job on my neck. Since I've got a book launch to attend tomorrow evening, it would be kind of nice not to look like someone just tried to strangle me."

Especially when photos would be taken that would appear in local newspapers and on various internet sites. The last thing she wanted was to give her poisonous fan the satisfaction of knowing that he had hurt her.

Luckily, her sweater had cushioned her neck and make-up would hide some of the marks, but if the bruising was too profound, the dark colour would still show through.

While she held the two packs of frozen vegetables in place, O'Halloran made calls, one to Auckland Central, one to McCabe. When he hung up, his expression was grim. "The police are sending someone out. He should be here in the next fifteen minutes."

O'Halloran relieved her of the job of holding the peas

at the back of her head. "Now tell me everything that happened from the time you walked inside."

As emotionlessly as possible, Jenna related the sequence of events. Going back over what had happened kept sending small shocks of adrenaline through her and she felt furious and shaky in turns. It was an interesting effect.

O'Halloran said something soft under his breath. "Honey, I'm sorry, but this has to be done. When the detective gets here, he's going to ask you the same questions. If we go over it now, it'll be easier when you have to give a statement."

"This is my problem." Jenna held out one hand. Despite her efforts she couldn't keep it steady.

O'Halloran grinned quick and hard. "I've got an idea that might help. Where do you keep your liquor?"

"There's brandy and sherry in the pantry."

He opened the pantry door and took down a bottle. "Which do you prefer?"

"Neither," she muttered flatly. "I use them for cooking."

"Too bad." She heard the click of a glass tumbler, the sound of pouring, and placed a bet with herself that he had chosen the brandy.

She was wrong, he had quarter-filled the glass with sherry.

"It's got 'fortified' on the label," he said dryly, "there's more sugar. That's key, so drink up."

"Is that an order?" With a grimace, she sipped. The rich, syrupy flavour spread across her tongue and flowed like liquid fire down her throat.

He replaced the cap on the bottle. "Last I heard women don't take orders anymore."

Jenna choked then had to cough. She hastily placed the glass on the table before she spilled the sherry. O'Halloran was being downright charming, but he wasn't flirting with her. He was just trying to help her past her little battle with shock.

He gave her a gentle thump on the back. "Better?"

She gave a hiccoughing gulp then drew a long breath. "*Distracted* is more the word."

"Good. I've got another remedy." Removing the bag of frozen beans from her neck, he tossed it on the table and hooked out a chair.

Moments later, he scooped her off her chair and sat down with her on his lap.

Chapter 10

Too surprised to protest, Jenna grabbed at his shoulders to steady herself. "I haven't heard of this remedy." The muscular hardness of his thighs beneath hers and the furnace heat of his chest and arms were not exactly comforting, but he had definitely driven out the shaky chills and given her something else to obsess about.

One big hand curled around her nape, pressing her head against his shoulder. "It's not textbook."

She inhaled O'Halloran's warmth and scent. Okay, now he was definitely flirting with her, but the rumble of his voice, the steady pound of his heart, was soothing. She gave up the idea of bolting and stayed in place. "I could use another drink."

He pressed the tumbler of sherry into her hands and waited until she drank. "Can you remember if he said anything?"

A flashback of the black balaclava and the pale glint of his eyes made her stiffen. She couldn't prevent the small shudder that went through her.

"Have another sip, it'll help."

Obediently, she took another mouthful of sherry, then a second, waited for the warming effect, then tried to think. "Other than a nasty name, nothing. The only thing I really noticed was that he was angry. Make that very angry, and it was personal."

Her stomach tightened at the thought that someone in her past hated her enough to break into her home, *wait there while she was in the house*, then attack her, even knowing O'Halloran was outside. "I must know him. When I looked into his eyes…" She frowned, trying to catch an elusive wisp of memory.

"We can work through that later. What else did you notice? The colour of his skin, the way he talked, the way he smelled."

She closed her eyes. The instant she did that, O'Halloran's heartbeat seemed louder. She forced herself to relax, concentrating on the soothing regular beat, the cosy encircling warmth of his arms.

Taking a breath, she deliberately visualised the moment she had stood in the doorway, poised to hit the stalker with the vase. She tensed as she recalled the blackness filling the doorway then the shock of realisation when she had seen the glint of his eyes. "European. He had light skin and eyes. He was tall, because I had to look up, but not as tall as you. Maybe about six-one."

She thought back and remembered one other detail. "He smelled like new appliances. When I bought a new dishwasher and washing machine for the house and unpacked them, it was that smell. The polystyrene packing, I guess."

"That gels with the vehicle he used to make his getaway. It was an appliance van."

She straightened and stared into O'Halloran's eyes. "You got the number."

His mouth kicked up at the corners in that mesmerising way. "I got the number."

A dizzying sense of triumph and satisfaction spiralled through her. As scary as the stalker was, she thought, he wasn't nearly as scary as O'Halloran. She had wondered what had been taking O'Halloran so long; now she had her answer. He had been busy outsmarting her stalker.

His gaze locked with hers. "Honey, I'm sorry I took so long to get to you. When I realized the house was in darkness, I almost had a heart attack. I knew he had to be inside."

Grimly she concentrated on the amber colour of the sherry. Unfortunately, the adrenaline-laced flashback to the moment his hand had clamped onto her throat was hard to stop. "He must have been inside already when we drove in. I didn't realize until I was upstairs. I think he was after my laptop."

His gaze sharpened. "Did he get it?"

"No way. I hid it under the mattress."

"Then you hit him with the vase." He grinned. "That's my girl."

Jenna tried to squash the burst of pure pleasure that glowed through her at the statement. Despite the fact that she was sitting on his lap, she was not by any stretch of the imagination "his girl." If she wanted to underline that fact all she had to do was recall that O'Halloran hadn't wanted to guard her and had done his best to fob her off on someone else. "I was going for his head. Unfortunately I got his shoulder instead."

The faint shaking of O'Halloran's chest alerted her to the fact that he was laughing.

Jenna blinked and tried to look away from the mesmerising glint of white teeth, the sudden glimpse of the carefree, younger O'Halloran she had once known, but the sherry had kicked in and she was feeling just the tiniest bit woozy.

Feeling suddenly, ridiculously self-conscious she relaxed back against his chest and tried not to love it when his arms tightened around her. "This could get to be addictive."

"Not as addictive as this."

Cupping her chin, he gently angled her head. "I'm going to kiss you. If you don't want it, just say so and I won't."

Her heart slammed once, hard. She found herself caught in the net of his dark gaze, riveted by the mouth-watering cut of his cheekbones and the sexy hollows beneath, riveted by his mouth. The fact that he had given her a choice, putting her in the driving seat with the kiss, was seductive in itself, and was more than a little manipulative, she decided. But even knowing that O'Halloran was managing her in a distinctly male way, just the fact that he *wanted* to do so had the effect of draining away any objection.

And she should have an objection. Over the past few minutes, O'Halloran had moved in on her in stages, holding her, caring for her injuries, sitting her on his lap. Allowing more was tantamount to giving permission for sex.

He lowered his head, his breath washed over her

cheek and, in that moment, Jenna knew she wasn't going to move, and she wasn't going to say no.

She was twenty-nine, and since O'Halloran, she had never been able to choose anyone else. She had never been able to even relax with any of the men she had dated, or enjoy being kissed, which had ruled out intimate touching and sex.

She'd been accused of being frigid, but she knew that wasn't the case. She wanted to fall in love. She wanted the dizzying highs and the gritty lows, the laughter and the tears and the tender moments, and she definitely wanted the sex.

She wanted to touch and taste and smell; she wanted the earthy, no-holds-barred intimacy of being naked with her man while he made love to her.

Dispassionately, she stared at the hard line of O'Halloran's jaw, the sexy five o'clock shadow. Her problem was that O'Halloran had spoiled her for anyone else. As hard as she tried not to, every time she met someone new, unconsciously, she compared him to O'Halloran.

Cupping his jaw with her free hand, she lifted up the last few inches and touched her mouth to his. She felt his surprise, the hitch in his breath. A split second later, O'Halloran's arms closed more tightly around her, although he kept the kiss soft, giving her the opportunity to draw back if she wanted.

A pastiche of conflicting emotions threw her back to the intense moments in the elevator, then further back still, nine years, to the incandescent lovemaking in his apartment.

Heat shimmered and pooled. Memories, new and old,

seemed to shift and meld as she wound her arms around O'Halloran's neck and gave herself over to the kiss.

His palm flattened in the center of her back, the heat of it burning through her sweater as he urged her closer. Her breasts were flattened against the hard wall of his chest, her nipples pebble-hard. The firm shape of his arousal against one thigh sent a sharp, hot pang through her.

Dimly she noted that it was time to stop, climb out of O'Halloran's lap and regain some semblance of control. But with O'Halloran still holding her with seducing firmness while his mouth settled more heavily on hers, stopping was rapidly becoming an abstract concept.

He lifted his head, his gaze narrowed and glittering, as if he'd divined her intention to stop. In that moment, Jenna realized that the concept of experimenting with O'Halloran was inherently, dangerously flawed.

She felt as if she'd been kicked in the stomach. She hadn't ever been able to forget O'Halloran for one very good reason. Nine years ago she hadn't just been attracted to him; she had fallen in love.

That was why it had been so difficult seeing O'Halloran and Natalie as a married couple, and why she had kept a careful distance.

The enormity of the mistake she'd made in falling for O'Halloran made her stomach hollow out. She should have met someone in a safe, steady, "normal" job. A man she could have settled down with and started a family.

To make matters worse, if anything, she was even more attracted to this older, grimmer version of O'Halloran.

O'Halloran reclaimed her lips and all of the reasons

she should pull back evaporated on a raw surge of heat. Instead, she cupped his face and kissed him back, wallowing in the scent and taste of him, his hard, masculine warmth.

O'Halloran hadn't come near her in years, now, within days of that meeting in the cemetery, he was making no bones about wanting her. And crazily, she was teetering on the brink of going to bed with him.

A vibrating pulse resonated through the kitchen.

O'Halloran lifted his head. "I need to answer that."

Calmly, he reached around her and retrieved the phone from the kitchen table, while keeping her on his lap, and answered the call.

The abrupt change from passion to calm neutrality, while O'Halloran fielded the call, was like a dash of cold water.

Not prepared to sit tamely on his lap while he talked business, Jenna unlooped her arms from around his neck and eased off his lap. Not quite saved by the bell, but close. She had forgotten O'Halloran's knack of switching from hot to cold. That macho, distinctly alpha quality had confused her in the past, but she was not prepared to be confused now.

Grabbing the rapidly thawing bags of frozen vegetables, she replaced them in the freezer then remembered to check the take-aways.

As soon as she opened the oven door and smelled the aroma of spicy Chinese, her stomach rumbled. Probably the reason she felt so shaky was that she needed to eat.

"Let me help you with that."

Jenna noted O'Halloran's watchful gaze, as if he was assessing her mood and had judged correctly that she had backed off. "If you want to help you can set the table. The plates are in the cupboard next to the pantry."

She grabbed an oven mitt and set warm containers of food on the kitchen counter, breathing a sigh of relief as O'Halloran began setting out cutlery and plates.

The intercom at the front door buzzed, indicating that someone was at the front gate.

Jenna's head came up sharply enough to send a throb of pain through her skull.

"I'll get it." O'Halloran's gaze was still oddly neutral, his voice deep and flat. "That'll be either Hansen or McCabe."

A small shudder of reaction went through her as he strode out of the kitchen to see who was out on the street. She was jumpy, but then a lot had happened in the space of the past forty or so minutes.

Leaning back against the counter, she felt the lump at the back of her head. Thankfully, it had responded to the ice and had mostly flattened out.

Although, that wasn't her only problem.

She touched lips that still tingled and burned from O'Halloran's kiss. After nine bland, benign years without any discernible emotional highs or lows, the past had come back and bitten her, with a vengeance.

She was still trying to figure out just where the biggest danger lay: from the masked intruder she had upset with her latest book, or the ex-boyfriend she had hired to protect her.

Marc stepped out into the rain and disengaged the manual lock for the front gate, allowing a sleek, black four-wheel drive to glide into a space beside his truck.

He wasn't surprised to see McCabe step out because

the SUV was his. What he hadn't expected was for Mc-Cabe to bring company in the form of Carter Rawlings and Gabriel West. Both former Special Air Service associates of McCabe's, Marc had met them a few years back during a dangerous situation that had developed when he had been staying in Carter's hometown, Jackson's Ridge.

Since then they had gotten into the habit of socialising on a regular basis. Marc had even found himself nominated for duty as a godparent for Carter's first child, a little hellion called Blake. Saying yes had been a tough moment, but Carter hadn't brooked a refusal. He had understood how much Marc had lost.

Marc lifted a brow at their evening clothes. "Looks like I interrupted something."

McCabe shrugged out of his jacket, jerked loose the knot of his tie and tossed both in the rear passenger seat. "We were at an SAS reunion dinner."

"More like a wake if you ask me." Carter, who had probably gotten rid of the jacket and tie at the beginning of the evening, walked around the bonnet of the SUV and clapped Marc on the shoulder. "Sadly, I didn't recognize anyone."

McCabe frowned. "I saw you talking to Oz."

"That wasn't Oz," Carter said flatly. "Oz had crazy eyes. Whoever was impersonating him looked—"

"Normal?" The third passenger, Gabriel West, by far the quietest of the three and, Marc had always thought privately, the most lethal, stepped just short of the light flowing from the porch. "You're right. No way was that the Oz we once knew. He was carrying an extra twenty pounds and driving a people carrier. I'm going with the alien abduction scenario."

Carter looked irritable. "He was bald, not green."

West shrugged and extended a hand to Marc. "Whatever. There was no pizza or beer at the reunion, so an executive decision was made."

Marc accepted West's brief handshake, automatically noting the way both McCabe and Rawlings had fanned out slightly. Even though the positioning was probably unintentional, designed to cover arcs of attack, it emphasised that, the banter aside, this was not a social visit.

He had requested backup and McCabe had brought it. All three had once been part of a tight and very successful SAS team. The tendency to fall into the natural rhythms and patterns of a patrol was probably as instinctive and natural to each of them as breathing.

He jerked his head in the direction of the house. "If you're hungry, there are Chinese take-aways in the kitchen."

The door opened, and porch light flared over Jenna, highlighting her delicate curves, the exotic slant of her cheekbones and dark eyes. Three sets of male eyes swivelled. Marc logged the small silence that followed, the automatic aura of male appreciation.

Jenna smiled coolly. "I take it this is the cavalry."

Marc stepped toward Jenna, the move instinctive, blatantly laying claim, he realized. If any of the three men wanted to shake hands they would have to get past him first.

He made introductions and watched over the brief exchanges as Jenna invited them into the house. Even knowing that McCabe, Rawlings and West were all happily married to women they were in love with didn't make any difference. They were competition, and Jenna was single and available.

Until about five minutes ago.

The decision he had made when he had picked up Jenna, sat her in his lap and kissed her, settled in more firmly. He had wanted to comfort her. He had wanted her, period. He didn't know where this would take them long-term, but he had his confirmation that Jenna wanted him.

Marc's jaw tightened at the careful way Jenna avoided his gaze. Now that he had made his decision, he was impatient to claim her, but he was aware that if he pushed too hard he could lose her.

Jenna's reserve had always been about protection, not frigidity. Nine years ago the reason he hadn't been able to reach beyond her reserve was that not only had she lost her father to the military, she had also lost a fiancé.

The situation had been frustrating, but at least he had finally understood why she'd been so wary of him. In retrospect, because he was a cop, it had been a small miracle that she had even consented to go out with him at all.

Discovering that Jenna had been a virgin when they had made love had been a watershed moment. The relationship had ended, but despite the passage of years he had continued to feel proprietorial about her. In a purely masculine sense, she had belonged to him.

Since then she would have had lovers.

Years had passed, and Jenna was single and gorgeous; he had to accept that fact, even if he didn't like it.

He watched as Carter, West and McCabe filed inside as meekly as if butter wouldn't melt in their mouths, when the reality was somewhat different.

Marc had heard some of the stories and read edited Reuters reports of a couple of the SAS missions they had been involved in overseas. They were his friends and no longer in the SAS, but that didn't change the fact that they had been, and still were, should the occasion demand it, bona fide predators.

Jaw tight, he followed them inside the house. Mc-Cabe, Rawlings and West wouldn't touch Jenna, but in that moment he logged a salient fact. The world was filled with men who would, in a heartbeat. If he left the way clear for them.

Over his dead body.

Chapter 11

Jenna saw a second vehicle arrive just as O'Halloran was about to close the front door. Her stomach dropped a little as she recognized Elaine Farrell with Detective Hansen.

She activated the gate to let them in the drive and stepped out onto the porch as O'Halloran shook Hansen's hand.

She had told them the intruder had been wearing gloves, so there was no fingerprint evidence to be collected. O'Halloran gave them the licence tag and description of the van.

Twenty minutes later, after giving her statement and having Hansen and Farrell check out her upstairs bedroom, they walked the property in the light, persistent drizzle that had set in, then left.

Jenna had insisted on accompanying O'Halloran and

the two police officers. She had needed to see where the intruder had gotten in, so she could make plans to make the fence secure.

A chill shot down her spine when she saw that the entry point was right across from her office window. Even if the stalker hadn't climbed over the fence, he had probably been able to watch her from the other side.

Wet hair trailing down her back, Jenna stepped into the light and warmth of the entrance hall. O'Halloran, his hair wet and his shirt clinging to broad shoulders, because he had walked through soaking foliage, glided in behind her.

Jenna grabbed towels from the downstairs linen cupboard, kept one for herself and handed the other to O'Halloran. As she strolled back into the kitchen, McCabe, West and Carter stepped in her back door. She saw that they were also wet. They had also been outside. They had obviously been checking out her property although she hadn't seen or heard them.

She collected more towels and handed them out.

Bemused, Jenna listened to the tales bandied back and forth about past operations. A lethal jewel thief who had tried to kill West's wife, Tyler, and the misplaced bullet that had ended West's reputation as untouchable in battle. The saga of the escaped ostriches in Carter's hometown of Jackson's Ridge.

The conversation switched to speculation about her stalker and possible avenues the investigation would take.

McCabe folded his towel when he'd finished with it and placed it neatly on the end of her counter. "If Farrell's got the case, this guy may as well give up now. The lady's got a reputation."

Carter folded his arms over his chest and leaned against the kitchen counter. "Farrell's a gunslinger. No sense of humour, though. The only time I ever saw her smile was when West got shot in the ass—"

A bunched-up towel hit Carter in the midriff.

When he spoke, West's voice was mild. "Do we have to talk about that?"

O'Halloran, who looked as if he was having trouble controlling his mirth, rubbed a hand over his mouth. "Pretty sure Farrell did a lot more than smile. I heard she used her phone camera."

Carter used the towel to blot his hair again then dropped it over the back of a chair. "She used it. I erased the evidence. She made the mistake of putting the phone down while she was booking some guy." He patted West on the shoulder. "You owe me, big-time."

West shot Jenna an embarrassed look. "Ignore them. I was protecting my wife."

McCabe, who had been talking into his cell out in the hall, stepped back into the kitchen. "And we all love it that you went to that extreme."

O'Halloran grinned. "All in the line of duty, and anything beats herding ostriches. I've still got *those* scars."

Jenna discreetly checked on the food in the oven. There wasn't enough for five, so she grabbed fresh vegetables out of the fridge to stir-fry and grabbed packets of instant noodles from the pantry.

O'Halloran joined her by the stove. "I'm no chef, but if you want stir-fried vegetables, I can do that."

She handed him a knife and board then put the noodles on to cook.

While O'Halloran chopped, Jenna got out the wok and some oil, and set it to heat. Carter and Mc-

Cabe found plates and cutlery and set the table, while O'Halloran cooked the vegetables. Minutes later, Jenna extracted the take-out containers from the oven that were filled with now sadly wilted Chinese and placed them on the table. Along with the large bowl of noodles and the stir-fried vegetables, there was enough food, but barely.

Her heart pounded just a little faster as O'Halloran held her chair for her then took the seat next to hers. He wasn't sitting any closer to her than Carter on her other side, but she couldn't help being ultra-sensitive to his presence.

From the moment he had stepped back inside the house after chasing the intruder, O'Halloran had been sticking close.

At first, she had thought it was just his natural protective streak. She had gotten hurt while in his care, so of course he would be careful that nothing further happened to her.

But his behaviour wasn't just about protection. From the time McCabe and his two friends had arrived, O'Halloran had made no bones about bluntly staking his claim on her in front of the other men. And since that kiss he had constantly invaded her personal space.

The physical closeness signalled a major step into uncharted territory with O'Halloran, and the message he was sending was loud and clear. She could delay the issue all she liked, but unless she came up with a definitive *no*, sex was going to enter the equation.

It was no longer a matter of *if* so much as *when*.

Marc ate slowly but steadily, despite his hunger, more aware of Jenna—the pure, elegant line of her profile, the faint flowery perfume that clung to her skin—than the taste of the food on his plate.

His phone vibrated. Excusing himself, he walked out into the hall and took the call. It was Farrell. They had checked out the registration plate and it belonged to a security company. They had rung the firm and one of the guys had just gone down to the compound and checked. The van wasn't in the compound. It had been left out on the road, with the keys under the mat.

Grimly, Marc hung up and walked back into the kitchen and related the news.

When McCabe heard the name of the firm he looked interested. "They do installations. I'll give Williams, the guy who runs it, a call. He'll let me look at his employee roster."

Carter picked up plates and carried them to the counter. "If the van was left outside of the compound, there's got to be some security footage."

Marc slipped his phone into his pocket. "Farrell's already covered that angle. Whoever used the van was smart enough to park away from the surveilled area."

West raised a brow. "So the guy returned the vehicle *and* knew where the cameras were. It's got to be one of the employees."

Jenna set her fork down and began stacking empty serving dishes. "Or someone in the security business, who's got access. If it helps, I've got a partial photo of him on my camera."

Marc suddenly thought of something that hadn't happened earlier in the evening, which should have. He caught Jenna's gaze. "When you left the house today, did you set your alarm?"

"It was on. I never leave the house, even to go for a walk, without setting it."

"When we got to the house the power was on, so the alarm was working."

She caught his drift immediately. "The alarm was set, but it didn't go off, even though he was inside the house when we got here."

Security alarms. He felt as if a piece of the puzzle had just fallen into place, crazily linking what was happening to Jenna even more strongly with his own investigation into Natalie's and Jared's deaths.

In that instant, he remembered why the guy wearing the ball cap at the cemetery the previous day had looked familiar. A couple of months earlier when he had been researching the firm that had installed the security alarm in his house, which had burned down, an employee in a ball cap had been spooked by his presence and had left in a hurry.

Marc had hit a brick wall when it had turned out that the guy he had seen wasn't an employee of the firm. He had assumed that whoever it was had probably been a customer who had recognized him as an ex-cop and made a quick exit. It happened occasionally, so he had written off that particular episode.

But not anymore.

The guy who was stalking Jenna wore a ball cap. It was a small point, but it was too much of a coincidence for him to ignore.

"That seals it. The odds are our boy works in security, probably selling or installing systems."

There was no other explanation. The man had bypassed Jenna's alarm, which was a good one, so that probably meant he knew his way around the interior wiring, or he had access to the manufacturer's master codes. First thing in the morning he would arrange to have the alarm removed and taken in for fingerprinting then have a new system installed.

Jenna walked through to her office, found her handbag and looked for her phone so she could provide the guys with copies of the photo. When she couldn't find the phone, she rummaged through the bag to doublecheck.

She became aware that O'Halloran was leaning against the doorjamb. "The phone's gone."

"Maybe you left it in your car."

"No. I always carry my phone in a side pocket in my handbag, specifically so I don't forget it."

A flash of memory came back to haunt her; the moment she had been spooked earlier, the creaking floorboards. "He was in here. I thought he must have been after my laptop, but it makes more sense that he was after the phone."

"And the photograph. Too bad we already downloaded a copy at Auckland Central. What kind of phone was it?"

Jenna set the bag down on her desk, suppressing the queasy desire to empty the contents of her bag on her desk and wipe everything down. Whoever he was, he had been wearing gloves, so his skin hadn't actually touched anything she owned; somehow that fact was important.

Jenna supplied the make of the phone. A quick rummage and she found the box and the book that went with it.

O'Halloran checked out the specs. "It's got Bluetooth and a GPS. Is your wireless connection active?"

"I never turn it off. When I'm away from my desk, the phone's my portable office."

"Good. I'll give this to West. He's got shares in a phone network and some scary software he developed for the military. If he can get an access code, we should be able to remotely activate the GPS function on the phone."

A flurry of rain hit her office windows. The cold air that went with the building storm seemed to seep through the glass. Jenna rubbed at her arms, to stave off the chill.

Her jaw clenched when she noticed that her hands were doing the shaking thing again.

O'Halloran said something soft beneath his breath, laced his fingers through hers and pulled her into a loose clinch.

Surprise gave way to warmth and tingling heat, pushing back the reaction that had gripped her when she had realized *he* had taken the phone.

She let out a breath and tried to relax, dropping her forehead on O'Halloran's shoulder and breathing in his scent. O'Halloran's palm curved around her nape, the fiery heat comforting.

The phone was just a possession. It could be replaced easily enough. It was the underlining of the fact that the stalker had been in her home and had systematically gone through her things—the sense of violation—that had upset her.

After a few seconds, when O'Halloran seemed content to simply hold her, she finally began to relax.

O'Halloran responded by easing her close enough

that one thigh slid between his and her breasts flattened against his chest. She could feel the masculine shape of him against one hip, but the semi-arousal aside, the hug still felt more about comfort than sex.

The fierce tension that had gripped her left her by degrees, making her aware of just how tightly strung she had been. Letting out a breath, she relaxed a little more, enjoying the feeling of being cocooned by O'Halloran's heat and strength.

His hand squeezed gently at her nape, adding to the delicious feeling of comfort. "I know it's a shock," he murmured. "The bastard's invaded your home and he seems to want to mess with your head, but he's not that smart. He's made mistakes, and he'll make more, guaranteed."

She tipped back her head and met his gaze. "How long does the GPS have to be on to pinpoint the location?"

"If we're scanning for the phone, all it needs is enough time to make the connection with the server, and we'll have the location."

Despite the comfort O'Halloran had been dispensing, his expression was grim and cold enough to send a shiver down her spine, although this time in a good way.

The guy who had broken into her home had thought he was targeting a lone, vulnerable woman. But with O'Halloran now in the picture she was abruptly certain that her stalker had bitten off way more than he could chew.

Chapter 12

After McCabe, Carter and West had left, Jenna locked the door. O'Halloran was still in the house. He was making calls and had his laptop booted up on her kitchen table, so she wasn't alone. The act of locking up should have made her feel safe, but she was suddenly all too aware that she wasn't safe in her own home and that she couldn't stay there tonight.

The thought of trying to sleep in her bedroom filled her with quiet dread. She hadn't cleaned up all of the pottery shards and broken glass. In any case, it would take a while to wipe the attack from her mind.

Once O'Halloran had checked through her email and her folder of negative fan mail, she would pack what she needed and check in to a hotel somewhere.

The act of making a decision, of taking back control, was steadying. Feeling calmer, she walked up to her room and stepped inside, tensing at the mess and the blank, cold view out onto her balcony.

Flicking on a light, she marched across to the French doors, checked the locks and drew the curtains. As she turned, she caught her reflection in her dresser mirror and caught her breath.

She was used to seeing herself casually neat, her hair brushed or coiled and, for want of a better word, *calm*.

In the space of a couple of hours, that had all changed.

Her hair was tousled, her face pale, but it was her mouth that drew her attention. Her lips were pale but a little swollen. She looked like she had just been kissed. Or as if she had just rolled out of bed.

Grabbing a loose jacket, she shrugged into it then dragged a brush through her hair and pinned it up into a coil. Unfortunately, with her new cut, the shorter tendrils wouldn't stick and cascaded around her jaw and nape, the effect somehow even sexier than just leaving her hair loose.

Sex. The thought—the hot, sweaty skin-on-skin reality of it—sent a quiver of sensation through her.

Putting the brush down, she stared at her reflection. The problem was, she thought grimly, that for O'Halloran casual sex might be no big deal, but for her it would be.

She was used to being solitary and alone. She worked alone, ate alone, slept alone.

A graphic image of what it would be like to go to bed with O'Halloran, to be naked with him on top, flashed through her on a wave of heat.

She realized how enclosed and "female" her world had become. She worked, exercised and socialised with women. Even her accountant and doctor were both female. The only contact she had with men was, literally, by chance, through her fan mail or the occasional date she got talked into. And none of those men were even remotely in O'Halloran's league.

Retrieving her laptop from beneath her mattress, she walked back downstairs. She collected the file from the bottom drawer of her desk and carried it all through to the lounge.

A Victorian carriage clock sitting on her mantel informed her that it wasn't late, barely ten o'clock, which was disorienting. After everything that had happened, it felt closer to midnight.

In the kitchen, she could hear the deep, cool sound of O'Halloran's voice as he talked on the phone. He would be leaving soon, but before he left, she wanted to show him the emails.

As she was booting up the computer, she remembered the conversation with Selene, and her conviction that her favourite fan could provide a clue to the identity of the stalker.

Offhand, she didn't think Lydell88 was stalker material. The conviction was knee-jerk, because every online or email conversation she'd had with Lydell had been positive and uplifting: she liked him. If he was a stalker, she was certain those traits would have revealed themselves over the years of correspondence, and they hadn't.

The other reason she didn't think it could be him was that he never pushed contact. Usually he only instigated a conversation when she had a book out. She in turn tried to limit her contacts to the times she needed police procedural information.

Placing the laptop on the coffee table, she booted it up and considered lighting the fire. It wasn't that cold, but with rain drumming on the windows and the wind building in intensity, the flickering flames would add a comforting glow.

Satisfied that the laptop battery was good for a couple of hours, she found her fan mail file, selected the one labelled Lydell and opened it up.

A few minutes later, O'Halloran joined her.

He flicked through a couple of the emails but didn't seem overly interested in Lydell, other than the fact that she had kept every email Lydell88 had ever sent.

Marc closed down Jenna's Lydell email file and opened her folder of negative fan mail and stared at the print copy of the email that contained her threat. He experienced the same cold sense of a missing piece of a puzzle dropping into place that he'd felt the first time he read the email.

Memory flickered, a series of freeze frames that made him go still inside.

Natalie sitting at her computer most nights when he had gotten in late. The argument when he had discovered that she was chatting with an online friend. A male friend.

Jenna frowned. "What is it?"

"I've seen that email address before, or something very like it. There's one change, an extra letter tagged on the end."

Maybe it was sheer chance, coincidence, and this was a completely different person, but he didn't think so. When he'd worked cases at Auckland Central and made a breakthrough he had felt the same sharp kick of instinct, the same inner certainty.

His decision at the cemetery to refocus his own personal investigation on Natalie's and Jenna's lives was confirmed. For six years, he had centered his hunt for the person who had killed his family on a criminal ring he had been investigating at the time. His spectacular lack of success was now explained. He had assumed that his house being torched was a crime of vengeance, directed at him.

Normally he worked only on facts. But in the aftermath of funerals and the slow, painful recovery from his injuries, he had made the fundamental mistake of making an assumption.

Now, finally, that assumption, which had stonewalled his investigation, had been cleared away. Marc hadn't been the target of the perpetrator. The murderer's focus had been Natalie.

"You've found something."

The flat certainty in Jenna's voice brought Marc's head up. He controlled his impatient need to start work on a list of men in both Jenna's and Natalie's pasts. If Hansen managed to match the fingerprints, that would be a step that was no longer required.

"That the criminals I thought were responsible for Natalie's and Jared's deaths, weren't."

The room seemed to fill with silence, punctuated by the slow tick of an antique clock.

"I'll make coffee."

Too tense to sit, Marc levered himself up from the couch and restlessly paced the length of the sitting room, his mind switching to the avalanche of new information that had, within the space of a few hours, changed everything.

He found himself staring at a small trio of family snapshots on an elegant corner table—one of the silver frames held a studio photograph of Natalie with their small son.

His chest tightened. He hadn't murdered them, but for years guilt had eaten at him. He had assumed they had died because of his work as a police detective.

The need to absolve himself, if only partially, had driven him to continue to search for evidence. He had hunted a phantom, one who had constantly slipped from his grasp.

The perp had been content to taunt Marc from a distance. But, finally, he had made a mistake. Probably because Jenna was a woman and lived alone, he had fallen into the trap of underestimating her.

The fact that he had turned up in person was a major breakthrough.

Marc now had motivation, an email, a photograph, video footage and, most importantly, with the cellophane on the rose, and the clipboard and pen he had found at the base of Jenna's fence, fingerprints.

Despite all of the fancy evidence-collection techniques that were so popular on TV shows, fingerprints remained the number-one method of obtaining a conviction. There was just no way of getting around the fact that fingerprints placed the perp at the scene of the crime.

Although none of the evidence was conclusive unless they got a match on the prints, and that might not happen. But at least he finally had enough information to put together a profile and prove that a murder had occurred.

Marc's jaw tightened. For the first time, he could see the man he'd been searching for.

By running a list of the men both Natalie and Jenna knew, by virtue of cross matching, he could isolate a list of suspects.

Then there was the aspect of Jenna's book. Something Jenna had included in her latest story had pushed a button, strongly enough that the perp had tried to intimidate her into removing the book from the market.

A sense of icy satisfaction filled Marc. He would go back through the book with a fine-tooth comb. Somewhere, there was information vital enough that the perp had seen the possibility of exposure and had moved to nullify the risk.

Jenna strolled back into the room and set a tray down on the coffee table. Marc set the photograph down and walked toward Jenna. As he did so, he became sharply aware that in the space of the few minutes it had taken her to make coffee, something had changed.

The glow of awareness was gone from her expression, turned off as efficiently as turning off a tap.

Jenna handed him one of the mugs, but instead of sitting next to him on the sofa, she retreated to an armchair, further emphasising the distance between them.

Frowning, Marc drank a mouthful of the coffee. "Natalie used to chat to some guy online. I'm pretty sure it's the same guy who emailed you."

Grimly, he noted that Jenna didn't look as surprised as she should have. "You knew she was talking to someone. That Natalie was involved with some guy online."

Shock jerked Jenna's head up. "I didn't know about the online part. All I knew was that she had met someone. She didn't say how."

"If Natalie was involved with someone then you need to tell me all the details. Forget that she and I were married."

The calm flatness of O'Halloran's tone was faintly chilling.

Keeping Nat's little secret had been a habit, made easy by her death. The way Jenna had seen it, you shouldn't have to tell on people after they had died, but she couldn't afford to hold back now. If Nat's illicit boyfriend and Jenna's stalker were one and the same, then that was a bona fide link.

"Natalie phoned me the day before she died to tell me she was considering leaving you to be with her new boyfriend. I didn't quite believe her." She shook her head. "I couldn't believe she would—"

O'Halloran picked up the copy of the email. "I need to know his name."

The remoteness of his gaze made the breath catch in the back of her throat. "She never gave me a name, but I didn't know he was an *online* friend. All I knew was that he had been sending her gifts and that Nat was... excited. She died the next day."

Jenna's stomach tightened. She literally felt sick at the implications. Now that it seemed clear that the house fire hadn't been set by the serial arsonist, the meeting with Natalie's online friend had taken on a new, potentially ominous cast. That didn't mean he was implicated in the murder, but he could be.

It was a connection she should have made and hadn't. The dangers of meeting someone off the internet swirled around in her head. She knew better than most how many crazies there were out there.

"Don't beat yourself up about it. I knew about the online friend, and I didn't connect him."

The flat acceptance in his voice stopped her in her tracks. She knew that Natalie hadn't been entirely happy in the marriage, but she had assumed that was because she had suffered from postnatal depression after having the baby.

She had never considered that O'Halloran might not have been happy. "I don't know. Maybe it was just talk. In any event there was no point mentioning it, because nothing happened—she didn't go with him."

And Jenna hadn't wanted to destroy his memories of Nat. After all, she hadn't done anything wrong. After she had died, the last thing she had wanted to do was despoil her cousin's memory.

O'Halloran was silent for a beat. "There was if he had anything to do with the gas explosion."

A chill went through Jenna at the soft, flat comment. On the heels of that another thought made her go still inside. "I used a couple of the things that happened to Natalie in *Deadly Valentine*, the secret admirer and the use of arson. If he's the same man, that would explain why he's so angry."

Because she had inadvertently revealed his crime, even if only in a fictionalised form.

Pushing to his feet, O'Halloran slid his phone out of his pocket. "Which will be why he wants your phone and computer, and anything else that might connect him to Natalie's death."

He short-dialled Farrell. When he got her voice mail, he left a message and hung up.

A heavy roll of thunder indicated that the storm had moved overhead. As Jenna pulled a curtain aside to stare outside, Marc gave in to impulse and walked over to her. He shouldn't touch her, but he found himself wanting to pull her close and soothe away the tension that was visible in the line of her back, the set of her jaw.

Her inability to meet his gaze brought his head up, sharpened all of his senses. In that moment, the small body language cues he had noted ever since the encounter at the gravesite—her pale face and abrupt change of mood when he had focused on Natalie—added up to a conclusion he should have arrived at earlier. Somehow, despite the passage of years and the fact that she had been the one who had ended it, Jenna still cared for him.

Cancel that: nine years had passed. She loved him.

Her shuttered gaze met his. Something about his expression must have alerted her that he knew, because she smiled brightly. "I'll make a copy of a couple of Lydell88's emails, if you want them."

"Great idea." Maybe it would stop him from doing something rash like reaching out, snagging her wrist and pulling her close again.

Jaw tight, he watched Jenna collect the file and walk out of the room.

The thought that they were close to lovemaking momentarily wiped his mind clean of anything else. The fierceness of his response set him on guard.

With the investigation now heating up, staying close to Jenna, and allowing her memory, and his, to unlock, could be the most effective way to finally capture the murderer who had eluded him for six years.

Like it or not, Jenna had become the key to solving the case. He couldn't afford to be separate from her right now.

If he made love with Jenna, maintaining any kind of professional distance would be impossible and, with the stalker now a tangible threat, he needed to maintain his clarity of mind.

Satisfaction eased off some of his tension. Decision made.

He wanted Jenna in his bed. And she wanted him, but they would have to wait. Protecting Jenna and making progress on the investigation had to take precedence.

He had already lost Natalie and Jared.

He couldn't lose Jenna.

Chapter 13

Jenna stepped back into the room just as the lights went out.

"Wait here," O'Halloran said quietly. "I'm going to check the fuse box, just in case."

She heard the faint sound of his footfall, felt the displacement of air as he glided past.

Not wanting to sit alone in the dark with the sound of thunder rolling overhead, she followed O'Halloran out into the hall and watched as he shone his flashlight into the fuse box. "It looks okay."

She trailed him to the kitchen and watched as he shrugged into the shoulder holster. The metallic click as he slid the clip home in the Glock sent a chill down her spine. She had watched O'Halloran unload the gun and place both the gun and shoulder holster on the kitchen counter; she just hadn't thought he would have to use it.

He paused at the kitchen door. "I won't be long. The whole street is in darkness, so he hasn't tampered with the power this time. I think this outage is genuine. A bolt of lightning probably knocked out the transformer."

The kitchen door shut behind him. Her spine tingled at the silent way O'Halloran had moved through the darkness. Unnerved by being alone in the dark, she found the penlight she had used earlier.

Swinging the beam around the kitchen, just to make sure she *was* still alone, she walked quickly to the kitchen door, opened it and stepped out onto the back porch. A blast of cold air and rain instantly soaked her.

O'Halloran ghosted in out of the pitch-blackness, his eyes shooting dark fire. "What are you doing outside?"

Jaw taut, Jenna ignored the question. She was in no mood to explain that after the episode with the stalker in the so-called safety of her house, outside had seemed a whole lot safer. "Did you find anything?"

"He's not on the property." O'Halloran stepped beneath the porch and slicked wet hair back from his face. His shirt was plastered to his shoulders, water trickled down his chin.

Lightning lit up the back garden with a searing white glow, and, a split second later, a crack of thunder made her jump.

He stepped inside, found the towel that he had used earlier and blotted his face and hair. "That's it," he said grimly. "You can't stay here. We can't stay in my apartment, either, because I can't guarantee that he doesn't know where I live, which means a hotel."

Jenna stepped into O'Halloran's apartment, a brief stop-off on the way to a hotel, while he packed a bag.

Curiously, she looked around as he led the way
through a large modern apartment with vaulted ceil-
ings and dark hardwood floors softened by rich Turk-
ish rugs. Warm lamplight glowed, pooling softly over
comfortable sofas and highlighting an array of interesting oils on the walls.

They stepped into a wide hallway. The white walls,
which would have been uncomfortably sterile if left
bare, again, were adorned with an interesting collection
of paintings. "I didn't know you liked art."

He paused by the doorway to a bedroom. "I like it. I
just don't know anything about it. Luckily, my mother
solves that problem. Every year she runs a charity art
auction. I donate, and she insists on turning the dona-
tion into a bid on a painting."

Jenna stared at the delicate watercolours lining the
hall. They all matched and she was suddenly certain
that O'Halloran was well aware of that fact.

The paintings gave Jenna an odd, narrow glance into
O'Halloran's family life. She knew from the careful selection that his mother had done her best to decorate his
walls with light and beauty, and to turn the sterile barn
O'Halloran had chosen, the very antithesis of a family
home, into a comfortable apartment. And O'Halloran
had let her.

The fact that O'Halloran's mother had a hand in dec-
orating also told her that O'Halloran lived alone.

The thought was oddly disturbing. She was used
to living alone. As a writer, solitude suited her for the
most part, but O'Halloran was different. Despite his
occupation as a cop, she had always considered him to
be a family man.

It was an odd moment to take her head out of the

sand and confront her phobia about being involved with either a soldier or a cop, because it was a fact that they needed their families more than most. The thought that at the end of a day of dealing with hardened criminals and maybe even the rawness of death, O'Halloran had come home to a cold, empty apartment made her chest squeeze tight.

Despite the art on the walls, the apartment was hollow, and it was lonely.

Within minutes, O'Halloran had what he needed. Glad to be leaving the too-revealing confines of his apartment, Jenna climbed back into his vehicle.

She studied street signs as he accelerated out of the center of town and found an on-ramp to the Southern motorway. "So…where are we going?"

He checked the rearview mirror then flipped open the glove compartment and extracted an accommodation booklet, which he handed to her. "Find a hotel or motel. I'm just going to drive for a while and make sure we're not being followed."

Half an hour later, feeling exhausted, Jenna walked into the double-room suite she had booked in the Lombard Hotel.

O'Halloran stepped in beside her and put their bags down. "Choose the room you want and I'll take the other."

Minutes later, after placing her bag in the nearest room and making a brief survey of the suite, which had a small kitchen, Jenna took a shower, changed for bed and brushed her teeth.

While she was in the bathroom, she took stock of her bruises. The ones around her neck hadn't developed much beyond red marks, so hopefully they would fade by morning, but her knee was a different matter. The dark bruise was large and spectacular, and the knee was still sore.

After rubbing in some arnica, which she'd brought with her, she quickly dried her hair then walked through the lounge to her bedroom. On the way, she glimpsed a slice of tanned torso as O'Halloran peeled out of his shirt. At that moment, his gaze snagged on hers for long enough that she froze in place and her stomach clenched. Then he looked away.

Cheeks burning, feeling like a love-starved voyeur, Jenna continued on toward her bedroom, closed her door and slid into bed. Flicking off the light, she lay in darkness and tried to relax, but her heart was still racing. She hadn't mistaken O'Halloran's initial response. His gaze had been narrowed and she had gotten the impression that he hadn't minded in the least that she was seeing him with his shirt off.

Somewhere in the distance she could hear O'Halloran taking a shower. Every time she thought about the comprehensive way O'Halloran had kissed her back at her house she melted down, although he hadn't pushed any further. Sometime during the evening he had seemed to back off, leaving her floating in limbo.

It didn't take a rocket scientist to figure out when and why the change had happened. When O'Halloran had made the connection about Natalie's online friend, his whole focus had altered.

She had felt his instant shift away from her and back to Natalie and Jared. When she'd seen him staring at Nat's photo, she had gotten the message loud and clear. No matter how focused O'Halloran was on investigating her stalking and protecting her—no matter how seductive that seemed—she couldn't allow herself to forget that his primary motivation was the same one that had driven him for the past six years. The need to solve the murder of his wife and child.

As powerful and overwhelming as the attraction was for her, she couldn't allow herself to forget that to O'Halloran her primary importance was as a lead in his investigation.

The following evening, after a day split between Auckland Central and putting together a comprehensive list of all of the men in both Natalie's and Jenna's lives, Marc surveyed the reception room at the Lombard Hotel. A combined book signing and literacy function was being held and the room was presently packed with an array of brightly dressed and heavily perfumed women. Because the hotel was also a casino, a smattering of other guests continually drifted through the door and mingled, a number of them men.

West and Carter were present, cruising the crowd and keeping an eye on the doors. Blade Lombard, part of the SAS team that Carter, West and McCabe had belonged to, and also the current manager of the hotel and casino, had also offered to help out with security.

Like Marc, Blade's gaze was fixed on the line of fans queuing to obtain a signed book from Jenna. A number of other authors were also part of the function, but none of them commanded queues that wound like a snake around the walls.

He caught Marc's eye, his own expression rueful. "Do you read her books?"

Marc automatically stiffened then allowed himself to relax. "Yeah, they're good."

"My wife writes the same stuff. I like her books, although the love scenes are a bit—"

Marc found himself grinning that Blade, who was normally eloquent, seemed to be at a loss for words.

Blade frowned as he saw what Marc had just noticed: a very masculine-looking woman wearing a heavy dress and a shapeless jacket was in Jenna's queue. "Do you think she's for real?"

Marc's jaw tightened as he noted her brawny shoulders and muscular calves. "What do you think?"

Blade shook his head. "No way."

By tacit agreement they moved closer, Blade strolling down one side of the queue, Marc taking the other. Marc still wasn't completely sure of gender, but he wasn't about to be caught flatfooted.

As the woman reached Jenna's table, her hand dived inside the left lapel of her jacket. Marc swore beneath his breath. A split second later, Blade, who was slightly closer and definitely more on edge, beat him to the punch and caught the woman in a wrestling hold. A strangled shriek rent the air as Marc jerked the flap of the jacket open and the "gun," in reality a battered copy of what looked like Jenna's first book, dropped to the floor. Jenna, looking gorgeous and sultry in a tangerine halter-neck dress, pushed to her feet.

The whole room seemed to freeze as the motorised click of cameras filled the air. Blade muttered a gritty, mostly indistinct word and let her go, and the now overloud hum of conversation broke over them.

The woman spun and confronted her attacker. "You're Blade Lombard, aren't you?"

Blade dragged at his tie, looking acutely uncomfortable. "That's right, ma'am."

"I read your wife's books."

A relieved expression flashed in his dark gaze. "How many copies would you like?"

The woman smiled determinedly. "I don't want a book. What I'd like is for you to do that hold again so I can get a picture."

"How about," Jenna interceded smoothly, "I give you a gift pack of all ten of my books?" She grabbed a wrapped box of books and handed it over. The woman, now thoroughly distracted, took the books. Blade, recognizing an out when he saw one, slipped away into the crowd.

With the woman mollified by the books, Jenna indicated to Marc that she needed to take a break. On edge, even though there hadn't been a threat, Marc stayed close as he walked Jenna to the ladies' room.

Jenna sent him a cool glance. "Did you have to attack her?"

"I'm not taking any chances."

Jenna was abruptly silent, and Marc cursed himself for being so grim. Up until now, Jenna had actually relaxed and she had been enjoying herself.

The corridor leading to the bathrooms was filled with a mixture of men. On top of the casino crowd, there was also a pharmacy convention running in an adjacent reception room.

Gaze cold as he skimmed each of the men, Marc made an executive decision. He couldn't afford to let Jenna go into the ladies' room without protection. Ignoring outraged gasps, he stepped into the pale pink bathroom and grimly waited.

As they exited the ladies' room, a barrage of cameras

met them. His annoyance growing, a cold itch down his spine, Marc escorted Jenna back to her table. Using his lip mike, he spoke to West and Carter and requested that they move in closer and watch anyone with a camera. A few years ago, McCabe had been shot at a fashion event filled with cameras. Just like the book signing, the fashion show had been a security nightmare.

Jenna's queue gradually reduced in size. Marc checked his watch as he grimly stood over Jenna, more than happy to make it plain that if anyone tried to harm her they would have to deal with him. The fact that more and more men had filtered into the room didn't make him feel any happier.

A pretty female reporter for a women's magazine asked if she could take a picture of Jenna. After Jenna had posed, she requested a second shot, this time with Marc.

Obligingly, Jenna looped one arm around his waist. Cameras whirred and clicked as more reporters moved in. In that moment, something shifted at the edge of Marc's vision, a reporter with a zoom lens that looked more like a gun than a camera, and his patience dissolved.

Chapter 14

Expression grim, O'Halloran's hand landed in the small of her back. "That's it, we're out of here."

West and Carter automatically fell in behind them. Somewhere, another camera flashed.

O'Halloran's jaw locked. He saw the distinctive outline of Blade Lombard's shoulders, the black gleam of his ponytail, heard a muffled epithet. A number of reporters had been asked to leave. At a guess, another had just been escorted to the door.

They reached the bank of elevators, and O'Halloran pressed the call button. Slow seconds passed before the doors swished open and he ushered Jenna inside. Carter stepped inside with them; West stayed downstairs. O'Halloran lifted a hand as the doors closed. West would keep an eye on anyone trying to follow them.

O'Halloran's arm locked around Jenna's waist as the

elevator shot up. Jenna didn't complain. She'd been on tenterhooks all night, mostly because of the danger, but also because O'Halloran had been the cynosure of a lot of female eyes and she'd finally had enough.

She had thought she could be adult and sophisticated about O'Halloran mixing with her mostly female audience, but a gorgeous, leggy brunette coiling her arms around O'Halloran's neck had been the last straw.

Natalie had been the exception to the rule, because she had been genuinely nice and Jenna had loved her, but with any other woman she found she was burningly, searingly jealous.

O'Halloran hadn't responded to the brunette—he had barely seemed to see her—but that didn't matter. The fact was, she had been a threat. For however long she and O'Halloran were together, he was *her* man, and she wasn't prepared to share.

Carter melted away as they reached their suite. O'Halloran unlocked the door then insisted on going in first.

O'Halloran's actions were like a dash of cold water, forcibly reminding Jenna of the threat. Following him into the suite, she closed the door behind her and leaned against it as she waited for O'Halloran to finish checking it out.

He stepped out of her bedroom, crossed the width of the lounge and looked in the second bedroom.

When he re-joined her in the lounge, he shrugged out of the shoulder holster and laid it and the Glock on the coffee table beside his laptop. Dragging his tie to loosen it, he simply walked to her and pulled her into his arms. Dropping her evening bag on the floor, Jenna closed her arms around his neck, went up on her toes and angled her jaw for his kiss.

After the past twenty or so hours, when O'Halloran had seemed to withdraw from her almost completely into the investigation and his role as bodyguard, she had begun to despair. She had understood his motivation, his driving need to bring the killer to justice, but she hadn't liked the feeling of being so easily sidelined.

They were going to make love, and the knowledge that they had finally reached that point made her feel wobbly with relief. After the misery of the previous night, spent tossing and turning in her room, considering the very real possibility that once the killer was caught O'Halloran could walk out of her life, there was no way she was missing a chance that might never come again.

From the time she had fished her latest book out of its box and been shocked by the likeness of the cover model to O'Halloran until now, her objections to falling for him had been systematically obliterated. Maybe it was as simple as recognizing just how lonely *she* had been. Whatever the catalyst was, inside she had changed and she couldn't change back.

She wanted him; she loved him, and the emotions were deep and painful.

She could back away from committing to sex, insist they wait and see if a viable relationship developed. The only problem was, neither of them was "normal" when it came to relationships.

They were both hurt and just a little dysfunctional. She had loved him for years. If she had loved him that long, chances were she wasn't going to fall out of love with him anytime soon.

Maybe what they would share wouldn't mean anything special to O'Halloran. The probability was that for him it would be nothing more than a fleeting affair.

Even so, that was a risk she had to take. She couldn't live with herself if she didn't at least try.

O'Halloran lifted his head, his gaze midnight dark. "If you don't want this, tell me now."

For an answer, Jenna fitted herself more tightly against the hard-muscled plains of O'Halloran's body, and pulled his mouth back to hers.

The passion was white-hot and instant. The relief of her breasts flattened against his chest, the scrape of stubble against her jaw, made her shudder. O'Halloran tasted as good as he smelled, clean and male and delicious.

As she lifted up against him for a second kiss, this one deeper, hotter, she wondered how she had managed to live without him.

His fingers tangled in her hair, holding her captive. She logged his groan of satisfaction as his mouth came back down on hers, and she found herself walked back a half step, then another, until her bare back came up against the cold solidity of the wall.

The relief of O'Halloran's weight pinning her, the heat blasting off him, the firm shape of his arousal pressing into her belly, sent a sensation jerking through her. She felt his fingers at her nape, the release of tension as the halter of her dress loosened then slipped down to hang around her waist, then his hands swept up to cup her breasts.

For a brief moment, time seemed to move with liquid slowness as he kissed her jaw, the curve of her neck.

The abrasive warmth of his palms, the sensual drag of his shirt against naked skin, made her stomach clench.

Dragging at his tie, she tossed it aside and unfastened his shirt.

O'Halloran said something low and rough. Bending his head he took one breast in his mouth. Her fingers clenched in his hair for long seconds then restlessly shifted to his shoulders as the aching heat in her belly coiled tight, and suddenly there was no air.

Jenna felt a tug, a rush of cool air, then fabric puddled around her feet.

Swallowing at the sheer vulnerability of being mostly naked while O'Halloran was still almost fully dressed, Jenna tugged at the buttons of his shirt until it hung loose from his shoulders. "I could do with some help here."

O'Halloran grinned quick and hard and shrugged out of the shirt then pulled her close. The heat of skin-on-skin contact spun her back nine years, to darkness and moonlight, an uncomfortable couch and too little time.

This time, she thought a little dizzily, as she dragged at the fastening of his trousers, they would have all night. She heard his swiftly indrawn breath, and then the room tilted as he swung her into his arms. Short seconds later, she found herself deposited on the cloud-like softness of the bed.

The room was dark, illuminated by the strip of light glowing in the door and by the bright moonlight flowing in off the balcony. She watched as O'Halloran stepped out of his trousers. She drew in her breath at the sleek width of his shoulders, the hard flatness of his stomach, the muscular length of his legs.

She heard a faint tearing sound. Dimly, she registered that O'Halloran had just sheathed himself with a condom.

She felt a tug at her hips and registered the glide of her panties as they slid down her legs and the cool wash of air.

For long minutes he simply held her close, kissing and soothing her and letting her explore. When her hand slid down over washboard abs and found him, he groaned and came down on top of her. She wrapped her arms around his neck, pulling him close. He lowered his weight, and her breath came in as she felt the nudge of his knee between her thighs.

Her stomach tightened at the sheer vulnerability of opening her legs, but that consideration evaporated as she felt the sudden pressure as he lodged in her opening. His gaze locked with hers as his weight settled more heavily on her.

The sheer intimacy of being this close with O'Halloran, gazes locked, breaths mingling, the sensual heat of his body pressing into hers, was seductive. She arched, wanting more, wanting him closer still, and with one heavy thrust he was inside her.

Time seemed to slow, stop, as she adjusted to the intrusion, part of her still reeling from the unexpected speed of his entry.

O'Halloran cupped her jaw, his gaze strained. "When was the last time you made love?"

Jenna sucked in a breath, her whole being still centred on easing the pressure between her legs. "Do I have to answer that?"

O'Halloran said something low and gritty. "I knew it. You haven't made love with anyone else."

She took another breath and moved her hips slightly. The pressure was easing, but just. "I've been…busy."

"Uh-huh. Writing about it."

She caught the edge of his smile, and the tension that had gripped her at the whole idea of making love evaporated. After all, it wasn't an exam she could potentially fail; it was something that was supposed to come naturally.

He cupped her jaw. "If you want me to stop, just say so. Otherwise, I'll take it slow."

Her gaze flashed to his. "Don't you dare stop."

In response, O'Halloran leaned down and touched his mouth to hers, the kiss oddly sweet. As he did so, he eased back then pushed in slowly. This time the entry was easier, smoother. O'Halloran continued the slow rocking for long minutes. Dipping his head, he took one breast into his mouth and bit down gently.

Sensation gathered, coiled tight, jerked through her in hot, dizzying waves. She gripped O'Halloran's shoulders. Moments later, he plunged deep and the room dissolved.

She must have fallen asleep, because when she woke, O'Halloran was withdrawing himself from her body by slow increments. He eased his weight off her fully and left the bed. Shivering a little at the loss of his body heat and the cool air-conditioning flowing over her damp skin, she dragged the coverlet over her.

She heard O'Halloran's voice as he spoke to someone on his cell. Minutes later, he returned and slid into bed with her.

"That was Farrell. They couldn't match the prints with anyone from the security company."

Even though she was sleepy, her brain automatically clicked into investigative gear. "What about associate firms? Suppliers?"

"Farrell's got a list. That's what I was doing last night. The checking is going to take some legwork."

She yawned and blinked as an idea popped into her head. "What about the list of registration plate names? There were a couple of companies listed."

O'Halloran shook his head. "You should have been a cop. One of the companies is a security wholesaler. Farrell's getting a warrant and putting together a team. That should be a go in an hour or so."

Now wide-awake, Jenna watched as O'Halloran pulled on dark pants and, not bothering with a shirt, walked back out to the lounge. She listened to his deep, cool voice as he made another series of calls.

After a while, tiredness caught up with her and she drifted into a light doze. The next time she woke, O'Halloran was sliding back into bed. Pleasure hummed through her at the sheer, comfortable intimacy of having him in bed with her. It was something she could get used to. "Did you make progress?"

"Some."

The neutral tone to his voice, the subtle distance, informed her that the breakthrough was significant.

As hard as she tried to keep it at bay, a tension she didn't want to feel crept up on her, dissolving the warm bubble of happiness she had been inhabiting ever since they'd made love.

She should be happy for them both. Her stalker would be put behind bars, and O'Halloran would find Natalie and Jared's killer. They would both have closure.

While she knew that O'Halloran's distance was just a

part of him she had to accept, a knee-jerk reaction after years of keeping details of investigations confidential, she couldn't help but resent the barrier it represented. Just when she had managed to get a tiny piece of his attention, the investigation was taking him from her, but she wasn't about to give up without a fight.

Rolling on her side, she ran a hand over his torso and chest. Lifting up on her elbows, her hair falling in a curtain around her face, she dipped her head into the muscular curve of his neck, and breathed in his scent, then explored lower.

One big hand curled around her nape. "You don't want to sleep?"

"No."

"Good, I don't want to sleep, either."

Extracting another condom from the bedside table, he sheathed himself.

Her reaction was at odds with common sense. Condoms were good, any person with common sense wouldn't go near sex without one, unless they were married.

What she was feeling was silly, bordering on stupid, but a part of her hated it that O'Halloran had sheathed himself, because the condom seemed to symbolise his control.

The second the thought occurred to her, she wished it hadn't. For most of the evening, she'd been able to calmly ignore the fact that O'Halloran would probably never feel about her the way she did about him. But that didn't mean she had to put up with him deliberately controlling his passion, which she was suddenly sure was the case.

Gaze oddly wary, as if he had caught her mood, he

pulled her down until she was sprawled across his chest, and kissed her slowly and languorously.

She shifted, eased up his body and straddled him, taking control of the lovemaking and taking her time, absorbed by the sensations.

O'Halloran groaned. His hands framed her hips, adjusting the angle. She felt him lodge deeper and drew in a breath as he began to move. The idea of control crashed and burned as he rolled, pulling her beneath him, and once again the moonlit room spiralled away.

Branden Tell turned down his street and braked behind a dark sedan that seemed to be going nowhere fast. Either that or they were lost.

After trailing behind the car for long seconds, he put the lights of his Hummer on full beam, just to be obnoxious, and studied the two heads he had spotlighted.

Not kids looking for a place to park; they were both adults, one male, one female, and *she* was driving.

The woman checked him out in the rearview mirror, although with several hundred watts of high-powered halogen light hitting her square in the eyes, she wouldn't be able to make out a thing.

On the verge of forging past, she foiled him by speeding up. Tell swore beneath his breath and drove up hard behind them. They had a powerful car, but his Hummer would drive right over the top of them if he put his foot down.

They slowed, forcing him to brake again, although this time Tell controlled his temper, barely. His drive was just meters away—no point in losing it now—and besides, another car had nosed in behind him. If he wasn't mistaken it was a police cruiser.

An indicator light flashing jerked his attention back to the car in front. All the hairs at his nape lifted as the dark sedan turned into his drive.

Adrenaline shoving through him, he dipped his lights and drove past. His gaze glued to his rearview mirror, he watched the police cruiser park behind what he now knew was an unmarked police car.

He had been found.

Cold shock hit him.

His planning had been close to perfect. There was no way O'Halloran could connect him. He had never used an email address that could be traced to him, and fingerprint evidence was worthless since he had never been booked so his prints were not in the police system. If he needed a vehicle, he usually stole one, and the photo Whitmore had taken of him had also been worthless, because his hand had obscured most of his face.

The answer was clear. The bitch Whitmore must have found something on her computer.

A horn blared. His foot jerked down on the brake. The Hummer rocked to a halt, and he stared, disoriented, at the motorway intersection he had almost driven through.

Directing a one-finger salute at the car he had almost T-boned, he reversed, spun the wheel and headed back to town.

A pulse jumping at the side of his jaw, he drove into the Lombard Hotel car park and cruised around until he found O'Halloran's vehicle, which he had followed earlier in the day.

Satisfaction eased the cold fury that gripped him.

Somehow O'Halloran and Whitmore had found him

and sicced the cops on him. If he had arrived home a minute earlier, he would have been caught.

Although it didn't matter now. He was almost ready to leave.

Now he would finally get to be James Holden, the name on his fake passport. Once he was in his new life, Jenna Whitmore's book, O'Halloran and the murder investigation would no longer be a threat to him.

All he had to do was focus on the next few hours, carry through with his plan to pay back both Whitmore and O'Halloran, torch his warehouse and make it look like that loopy serial arsonist did it. It had worked for him once before, it would work again. Then he would leave on the first available flight out.

He drove until he found a parking space that afforded him a view of O'Halloran's vehicle and the exit lane.

It was the middle of the night, but if he didn't miss his guess, O'Halloran would be getting a call from the cops who were staking out his house. O'Halloran wouldn't be able to resist wanting a piece of the action. And if he had found his house, Tell was willing to bet the clever bastard had found his other bolt-hole.

A shame O'Halloran didn't know about the third one.

Dousing the Hummer's lights, Tell set himself to watch.

Chapter 15

The vibration of his phone brought O'Halloran out of a light doze.

Jenna moved sleepily as he slid his arm out from beneath her head, but she didn't wake. He padded out to the lounge, picked up his phone and texted West, who he'd arranged to meet down in the lobby.

Earlier in the evening, they'd managed to cross match the wholesaling company on the list of car registrations he had compiled with another firm that imported security alarms and the name that had come up had made all the hairs at the back of his neck stand on end.

Branden Tell was a name from his, Natalie's and Jenna's pasts. A sports jock with a number of minor disabilities, including colour-blindness and mild dyslexia, which had kept him out of the military and the police force, he had tried to date Natalie when she had been a student.

Marc hadn't thought of Tell because Natalie had been popular. The list of men who had wanted to date her had stretched from here to next week. He could remember Natalie commenting that she hadn't been interested in Tell, not because of the disabilities, but because he had been something of a cold fish until he had gotten her alone.

Finding Tell didn't make the past any easier to accept, but it had finally supplied Marc with a logical motivation for Natalie's and Jared's deaths.

Rejected by the military and the police, ultimately rejected by the woman he had wanted, Tell had decided to take revenge.

But Natalie hadn't been the only one Tell had targeted. Nine years ago he had taken Jenna out, on the night of the ball and she, too, had dumped him.

If he hadn't gotten worried and gone after Jenna with the intention of giving her a lift home, she would have been hit and killed or knocked into the river and drowned. Marc was willing to bet that the driver had been Tell and that, like the incident at the mall, he had meant to hit Jenna, both times.

He had called Farrell to bring her up-to-date with the development. She'd sent out a car, but evidently Tell hadn't been at his house or his place of work.

Not bothering to switch on a light, because his eyes were adjusted to the darkness and he didn't want to wake Jenna, he dressed quickly in a black T-shirt, pants and boots.

He shrugged into the dark webbing of his shoulder

harness, holstered the Glock, put on a loose black jacket and he was ready to go.

He walked to the bedroom door and checked on Jenna. Her hair was fanned out on the pillow, one arm draped over the end of the bed. His chest tightened as he noted that since he had left the bed, she had rolled over and now occupied the place that he had vacated. Even in sleep it seemed that she gravitated to him, as if unconsciously she was drawn to his warmth.

The idea of *her* warmth was seductive. She had held him and enfolded him in a gentle warmth that he was in danger of becoming addicted to. Tonight, even knowing that he had needed to restrain his libido and take things slowly, he'd had trouble controlling himself. If they stayed in bed for a week, he didn't think he would be able to have enough of her.

She loved him.

She hadn't said as much, but Marc couldn't dismiss the knowledge. Even if he hadn't come to that conclusion, he couldn't dismiss the fact that Jenna had never slept with another man, she had only ever been his.

Maybe it was a little primitive and old-fashioned of him to be happy that she had only ever belonged to him, but O'Halloran didn't care. On that point, his feelings were straightforward and uncomplicated and making love had just cemented what he wanted.

If Jenna was prepared to take the risk and give him her love, then he was taking it.

His phone vibrated again.

Backing away from the open door, Marc strolled to his laptop, which was on the coffee table. He flipped open the computer. It was on sleep mode, so the screen saver flicked off and he went straight into his mail program.

With any luck he would be back before it was fully light, but just in case he typed a quick email and pressed the send button.

Leaving the laptop open on the coffee table, he stepped quietly out of the door.

West and Carter were waiting in the lobby. Minutes later, they walked through to the underground parking lot, climbed into Carter's sleek black utility truck and headed towards the southern side of town.

Tell had a street office and owned a house under his own name, which Farrell had under twenty-four-hour surveillance. But West, with his uncanny nose for tax and business scams, had been able to unearth the interesting fact that Tell filtered most of what he earned through some murky trust, which just happened to also own a warehouse at a third address.

It was growing light as they pulled up a block short of the warehouse premises.

Carter stared at the roofline in the distance. "I'm taking it we're not allowed to shoot this guy."

Marc flipped back the lapel of his jacket. "I've got the gun."

Carter waited for West to exit then extracted a duffel, which he slung over one shoulder before locking the truck. "If Tell's got a gun, my wife is not going to be happy. She thinks I'm at a reunion, hanging out at a hotel bar, swapping stories."

West turned his head, as movement registered off to the left. "Just hold that thought and try not to get shot."

A group of joggers appeared out of the mist, most of

them older women with toy dogs on leashes. They were followed by a group of power-walking senior citizens.

Marc checked his watch and began to walk. They passed a sign that announced that they had just entered the Sunnyvale Retirement Village. He studied the surrounding houses. To go with the retirement village theme, they were all similar-sized cottages painted in soft pastel colours. Plantings of petunias were popular.

Carter lifted a hand to an old lady wearing a bright red bandanna who was lagging behind the rest of the power walkers.

A pink cottage with large, painted butterflies adorning the front porch loomed. Marc stepped around a tiny pile of dog droppings that was probably going to get some senior citizen blackballed from the village before the day was out.

His gaze caught on Carter's faded rucksack. "What have you got in the rucksack?"

He snagged it off Carter's shoulder before Carter could protest, although Marc did it carefully. He had heard stories about Rawlings, and quite a few of them had involved explosives, because that had been one of his particular skills in the SAS.

Dragging open the flap, Marc peered inside. There was a lump of what looked like putty wrapped in plastic in the bottom. There was also a separate package that had to contain detonators.

He had told Carter to leave his gun at home. He had just forgotten to rule out fireworks. "Where in hell did you get C4?"

Carter reclaimed the rucksack with barely a flicker. "A friend had it in his garage. He was worried one of the kids would get their hands on it, so he asked me to dispose of it."

Marc moved sideways on the path, giving Carter extra room. "Don't tell me it's past its use-by date."

Carter's expression was scarily neutral. "With any luck, that could be today."

Marc stopped at the neatly hedged rear of a large building that stood cheek by jowl with the butterfly cottage.

Shaded by thick trees and with tightly controlled and manicured shrubs that were clearly tended by the village residents, it could almost pass for a modern barn-style house. In reality, it was the edge of a light industrial area. "This is it."

West surveyed the building. "Looks like a garden center."

Carter stepped into the deep shade of a tree. "Cool. Since we don't have guns, maybe we'll get lucky and find some gardening implements of some kind."

Marc ignored the banter.

There was no guarantee they would find Tell, but he hadn't vanished into thin air. Tell had to be basing himself somewhere in town. If they found him, Marc wasn't about to worry about the legalities of the situation. They would grab him *then* place the call to Farrell.

Tell strolled into the Lombard Hotel dressed in a business suit and carrying a briefcase. He had already made a reservation over the internet, using his new identity, so signing in and picking up his key was just a formality.

He didn't intend to stay. Not very long, anyway.

The room key was just a convenience to get him

up to the concierge floor where, according to one of Jenna Whitmore's most popular fan sites, she was staying the night.

While the fan site had proved a useful resource for tracing Whitmore's movements, it hadn't been able to supply him with the exact number of the room. Although finding it shouldn't be a problem. It would be easy enough to pinpoint the room by the security outside.

He took the lift, checked his room key then strolled slowly down hushed, thickly carpeted corridors. The Lombard Hotel was five-star and swanky—even the air smelled expensive.

He passed a darkly suited security guard. Two doors down, he found his room.

The coincidence that he had been placed so close to Whitmore made up for the inconvenience of having to pay the exorbitant price for the room.

Checking his watch, he stepped inside, closed the door behind him then, with quick deft movements, unpacked and assembled the 9mm Browning he had tucked into his briefcase. A handgun he had chosen specifically because it had originally been designed for the military, the Browning was a thing of beauty.

Walking through to the bathroom, he glued on a fake moustache, and fitted in contacts that changed the colour of his irises from light blue to brown. When his eyes had stopped watering, he slipped on a pair of glasses that had a faint tint, enough to distract anyone who took a second look at him.

A thrill shot down his spine as he slid the gun into the shoulder holster he was wearing and surveyed the effect in the mirror.

According to Whitmore's schedule, she would be leaving the hotel to catch an early flight south just after breakfast.

She wasn't ever going to make that flight.

Sunlight flowing across the bed woke Jenna. Rolling over, she discovered that she was alone and from the coldness of O'Halloran's side, he had been gone for some time.

The faint stiffness of various muscles and the definite feeling of tenderness between her thighs sent hot memory flashing through her. They had made love three times, the third time sleepy and prolonged and intense as they'd lain in the dark, almost more content to hold each other than move. In those long, drawn-out moments it had been easy to imagine that O'Halloran really did love her, that what they had would magically metamorphose into a real relationship.

Stepping out of bed she searched for something to wear and settled on one of O'Halloran's business shirts, which was still folded neatly in his suitcase. White and crisp with a thin blue line, it was clean but it still had the subtle, stomach-clenching smell of O'Halloran.

Maybe it was a cliché to wear it. She didn't care. She was still high on the humming delight of having spent an entire night in bed with her man, and she was determined to wallow in the experience while she could.

Hugging the shirt close to her skin, she strolled to the bathroom, refusing to think about an end to her time with O'Halloran. As she stripped off, she glimpsed herself in the vanity mirror. Her hair was a languorous tangle, her mouth pale and swollen, a faint red mark decorated the side of her neck where O'Halloran's jaw had scraped her tender skin.

What they'd done together was imprinted all over her and, in that moment, she knew that no matter how modern or independent she strived to be, in her heart all she wanted was a life with O'Halloran. She was in love with him and the emotional risk was huge.

If she couldn't have him, she already knew that she wouldn't have anyone else. She wouldn't ever get married and, unless she could achieve a solo adoption, she would never have the family she craved.

She didn't know why O'Halloran had touched her so deeply. It was a fact that they had never ended up spending that much time together. She knew more about most of her casual friends than she did about O'Halloran.

Maybe it was simply that she had been so vulnerable when she had met him, or because when she had ended the original relationship she had still been in love with him and had never gotten closure.

Whatever the reason, at some deep, bedrock level, a stubborn part of her had taken one look at O'Halloran and chosen him.

After showering, she quickly changed into a business suit, because she would have to leave to catch her flight straight after breakfast.

She checked her watch and frowned. She had assumed O'Halloran had gone down to breakfast early, but if that was the case, he would have been back by now.

Frowning when she remembered she didn't have her phone, she walked out to the lounge and quickly checked her email.

A long list of social networking prompts flowed in with regular emails. She ran her eye casually down the list, automatically designating everything as non-urgent until her gaze snagged on Lydell88.

An automatic warm glow flowed through her. Lydell must have read her book.

She checked her watch. She had a few minutes before she needed to go down for breakfast.

When she opened up the email, the message was simple and succinct. Check the mail program on the laptop next to yours.

She frowned, briefly confused. Although there was only one logical reason for Lydell to know that there was a laptop sitting side by side with hers on the coffee table.

Taking a deep breath and feeling suddenly shaky, she bent down and activated the touch pad of O'Halloran's laptop. It flashed off sleep mode and she found herself staring at O'Halloran's mail program, which was already open.

And which also happened to be Lydell88's mail program.

Legs feeling a little wobbly, she sat down on the couch and simply stared at the file of emails that O'Halloran had left open for her to see. Tears burned her eyes, trickled down her cheeks.

She had emailed Lydell88 for years, slowly nurturing the building friendship with him. She had been careful. She hadn't wanted to impose or ask more than he'd wanted to give. From the careful way he'd never allowed the online friendship to cross over into a real personal relationship, even though they both lived in Auckland, she'd known that he was wary of intimacy.

She'd respected his need for distance, but it was a fact that most of the correspondence had been instigated by him. Sometimes, on rare occasions, they had even chatted on live forums she had hosted then afterward continued on into the night on her website chat line.

The conversations had never gotten too personal, but in an odd way they had become her emotional lifeline because underneath the police procedural information and the technicalities of plot, she had been aware that Lydell88 *cared*. In a quiet low-key way, he had been the closest thing she'd had to a relationship in years.

She wiped tears from her cheeks, careful not to smudge her mascara, and found herself grinning like a loon as she began opening and reading the emails *O'Halloran* had sent to her.

Her heart pounded as she stopped reading and scrolled down the file, trying to count how many, like a miser gleefully counting dollar bills. There were literally hundreds.

O'Halloran read her books. He *liked* them.

Dazed, she reflected that it was no wonder she had fallen in love with him, because he really was perfect for her.

Outside in the corridor she registered the rattle of a room-service trolley. A knock on the door distracted her from her all-important tally.

Still feeling like dancing a jig because she was so happy, Jenna answered the door, drawn by the only thing that could drag her away from O'Halloran's entrancing laptop: the possibility that it could be the man himself.

The door swung open and was immediately jammed by the trolley she'd heard out in the hall.

A tall, suited guy, who looked nothing like the bodyguard O'Halloran had introduced her to last night, pointed a large handgun at her head.

"Good morning, Jenna." He shoved the trolley, forcing her back into the room as he kicked the door shut behind him.

Jenna stared at the glinting glasses and what was obviously a fake moustache. He looked different, his eyes were dark, not light, but she would know him anywhere. "Branden Tell."

"That's right. Not the hero, the villain."

Chapter 16

Sunlight beamed through chinks in the dusty little room Branden Tell had dragged her into, shortly before taping her to a chair, taping her mouth and leaving.

She knew he hadn't gone far, because periodically she could hear a soft tapping sound, as if he was typing, and once she had heard him speak on the phone.

She had strained to hear what he was saying, but his voice had been too muffled, indicating that there was at least another room separating them.

That suited her just fine; she didn't want him close. Long minutes of being clamped against his side while he'd urged her into a service elevator, the barrel of the gun digging into her side, had been enough. Nine years ago she hadn't particularly liked Tell. Now she definitely didn't like him.

Rocking the chair slightly, trying to make as little

noise as possible, she managed to shimmy around in a painful circle, so she could get a good look at her surroundings.

Not inspiring. A concrete floor and one corrugated iron wall through which tiny beams of sunlight glowed. The only positive was that there was a nail sticking out of one of the timbers. It wasn't much to pin her hopes on, but the rusty old nail, combined with the fact that Branden had only taped her wrists, not tied them, provided some hope.

That, and the fact that Branden had made her chew sleeping pills, thinking they would knock her out.

The pills, depending on which one—and she had tried them all—did make her drowsy, but the effect never lasted long. Her doctor had given up prescribing them for her occasional insomniac episodes, because usually half an hour after taking one she was as wide-awake as ever.

From the bitter taste in her mouth, the dull headache and general feeling of lethargy, she concluded that Tell had given her one of the stronger formulations. Although that had been a good hour ago now. Tied up in the back of a military-style Hummer, she had fought the drowsy effect of the pill in an effort to see exactly where Tell was taking her. Although every time he had checked on her she had played dead for him.

She had decided that if he thought she was unconscious then that was an advantage of a sort. Given that she was pretty sure Tell didn't mean her to live, she needed to exploit every advantage if she was to have any hope of escape.

She had timed the drive, which had been a good forty minutes, and she knew from overhead signs she'd glimpsed that they had been on the Southern motorway. The change from the roar of motorway traffic to sporadic passing vehicles signalled that Tell had turned off into one of the suburbs south of Auckland.

Working the chair until she was backed up to the nail, she tried to catch the edge of the tape on the nail head. The process was awkward, because she couldn't see what she was doing and had to work by feel. Added to that her hands were starting to go numb, which meant she had to work quickly. If they went completely numb she wouldn't be able to feel where the nail head was.

After the first few minutes her shoulders and arms began to burn, but she gritted her teeth and kept rubbing the tape back and forth on the nail. Every now and then she slipped and the nail scraped over her skin, but she ignored the discomfort.

Stopping to rest her shoulder muscles, which were starting to cramp, she tried pulling her wrists apart. Before there hadn't been any movement, now there was enough flexibility that she could wiggle her wrists a little. It was definitely working because feeling was pouring back into her hands in the form of fiery pins and needles.

Jaw gritted, she started the sawing process again. Time crawled by. Her shoulders and back ached and the effort made her break out in a sweat. Her wrists and hands felt like they were on fire, but she was eventually rewarded with a sudden loosening.

In the distance she heard a rumble, as if a large roller door had been activated, and the sound of a heavy truck. Abruptly, the sporadic sound of vehicles fell into its context. She wasn't hearing road noise. The building must be part of an industrial area somewhere.

If it was a warehouse of some kind that meant it would be one of many. So there had to be people nearby, and they were probably ridiculously close. All she had to do was get free and find some way to sneak past Tell.

The heavy detonation of an explosion jerked her head up, followed by the rending shriek of metal, so close it hurt her ears. She could hear footsteps.

Heart pounding so hard she could barely breathe, eyes wide, she stared at the shadows that filled the doorway, hope and a fierce exultation filling her.

O'Halloran.

She knew it. He had come to get her.

O'Halloran stepped through the twisted ruin of the door Carter had just blown off its hinges into the cavernous space of the warehouse.

Carter and West flowed in behind him. Moving quickly, they checked the series of storerooms that opened off the main area.

Kicking open the final door, O'Halloran stared into an empty room. The place was dusty and the only footprints were theirs. Tell hadn't been here for weeks, if not months.

Knowledge nagged at the back of his mind. He had made the mistake of remembering Tell as he had been years ago, an unassuming student, and not overly bright. But Tell had been smart enough to elude Farrell, and Marc couldn't forget that he had kept *him* on a string for six years.

West walked up behind him. "He's not here."

O'Halloran holstered his gun and checked his watch. "Nope, he's somewhere else."

Now that they'd exhausted this avenue he needed

to get back to the hotel, because Jenna had a flight to catch. Farrell had a watch on the airports and Tell's house and an APB out on Tell's vehicle, which apparently was a Hummer.

A shadow falling across the sunny entrance to the warehouse made Marc stiffen. An elderly man was poking his walking stick at the remains of the door.

He fixed Carter with a beady eye. "This doesn't belong to that crook Morrison, or his son. We made him an offer he couldn't refuse. It now belongs to the Retirement Village Trust, as of last week. Planning on turning it into a community hall."

Carter had the grace to look guilty. "Uh, sorry about that—"

"I hope you're going to fix the door."

"Sure, I've got tools in the truck. Will tomorrow do?"

"It will, and don't think about weaselling out of the job. We've got your licence tag and security footage. The neighbourhood watch is on the ball around here."

Marc's attention sharpened. "Morrison? Was that the cop?"

"That's right. Got indicted for extorting money from organized crime figures and gangs."

"I remember." He should. He had made the arrest and filed the charges.

As they walked back to Carter's truck, disparate pieces of information began to fall into place. Tell had been illegitimate, but he had let it be known that his father was a cop, which was why he had wanted to follow him either into the military or the police force.

The same year Natalie had died, Marc had prosecuted a crooked cop by the name of Branden Morrison.

Sliding his phone out of his pocket, he short-dialled

Farrell. A few minutes later, she called back, confirming that Morrison was Tell's father.

His stomach tensed at the implications as he swung into the passenger seat of Carter's truck. He had been looking for motivation and a way to tie Tell into both Natalie's and Jared's deaths and Jenna's stalking. He had thought it had to be Tell's fascination with Natalie, the added resentment that Marc had the career that Tell had been shooting for, combined with his fear that Jenna's book might expose his crime.

The only problem with that scenario was, why risk exposure by going after Jenna now, when it was too late to stop the book being published anyway?

It would have been far better if Tell had stayed quiet and let the whole thing fade. After all, the book was fiction. As closely involved as Marc was, he had read it and not connected the dots.

Tell could have quietly sold up all of his assets, emigrated and dodged possible charges, but he hadn't; he'd stayed because he'd always had another, ultimately more powerful motive: revenge.

The yearly emails from Tell were the clincher. He had never had any intention of fading into the background. All Jenna's book had done was present him with another platform to act out that revenge.

The link that strung Tell's crimes together was simple: it was him.

Marc stared out of the window at the heavy morning traffic on the motorway—rush hour was getting underway.

Checking his watch, he tried phoning the hotel room again, then Dawson's phone. He frowned. Jenna should have picked up, she would be anxious to leave, and should have phoned him by now. Something was wrong.

Before he could dial Blade's cell, his phone vibrated again.

It was Blade. Dawson was down, with a concussion, and Jenna was missing. He had checked security tapes and found the footage. A tall guy dressed like a body-guard had taken her down a service elevator into the underground garage. The guy had looked nondescript apart from a moustache, which had obviously been fake, but he had been driving a military-style Hummer.

Chest tight, heart hammering, Marc hung up. He stared blankly ahead, no longer seeing the interior of the truck or the cars and buildings flashing by. Grimly, he tried to think.

He could second-guess Tell, he'd done it often enough with other criminals. All it took was careful analysis, but for long seconds all he could think about was the way Jenna had trusted him last night. The moment this morning when he had watched her roll over in bed and reach for him. And he hadn't been there.

In that moment he realised, too late, that he wanted to be there for her—personally, professionally, every way there was.

The enormity of the mistake he had made in going after Tell instead of leaving the enforcement work to Farrell sank in a little deeper.

For long seconds, he was flung further back into the past, to a burning building and a wife and child who had needed him. He hadn't been there for Natalie and Jared.

Knowing that Tell had murdered them had made a difference. Looking back, there was no way he could have known his arrest of Morrison would have a backlash. Tell would have staked out the house. With Natalie keeping her correspondence with him secret, Marc had been cut out of the loop, literally.

But that wasn't the case with Jenna. She had shared everything with him: her fear and distress, her passion and love.

His fingers closed into fists. She had even helped him with the investigation.

Natalie and Jared's loss still hurt, but he'd had years to come to terms with it. But the prospect of losing Jenna filled him with desperate fear.

In her quiet way, Jenna was his, more intimately and completely than any other woman had ever been. Over the years, he had gotten to know every nook and cranny of her mind, her quirky humour, the softness of her emotions, the steely way she had refused to allow any guy to rush her into bed unless *she* wanted to go there.

And she hadn't. Instead, she had saved herself for him.

He would get her back.

He had to. He loved her.

The realisation hit him like a kick in the chest.

It explained why he had never been able to forget Jenna, even down to emailing her under an alias so even if it was only in a small way, he could continue to be part of her life.

Carter glanced at him and softly swore. "What's happened?"

Keeping his voice toneless, Marc related the bare details Blade had given him.

Carter pulled over. "What do you want to do?"

"Blade's already called Farrell. She's put an APB

out on Tell. He's driving a Hummer, so he should be easy to spot."

The military fetish fitted. Unfortunately, a whole lot of things fitted, now that it was too late.

Too late. The words haunted Marc. Six years ago he had been too late for Natalie and Jared.

He had no intention of being too late for Jenna.

Grabbing his briefcase, he flipped it open and dug out his iPad. Using the software that West had supplied, he checked to see if coordinates for Jenna's phone had been recorded. The result was still negative.

He would keep checking, but time was passing. If Tell had intended to turn on the phone, he would have done it by now. Chances were, he had tossed it.

Marc flicked back to his server and typed in Google. "Tell has another bolt-hole. We just have to find it. His father extorted a lot of money from organized crime figures, which could never be recovered because he tied it up in family trusts. The trusts owned a number of properties. All we have to do is search for property holdings under the name Morrison."

The hits were numerous. A lot of people had been outraged by Morrison's greed. Within seconds, O'Halloran found what he wanted in a sensationalised press offering that had completely ignored the idea of confidentiality and had published a list of Morrison's assets.

With a sense of disbelief, he noted that there was also an exposé on Morrison's illegitimate children, three at last count, including Branden Tell. Now wasn't a good time to reflect that if he had read the Sunday papers six years ago, he could have solved the case.

He wrote down the addresses of a number of properties in South Auckland, all of which sounded industrial.

Picking up his phone, he called Farrell. She agreed to dispatch cars to check out the addresses he had given her, but at present, thanks to the arson investigation, she had limited manpower.

Jaw locked, Marc gave Carter the nearest address. It was a long shot, but they had to start somewhere. He had a cold itch up his spine. Time was important.

He needed to find Tell before the man had time to put the next part of his plan into action.

And Marc was convinced that Tell had something planned. Otherwise, why bother to kidnap Jenna?

If Tell had wanted to extract a simple, straightforward revenge he could have obtained that by shooting Jenna in their hotel room.

Chapter 17

Jenna's hopes plunged as Tell, not O'Halloran, stepped through the door of her dark little cave of a room. Without the moustache or the glasses, but dressed neatly in a suit, he was all too familiar, shoving her back to the past.

Back to the night of the ball, when Tell had been her escort and she had almost been run down in the dark. Back to just days ago, the chilling replay in the mall parking lot.

Fury poured through her. It had been Tell behind the wheel each time. Of course it had been; the wonder of it was that she hadn't managed to see it before now. As a suspense writer she was used to drawing together disparate pieces of information, looking for patterns, she just hadn't been capable of doing it with her own life.

If she could have spoken, she would have coldly

stated that she knew exactly what he was, what he had done not just to her and her family, but to O'Halloran, but all that came out was a strangled, muffled sound.

Tell frowned. "Damn, you're awake. Not that it matters. It'll only make the show more interesting."

He cocked his head to one side as if listening for her reply, then grinned. "Sorry, forgot you can't talk. Bet that must be a novelty."

He moved forward with a deceptively fast, gliding step that made her heart freeze. She thought he was going to hit her, but instead he ripped the tape off. "Although, I guess as a writer you're more concerned with writing trashy novels than talking to actual people, which would be why you've never managed to find anyone."

Jenna gasped at the burn across her mouth from the tape. She didn't think he had actually taken any skin off, it just felt like it.

Forcing herself to ignore Tell's jab about her personal life, and the chilling knowledge that he had obviously kept tabs on her over the years, she sucked in a lungful of stale air and slumped a little, as if the defiance she'd just shown had exhausted her and she was fighting sleep. "If you don't like books, don't read."

"Good advice."

He stared at her and frowned. Adrenaline surged through her as he continued to stand over her. He hadn't seemed to have noticed that she had moved the chair, but if he did, it wouldn't take him long to put two and two together and check her wrists.

Another rill of panic shot through her as he bent down, but he didn't check her wrists, he simply picked up the chair with her in it.

Jenna's stomach lurched as he carried her, although she was more concerned that he might notice she had practically sawed through the tape binding her wrists.

Seconds later, he set the chair down by a stack of cartons in what looked like the main room of a warehouse. A bare, iron roof soared overhead. The Hummer he'd used to transport her here was now parked inside and occupied one end of the room. Boxes of varying shapes and sizes were stacked at the other end.

Jenna's blood ran cold when she noted the contents: security systems.

The connection she had made when she'd been half-asleep the previous night had been heart-poundingly correct. Hope surged afresh, sending blood pounding through her veins, burning through the dull, heavy lethargy the pills had induced.

O'Halloran had taken her suggestion that Tell could be linked somehow with security systems rather than firms seriously enough that he had gotten out of bed and started making calls. He had come back to bed, but left in the early hours. The conclusion was obvious; he had a lead on Tell.

He would be searching. She knew better than anyone what O'Halloran was like. He was dogged, relentless. If anyone could find her, he would.

Letting herself sag a little farther in the chair as if she was fighting the effects of the sleeping pills Tell had given her, she continued to take stock of her surroundings.

There was a desk neatly piled with papers and what looked like order books. An expensive laptop sat next to a printer and modem and other various pieces of office paraphernalia.

Her gaze snagged on the sleek shape of a stylish white phone. *Her phone.*

She jerked her gaze away in case Tell noticed that she'd spotted it, but she needn't have bothered. He was busy loading a stack of folders and boxes into the back of his Hummer.

Getting ready to leave.

Taking a deep breath, she forced her wrists apart as far as they'd go. Frustratingly, the tape had stretched, but hadn't broken. Closing her eyes, she sent up a desperate prayer. She needed help, and she needed it soon.

She needed Tell to leave the room for one minute, two at the most. She was pretty sure she had enough stretch in the tape that she could shimmy out of the chair, get over to the desk and switch on her phone.

Long minutes passed while Tell continued to load the Hummer. The soft burr of a phone saw him straightening. He answered his cell, a call that seemed to be about flight details, then had to set the phone down while he searched for a file he must have stacked in the backseat of the Hummer.

Another loud detonation made her jump. From the rending sound of metal being crushed, she guessed that the building was cheek by jowl with a car-recycling plant.

Tell was busy, with his back to her, and there was enough sound that he wouldn't hear the noise she was bound to make getting loose from the chair. She would never have a better chance.

Giving the tape around her wrists a final stretch, she planted her feet firmly apart on the concrete floor, braced herself and pushed upward. She managed to slide her arms and wrists up a few inches, then, in order to clear the top of the chair, she had to shimmy and straighten by increments. In the process, the chair wobbled and banged on the concrete.

Adrenaline flowing, she darted a glance at Tell, who was still rummaging in the backseat of the Hummer, as she pulled hard at the tape. It had stretched enough that she could step backwards through the loop of her arms. She was still tied, but now at least her hands were in front.

Walking quickly to the desk, she picked up the phone and depressed the start button. She had a moment to wonder if Murphy's Law had struck and the battery was flat, then it activated with a soft glow and a faint musical chime.

She debated making a run for it with the phone, but the distance to the door was a good fifteen meters, Tell would catch her before she could reach it.

Her priority had to be ensuring that the GPS search program had enough time to connect with her phone and download her location. Working quickly, she scrolled through to settings and turned off all of the noises the phone made. Setting the phone back on the desk, she placed an invoice book on top of it to hide the faint glow that signalled it was on.

Just as she was about to return to her chair she saw the small squat shape of a box-cutter blade.

A sharp thunk signalled that Tell had shut the door of the Hummer. Her heart slamming hard in her chest, Jenna snatched up the box cutter and covered the four paces to her chair. She sat down a split second before Tell half turned to check on her, a document in one hand, phone to his ear.

He stared at her then looked away. Jenna went limp

as a noodle. The box cutter was hidden in the folds of her skirt, and he hadn't noticed that her hands were tied in the front, not the back.

Working quickly, she slit the tape, wedged the box cutter between the small of her back and the seat then clasped her hands together behind the chair as if they were tied.

Tell's laptop pinged, indicating he had mail. He hung up from his call and strolled past her to his desk. Apart from raking a cold glance over her, he barely seemed to notice she was there.

He refreshed the screen then muttered a hard, sharp word. "Damn, how did he manage to find my email address?"

Attention riveted, Jenna stared at the laptop screen as Tell scrolled down. The email appeared to be blank.

Frowning, he opened up the attachment that had come with the email. A photograph of Jenna opened up, filling the entire screen.

Cursing beneath his breath, Tell hit the delete button. The photo and the email winked out as he slammed the laptop shut, but it was too late, she'd already seen it.

He might have emailed Tell, but the message had been for her.

Fierce satisfaction filled her, although she kept her expression carefully blank. The email informed her that O'Halloran had gone through Tell's life with a fine-tooth comb and had found his business email address. When it came to research and investigative method, O'Halloran was clinical and focused. By now, what he didn't know about Tell wouldn't fit on a postage stamp.

Tears filled Jenna's eyes and made her feel shaky inside. For O'Halloran to have sent the email at that moment meant he must have been monitoring the GPS program on her phone. He couldn't know who had turned on the phone and he hadn't risked calling her number, because if Tell had been using the phone, that would have alerted him. Instead, he had put a call through to her in the only way he safely could, by emailing Tell.

He had the coordinates, which meant he was on his way. She didn't know how long she had to wait, but at a guess based on the time it had taken Tell to drive here, it would be half an hour or so.

Her chest squeezed tight. The photograph O'Halloran had used was an old one, nine years old to be exact. She remembered when it had been taken, during a carefree, impromptu picnic at the beach.

Despite the fact that O'Halloran would be working hard and literally have no time, he had somehow managed to find a photo of her from the time they had dated and send it out into cyberspace.

It had been a crazy, quixotic, *romantic* gesture. There was no guarantee that Tell would have even accessed his email. Even if he had, the chances were that she wouldn't be in a position to see the photograph, but still, he'd sent it. And in that moment she saw another side to O'Halloran.

He was in turns frustrating and uncomplicatedly, ruthlessly male. He was her lover, friend and protector. Most importantly, he was *hers*.

The concept settled in, filling her with a fierce sense of certainty.

O'Halloran hadn't ever given her any words of love. When it came to emotional discussions, he was the original Sphinx, but that didn't matter. He was hers in all the ways that mattered. Maybe it would take him a little time to get around to telling her. That was fine; she could wait.

All she had to do was get out of this alive.

Tell checked his watch then walked back in the direction of the Hummer to make another call. The sound of a large truck backing up to the roller door stopped him in his tracks.

Tell spun. Instead of going to the door, he picked up a can, unscrewed the lid and tossed it away as he walked toward her.

Horror filled Jenna as he began dousing the stacked boxes next to her with gasoline.

Marc and members of the Special Tactics Squad he used to command fanned out like dark shadows, flowing around the warehouse to key entry points: a rear window, a side door and either side of the main roller door. Seconds later they were all in position.

Cornell, the senior detective at Auckland Central, hadn't been happy about Marc's insistence that he be included in the team, but in this instance he'd allowed it because Marc knew Tell, and he'd also added the condition that he couldn't personally shoot anyone.

Marc hadn't made that promise, and Cornell hadn't pressed the point. He knew what Marc had lost at the hands of Tell better than anyone.

Marc spoke into a lip mike. Carter and West had driven the large delivery truck, which was presently parked hard up against the roller door of the warehouse. If Tell tried to escape, he'd find that avenue blocked.

There was a moment of quiet, until the team sniper indicated that he was in position.

O'Halloran gave the order to proceed. In the same instant, he smelled smoke.

Panic gripped him, the kind of icy, bone-deep dread that had hit him six years ago when he'd arrived home to find his house ablaze.

He smashed the rear window and climbed through into a dark room that was already filling with smoke. A second team member, a young ultra-fit officer called Trent who was relatively new to the squad, followed a half step behind, covering him.

Glock held in a two-handed grip, Marc stepped through an open door into a corridor. He checked what looked like an empty storage room and kept moving. When he saw the leap of flames, he roared Jenna's name.

Sucking in a lungful of smoky air he called again.

The sound of a vehicle filled the air as he stepped into a room that was rapidly turning into a blazing inferno. Flames and black smoke poured from a central pyre, licking up the walls.

Someone said his name, the sound hoarse. A split second later, Jenna loomed out of the smoke.

Marc grabbed her, one arm snaking around her waist and hauling her in tight against him as he dragged her and half carried her back the way he'd come. Seconds later the Hummer, engine screaming, smashed through the far wall of the warehouse.

Marc had a moment to haul Jenna in against the wall of his chest and wrap both arms around her before the sudden gush of fresh air sent flames whooshing.

Heat singed Marc's skin even through the fire-retardant overalls, which were standard issue, and the body armour he was wearing. Coughing, eyes running, he swung Jenna into his arms. Almost totally blinded by the smoke, he found the room where he'd entered the warehouse by following the draught of air flowing from the window.

He handed Jenna through the window, then clambered after her. Seconds later, they were outside on the cool green grass, the blue sky arching above, cloudless except for the pall of smoke that funnelled up from the burning warehouse.

When he could breathe without coughing, Marc studied the burning building, a sight he profoundly hoped that he would never see again.

"Are you all right?"

Jenna's hand linked with his. He looked into her concerned gaze and his heart locked up.

He didn't know how, but she knew what the fire made him feel, the memories that seared him and the grief that should have made him drop dead in his tracks. But it hadn't, he had kept breathing, kept living. Life moved on and now he was happy that it had.

He cupped her face, which was pink from the heat, and sooty. It didn't matter, Jenna had always been beautiful to him. "I love you."

She smiled, tears tracking down her cheeks. "I know. Thank you for the emails, Lydell88."

He found himself smiling into her eyes. The email correspondence had started out as a way to keep tabs on Jenna and make sure she was okay. He had never intended for it to develop into anything more, but somehow the exchanges had metamorphosed into an addictive habit he'd had a hard time controlling. "I wasn't sure if you had time to find them."

"I'm glad I did. It kept me going after Tell busted into the hotel room." Reaching up, she slid her fingers into his hair. Cupping his skull, she gently pulled his head down until his forehead settled on hers. "I love you, too, and have for a long time now."

Going up on her toes, she sealed the words with a kiss that was soft and gentle and filled with the kind of promise he thought he'd given up on a long time ago.

She eased back a few inches. "Don't you want to go after Tell?"

He rubbed his thumbs across her cheeks, wiping away the tears. "Nope."

The relief in Jenna's gaze made his heart squeeze tight. In that moment, he made a second vow. From now on, Jenna came first. Happily, he had enough money that he could afford to follow McCabe's example; the business could go hang.

She smiled. "Good, because I think your friend Carter took care of that. I don't know if you've noticed, but he kind of ran over Tell with that truck."

Jenna strolled over to the two vehicles with O'Halloran, happily leaning into his side and enjoying the feel of his arm clamped possessively around her waist. She was barefoot, bruised and scraped, her hair was singed and she looked like a chimney sweep, but she was almost dizzy with happiness.

In the oddball way that it worked, her writer's mind threw up a question about the past that had been niggling at her off and on. "Just one thing. When, exactly, after we first broke up did you visit the air base to find out about my family background?"

"And Dane Hawkins."

She drew in a sharp breath at the sudden visual of Dane: warm brown eyes, brown hair shot with surfieblond streaks. But like the sepia-toned photographs lining her stairwell, the image now seemed faded and distant, a pleasant memory rather than a wrenching one. "And Dane."

"A couple of days after we broke up. Why do you think I was worried enough to follow you when you left Tell at the ball that night and walked home alone?"

She gripped the lapels of his overalls. Her eyes were burning with tears again, her chest squeezed tight. She couldn't help it, she felt like she'd just stepped out of a dark tunnel into blinding sunlight. "So you knew what had happened before we made love."

Again it hit her. That was why he had been so silent and withdrawn, and why he had let her go with barely a word. Not because he didn't care, but because he did.

His gaze was dark and impossibly soft. "I knew you didn't want the relationship because I was a cop. Up until then the way you were hadn't made sense because I knew you wanted me." His hands curled around her arms, pulled her close. "We shouldn't have made love. I shouldn't have touched you, but the near accident pushed things over the edge. And," he admitted, "I hoped that if I made love to you it might be enough for you to leave the grief behind."

And choose him.

Coiling her arms around his neck, Jenna answered the question in his eyes, the one question she knew he wouldn't be able to ask. "Dane had been gone for almost two years when you first asked me out. I knew you were a cop, and still I agreed, which should tell you something. I wasn't ready for a relationship with anybody, most especially a soldier or a cop, but it was a fact that I couldn't resist you. That night we made love, Dane didn't come into the equation."

Relief flared in his gaze. "That's why I didn't come near you again, until I started dating Natalie."

"And then Nat was a good friend. Trust me, I know. After I lost Dane, I wouldn't have gotten through it without her."

His forehead dropped on hers. "Did I tell you that I loved you?"

She couldn't stop smiling. O'Halloran loved her. He had always loved her. She knew he had loved Natalie and Jared, too, and that they would always have a special place in his heart. But, like her time with Dane, that part of his life had come to an end and couldn't be gotten back.

Now that they had found each other for the second time, the future stretched forward, almost unbearably bright. It seemed almost impossibly greedy, that after nine years of waiting she could finally have the man she loved with all her heart, and the family and life she craved.

Marc kept Jenna close as he joined the members of the STS, who were gathered around the truck and the Hummer, lethal automatics held, barrels pointing to the ground. Like him, they were all, except for the sniper who had been holed up on a roof across the road, singed and covered with soot.

In the distance, sirens wailed. The fire trucks were on their way. Not that there would be much for them to do by the time they got here. The warehouse was little more than a shell and was already close to totalled.

Marc lifted a brow at Carter as he checked out the

odd configuration of the two vehicles. "How did you get the Hummer wedged underneath like that?"

Carter leaned against the truck, which Marc had borrowed from one of their security suppliers and which he was now going to have to pay to have repaired.

He didn't care. He had more money than he needed, and if Carter hadn't pulled the stunt with the truck, Tell might have gotten away. Hummers were notoriously difficult to stop. Using the truck to cut him off had been a one-shot chance, and it had paid off.

Carter had an innocent look on his face, which, for a hardened former SAS assault specialist, was difficult to achieve. "It's all a bit confusing now, what with the smoke and everything—"

"It's not an insurance job. I'm paying."

"Cool. Then I drove him down."

A cop cruiser pulled in at the curb. Farrell and Hansen climbed out. Marc grinned when he noticed Farrell was driving.

He checked in the cab. Tell was pinned by the steering wheel and crumpled metal. Stuck like a sardine in a can, he was conscious and definitely unhappy.

West braced a hand on the Hummer and peered in. "I guess we should call an ambulance."

Carter shrugged. "I'm thinking we should run it past Farrell first. She won't be happy if we make a decision without her."

West nodded. "That is absolutely right. We should wait."

Farrell put the cell she had been talking into in her pocket as she came to a halt by the wreck of the Hummer. Hansen strolled around the vehicle and checked out Tell. "Looks like we won't need the cuffs. Shame, I was looking forward to the moment."

Farrell dug in her pocket and handed Marc a sheet of paper. "That little ritual was reserved for O'Halloran, anyway. But maybe if you talk to the firemen nicely, they'll give you a turn with the Jaws of Life." She shot Marc a look that, for Farrell, who was the ultimate professional, was oddly soft. "Hey, good job."

Marc studied the sheet, which was a list of more than twenty unsolved crimes.

Farrell smiled grimly. "Recognize some of those? We worked a few together. I ran a list of crimes using the security system as the common denominator, like you suggested, and bingo. Our mystery burglar turned out to be Tell. At current estimates, he's stolen more than a million dollars' worth of high-end appliances, cash and fine jewellery."

"Murder, attempted murder, burglary and arson." Satisfaction took some of the edge off the anger that had burned through him when he had realized that Tell was the perpetrator. "With any luck, by the time he gets out, he'll be an old man. Did you realize his father was Morrison?"

He saw the moment Farrell put it all together. "So that's why he went for you. You put his father away."

Marc tightened his hold on Jenna, her warmth and softness reminding him of the single most important fact. She was safe, and she was his. "Except he couldn't quite bring himself to attack me directly, instead he attacked the women in my life."

"A coward." Farrell smiled coldly at Hansen, who had straightened from checking on Tell's condition, and who now had his phone out. "Hansen, make that a big wait on the ambulance."

Epilogue

The wedding was held in the little church just down the road from Jenna's house. Old and beautifully kept, with soaring stained-glass windows, the church was big enough to hold all of Marc's and Jenna's families and friends.

McCabe, Blade Lombard and West and Carter were there, along with their wives and families. Elaine Farrell had also accepted the invitation, along with her partner, a sleek well-groomed businessman.

The ceremony was traditional; the bride wore white. As Marc slipped the ring on her finger and Jenna, in turn, placed a ring on his, the vows they made echoed softly.

Minutes later, Jenna caught the misty smile on her Aunt Mary's face. As she and Marc walked into the vestry to sign the register, a fine tension she had barely been aware of dissolved. Aunt Mary was intensely maternal. Jenna knew she had found it hard to let go of each and every one of her children. She knew Aunt Mary loved her as if she were her own, but that she also loved both Natalie and Jared with a fierce devotion.

The week before the wedding, Mary had invited both Jenna and Marc over for lunch then, out of the blue, she had suggested a visit to the cemetery. The few minutes at the gravesite had been difficult and emotional, but now Jenna understood what Mary had done. There had been no wreath, no soft toy, just a simple bunch of flowers, which she had combined with Marc and Jenna's offering in the little stone vase off to one side.

She had let Natalie and the baby go.

When the signatures were done, and while they waited for their witnesses—McCabe and Jenna's editor, Rachel—to sign, Marc pulled her close. "Are you all right? You look a little pale."

Jenna smiled into his dark eyes, her own misty. "Never better."

And to improve on what had so far been the most sublime day of her life, she reached into the tiny pocket she'd gotten the seamstress to sew into her dress at the last minute and extracted a small blue object. "I have a gift for you."

She handed the baby rattle to Marc. For a split second, his expression was perfectly blank then his piercing gaze shot to hers. "Are you sure?"

"Positive."

With a whoop, Marc swung her into his arms then finally, achingly, he kissed her. From the hubbub of noise and a series of frantic motorised clicks Jenna was dimly aware that some of their guests had crowded into the vestry and the wedding photographer was capturing every angle of their private moment. She didn't care.

Somehow they had come full circle and she was back exactly where she wanted to be, in O'Halloran's arms.

*   *   *   *   *

"Aaron, stop."

Her voice was breathy, aroused.

"Don't try to tell me you don't want me, Camille. I know you better than that."

"You don't know me at all."

What a load of crap she was feeding herself. He'd spent every moment of the past week memorizing her—from her body to the cadence of her speech, every sigh and every look. He'd lain awake each night listening to her breathe, drenching his senses with her. He knew Camille Fisher as well as he knew himself, better perhaps. "What have you convinced yourself of? What's going on in that sharp mind of yours?"

"I..."

As she searched for words, he cradled her foot, warming it.

"I don't want this between us."

He tipped her chin up until she looked into his eyes. "Baby, it's already between us."

The torment in her expression spoke of a battle raging within her. She knew he was right.

Dear Reader,

Luck is one of life's big mysteries. Some people believe we make our own luck, while others seem cursed with bad luck their whole lives. We all know people who seem to skate through life with golden tickets. Not that they don't earn their successes, but they seem flat-out luckier than the rest of us. One such person I know became the inspiration for the hero in *Seduction Under Fire*, park ranger Aaron Montgomery.

Aaron's life is one golden opportunity after another. He's on the fast track at work and, to top it all off, he's gorgeous (and knows it). Anything he's ever wanted, he's gotten…except the attention of his best friend's sister-in-law, Camille Fisher—and this ticks him off.

Camille is the unluckiest person she knows. All she ever wanted was to be a cop, but a freak accident has relegated her to a desk job—permanently. Nothing ever goes her way, and Aaron, with his golden goodness and perfect life, irritates her like salt in a wound. These two can't stand each other, but when they're targeted by a cartel, they're forced to rely on one another to survive. If they can find luck in love along the way, so much the better.

Happy reading!

Melissa Cutler

SEDUCTION UNDER FIRE

BY
MELISSA CUTLER

First published in Great Britain 2013
by Mills & Boon, an imprint of Harlequin (UK) Limited,
Eton House, 18-24 Paradise Road, Richmond, Surrey TW9 1SR

© Melissa Cutler 2012

ISBN: 978 0 263 90350 8
ebook ISBN: 978 1 472 00704 9

46-0313

Harlequin (UK) policy is to use papers that are natural, renewable and recyclable products and made from wood grown in sustainable forests. The logging and manufacturing processes conform to the legal environmental regulations of the country of origin.

Printed and bound in Spain
by Blackprint CPI, Barcelona

CHOICE OF
TWO
GIFTS!

A **treat**
from us to
thank you
for reading
our books!

Turn over **now**
to find out more

Thanks for reading!

We're treating you to **TWO** fabulous offers...

Melissa Cutler is a flip-flop-wearing Southern California native living in San Diego with her husband, two children and a nervous Siamese cat. She spent her teenage years on the floor of her local bookstore's romance aisle making tough choices about which novels to buy with the measly paycheck from her filing-clerk job.

Her love for happily-ever-after stories continued into her job as a high school English teacher, and in 2008 she decided to take her romance-novel devotion to the next level by penning one herself. Halfway through that first book, she thought, *This is what I want to do every day for the rest of my life,* and she never looked back. She now divides her time between her dual writing passions—sexy small-town contemporaries and edge-of-your-seat romantic suspense.

Find out more about Melissa and her books at www.melissacutler.net. She loves to hear from readers, so drop her a line at cutlermail@yahoo.com. You can also find Melissa on Facebook and Twitter.

To my two beautiful kids, who cheer me every step
of the way while I chase down my dreams.

Chapter 1

Camille Fisher stood in a bathroom stall wearing the navy blue suit she'd picked out from a JCPenney clearance rack. The jacket buttoned across her chest, but it was a tight fit. With any luck, it would hold until after the press conference. She smoothed a hand down her skirt to make sure it covered her scar. It did, but she scowled at the streak of sweat her palm left on the polyester. Running too late to do anything more about the way she looked, she shielded her eyes from the mirror over the sink and reemerged into the bustling precinct.

Her boss caught up with her in the hallway, wringing his hands. "Look, I know public speaking isn't your cup of tea, but I think it's a good move for you. Gets you out from behind your desk for a change."

Camille stopped short, reeling at the note of sympathy in his tone.

"I only agreed to this arrangement because a child's involved. I happen to enjoy working the dispatch desk." That was a whopper of a lie, but how dare Williamson pity her.

Five years ago, she was a force to be reckoned with, the youngest officer and only female ever promoted to the Special Forces unit in San Diego law enforcement history. As happened every time she thought about those days, the best six months of her life, she experienced a split second of exacting pain in her heart. Not a widespread pain like the bullet had been, but that of a needle. Worse than the pain, reflecting on her past left her feeling weak.

Above all else, Camille hated feeling weak.

"No need to get your back up, Fisher. We all appreciate you stepping up to the plate on this one. I'll see you out front in five."

Inside the lobby doors, Camille opened the three-day-old kidnapping file with trembling hands. She ran her fingertip around the edge of the glossy photo clipped to the front. If Williamson thought her involvement improved Rosalia Perez's chance of being recovered alive, then she owed it to the five-year-old smiling at her to do everything she could.

She pushed the double doors open and froze, stunned by the scene before her. The space between the San Diego Central Precinct and the surrounding high-rises was packed with spectators and journalists. The odor of hundreds of people standing in the midday sun swirled with the stench of car exhaust and city grime. Already on the verge of losing her breakfast, she gagged a little as she took her place in the line of law enforcement officers and government officials.

Camille didn't recognize the man dressed in civilian clothes who stepped to the podium. She tried to concentrate on his introduction of her, but she was working so hard to look confident that it took a nudge from Williamson for her to realize it was her turn to speak.

"Uh...I mean...welcome." She cringed. So much for a smooth beginning. The stares and expectations of the audience bore into her and she shuffled her notes, dumbstruck. Then she noticed Rosalia's photograph peeking out from behind some papers.

This one's for you, Rosalia.

With a deep breath, she squared her shoulders and began.

"At approximately eight o'clock on the morning of Tuesday, February 10, Rosalia Perez boarded a school bus to Balboa Elementary. When class started at eight-thirty, she was marked absent by her teacher. Following the school's unverified absence protocol, a phone call was placed to her home at eight-forty-five and was answered by Rosalia's maternal grandmother, who is a non-English speaker. An interpreter at the school was summoned and a second phone call was placed at nine o'clock, during which the grandmother said that Rosalia had ridden the bus.

"The school bus driver confirmed that his bus dropped Rosalia off in front of Balboa Elementary at eight-ten. By nine-thirty, the girl's mother, Maria Delgado, had arrived at the school. She, along with the school secretary, contacted the police to report her daughter missing. An Amber Alert was issued at nine-forty-five.

"Rosalia Perez is five years old, weighs fifty-one pounds and stands forty-four inches—or just under four feet—tall. She has shoulder-length brown hair and a strawberry-colored birthmark on her forehead above her left eyebrow. You'll find a photograph of her in your press packet.

"Interviews conducted with adults present on the Balboa Elementary campus that morning yielded no information regarding Rosalia's disappearance, but two student eyewitnesses report seeing Rosalia, before school, approach a brown two-door sedan driven by a dark-haired man.

"At this time, our main suspect is Rosalia's biological father, Rodrigo Perez, aka El Ocho, a member of the crime organization in Mexico commonly known as the Cortez Cartel. He is suspected of being in the United States illegally. He is approximately five feet eight inches tall with light brown skin and short, black hair. In every photograph we've acquired, he's wearing black leather gloves. He is considered armed and extremely dangerous.

"I will be conducting briefings at twelve o'clock each day in the main conference room of this precinct to keep the public as informed as our investigation allows." She glanced around for the man who had introduced her. "Am I taking questions?"

He nodded and the entire throng of reporters stood at once, shouting.

Camille gestured to a woman wearing a red suit in the front row.

"How can the police be sure Rosalia hasn't been taken to Mexico by her father?"

"The Border Patrol is immediately notified of all Amber Alerts, but with the nearly two-hour gap between the time Rosalia was last seen and when she was reported missing, we have no way of knowing whether she was taken out of the country, especially since the abduction site is only twenty minutes north of the Mexican border. We are working to gain permission from the Mexican government to widen our search to include Baja."

Camille took a dozen more questions before gathering her notes and giving the podium over to the man who introduced her. Trembling with adrenaline, she nodded to her boss and walked past the line of officials and back through the double doors.

The relative silence of the precinct was a relief. Mostly, she couldn't wait to change out of her suit. From the chair at her desk she grabbed her duffel bag and heard her cell phone ringing in her purse.

When she saw the text message, she smiled and snagged Williamson as he walked by. "I just got word my sister's in labor. I'll be back at work tomorrow in time for the press briefing."

"Congratulations to your family. And give your dad my best. Remind him I still owe him for the burger he bought me last month."

Camille's father was retired, but his years on the force were legendary. She was constantly asked by her superiors to give her father their regards or forced to sit patiently through retellings of his most heroic moments. There had been a time Camille dreamed of following in his footsteps. The familiar needle of pain pierced her heart, but she refused to dwell. No more thoughts of dying dreams, not when she was about to become an aunt.

Juliana was two years Camille's junior and as different from her as a sister could be. A lifetime of strained relations had finally given way to friendship two years ago, after Juliana fell in love with Camille's former partner, Jacob. That he was the man responsible for Camille's accidental shooting was immaterial. She'd known the risks of her high-stakes job when she signed on.

She grabbed her duffel and kept moving. She'd change out of the uncomfortable skirt and flats after she checked in with her sister.

Aaron Montgomery's eyeballs hurt.

He could barely see the sun through the heavily tinted windows of the meeting room, yet it was still painful. Not even his special hangover energy drink helped when his head ached this badly. Sure he'd wanted to celebrate Tuesday's big arrests, but what in God's name made him down those last three tequila shots instead of calling it a night?

The answer, of course, was a petite college senior—at least, that's what he thought she said—with long chocolate-colored hair and a waistline so tiny that when she ground against him on the dance floor, her little black skirt kept sliding down to reveal her thong.

Ah, good times.

"Something funny, Montgomery?" barked Thomas Dreyer, the ICE Field Office Director, who stood at the head of the table.

Aaron mashed his lips together in an effort to stop smiling. "Just thinking about how those cartel runners almost crapped their pants when we caught them, sir."

"Add those two to the ten we expedited in December and we're starting to send a clear message that these low-lifes can't move guns through our country's deserts and get away with it. If the cartels want to wage war against each other in Mexico, I'll be damned if they're going to do it with American firepower."

"I couldn't agree with you more, sir." Staying on Dreyer's good side was proving to be a tricky act—the man had no sense of humor—but Aaron was an expert at being a team player. And this was a team he was determined to rise to the top of.

As was usually the case in his life, Aaron had been handed the opportunity. His best friend, Jacob, referred to his luck as Aaron's Golden Ticket. The label was fine for a joke, but Aaron knew better. He didn't wait for luck to strike him where he stood, but instead kept his eyes open, ready to move into the path of the bolt at the first sign of a spark. So when, a year ago, the Federal Immigration and Customs Enforcement agency, better known as ICE, handpicked him to participate in a regional joint task force to combat drug, guns and human trafficking through the Southern California desert, Aaron seized the opportunity.

And he had a goal for himself. A big one.

He had no interest in being a boss man, standing at the head of the table as an administrator like Dreyer. His ultimate goal was to prove his worth as an ICE field agent. Maybe undercover. Definitely abroad.

As one of two Park Rangers on a unit comprised primarily of Border Patrol officers and ICE intelligence agents, Aaron was in ambitious company. Although he came to the unit with thirteen years' experience as a Backcountry Park Ranger, he'd invested months of rigorous field training in weaponry and combat tactics and countless hours of classroom time to understand border policing laws so when the opportunity to transfer from Park Ranger to ICE agent presented itself, he'd be ready.

The challenge couldn't have come at a better time. The diversions that used to satisfy his wanderlust had lost their flavor. Though he still thought his Mustang Shelby GT 500 was the best money he'd ever spent, he no longer took it for day trips simply for the thrill of the drive. Even the club scenes he frequented felt like a waste of time. Rock climbing, speedboating, skydiving—nothing he tried could take away the restless dissatisfaction that had settled into his bones.

Last night, he'd stayed out way too late with Little Miss Thong because she was exactly the type of girl that got his blood pumping. But sometime during the night, the pointlessness of what he was doing dawned on him. Time and youth were slipping away from him at an alarming rate, a revelation he counteracted by drinking and dancing more than usual.

Since Jacob's wedding a year and a half ago, Aaron felt *off*.

At first, he thought it was because Jacob no longer had much time to spend with him, but it was more than that. Maybe he was subconsciously jealous of Jacob's marital bliss or maybe Aaron was bored, but the discontent that had dogged him since his friend's wedding was damned annoying.

"As I was saying," Dreyer said with a hard glance at Aaron, "the latest intel is that the Cortez Cartel's weapons distribution operation is being headquartered near the Baja capital city of La Paz, along the Sea of Cortez." He pushed a button on his laptop and a satellite image of the Baja peninsula projected onto the wall behind him.

"As we already suspected, the Mexican government's crackdown on cartels within Baja's border cities has spurred them to move to obscure locations and utilize more creative means to smuggle weapons into their country."

With another push of a button, Dreyer projected a grainy photo of a Hispanic man with jet-black hair and a round, oily face. "This is our next target, Rodrigo Perez, Alejandro Milán's second-in-command. Perez has been running the weapons-smuggling division of the Cortez Cartel for approximately one year and manages a crew of at least thirty men."

Aaron felt the vibration of his cell phone in his shirt pocket. He flipped it open to find a short text message—*Jul n labr.*

"Look at that," he muttered to himself. "I'm about to be a godfather."

He caught the eye of Nicholas Wells, the other Park Ranger in the unit, and held up his phone. "Family emergency," he mouthed, scooting out of his chair. He opened the door and slipped into the bright afternoon, his headache forgotten.

She should have known he'd be at the birth of Juliana and Jacob's child—he was her brother-in-law's best friend, after all—but Camille's stomach still lurched when she heard the deafening rumble of Aaron's obnoxious car pull into the hospital parking garage behind her.

Unwilling to park on the same level as him, she drove past whole rows of available parking spots, waiting for him to choose one first. To her chagrin, he passed every open spot, too. In her rearview mirror, she saw Aaron chuckling behind his wraparound sunglasses and knew he was onto her plan. Even in the dim light of the garage, his dimples sparkled. The man was like a barbed thorn in her side—irritating and impossible to dislodge.

Finally he conceded and pulled into a space on the fourth level. Camille drove to the roof.

Then it occurred to her that in a matter of minutes, she'd be sitting in a waiting room with the man she'd successfully avoided for over a year. She thunked her forehead on the steering wheel and groaned.

She first met Jacob's best friend two years earlier, and it had been a miserable experience. Simply put, Aaron was the most arrogant man she'd ever known. Handsome to a fault, with wavy blond hair and a body so meticulously ripped it was the perfect advertisement for his bloated ego, he'd made her feel like a piece of meat from the moment he introduced himself without raising his eyes higher than her chest.

When he figured out she wasn't going to drool all over his showy muscles, lame jokes and expensive car, he'd been equally put off by her.

At Juliana and Jacob's wedding, Camille put on her game face and tolerated Aaron for the single dance required of the maid of honor and best man, then spent the rest of the reception watching him hit on all the young, single women in attendance. She couldn't believe how easily they fell for his boyish good looks and perfect body. They didn't even notice he was treating them like interchangeable objects. She made a game of predicting which one he'd invite to his room that night. Because the wedding party had rooms on the same hotel floor, it was an easy mystery to solve.

And her prediction had been correct.

She knew Aaron thought she was a killjoy, but unlike the girls falling all over him at Juliana's wedding, Camille didn't require the validation of a man. And it was a good thing, too, because being a young female cop with a statuesque figure was like being an island in a sea of chauvinism. Why this particular chauvinist rubbed her the wrong way, Camille wasn't sure. Frankly, she tried not to think about it—ever.

She grabbed her bag of clothes and purse and locked her car. When she got to the stairwell, she paused. Which would Aaron be less likely to take—the stairs or the elevator? She decided to take the stairs, even though her dressy shoes were beginning to rub, because it would preclude any chance of being stuck in the tight confines of an elevator with him. If he chose the stairs, she could hang back and let him go first.

As she turned the corner onto the fourth level landing, Aaron materialized in the stairwell.

"Camille, what a…pleasant surprise," he deadpanned, falling into step beside her.

"I see you're still compensating for your shortcomings with that offensive car."

He chortled. "It's good to know time hasn't softened your icy heart."

Narrowing her eyes, Camille picked up the pace. So much for hanging behind; she wouldn't give him the satisfaction. She motioned to his dark glasses. "Are you hungover again? Funny how every time I see you, you've been drinking too much. Maybe I'll send you an AA pamphlet."

With her skirt and shoes slowing her down, Aaron paced her effortlessly.

"Gee," he said, "that's a nice suit you're wearing. Borrowing your grandma's clothes again, are you?"

"You're such a pig."

"And you're still a shrew, so we're even."

That was enough for Camille. "Out of my way," she snarled. Elbowing him in the chest, she propelled herself into the lead.

He quickened his steps to match hers. "Always such a

bully. When're you going to figure out no one likes a bully, Blondie?"

"When're you going to figure out I hate you, you misogynist prick?"

"Sweetheart, I figured that out the day we met, and I dropped to my knees, thanking the Lord for small favors."

They broke into a sprint, their feet flying and their knees pumping like football players running a high-step drill. Camille knew she was acting immature, but she simply had to be the first person to the bottom of the stairs, the first person through the hospital doors, the first one to reach Juliana's bedside.

As they traversed the last flight of stairs, Aaron shouldered past her, taking the steps two at a time. When Camille tried to match his stride, one of her shoes flew off. She grabbed the railing to keep from pitching headfirst to the ground.

Aaron reached the bottom level of the parking garage and scooped up Camille's shoe. He turned to face her with a smug smile. "I'm sure your grandmother will want this back."

Gasping at the insult, she yanked her other shoe off and hurled it at him.

He ducked, but his laughter was drowned out by a revving engine, its echo thunderous in the confines of the garage.

A white minivan screeched to a halt behind Aaron as its side door opened. Two masked men armed with fully automatic assault rifles were staged inside. Aaron whipped his head around, but it was too late. The men pulled him in and pointed their guns at Camille.

"In the van, *puta*. Now!" one of the men shouted at her.

Impossible. This couldn't be happening. She was there for the birth of her niece.

"Camille, run," Aaron called from within the van.

Run? Where? The only route was back up the stairs and then she'd still be trapped in the garage. Her eyes settled on the rifles, AK-47 knockoffs, probably Romanian. Wherever they were from, the guns made her only choice perfectly clear. Numbly, she got into the van.

Aaron sagged against the floor with half-closed eyelids as though he were drifting to sleep. "Aaron, what...? Why are you—" She yelped, turning toward the pain in her upper arm. An unmasked, baby-faced man with slicked-back hair was plunging a needle into her.

"Oh, God, no." Then her tongue, along with the rest of her body, grew heavy, and she crumpled over Aaron's limp form.

Chapter 2

Body odor. Not the occasional whiff of someone who forgot to apply deodorant, but the cloying, inescapable stench of people who, as a habit, did not bathe. The smell was so pungent, Aaron tasted it in his mouth as it hung open, slack and drooling due to the drug he'd been injected with.

Time passed indeterminately. Perhaps they drove for an hour, maybe longer. He couldn't see anything except the booted feet of his captors, nor feel anything except the weight of Camille sprawled over him. No one spoke except for comments in Spanish said in whispers too soft for Aaron to translate, though he was adept at the language.

When the van stopped moving, the kidnappers stirred.

"Ustedes dos llévense al hombre." You two take the man. *"Cuidado, Perez lo quiere ileso."* Careful, Perez wants him unharmed.

Rodrigo Perez.

With the mention of that name, Aaron knew why he'd been taken and what they were going to do to him. As the

man who arrested two of Perez's operatives, Aaron was
going to help the cartel send a message to the U.S. government. Today he was going to die. Probably beheaded. Most
likely paraded around the streets of Tijuana on a stick. And
Camille, poor unlucky Camille, was going to die, too.

He was dragged from the van to a small plane on a
cracked blacktop runway in the middle of a lettuce field.
Camille was slung over the shoulder of a short man, her legs
dangling and her skirt bunched, revealing the white of her
panties. Another man walked to her, chuckling, and pulled
her skirt higher.

Realization of his powerlessness crashed over Aaron.
These men could do whatever they wanted to Camille—
rape, kill, anything—and Aaron couldn't protect her. It was
one thing to die as a result of his dangerous job. It was
something much worse to watch another suffer, particularly
a woman, for no reason other than her close proximity to
trouble when it struck.

He was shoved through a side door in the plane and
dumped on the floor. Camille was dropped at his side. With
much effort, he turned his head to see her. Her eyes were
not glazed over from the drug, nor did she look afraid at
all, which threw Aaron off. He'd been prepared to console
her. Instead she met his look with a sharp, confident gaze,
as though she was trying to give *him* courage.

The plane taxied, then angled into the air. Aaron shifted
until the back of his arm touched Camille's hand. She wiggled her fingers against his skin. Of all the people in the
world to be the last each saw before dying, that they were
stuck with each other was definitive proof that God had an
ironic sense of humor.

When the plane reached cruising altitude, someone
moved between Camille's legs. Aaron could tuck his chin
enough to see the man's slim form, but not what he was
doing. He had a pretty good idea, though. Against the back

of his hand, he felt her skirt being raised. Someone Aaron couldn't see laughed and whooped. Aaron took Camille's hand firmly in his and looked into her eyes. For the first time, she seemed afraid.

Don't think about it, Camille. Look at me and turn your mind off.

After a minute, her look of fear evolved into confusion. The man above Camille smacked Aaron's hand away and rolled her to her stomach. Then Aaron saw the harness.

Black straps looped around her thighs and shoulders, meeting in a rectangle of material against her back with attachments for the master jumper. Camille was being fitted with skydiving gear, the kind used in tandem jumps. When her harness was on, the man left her on her stomach. She turned to Aaron, her expression questioning. Aaron tried to speak, but his words came out distorted beyond understanding.

The same man moved over Aaron, lifting his legs and putting his tandem harness in place. Aaron had enough experience and skill to be a solo jumper, but like most people, he'd started with tandem jumping, where the novice is strapped to the front of an experienced jumper—the one with the parachute.

Aaron's master jumper began the process of binding them together. Aaron had read reports of instances where this hadn't been done correctly and the results were as gruesome as one might imagine. Hopefully these guys knew what they were doing.

The door of the plane opened and the howl of air moving at a hundred miles per hour eclipsed all other sounds in the cabin. The kidnappers heaved two wooden crates fitted with chutes through the opening. Too bad Aaron would never have the chance to tell his team about the Cortez Cartel's method for smuggling weapons into Mexico.

Goggles were put on Camille and Aaron, which seemed

like an odd bit of caring for hostage-taking narco-terrorists, and they were hauled to standing on weak but functioning legs. With the press of the master jumper's belly nudging him, Aaron dragged his heavy feet toward the open door. He remembered how intimidating that opening, with the scream of the wind, looked on his first jump, and turned, seeking Camille to bolster her courage.

She stood behind Aaron, lining up for her jump. Though he was pretty sure she'd never been skydiving before, he shouldn't have been surprised by the look of steely determination on her face. She might be the most grating woman he'd ever met, but he had to admire her fortitude. Camille was one tough broad.

She dipped her head in a terse nod, then shrank away with the rest of the plane as Aaron fell into the infinite blue horizon.

Camille's heart pounded in her ears as she fell to earth. The fear of not knowing if the chute would open or if her harness would hold overrode all other thought during the free fall that seemed to last an eternity. Finally, the force of the unfurling chute jolted her back. Cold air whipped at her bare legs and feet. She was probably the first woman in history to skydive in a business suit, which was an honor she could have done without—and a perfect example of her rotten luck.

Camille used to believe she had fantastic luck. Five years ago, while lying in a hospital bed, she felt lucky to have cheated death, lucky that when Jacob misfired his gun, the bullet ripped through her thigh and not her head or an artery. In the days following the shooting, she felt lucky to keep the leg with the promise of walking again.

But as weeks and months passed, luck abandoned her. Oh, she could walk—for a little while before the throbbing pain became unbearable. And she could run—for a minute or two at a time. Soon, her recovery stalled.

What crushed her the most was the damage to her right hand, even though the bullet hadn't come close to it. No matter how diligently she worked in rehab, her right hand shook uncontrollably when she held a gun. She discovered that little nugget of joy four weeks after the accident, her first time back at the firing range. She tried to load the magazine of her Glock 23 and her hand shook like there was an earthquake inside her body. She couldn't even get a round off.

Her mandatory, department-issued therapist called it post-traumatic stress disorder. That sounded pretty official and all, but giving a name to her problem didn't magically fix her.

Nothing could fix her.

Just like that, Camille's temporary assignment to the dispatch desk took on the horrible stench of permanency. Her family encouraged her to pick a different career—if she ever heard the saying *When one door closes, another opens* again, she'd hang herself—but being a top-rate police officer was all she'd ever wanted. It was her one thing, her only thing.

She knew why she'd been kidnapped. Her image was splashed on the news naming Rosalia Perez's father as a suspect, and a few hours later she was snatched by a group of Spanish-speaking thugs with the financial resources to own a private plane and an arsenal of assault weapons.

Her remorse was solely for Aaron, whose only offense was arriving at the hospital at the same time she did. At least he had the good fortune to be taken hostage with a former Special Forces officer. If even the smallest opportunity for escape opened, Camille would try to get Aaron to safety. She might hate the guy, but no one deserved to die this way. She had a vague recollection of Jacob gushing about Aaron's assignment as a Park Ranger to an ICE task force, but she had no idea if he possessed skills that could aid their escape. The only Park Rangers she'd ever met had been a pair of granola-eating trail guides.

During the five-minute descent, she focused on determining their location. The ocean sat to the east and a long range of foothills sprawled over the west and south. What really struck her about the landscape was its desolation.

Save for a large city to the south along the shoreline and a highway running north and south, there wasn't much to see. No suburban developments and few signs of life. The ground, from the shoreline to the tops of the foothills, was blanketed with rocks, tall-reaching cacti and scruffy desert plants. This had to be Mexico. Nowhere in America would such a large stretch of land abutting the ocean be free of people.

Before Camille touched down, she saw they were met by six mangy horses, one of which had a rider, a stout middle-aged Latino man with a thick mustache and a wavy shock of black hair. Two horses were strapped to a wagon laden with the wooden crates. The remaining horses were riderless and saddled.

She landed hard and grunted in pain when her knees hit gravel. The jumper attached to her toppled over her and shouted something in Spanish, then detached their harnesses and hauled her to her feet. Aaron stood nearby, a rifle pressed to his back. Despite it being February, the desert sun blazed against Camille's fair skin. She licked her dry, cracked lips and tried unsuccessfully to swallow.

When someone shoved her toward him, her jelly legs lurched and she tripped over a rock. She would have fallen except Aaron reached out and caught her. With an expressionless face, he pulled her to his side and maintained a steadying hand on her elbow.

Mr. Mustache gestured to a chestnut-colored horse. With tentative steps, Camille approached it. She wiggled a foot into the stirrup and tried to hoist herself on, but her muscles refused to comply.

Aaron's hands encircled her waist. "I've got you," he whispered.

As he lifted, Camille hefted her leg over the saddle. Aaron swung behind her. It was the closest she'd been to a man in a long, long time. Check that—ever. She squirmed, desperate to put an inch or two between them.

"Easy there," he muttered. To Camille's mortification, he grabbed her hips and pulled her onto his groin. "Sorry." His breath on her skin sent an involuntary shudder through her spine. "This saddle's too small for the both of us."

No kidding. "Just keep your hands to yourself."

He responded with a quiet snort. "We're going to die, Camille, and even if we weren't, you're not my type."

"Believe me when I say that's a relief."

With Mr. Mustache holding the reins of Camille and Aaron's horse, the caravan began a slow trot into the foothills, away from the city she'd seen in the distance.

As they rode in silence over an endless expanse of shrubs and sand, Camille caught a whiff of Aaron's scent for the first time—clean, like freshly laundered cotton. Discreetly, she turned her face toward his neck and inhaled. No doubt about it, despite their ordeal, the man smelled like laundry straight out of the dryer. She squeezed her arms down, certain she didn't smell as nice.

She'd learned the hard way that when men were as good-looking as Aaron, they were used to getting whatever they wanted. Aaron, in particular, oozed entitlement from his every pore. As though being born beautiful was anything more than lucky genes.

It irritated Camille to be the foil to his physical perfection. She neither looked nor smelled as good as he did. She felt awkward and unnatural on the horse while he was graceful and practiced. It was not an exaggeration to say he made being taken hostage look elegant and easy. No wonder she'd avoided him the past two years. His very existence felt toxic to her own.

When the trail turned steeply upward, Camille was forced to lean into his chest. He tensed in response. She turned to find him scowling.

"Don't worry," she growled, "it's not a come-on. You're not my type either."

Not that it mattered in these last few minutes of his life, but no way would Aaron embarrass himself by sporting an erection while sharing a saddle with Camille Fisher. There would be no masking it since she was sitting on his lap, a position only slightly more comfortable than enduring the constant wiggling of her derriere.

Somehow, he had to figure out a way to stop his body's reaction. First, he needed to quit smelling her hair, which was difficult because it was the most exquisite head of hair he'd ever seen, hanging in thick tresses down her back, inches from his nose. As the trail turned steep, Camille reclined into him and it took all his mental wrangling to not bury his face in it.

The second key to his success was not looking at or touching her long, perfectly toned legs to see if her skin was as soft as it looked. He remembered those legs from Jacob and Juliana's wedding, how they looked holding up her red dress. What a waste, he'd thought at the time, to give such a body to a foul-tempered harpy.

The moment they crested a hill and a compound came into view, nestled in a narrow valley, Aaron began searching for a weakness in the layout he could exploit as an escape route. If there was one, though, he couldn't find it. The towering cinder-block wall surrounding three squat, houselike buildings was topped with thick ropes of barbed wire. The iron-barred entrance gate on the east side, currently guarded by two men with rifles, was the only break in the wall.

The horses were led to the south of the compound, under a lean-to that served as a stable, where a pudgy man with wide-set eyes and a long, thin mouth like a frog took the reins. Aaron hadn't seen a single car yet, which meant they would have to flee on horseback. With that in mind, he made damn sure he knew where the tack and saddles were stored before he and Camille were dragged from the horse and marched toward the entrance gate.

Barefoot, Camille stumbled along the inhospitable desert terrain. Aaron kept a firm hand on her elbow, steering her around the worst of the rocks and prickly cacti blanketing the ground, but her lack of footwear was one more strike against the probability of a successful escape, as if the odds weren't impossible already.

By the time they reached the courtyard created by the buildings' U-shaped layout, his hope for freedom had evaporated. The barbed wire-topped fence looked even more ominous up close and, with every step he took over the bullet-casing-littered ground, he counted another man and even more guns. They didn't stand a chance of escaping this place with their lives.

They were prodded past an unmarked white delivery truck and a table loaded with what looked like satellite communication equipment and into the largest building that seemed to serve as the living quarters. Halfway down a dim hallway, they were muscled into a room that was empty save for the rusty metal chair Aaron was shoved into.

With a half dozen armed men surrounding him and a gun nudging Camille's back, he didn't put up a fight. Not even when a man with heavy acne scarring, holding a white rope, stepped forward to bind his hands behind the seatback and his legs to the legs of the chair. Within minutes, a second chair appeared and Camille was similarly bound.

Aaron met her gaze. The toughness he'd come to admire was still there, but shadowed by a hint of fear. As if maybe she'd done her own assessment of their odds and found them as bleak as he had.

From behind the cluster of men, a little girl with round, fearful eyes shuffled forward.

A tall, wiry man knelt next to her, whispering. She looked as though she was ready to run, but the man gripped her soiled red shirt tightly. She looked at Aaron and two tears rolled down her cheeks.

With a push from the man, she spoke in a mousy whisper in English. "We will send your picture to the American government." After more prompting in Spanish, she continued. "Your government has one day to free the prisoners you took this week." She paused and shook her head as more tears fell.

The man grabbed her frizzy black hair and shook her hard. *"Habla ahora o no comerás esta noche."* Say it right now or you will not eat tonight.

For the first time in his life, Aaron wanted to hurt another human being. His nostrils flared as he struggled for self-control.

"Or…or…" the girl continued softly, "you will die."

A man stepped forward with a camera and clicked twice. Aaron was certain he was captured in the picture displaying a sneer that matched the rage he felt. He wanted to shout at these men for defiling the girl's innocence, but it would be stupid to reveal his understanding of their language. So he held his tongue as the man dragged the girl from the room. The rest of the crowd filed out and multiple locks clicked into place.

The atmosphere was heavy after the men left, punctuated only by the sound of Aaron's labored, anger-fueled breathing.

"I know that girl," Camille said, staring vacantly at the door. "That was Rosalia Perez."

Chapter 3

Camille was looking for a flaw in their captors' plan, an opening in their defense—anything to take advantage of. Now that the drug had worn off and her mind and body could work in harmony, she began to think in earnest about escaping.

Almost a perfect square, the room showed little promise for their freedom. Though it had two doors, the one they'd entered through and another that opened to the courtyard, judging from the barred window adjacent to it, she felt safe in assuming both were locked. The concrete floor was barren except for their chairs. Not even a nail hung from the cracked cinder-block walls. No electrical outlets, no lights—nothing.

She squirmed, testing the knots, and felt a stinging pain in the side of her right hand. She groped with her fingers and found the source, a sharp barb where the rusty metal of the chair had eroded. That, she could work with.

Aaron's voice cut through the silence. "I'm sorry I got you into this mess."

Camille blinked. "*I'm* the one to blame. Whatever prisoners they want released, they must think I'm a good pawn since I went on national news today implicating Rodrigo Perez in the kidnapping of his daughter. He's a major player in the—"

"I know who he is. He's the next target of my task force because he's running weapons through the desert. I'm the one who arrested the prisoners they want released."

"Oh." She pulled her face back, shock rendering her momentarily speechless. "Jacob said you'd joined a task force, but I didn't know you had the authority to make arrests."

"What did you think I do for a living?"

"You're a Park Ranger. I figured you were cataloging cacti and leading hikes. How was I to know you were in the field hunting international fugitives?"

Aaron huffed. "You had no idea Park Rangers are fully sworn-in peace officers, same as you?"

"Er, nope." *And you can shut up about how ignorant I am, Mr. Perfect.*

"I'm sorry to burst your bubble, but you don't get to take credit for getting us killed."

She wiggled the rope. "Hey, we're not dead yet. You can only take credit for getting us kidnapped."

"We're tied up in a barbed wire-rimmed compound in the middle of the Mexican desert, surrounded by men with assault rifles and God knows what else, without any money or transportation. Excuse me for not feeling very optimistic."

Camille shrugged noncommittally. "Any idea where we are?"

"The Cortez Cartel has a stronghold in La Paz. Given the orientation of the water and the sparseness of the population, that's my best guess."

"I've never heard of La Paz."

"It's not very touristy, not like Cabo. ICE thinks the cartel works it like a mafia, with their fingerprints everywhere, even in the local police."

"Is the Cortez Cartel Mexico's most powerful?"

"Not by a long shot. That would be the La Mérida Cartel. Before he was arrested, their leader, Gael Vega, started his own militia that rivals the Mexican military in power."

They were warned of their captors' return by the sound of boots in the hall followed by clicking locks moments before the door opened. The man who had taken their horses entered holding a bottle of brownish water and a bowl of rice, followed by an armed guard who stopped in the doorway.

He held the water to Camille's lips. She turned away, not about to let it pollute her body. The man chased her mouth with the bottle and nudged at her closed lips a few times. Poking her with a spoonful of rice, he shouted in Spanish and gestured to the window. When she didn't relent, he moved to Aaron, who also refused. Only two minutes after arriving, the man and his guard left.

"Wish I'd paid more attention in my high school Spanish classes," she grumbled.

"He said this is your last chance for food until he returns tomorrow morning. And that you would be stupid to refuse."

Of course the Golden Boy spoke fluent Spanish. But she had to admit, the skill might come in handy when they escaped. And they would escape, she thought as she wiggled her wrists, teasing the rope against the barb.

Hours later, long after the room had gone dark and Aaron was only an outline as he sat in silence a few feet away, Camille felt the rope finally give. Her hands bore the evidence of her effort with countless scrapes and puncture wounds from the rusty barb. Thank goodness she kept up with her tetanus shot.

Once free, she bent to work on the ropes binding her feet.

"What the…?" Aaron said.

"Those idiots shouldn't have used such old chairs. Mine had a sharp edge perfect for sawing rope."

"Good thing, too, because the clock's ticking, Blondie. We don't have time—"

Camille's first order of business as an escapee was to make one minor but vital point with Aaron. "Let's get something straight—don't ever call me Blondie again. Or *Sweetie* or *Doll* or any of those derogatory nicknames you're so fond of. I hate it. Understood?"

"Okay, I got it."

Satisfied, Camille began untying the rope around Aaron's wrists.

"Like I was saying," he continued, "we don't have much time before frog man and his bodyguard bring us breakfast at gunpoint."

Camille looked out the window at the first glow of predawn. If they were lucky, they had maybe an hour or two to devise a plan. "As far as weapons go, we've got this rope and these chairs, but that's not enough. I've got another idea, but it'll take some time to prep."

"Care to explain?"

"Not yet." What she had in mind would open her up to all kinds of ridicule, so she decided to keep mum until she was certain it would work. While Aaron freed his legs from the chair, Camille slipped to the darkest corner of the room and took off her bra.

Aaron's heart pounded so loudly, he was surprised Camille couldn't hear it. Without weapons to defend themselves, they were as good as dead. And what weapon could they find in this room that would be any match for automatic rifles?

The chairs were too ungainly. The guard would have plenty of time to react if he saw a twenty-pound metal chair coming at him. He tested the individual spokes and chair legs, hoping to break one off and use it as a club or knife, but no such luck. He could wield a shard of glass from the window, but if anyone were in the courtyard, they would hear it break.

"Camille, I'm running out of ideas." He glanced in her direction.

What he saw was so at odds with what he expected that words died in his throat. Trying to ignore the taut points of her nipples beneath her thin white camisole, he watched her bite a hole in the beige bra she held.

"You got a weapon stashed in there or something?"

She ignored him and pulled a long, thin wire from inside the bra cup, then snapped it in half. "Bet you didn't know underwire is flat like a screwdriver."

"No, can't say I've thought much about bras except how to get them off as quickly as possible."

Rolling her eyes, she turned away and put her bra on. Still confused, Aaron gaped at her back. Once she'd righted her clothes, she knelt before the door that led outside. Using the blunt end of the underwire, she loosened the doorknob's screws.

"Throwing a doorknob at them is better than nothing, but hardly game changing, MacGyver."

She glanced sideways at him. "You're a dense man. We've been over this already. I hate nicknames. Take off one of your socks so we can put the doorknob in it. We can do serious damage to someone's head that way."

Aaron grinned, genuinely impressed. Even so, he couldn't stem the urge to tease her. "I didn't think a chick would be so handy to have around."

She jumped to her feet and rushed him. With fiery eyes, she poked him hard in the chest and waved the underwire beneath his nose. "You ought to show more respect to the person who's saving your life." She poked him again. "I'm not one of those helpless cupcakes you waste your time with.

I graduated head of my class at the police academy and was the first female Special Forces Officer in San Diego. Those sons of bitches have no idea what a mistake they made messing with me."

Aaron held up his hands in surrender. The gesture lost significance by the fact that he was chuckling. For some sick and twisted reason he didn't care to analyze, he liked her when she was all riled up this way. "Cupcakes?"

Camille snorted and went back to work on the doorknob screws. "Yeah, well, that's what they look like to me with their poofy hair and fake nails and fluffy clothes—little pink frosted cupcakes with sprinkles. Completely free of substance."

Aaron gawked at her. Not for the first time since their ordeal began, she'd rendered him speechless.

She was right. Most of the women he knew were a bunch of cupcakes compared to her, a woman so self-sufficient and physically capable that she was the one planning to save *his* life. She was the one fashioning tools out of her bra and improvising weaponry. He supposed he hadn't noticed sooner because they'd never been in a clinch situation before, but the lady was a badass.

He was fascinated…and irritated as hell to realize it.

Well, he had no intention of standing around and letting Camille be the only hero. While she finessed the external doorknob to stay in place, he removed his sock, slid the interior knob inside and took a few practice swings. As far as bludgeons went, this one would do nicely.

"The guard'll have a gun, so the trick will be to catch him unaware," he deliberated.

Camille stood and adjusted her skirt. "I thought of that, too. That's where our rope will come in handy."

Their animosity forgotten, they scooted their chairs together and hashed out a plan. Stripped of sarcasm and defensiveness, Aaron was surprised by how similarly their minds worked. Within minutes, they knew how to proceed and the role each would play.

They took positions on either side of the hallway door and waited. Feeling more confident than he had since being taken hostage, he smiled at Camille, who responded with a sly grin of her own.

In the two years he'd known her, this was the first time he'd ever seen her smile. He liked the effect it had on her features. It didn't soften her but made her look more powerful and capable and all those things Aaron was discovering this extraordinary woman was beneath her cold exterior. He studied her, mesmerized by her complexity, as she stood with a rope in hand, ready to spring at her enemy.

They had plenty of warning when it was showtime. Boots in the hallway, a lock rattling. With the click of the second lock, Aaron's muscles tensed. Camille crouched, leaning toward the door, the rope tight in her hands.

This was going to be fast.

The whole choreographed sequence would take less than a minute. The placement of their footfalls and the timing of their moves had to be exact. He and Camille would have to work as though they were breathing in unison.

The door swung wide, hiding Aaron behind it. Holding his position, he gripped the bludgeon and prayed.

Camille let the man get both feet in the room and register that the chairs were empty. She dropped the rope over his head and pulled him against her, strangling him as she moved backward three steps.

The guard played his part perfectly. He ran into the room and faced Camille and her hostage, his finger on the trigger of his rifle, shouting at her in Spanish.

"In," Camille said.

At her cue, Aaron kicked the door closed. With unflinching purpose, he brought the bludgeon down on the guard's head, felling him instantly. Then, working in perfect synchronization, Aaron straddled the guard and swung the bludgeon as Camille pushed her captive toward him. It took two thumps with the doorknob before he crumpled atop the unconscious guard.

Aaron stood over the two fallen bodies looking the part of a victorious warrior, surveying his conquered foes. Camille tried to be subtle about it, but she couldn't take her eyes off him. He gripped the bludgeon in his hand, and her gaze followed the sinews of his arm to his massive biceps and broad shoulder—muscles that no longer seemed like a sign of his vanity, but weapons in his arsenal. Despite all they'd been through, the shadows of his dimples remained and his wavy blond hair still looked boyishly carefree, but the planes of his jaw were rigidly set and the expression on his face was one she'd never seen on him before—hard and dangerous.

He raised his eyes and caught Camille staring. She wrenched her gaze to the window, her whole upper body flushing hot.

The guard moaned, snapping Camille back to the moment. She lunged for his gun at the same time Aaron did, but he reached it first. The guard moaned again before Aaron knocked his head with the butt of the rifle, sending him out cold once more.

Camille searched the men for weapons and discovered a short-barreled .38 Special. She spun the cylinder to check for bullets, which was no easy task given the way her hand shook. *Here we go,* she thought, snapping the fully loaded cylinder in place. The last thing she wanted to do was reveal this weakness to Aaron.

You see, I have this condition called post-traumatic stress disorder...

She cringed. Then she had an idea. "Aaron, you mind trading guns?"

He *tsk*ed in protest, but held the rifle out. "I guess size really does matter to a lady."

With the rifle, Camille felt better. She could hold it with both hands instead of one and steady it against her shoulder when she fired. Besides, one didn't need to strive for accuracy with an M16. She slung the gun's strap over her head and pushed the rifle around to her back. Squatting, she removed the guard's shoes and black jeans.

"What are you doing?" Aaron asked.

"I hate wearing skirts." She unzipped the offensive garment and pushed it down an inch before remembering her audience. Aaron's face was frozen in a grimace. So she disgusted him, what else was new? She couldn't escape shoeless, wearing a skirt. "Do you mind?"

"Do I mind that you're about to put on those nasty pants? Hell, yeah. They look like a biological superweapon."

"No, wise guy. Do you mind giving me some privacy?"

He faced the wall. Ignoring the foul odor wafting from the pants, Camille donned them and folded the waist to help with the fit.

"You can turn around now."

She tried on the other man's sneakers and was grateful they were a near fit.

"That's quite a look you've created."

She brought the rifle forward, gripping it tightly with both hands to keep the shaking to a minimum. "Yeah, I'm a real fashion maven. I'm calling this look *Cartel Chic*."

Aaron chuckled and Camille surprised herself by joining in. She did look pretty awful.

Too soon, the moment passed as they remembered where they were and what they'd done. Both sets of eyes returned to the unconscious figures on the ground.

"That was almost too easy," Camille said.

"We're not done yet, Blondie. We still have to escape from the compound."

Chapter 4

Camille was ready. She rolled her shoulders and felt the slide of her muscles against her camisole. Maybe it was only the effect of the adrenaline surging through her system, but she felt her position of power all the way to her toes. This random fate that had befallen her, to die at the hands of a bunch of criminals for a cause that wasn't her own, was about to get the shaft.

She walked to the door. "Ready?"

Aaron stood behind her, the .38 Special brushing her shoulder. "Let's do it."

She opened the door a crack, listening. A television set blared from the direction she and Aaron had been brought into the building, with a woman shouting in Spanish like a game show announcer might, against a background of hooting and cheers from an audience. Unable to hear anything above the din, she nosed her head through the doorway.

Somewhere nearby, a door banged closed. Camille flinched and pulled back, listening until she picked up the barely audible sound of a man's voice amid the television's noise. Then a second person spoke. A child. At the sound of Rosalia's pixie voice, Camille ached. She wanted to scoop the little girl up and run with her back to California, straight to the loving arms of her mother. But instead of acting impetuously and getting them all killed in a firefight, the best she could do for Rosalia was escape and tell U.S. authorities where to find her. Still, it was heart wrenching to leave her behind.

They crept into the hallway and turned right, toward three closed doors. It felt like Russian roulette, picking a door to open not knowing who or what was on the other side, but they had no other options.

Camille turned the knob of the first door. Aaron placed a hand on the small of her back and the barrel of his gun on her shoulder, angling it through the opening. She scanned the darkness. Someone slept on a cot along the wall. He stirred and rolled on his side. Holding her breath, she closed the door.

They tiptoed to the next room, though the blaring television program masked the sound of their movement. Aaron placed his hand on the doorknob. Camille wasn't tall enough to aim her weapon over his shoulder, so she slid it along his side, under his arm. The knob turned; the seconds ticked by. Aaron stuck his face through the crack. He smiled at Camille and stepped inside. Camille followed, closing the door behind her.

This room was not as dark as the first. The window was uncurtained and unbarred. A row of wooden crates identical to those pushed out of the plane sat along one wall, stacked two high. On another wall stood a table weighed down with piles of American cash.

Camille walked to the crates and tried to lift one. "Help me with this."

"What are you doing?"

"These guys are weapons smugglers, right? So what do you think's in these boxes, donations to Goodwill?"

"You guard the door. I'll look inside." He tucked the gun into his waistband. Camille tried to ignore the zing of desire that hit her at that maneuver. What a stupid thing to think about when their lives were in danger. On second thought, it was a stupid thing to think about *at any time.* She had no business *ever* thinking about Aaron's pants or what he put in them.

He lifted a box to the ground and dumped packing peanuts on the floor.

"This was the best idea you've ever had, Blondie."

With her rifle aimed at the closed door, she walked backward until she stood over the box. Aaron was right. This was the best idea she'd ever had. She didn't even care that he'd called her that terrible name again because in the box, nestled in a black nylon bag, were ten Smith & Wesson M&P 9 mm pistols. With silencers. And boxes of ammunition.

Aaron moved the .38 from the front of his waistband to the back. He screwed a silencer on to a 9 mm and loaded the magazine. Repeating the process with a second pistol, he handed it to Camille. She tucked it into her jeans.

"Don't you want to trade up for the silent model?" Aaron asked with honest surprise.

Camille wasn't about to admit her gun-handling defect. "Like you said, size matters."

He snorted and moved the bag to the table. "I'll look in the next box. You load this with cash."

They set to work. Within the span of a few minutes, their luck had improved tenfold. Instead of two guns with limited ammunition, they now had two AR-15 assault rifles, four 9 mm pistols with silencers, countless rounds of ammo, four grenades and—by Camille's hasty count—two hundred and fifty thousand U.S. dollars.

The grenades were an interesting find. Camille would

have had no moral qualms against blowing up the compound and everyone in it if Rosalia hadn't been present. Then she had another idea. It would be extremely risky, but still, it might work.

"Aaron, are there any more grenades in those boxes?"

The woman had balls, figuratively of course. Aaron was sure he couldn't have come up with a better plan if given a week to think about it. He rummaged through the boxes until he found another grenade, which he handed to Camille. Replacing the lid, he moved the box under the window to use as a step.

"I'll be right back," she whispered.

Her destination was across the hall, to the room that had been their prison. They were about to kill two people and Aaron couldn't find it in his heart to be upset. He was more disturbed that it didn't bother him.

Rifle in hand and the game-changing bag of booty slung over his shoulder, he stood on the box. From the looks of it, the rear wall of the house ran parallel to the western wall of the compound, with about three feet between the two. Plenty of room to jump and run.

Camille returned, sprinting through the door and kicking it shut as the grenade detonated. The explosion was earth-rattling. Aaron's ears rang and the door nearly came off its hinges. He slammed the rifle butt into the glass. He couldn't hear it break over the din of the explosion but felt the pane give way. After sweeping the rifle across the window to clear it of glass, he moved out of Camille's way.

In a flash of golden mane and lithe limbs, she jumped out the window. Aaron landed behind her and they ran, staying low under the windows along the north side of the building. Aaron peered around the corner at the crowd in the courtyard surrounding the crater that used to be their hostage-holding room.

A five-foot gap loomed between the house and a shed. Though Camille's ruse was working, it was still a leap of faith to zip between the buildings in plain sight. If only one man looked in their direction, they were dead. Aaron went first, holding his breath for the three steps it took to make the pass. They followed the path of the compound wall to the end of the shed, which still left them with a solid two car lengths of empty space to reach the entrance gate.

A burly man with a full beard and a rifle was standing inside the locked gate, yelling and gesturing to the men at the explosion site. Aaron knew what needed to be done and said a prayer for forgiveness. He'd never been a particularly religious man, but he was about to murder someone point-blank. At least with the grenade, Aaron didn't have to watch anyone die. This time, though, he was going to look a man in the eyes and shoot him.

"I got this." He picked up a rock and threw it against the wall, waiting for the guard to investigate. His heart pounded out of control and his hands were sweaty, but he wiped them on his jeans and manned up. Their lives depended on this and he wasn't going to act like a sissy by getting all shaky and nervous.

The guard's shadow gave him away first. His stomach came into view, then his arms and gun. Aaron fired two rounds, one into his head and the other into his chest. Though the sound of the shots was blunted by a silencer, the *plunk plunk* still echoed between the shed and the compound wall.

Aaron worked hard to ignore the significance of what he'd done as he frisked the dead man for keys, finding them in a pants pocket.

"Anyone onto us?" he asked Camille, who had chanced a look around the corner.

"We're good. They're putting out a fire on the roof."

"Then we keep moving." He sprinted to the gate with

a key in his outstretched hand. *Please let this be the right key....*

It was not. He jerked the key out of the padlock. His fingers found the next key on the loop and jammed it into the lock. It gave way this time. The chain dropped to the ground and they were through.

Aaron's and Camille's feet slipped on the loose gravel, but they maintained their breakneck speed to the lean-to. While he ran, Aaron scanned the half dozen horses. The dark brown steed appeared to be the healthiest of the bunch, with muscular legs that looked ready to fly over the terrain. He skidded to a stop and dropped their cache to the ground.

Camille was right behind him. "Okay, you're the horse expert. Go for it."

He hunted through a crate for a saddle, blanket, bridle and harness, and made quick work of readying the horse to ride. The memory of Camille's struggle to mount their last horse was still fresh in his mind, so he grabbed her around the waist and tossed her up.

She yelped in protest.

Aaron pushed the bag of guns and money onto her lap, then swung up behind her. "If I'm in charge, then we're doing this my way."

Camille must have thought better about arguing because she silently lifted herself from the saddle so he could get comfortable, then settled onto his groin as she had the day before. Aaron reached around her, grabbed the reins and spurred the horse into a gallop.

Their destination was east, to the ocean. Once the compound was no longer visible, he slowed the horse, setting a reasonable pace to conserve the animal's energy in the stifling, midmorning heat.

Aaron loved to ride and had been doing so since he could walk. There weren't many activities for desert kids like him in a one stoplight town, but he had the State Park at his doorstep. His parents took full advantage of that fact and made sure he and his younger sisters could ride and hike like pros.

Miles of desert disappeared behind them. Their steed easily avoided the thick blanket of shrubs and giant cardón cacti, which stood with long, green arms reaching for the sky like an army a thousand strong. Aaron found no signs of human existence, just acres and acres of pristine wilderness.

Camille's hair was as untamable as the land. It whipped and tickled Aaron like a cruel taunt. Unable to resist, he covetously gathered it in his free hand. He was such a fool to do that. A certifiable idiot. But he did it anyway, burying his nose in the locks before letting them slip through his fingers to blow in the wind.

Camille hadn't noticed, and while he was relieved, her obliviousness made him greedier. He felt himself harden and hoped she was oblivious to that, too. He gathered her hair again and glimpsed the creamy skin of her neck. His mouth watered at the thought of kissing it, which was even more certifiably idiotic, given that Camille was heavily armed.

At that inopportune moment, their horse lurched and he accidentally tugged her hair.

"What are you doing?"

"Trying to get your hair out of my face," he replied gruffly.

"Oh, sorry." She twisted it and stuck it down her shirt. "That's the best I can do for now."

That solved the hair problem. Now how was she going to stop the friction of her hips rocking against him or the agonizing heat passing from her body to his?

She relaxed against him, wiggling her backside as she settled. Choking back a groan, he looked heavenward, hoping they'd reach the ocean soon. He needed to get off this horse before he did something he'd spend the rest of his life regretting.

Aaron would never forget his first time meeting Camille

at Juliana and Jacob's engagement party, though not for its pleasantness. Aaron had taken one look at her standing on his parents' patio and targeted her as his next bedmate.

Like the fool he was around pretty girls, he cranked up his charm wattage, swaggering and openly praising her voluptuous attributes. And there was a lot to praise about Camille's body. She was, without a doubt, one of the most beautiful women he'd ever laid eyes on, with legs that went on for miles, curves custom-made for a man to wrap his hands around and full, pouty lips. Then she opened them and it was all downhill from there.

Apparently, his charm was too much for Camille to handle because the more charismatic he was, the more pungent she became. After that party, they'd seen enough of each other to last a lifetime. Aaron decided that no woman, no matter how stunning, was worth battling with such a sour disposition.

He smiled at the memory and might have laughed except Camille would want to know what was so funny. He'd thought about it in the plane and it struck him again how ironic life could be. He was racing across the Mexican desert with the only woman he'd wished to never see again.

And he was more attracted to her than ever.

Finally, the horse crested a ridge overlooking the beach. A temperate ocean breeze puffed at them, cooling Aaron's sunburned skin.

"We should ride in the surf to erase our tracks, in case they're on our trail," Aaron said as their mount picked its way down a canyon.

"Which direction do you think we should go?"

"If my bearings are correct, then the city we saw when we jumped is to the south. Let's see what we find." He tugged the reins.

Ahead of them stretched a pristine yellow-sand beach edged by cliffs and the endless ocean, which sparkled in the bright afternoon sun. It was lovely, really. Only a few hours earlier, he'd faced his own death, yet now he was riding horseback with a gorgeous woman along an empty beach. He closed his eyes and basked in the moment. Then the butt of Camille's rifle poked him in the ribs.

"You know, when I fantasize about riding with a woman through the surf in Mexico, she's not usually carrying a rifle."

She twisted to look at him, wearing a wicked grin on her lips. "Sounds like you have boring fantasies."

Aaron threw his head back and laughed. Leave it to Camille to surprise him again. He thought of a good comeback, something snarky and full of innuendo, but decided against voicing it. *This is good enough for now.*

He settled his arms more comfortably around Camille's sides, took another furtive inhale of her hair's magnificent scent and looked to the horizon, waiting for any vestiges of civilization to come into view.

Not five minutes later, he heard, then saw, an approaching vehicle in the distance. With a quiet curse, he turned their horse toward the cliffs lining the beach and found a concave section of cliff face. They dismounted, firearms ready. Besides the roar of the vehicle's engine, Aaron heard voices whooping and hooting. *Odd...*

He tipped his face around the corner. "It's a Jeep with at least four people."

"Why are they shouting?" Camille asked.

"I have no idea."

"I hear something else, too. What *is* that?"

Aaron shook his head. "I can't quite make it out."

They stood and listened. Aaron glanced at Camille's hands, which had started to shake, but decided against asking her about it.

The sound that had been so faint over the thunder of

the waves and the hollering and the Jeep's engine became clearer to Aaron. "It sounds like...huh?"

He and Camille looked at each other, their faces screwed up in confusion.

"Bruce Springsteen?" they exclaimed in unison.

Chapter 5

"Hide the guns. No way are these people cartel hit men." Aaron held the bag open and Camille wedged her rifle inside. She flexed her fingers, the weight on her chest lighter with the gun out of her hands.

The Jeep hurtled toward them, spitting sand in its wake and blasting Bruce Springsteen. Aaron grabbed the bag and the horse's reins. Walking the horse behind them, they planted themselves in the path of the joyriders. The music went dead and the Jeep crawled to a stop a few yards in front of them.

The man behind the wheel looked about fifty, with gray streaks in his brown hair, a softened body and the laid-back disposition of a man embracing his inner-Jimmy Buffett. The two women in the backseat looked young and were exactly the type of cupcakes Camille had railed against that morning. Clad in bikinis topped with cover-ups that didn't actually cover anything up, they were overdone in every way—too much makeup, too many artificial highlights in their hair and massive designer sunglasses.

"Hello there," the driver said. "You two look like you might need some help. Am I right?"

Aaron answered. "You guessed it. We came down to Baja with friends to go camping and when we left on our horse for a ride along the beach, they ditched us."

"They don't sound like very good friends."

"No kidding," Aaron said.

The driver rubbed his goatee. "Tell you what. We're pretty close to our camp. Would you and your girlfriend care to follow us back? I bet we could rustle up a cell phone for you to call your friends, and you can have a bite to eat and let your horse rest."

"I think we're done with those particular friends. Maybe we could borrow that phone to make other arrangements?"

"We can do that, too."

"Thank you." Aaron smiled wolfishly at the cupcakes. "Oh, and for the record, Camille and I are only friends. We're not…"

"Friends riding together on a horse?" one of the cupcakes asked.

"Yeah, her horse took off. We didn't have a choice."

Camille shifted her gaze to the rusty brown cliff face, regrouping. It wasn't that she cared about Aaron's enthusiastic clarification that they weren't involved—it was the truth, after all. And she didn't mind that the girls were angling for a better view of him. He was the most magnificent-looking man she'd ever seen, too. It was just that she was disappointed to have been wrong about him.

Since being taken hostage, she'd started to believe he'd changed, that underneath his party-boy persona was a respectable man capable of so much more than preening and seducing women. She'd begun to think of the two of them as a team. But she'd been wrong and the misjudgment stung.

But she had more important issues to worry about than a man so easily distracted by pretty girls.

Her thoughts returned to Rosalia, alone and frightened in the compound. Camille hadn't considered it before, but maybe she'd been dropped in the middle of the Mexican desert for a reason. Maybe this journey wasn't another case of her rotten luck, but a chance to redeem thirty wasted years. Maybe she needed Rosalia as much as the little girl needed her. A new plan began to take shape in her mind.

The driver offered his hand to shake. "The name's Charlie. In the back we've got Ana and Sarah."

"I'm Aaron and this is Camille." He waved to the cupcakes, and added a wink for good measure.

Unbelievable.

Charlie must have noticed Camille's discomfort because he patted her hand. "Would you like to ride with us? We have room."

His palm was sweaty and his fingers bloated, but he might prove to be a valuable component to her plan.

"Thank you, Charlie." And though she wanted to yank her hand away and wipe it on her pants, she gave his fingers a little squeeze. She even pulled off a convincing smile.

He wasn't being manipulative—that was such an ugly word—but Aaron knew how to be persuasive to women. He knew what they wanted to hear, what little looks and touches would turn them to putty in his hands. Except for Camille. Nothing softened her, but that was beside the point.

As soon as Aaron saw the women in the Jeep, he knew they were his and Camille's ticket out of Mexico. All he needed was a little time with them to parse out the details. He regretted Camille's embarrassment when he distanced himself from her, but he needed the women to think he was available, not some letch trying to cheat on his girlfriend.

Charlie's eyes had turned hungry at the revelation he

and Camille weren't an item. Aaron hadn't counted on that. She'd already proved she could kick ass and take names, but it went against his basic instincts to throw any woman to the wolves, even a cop.

Not that she seemed to mind. She was laughing and making flirty eyes at Charlie while Aaron was forced to watch through the rearview mirror as he followed the Jeep on horseback. Charlie wasn't remotely attractive and he was at least twenty years her senior. He seemed like a nice guy, sure, but as spineless as they came. A man like that could no more handle a woman like Camille than a child could handle a pet tiger.

The camp, though visible from the beach, was nestled into a valley between two foothills and demarcated by two palm-thatched palapas on the beach. One shaded a hammock. Aaron followed the Jeep onto a dirt road that wound among the homes, if he dared use such a polite word to describe the dwellings. Reeking of seaweed, the after-odor of bonfires and marijuana, the settlement was the housing equivalent of a pack of stray dogs. Of the twenty or so places, some were less flea-bitten than others, a few even looked rather domesticated, but the whole lot of them was a mangy bunch of misfits.

Charlie directed Aaron to the sea-green shack of some absentee neighbors who often brought their horse with them. Sure enough, a wood-and-wire fenced corral was sandwiched on the side of the property. No doubt the animal would be well cared for here. It didn't seem to have any identifying marks that might prove dangerous if the cartel went on the prowl for their stolen horse, which was a small blessing. To repay this community with the wrath of a vengeful cartel would be unforgivable.

The hardworking horse had one task left before it could rest, though. Aaron tugged the reins and set off for the perimeter of the settlement to take note of all the paths leading to and from the camp, should they need to make a quick getaway. Jacob would've said it was Aaron's Golden Ticket at work again, but nevertheless, Aaron was relieved to discover only one access point from the west, a steep dirt road leading out of the valley. Perfect.

He returned to the corral, found feed and grooming supplies and set to work tending the horse.

"You're a sneaky man," a heavily accented female voice behind him said. Ana, if he remembered correctly. "We've been looking everywhere for you."

Seducing these women would be a piece of cake if they were going to throw themselves at him. He kept scrubbing, to see how hard they'd work to get his attention. "Responsibility before pleasure, as they say."

"How sensible of you," she purred. A darkly tanned Latina, she was taller than Sarah and looked to be in her late twenties, with long black hair and a temptress's body. Not too long ago, Aaron might have quit his job and moved to Mexico for the promise of this woman's company. But his responsibility to Camille and his desire to make it out of Mexico alive superseded everything else.

"This horse worked hard today. It deserves a little pampering."

"I think I'm jealous of the horse," Sarah, obviously American judging by her voice, said. A pair of trim, tan legs came into view, complete with a Tinker Bell ankle tattoo. Aaron let his gaze roam over her body, hoping she couldn't tell how artificial his perusal was.

"When you're done here, would you like to freshen up at our place? We have a cell phone you can use to make those other arrangements you mentioned," Ana said.

"That would be wonderful. Speaking of other arrangements, how far from the city are we?"

"We're fifty miles north of La Paz, where we're from."

The women watched him clean the horse's hooves. "Fifty

miles isn't so bad. I'm thinking my friend and I could hitch a ride with someone and come back for the horse with a trailer."

"We'd be happy to give you and your friend a ride. We're going home tomorrow afternoon."

So far, so good. He put away the grooming supplies and gave the horse a second generous scoop of food.

"I'm ready to get cleaned up. Lead the way."

Sarah and Ana took him by the arms. As they strolled, Aaron asked, "Which one of you owns the house?"

Sarah answered. "Ana's brother owns it. He lets us use his place anytime we want."

"What kind of work do you do?"

"We're both high school teachers, English," Ana said.

"I'm from Arizona," Sarah explained. "I'm teaching here on an exchange program."

"It's a good thing I never had teachers like you two. I would have been a terrible student."

"Why is that?" Ana asked, giving his arm an extra squeeze.

"Just so you'd keep me after class."

The women giggled right on cue. At that moment, Camille came into view, standing by herself in front of Charlie's powder-blue trailer. She tracked his movement with wary eyes.

"Here's our place." Ana led him to a cottage across the courtyard from Charlie's house.

He glanced over his shoulder at Camille. A wrinkle of worry had appeared between her eyebrows. Reluctantly, he turned his back on her and climbed the rickety wooden porch steps. He sure hoped she was smart enough to figure out he hadn't abandoned her.

Loneliness wasn't a new emotion for Camille, but one that hit her hard as she watched the door close behind Aaron.

Loneliness and betrayal. She stared at the door for a long time while she reined in her emotions and considered her next move.

A hand brushed her shoulder. Her reaction was instinctive and immediate. Angling her elbow at a point, she whirled to jab her assailant in the stomach.

"Whoa." Charlie jumped back with his arms up in surrender.

"Sorry. I'm a little on edge today."

"No harm done. Where'd you learn a move like that?"

"Self-defense class. A girl can't be too careful these days."

"Right you are. I came to ask if you wanted to get cleaned up at my humble abode."

"Thanks. That would be wonderful."

He pointed to the black bag at Camille's feet. "I'm guessing you don't have a change of clothes in there."

"No, I wish."

"Well, last year a lady friend came to stay with me, but she left in a huff." He smiled as though recalling a private joke. "Didn't take her suitcase. I bet you could find something to fit you."

Camille nodded, grateful for the opportunity to shed the nasty jeans. "Thank you, not only for the clothes, but for giving us a place to regroup."

"It's not often a man stumbles on a lovely young lady in need of rescuing." He draped an arm across her shoulders and guided her to his house.

Camille tried to fit the image Charlie had of her by acting sweet and demure. She wasn't used to playing the unsavory role of a damsel in distress but had a lot riding on his belief that she was. Maybe he'd forget she tried to gut him with her elbow.

At sunset, Aaron sat in a white plastic patio chair and wolfed down a second plate of food at the traditional Sat-

urday night communal barbecue. Strands of white lights
rimmed the sprawling courtyard and classic rock filtered
out through the windows of Charlie's trailer. Twenty or so
people were in attendance, mostly adults with a few kids
thrown in. Charlie manned a charcoal grill on his porch
with a beer in his hand.

The shower Aaron took at the teachers' cottage had been a
godsend and Ana had allowed him to rummage through her
brother's closet for clothes. Though he was still exhausted,
at least he was clean and fed. He hadn't seen Camille since
freshening up and was beginning to feel uneasy about her
absence. He had no time to look for her, though, because the
teachers didn't grant him the tiniest bit of breathing room.
As though in competition, they seemed afraid to leave him
alone lest the other one gain the advantage.

He frowned as he scanned the crowd for the thousandth
time. Camille had another five minutes to materialize before he went in search of her.

"What do you think? Aaron, are you listening?" It was
Ana.

"Ask me again?" He'd have to be more attentive if he
expected Ana to offer Camille and him a ride to La Paz the
next day. Borrowing Sarah's phone earlier, he'd briefly
touched base with Dreyer to explain what happened and
where they were. Then the teachers were back in the room,
preening and posing, and he'd hung up after agreeing to wait
in La Paz for further instruction on the safest and most discreet way for ICE to get them out of the country.

"I asked, what do you think of our little vacation spot?"

"I've never seen another place—"

At that moment, Camille appeared out of the darkness.
She filled a plate from the buffet table and took a seat on
the edge of the courtyard. Aaron's relief at seeing her hit
him hard enough that he sighed audibly. She'd changed into
a floral skirt and a red tank top, which were terrible cloth-

ing choices. Not only was the skirt impractical, but if she was trying to be inconspicuous, this was not the top she should've chosen. Couldn't she have found a baggy sweatshirt to borrow?

Ana traced his line of sight to Camille and stood. "Enough talk. It's time to dance."

She led him onto a clear section of concrete where a few other couples swayed to the music. Sarah followed close at their heels. Camille was grimacing at her food and had yet to acknowledge his existence, which bothered him, although he wasn't sure why. He wasn't acknowledging her either, which he decided to correct after the next song ended.

Ana and Sarah danced against him with borderline desperation. Sarah wasted no time making sure Aaron knew precisely what she wanted from him. When grinding against him failed to hold his attention, she threw her arms around his neck and caught him in a surprise kiss.

Her breath reeked of cigarettes and tequila, like the girls in the dance clubs all smelled. Disgusting. But Sarah was the one with the cell phone and he needed to make a second expensive international call to Jacob later that night, so he kissed her back. When Sarah let go of him and Ana took her place, his eyes found Camille again. She was still scowling at her untouched food.

He couldn't decide if she was nervous about the possibility of the cartel finding them or merely irritated that other people were enjoying themselves. Actually, it reminded him of the way she looked at Juliana and Jacob's wedding reception, as if she'd decided beforehand to have a bad time and resented the other attendees for choosing otherwise.

More than any other aspect of her personality, her tendency to act put-upon really pissed him off. If she could change that one thing about herself, she'd be the total package—beautiful, intelligent and fun to be around. But two out of three was like being served a decadent dessert covered in mold.

Sarah, cutting off his line of sight, ran her fingers through his hair and turned his face toward hers.

He forced a smile. "Think I'm going to take a break, ladies."

Ana slipped her foot up his leg. "Don't be too long. Sarah's been greedy for your attention and I'm starting to feel lonely."

Oh, brother. "I'm going to get a drink and borrow Charlie's facilities. When I get back, you and I will dance again."

At the drink table, he mixed a margarita in a plastic cup for Camille. He planned to stay stone-cold sober to keep a lookout for the cartel, but a little alcohol would be harmless for Camille and might help her sleep. At the very least, she might stop looking like someone ran over her dog.

He reached her chair and found it empty. Scanning the crowd, he spotted her on the dance floor, her arms around Charlie.

Charlie was a terrible dancer and his hands were way too close to Camille's butt to be gentlemanly. Aaron glared at them, trying to catch Camille's attention. What the hell was she thinking, throwing herself at a sweaty, middle-aged pothead while their lives were in danger?

At least her hair was in a ponytail. Crazy that it mattered to him, but if Charlie laid a finger on Camille's hair, Aaron wouldn't be able to stop himself from dragging her away and shaking some sense into her. As long as he and Camille were in Mexico, her hair belonged to him alone.

He huffed, disgusted as much by his train of thought as the sight of Charlie's hands all over Camille. After downing the margarita, he crushed the cup and marched back to Ana, thumping Charlie's shoulder hard with his own as he passed.

Ana welcomed him with open arms. "You've come back to me."

"I have."

If anyone could distract him, it would be Ana, whose sexuality oozed like honey from a comb. He put his hands on her hips and pulled her hard against his thigh, moving them as a unit to the beat of the music. *To stop thinking about her for just one song, I'll push this as far as it will go.*

Camille hated dancing, always had. So it was hard to contain her revulsion when Charlie asked her to dance. But she couldn't say no, not when he'd agreed to loan her his Jeep the next morning.

At first, she was relieved that he initiated only the slightest sway of movement. Then she felt his hands getting friendly with her backside. As she smiled and made flirtatious conversation, she made a mental list of all the reasons why she was allowing herself to be treated in such a demeaning way. Still, the urge to break Charlie's hands made it challenging to maintain a façade of sweetness.

Halfway through the song, she looked over Charlie's shoulder and spotted Aaron walking in her direction. He sent her a murderous glare before wrapping one of the cupcakes around his body and practically screwing her right there on the dance floor. Like watching a car wreck in progress, Camille was powerless to look away.

Charlie, with a finger on her chin, forced her focus back to him. "He said you two weren't an item."

"Trust me, we're not."

"Then why are you jealous?"

"Oh, no. I'm not jealous. Just disappointed."

"Sometimes people don't turn out to be who we expect them to."

She wound her arms around Charlie's neck. "And some people are *exactly* who they first appear to be."

Charlie smiled. "You sure you don't want my help tomorrow looking for your lost horse?"

"Thank you, but I'd like to go alone. I'll bring some rope and tether it to the rear of the Jeep for the trip back to camp. I can't tell you how grateful I am for your help. I'm so lucky you found me on the beach." Stifling a cringe, she stroked his jaw and tried to fill her eyes with the promise of reward for his generosity.

A loud giggle from Aaron's groupies reclaimed Camille's attention. The American girl was attached to him again. Aaron must have said something really funny because both girls were tittering and playing with their hair.

That was enough for Camille. She kissed Charlie on the cheek. "It's my bedtime. Thanks for the dance...and the Jeep."

"You're welcome to sleep at my house, you know."

Nice try, buddy. "The beach beckons."

As soon as Charlie moved into conversation with another couple, Camille strode into Aaron's circle of hedonism and grabbed his arm. "Sorry to interrupt. I need to talk to Aaron. Don't worry, I'll return him to you in a sec."

She marched him by the elbow toward the water, where the sound of the waves would drown out their words, and spun to face him. "I've seen enough of your disgusting display."

"Aw, how sweet, you saved all your nastiness for me. Don't I feel special."

"If you want my advice, I think your best chance is with the American. She seems to have the lowest self-esteem of the two."

Aaron threw his arms skyward. "That's how little you think of me? You really believe that after all we've been through, I'm trying to get laid?"

"Isn't that what you're all about?"

"It shouldn't surprise me you feel that way."

She folded her arms across her chest. "What's that supposed to mean?"

"It means that your self-absorption distorts your perception of everyone else around you."

"You think *I'm* self-absorbed? No human being on the planet is more vain than you are."

"Are you kidding me? You've invested years in this whole martyr charade. Do you wake up feeling miserable or is that something you have to work up to over breakfast?"

It had been a long day. The ground looked fuzzy to Camille's weary eyes. Despite how well they worked together to escape the cartel's compound, interacting with Aaron was proving to be as toxic as ever. With what she was planning to do the next day, wasting her energy arguing with him was the last thing she needed.

She pinched the bridge of her nose. "You think your new friends will be willing to give you a lift to La Paz?"

He eyed her suspiciously. "They've already offered, and I accepted on both our behalf."

"Good. ICE will get you home safely from there." It was a burden off her mind that she didn't have to worry about him making it to California in one piece. Knowing Aaron had ICE backing him up, she could better concentrate on her plan.

"What's going on, Camille? Why are you talking like you're not coming with me?"

She straightened, trying to look as strong as she wished she felt. "Because I'm not. This is where we part ways. I'll only take my fair share of the money and weapons. The bag's behind the couch on Charlie's porch." What more could she say? It was great being kidnapped with you? "I've got a lot to do tomorrow, so I'm going to get some rest. Take care of yourself."

She took a step back. The cool sand trickled into the sandals Charlie loaned her.

"Camille, what the hell are you talking about?"

"Goodbye, Aaron."

She slunk sideways around his broad body, being careful not to touch him or smell his clean-laundry scent. Without looking back, she walked into the darkness.

Chapter 6

Feeling Aaron's eyes on her, Camille trudged through the sand to a hammock she spied earlier beneath a palapa. Was he relieved to be rid of her? Maybe, but what a dismal thought. She couldn't afford to dwell on the cruelty of the world, on what she'd lost and what she could never have.

She didn't need Aaron, she reminded herself. She didn't need anyone.

The hammock rocked as Camille sat, removed the band from her hair and ran her fingers through the hopelessly tangled tresses. If she survived until she reached La Paz, she'd cut it all off—a present to herself for beating the odds, which were perilously stacked against her.

She moved the pistol to her stomach for easy access during the night. With a yawn, she settled back with an arm behind her head.

A figure loomed over her. Camille gasped and grabbed for the gun, but Aaron disarmed her handily.

He crossed his arms and frowned at her. "What, specifically, do you have planned for tomorrow?"

With the express purpose of making him go away, she decided to give it to him straight. "I was leading Charlie on so he'd loan me his Jeep."

"Why?"

"I've decided to return to the compound to gather intel. The more data I can pass to U.S. authorities, the better Rosalia's odds for rescue. Then I'll drive the Jeep to La Paz and contact my team in the States to report my findings and get our families into protective custody so the cartel can't hurt them to punish us. What happens after that depends on what my bosses want me to do toward her rescue. But I've decided I'm not leaving Mexico until Rosalia's safe and I've done everything possible to help bring down the Cortez Cartel."

His scowl deepened. "I've already contacted my ICE team about Rosalia and protection for our families."

"You made a phone call? How?"

"Sarah let me borrow her cell phone. ICE has agents that specialize in rescue ops—to get both Rosalia and us out of Mexico. Look, it's virtually impossible to bring down a cartel. If it could be done, then the U.S. government would have already, trust me. There's no need to put yourself in more danger."

Camille gave a hard laugh. "*More danger?* You're kidding, right? We couldn't possibly put ourselves in any more danger if we tried. Even after Rosalia's rescued, do you honestly think the cartel will leave us alone? Do you think they stood around the hole from the grenade explosion and said to each other, 'They stole our money and guns and escaped. Oh, darn.'" She shook her head. "Aaron, they know who we are and where to find us. Maybe living in WitSec with your family for the rest of your life is acceptable to you, but it's not to me. I'm going to stay and fight."

Aaron was quiet for a long time. He dropped his arms and looked at the ocean.

To fill the silence, Camille kept talking. "I don't care if you think I'm doing it because I'm bent on being a martyr or whatever your opinion is of me. Rosalia deserves better. And I do, too. I may have a crappy life, but it's mine and I won't have a bunch of criminals dictating the terms. Maybe I'll end up a legend on the force like my old man after all."

He rubbed his chin, nodding. "What time do we leave in the morning?"

"What?"

"I'm in. What time do we leave?"

"What do you mean you're in? You're not invited."

"Have you ever driven off-road?"

"No, but—"

"I happen to be an expert at that. What time do we leave?"

Camille sighed. Of course the Golden Boy was an expert at off-roading. "Before dawn."

Aaron returned her gun and walked away, toward the party and his nubile teachers.

"I don't need you, Aaron," she called after him.

He turned around and walked backward through the sand, wearing a hard smile. "Yeah, well, I don't need you either, but here we are."

The breezeless beach was heavy with moist, salty air as Aaron maneuvered the Jeep over the sand in the predawn darkness. "I'm going to retrace our escape route to make sure I can find the compound again."

Yawning, Camille nodded her consent and ran a hand over the blue T-shirt and yoga pants she'd pilfered from Charlie's stash of clothes the night before. Though still groggy, she had woken with no trouble, which was out of character for her. She was typically such a heavy sleeper that waking enough to drag herself out of bed was the most difficult part of her day.

Under the pretense of looking at the ocean, she studied Aaron. She liked him like this, not the arrogant rake he'd been last night, but a serious, focused man. She had the sinking suspicion she could spend many content hours studying the small wrinkles that textured his face and made him appear less debonair, more distinguished.

The sun punctured the hazy sky as Aaron turned west through a dry riverbed between the cliffs separating the beach from the desert. They drove away from the light and into the gray-black darkness of endless foothills, toward danger that left no guarantee of their survival.

"I called Jacob last night."

Camille grinned. "Are Juliana and the baby okay? Is it a boy or girl?"

"A girl. Alana Rose. Jacob and Juliana are tired and worried about us, but everyone's healthy and safe. With your dad's police connections, Juliana's hospital room went under immediate guard. They'll move to the secure location my family's at once they're cleared by the doctors. Everyone's pretty pissed about our choice to stay in Mexico, but Jacob agreed to overnight my passport and the purse you dropped in the hospital parking lot to La Paz. The package should reach the city by tomorrow morning."

"That could be really useful. Thank you."

"One more thing. I don't think we should steal the Jeep. Charlie could contact Mexican authorities, and the last thing we need is to be arrested for grand theft auto. Ana offered to give us a lift this afternoon. She even suggested we spend the night at her place. I think we should take her up on it."

Camille snorted. "Judging by the way you two were dancing last night, I feel safe assuming she wasn't including me in her sleepover invitation."

Ugh. Why did she go there? She had about as much impulse control as a teenager.

Aaron rolled his tongue over his teeth. "I'm sure she has a sofa you can sleep on while she has her way with me in the bedroom. We'll try to keep the noise down."

Camille felt her face heat up and fixed her gaze on the foothills to her right.

"So...this is your first time in a foreign country?"

"Huh?" He made it sound as if they were on vacation.

"When I called Jacob, your sister said she didn't think you had a passport. Is this your first time out of the U.S.?"

"Yeah. I've always wanted to travel, but I've never had the time."

Aaron scoffed. "Never had time? That's a bunch of bull. People who really want to travel make the time."

"What a pretentious thing to say. I suppose you're a world traveler?"

"I've been around. Still plenty of places I want to see, though. What else is on your bucket list besides travel? Any goals or dreams?"

"You mean, besides surviving today?" She shrugged. "The only dream I ever had was to be a cop. As far as goals, I'm a member of the hundred-mile club at my gym. You know, people who swim the equivalent of a hundred miles of laps annually."

Aaron shook his head, frowning as if she'd given the wrong answer.

"Do my life choices offend you?"

"How old are you?"

"Just shy of thirty. How old are you?"

"Thirty-four. What about a boyfriend?"

"My love life is none of your business." Not that she'd ever had a love life to worry about.

"That's a no. Hmph." His frown deepened.

"What about you? Anyone special waiting for you at home?"

"No—and that's the way I like it. Monogamy's not my gig."

She chortled. "You're going to end up being one of those pathetic middle-aged men with a showy sports car and a twenty-year-old girlfriend. You know that, right?"

"Sounds fantastic." He ignored her conspicuous eye roll. "What about kids? Do you want to start a family of your own?"

"Why are you asking me all this stuff?"

"Answer the question, Camille."

"I don't know…maybe. But what's the point in hoping for something that may never happen? I'm done talking about this stuff. I don't appreciate what you're doing."

"What am I doing?"

"You're compiling a list of how pathetic my life is."

"I'm curious, that's all," he said.

"No more questions."

"Fine with me. We're getting close. Get your gun ready in case we run into any unfriendly search parties looking for us."

Camille armed herself and scanned their surroundings. The landscape looked like all the other foothills they'd traversed in the past few hours, rolling slopes carpeted with tall cacti and short, scrubby-looking trees. Before this week, she thought she had a good sense of direction. Out here, surrounded by nothing but monotonous desert, she wouldn't have stood a chance without Aaron's help, not that she was going to mention it. She was still smarting from his cringe-inducing questions.

Aaron parked the car and lifted the weapon bag to the ground, where they finished prepping their guns. Each would approach the compound with a rifle and two pistols, carrying a grenade in one pocket and extra ammo in the other. Their goal was to sneak near enough to get descriptions and numbers on the cartel operatives.

Camille closed her eyes and took a moment to remind herself why she was doing this—for herself, for her family, for Rosalia.

Lips brushed hers, accompanied by the scratch of stubble. Her eyes flew open. Aaron's brown eyes stared back, challenging her to resist his charm.

Or, possibly, to succumb to it.

Panicking, she tried to move away but Aaron maintained a firm hand against the small of her back. Evidently, all those muscles weren't just for show.

She socked him on the shoulder but he was unfazed, pushing his lips to hers while he stroked her jaw, coaxing it to relax and open. She refused, but found herself wondering about his tongue. All she had to do was part her lips and she bet he'd show her exactly how masterful his tongue was. She shivered, thinking about that tongue, those lips, his stubble abrading the skin above her lip, every hard, solid part of him. To her mortification, her nipples hardened in response.

What a nightmare.

It was all that talk about bucket lists that made him do it. That coupled with the fact that in the past forty-eight hours Aaron had stared down his own mortality more than once. He'd obsessed for two straight years about kissing Camille Fisher and here she was before him, her eyes closed, her face turned skyward, her luscious lips calling to him. Any minute, they could die. So why not go for it while he had the chance?

Now or never, man. If you want that kiss, you're just going to have to take it.

So he did.

And, good God, she felt better than he'd imagined, pressed to his body, even with her stubborn mouth refusing to yield. She raised her hand to his face, as if maybe she was trying to pry him away, but he knew she needed this moment of connection as much as he did. Taking her wrist in hand, he brought it behind her, tipping her back and thrusting her breasts against his chest.

Holy hell.

Then her mouth opened and he seized the opportunity to slip a finger between her parted lips, applying gentle pressure until—finally, *finally*—her mouth surrendered to his demand. Adrenaline coursed through him, leaving him breathless as he plundered the depths of her, demanding and exploring her warm, wet mouth. Memorizing the taste of her.

She slung an arm around his neck with a moan and something inside Aaron broke free. Crushing her supple, gorgeous body to his, he bowed her back even farther until they both teetered on the edge of falling.

When Aaron released Camille, he took a couple of swift steps back, probably fearful that she was going to knee him in the groin. Which she would have done had her legs not been so weak. She concentrated on staying upright and breathing. Keeping her eyes on Aaron, who seemed to be struggling toward that same end, a single, fleeting thought darted across her mind—she'd been right about his tongue.

As soon as she regained her composure, she shot him her best withering glare. "What the hell was *that?*"

"We might die at any time and I decided it would be nice to kiss you first."

She grabbed her rifle from the weapon bag. "Don't ever do that again."

"Yes, ma'am."

She didn't buy his easy concession for a second. The man looked about as remorseful as the Devil. He brushed past her, toward the peak of the hill. Still not sure her legs would carry her, she touched a finger to her swollen lips and watched Aaron walk. Then she realized she was staring at his perfect, firm backside. As if he were God's gift to women.

As if.

With a snort of disgust, she jogged to catch up.

"That's odd," Aaron whispered from where he lay on the ground at the top of the hill, his eyes on the valley to the west.

"What's odd?"

"No guard and no horses in the lean-to. In fact, I don't see a single person."

"Huh. Let me take a look." She left a good five feet of space between them as she army-crawled into a surveillance position. "There aren't any vehicles in the courtyard either." The place looked like a ghost town. Camille's hope disintegrated. Unbelievable. Could her luck get any worse? She kicked a rock and watched it tumble past the Jeep, down the hill.

"Let's go in for a closer look," Aaron said, his tone laced with disappointment. He blazed the way through a narrow canyon in tense silence.

They needn't have been quiet, though. Camille felt the vacancy in her bones as she neared the outer wall. She confirmed it after Aaron boosted her to look over the wall at the empty courtyard. No satellite equipment, no vehicles, nothing.

The hole created by the grenade explosion dominated the scene and offered a strange, grotesque view into the house where none should exist, like an eye socket without an eye. Burned bits of bone dotted the courtyard. Whether they were scattered by scavenging animals or the initial blast was a forensic question beyond Camille's knowledge set.

With their rifles ready, Aaron preceded Camille through the front gate. They opened the shed doors, then wandered into the house. The furniture had been left behind—sooty sofas in the living room, a scarred wooden table in the kitchen, unmade cots in the bedrooms. All the boxes had been cleared out of the weapon storage room.

Resolve—tenacious and angry—pierced through her disappointment, steeling her heart. Somewhere in this desert, a scared little girl needed saving. Camille wasn't about to let anything, even this seemingly insurmountable complication, derail her mission.

Returning to the courtyard, she found Aaron staring at the ground behind the shed, at the burned remains of the guard he'd shot and another poor soul who'd been added to the pyre.

"This doesn't change anything for me," she said, determination hardening her tone. "It makes it tougher, for sure, but I won't give up on Rosalia."

Aaron didn't say anything, didn't even nod. He just stared at the corpses.

Camille strode from the compound. Though her bum leg ached, she pushed the quarter mile to the Jeep, hauling her body painfully over the steepest part of the hill as her adrenaline finally crashed. Damn, but her stupid leg was killing her. What she wouldn't give to prop it up on a sofa, down some ibuprofen and sleep for a day.

When she reached the Jeep, she braced her hands against the dusty metal frame. Too many thoughts crowded her brain for her to sit patiently while she waited for Aaron. Shifting her weight to her good leg, she picked up her left foot and kicked the rear tire with a bouncy rhythm. The sizzles of pain felt good. Necessary.

Charlie's clothes stash hadn't included any sneakers and so she wore the dead man's shoes today. She stared at them with disgust. Maybe she'd burn them tonight. Or throw them out the car window on the way to La Paz. Her first order of business in the city would be to buy herself an outfit or two. And she was definitely going to cut her hair.

She kept her eyes on her bouncing foot, affording Aaron's boots only a nominal glance when they appeared at her side. When the minutes stretched on and Aaron still didn't speak, she looked at him. Leaning against the Jeep, he watched her with a look that could only be described as sympathetic. As if she was a shelter dog or a beggar. It was illogical for him to feel that way because he was in the same boat as she was.

"Don't look at me like that."

"Like what?"

"Like you pity me."

"I do pity you."

"You're such a jerk." She pushed off the Jeep and put some space between them.

"Let me explain."

She whirled on him. "Do I have a choice?"

"That's my point."

"What are you talking about?"

"You haven't had a choice in any of this." His voice was firm, angry. "You were right last night, you know. Our number was up the second they took us hostage. We can never go home unless the cartel is miraculously destroyed. And here's the part that really gets me—they weren't even after you, Camille. You were literally in the wrong place at the wrong time. Like when you were shot. Wrong place, wrong time."

"You don't know anything about me or the accident."

"Jacob told me everything about the accident that ruined your career. About the shoot-out at the meth house you were raiding, how you two positioned yourselves in a bathroom but forgot to check the tub. I know about the little boy hiding inside, how he pulled Jacob's arm when he tried to fire into the hallway.

"He hit you instead. It about killed Jacob to watch you bleed out on the floor of that filthy bathroom while they secured the house. He said you didn't complain once. He said you insisted the paramedics take the boy away first."

"Any cop would've done the same."

"All you ever wanted to be in life was a police officer— you said it yourself today. That was your only dream and it died the day Jacob shot you. Don't play me the fool by pretending your career is still on track. I know better."

"My past has nothing to do with this." She spread her arms, indicating the compound and the surrounding desert.

"You think one has nothing to do with the other? You don't think I notice your hand shake when you hold a gun? Or that your limp gets worse with every step you take? Your leg hurts pretty badly right now, doesn't it? Tell me I'm wrong."

"Shut up about how broken and pathetic I am."

"You're missing my point."

"Is that so? Because all I'm hearing is that you're a dirt-bag."

"Camille, I pity you because you haven't experienced enough happiness. Your whole life has been one letdown after another. All responsibility and pain, no joy. And what do you do for fun? Swim back and forth in a pool?" He swiped a hand across his forehead. "You need a life, and I stole any chance you had for one. Any chance you had to find some happiness, *live a little,* was destroyed because the day Juliana went into labor, you got to the hospital at the same time I did. Wrong place, wrong time. Boom, your life is over. It's not fair."

Camille's insides had turned to fire. The exacting pain she usually felt with the memory of her accident was more akin to a match, igniting flames of rage that licked at her heart and lungs. She yelled with all the strength left in her. "Stop. Shut up. Just shut up."

She couldn't even see Aaron clearly, her eyes were so

clouded by anger. She clenched her fists at her sides, trying to keep from attacking him like she wanted to.

Aaron took a tentative step toward her. "I pity you because you deserve so much more than the hand you've been dealt."

The pain in Camille's leg returned to her attention in full force. She was exhausted and hurt—physically and mentally. She sat where she stood, stretched out her left leg, drew her right knee in and rested her head in her arms. She didn't want to look at Aaron anymore. Or the vacant cartel compound. She didn't want to see the never ending desert or the brilliant blue sky.

"Camille, listen to me. You're the bravest person I've ever met. And I know a lot of men who've been in battle, a lot of men who go up against murderers every day. You trump them all. You don't let anything stand in your way, not a shaky trigger finger or a bum leg. I just… I respect that. You were caught up innocently in this whole mess, but without you, I'd probably be dead."

Camille's eyes brimmed with moisture to the extent that she stopped blinking, lest a drop jar loose to slip down her cheek.

"After everything you've been through in your life, you don't deserve to be in the middle of the Mexican desert fighting for the right to live peacefully. You should be in California holding your niece and getting your goddamned passport so you can start traveling." His voice was low but harsh. "You need to quit the effing police force and meet someone to start a family with—and spend every day for the rest of your life figuring out what makes you happy. Anything but this."

He exhaled deeply and paced in front of her.

Camille understood his argument. He pitied her mess of a life. How humiliating, but how true. There were so many times she could have curled in a ball and had her own pity party. But it wouldn't have done one bit of good—not then and not now either. She and Aaron needed to look to the future, to figure out how to rescue Rosalia and destroy the men who had marked them to die. They needed to deliver an epic cartel beatdown, not dissolve like a couple of wimps.

A rogue tear escaped from her eye.

"Don't you dare start crying," he commanded, stopping in his tracks and pointing a finger at her. "Or so help me, I'm going to hug you."

Camille smiled at the earnestness of his demand.

Aaron didn't return her smile, but offered her a hand. She accepted his help and didn't protest when he draped his arms over her shoulders.

"I'd insist that you let ICE take you home, and allow me to make things right for both of us, but I'm guessing you wouldn't go for that," he said.

"No way. We're in this together."

They stood, embracing, until the cry of a bird in the distance interrupted the moment. With nothing left to say, Camille walked around to the passenger side of the Jeep. She tried hard not to limp, but failed miserably.

Aaron, still looking at her way too seriously, opened her door. She let him, but as soon as he started the engine, she put her hand on the steering wheel to make sure she got his undivided attention.

"Aaron?"

"Hmm?"

"Don't ever pity me again."

"Yes, ma'am."

Then he smiled.

Chapter 7

With Baja's combination of dirt roads and pothole-riddled byways, it took Ana, in her ancient Pontiac hatchback, three hours to drive fifty miles. Three hours Camille spent in the backseat next to Sarah, who Camille hoped earned a back-ache the next day from constantly leaning forward to fondle Aaron's shoulders, neck and hair.

The city of La Paz unfolded gradually, with the occasional shack giving way to dirt roads lined with them. Ana's car thumped onto the first paved road after two hours of travel. The road gradually morphed into a bona fide high-way and the real city started, with gray cinder-block houses and markets, auto repair garages and clothing stores sporting barred windows and half-empty shelves.

Throughout the drive, Aaron peppered Ana with questions about the city. La Paz had a population of roughly two hundred thousand people and sat on the southeast edge of the Baja peninsula at the back of a long, narrow bay fed by the Sea of

Cortez, nine hundred miles south of the Mexican-American border and an ocean away from the Mexican mainland.

While the outlying sections of the city were relatively flat, the closer Ana drove toward the bay, the greater the downhill grade became, as if the whole of La Paz would eventually slip into the water. After going out of her way to give Aaron and Camille a mini-tour of the city, she turned away from the nicely maintained downtown district and into a less-picturesque urban neighborhood.

The houses were small and run-down, the streets narrow and jammed with parked cars. Save for the new Walmart and Costco Ana pointed out, this section of the city boasted no trendy shops like downtown, just taco stands and mini-marts, crumbling schools behind chain-link fences and drab apartment buildings. They dropped Sarah off in front of a freshly painted cottage with a weed-riddled yard and continued a few blocks more to Ana's apartment.

Camille hated the lack of security that came with arriving in broad daylight. After exiting the car, she scanned the sidewalks and apartment windows for sinister-looking faces. Nothing appeared out of the ordinary.

Ana chuckled at something Aaron said and for one sinking moment, Camille second-guessed their new friend's trustworthiness. What if Ana had ties to the Cortez Cartel? What if she and Aaron were walking into a trap?

Whoa there, girl. Deep breath.

So what if they might be ambushed by a bunch of Mexican mobsters? The faster she found the cartel, the sooner she'd rescue Rosalia. Besides that, it wasn't an ambush if she was armed and ready to fight back. With a hand on the grip of the gun in her pocket, she followed Aaron up a set of stairs to Ana's second-floor apartment.

Ana's place was small and tastefully decorated, with a living room that fit a sofa but little more and a bathroom that was only reachable through the single bedroom. Camille had the honor of using the bathroom first and let her eyes roam over the framed photos, knickknacks and books that topped Ana's dresser. She managed to resist the urge to rummage through the bathroom cabinets, a decision she felt quite mature about.

She returned to the kitchen several minutes later. "Okay, Ana, the bathroom's all yours."

"Thank you, Camille, but Aaron was about to explain why the front page of yesterday's newspaper contains a picture of you two being held at gunpoint."

Camille sank into a chair and angled for a view of the newspaper. The grainy color photo showed the two of them at their worst—snarling, caged animals that had been put through the wringer.

"You know." Aaron swatted the air with his hand. "Yesterday's news."

"The article claims you two are being held hostage by the Cortez Cartel. It seems that the cartel emailed your picture to both Mexican and American news sources and the American police, demanding that two men arrested earlier this week in California be released or they will kill you. Is it true? Were you kidnapped?"

"You'll be safer not knowing the details," Camille said.

"I deserve to understand the danger I bring into my home."

Aaron rose, wiping his palms on his jeans. "You're right about the danger. We'll show ourselves out."

Ana held her arm out to stop him. "Oh, no, you don't. I want answers or I'll call the police."

Camille had no idea why Ana didn't simply let them disappear into the night, but they couldn't afford any involvement from the Mexican police. Aaron must have reached the same conclusion, because he dropped back into his chair.

"Start at the beginning," Ana said. "Why did the cartel kidnap you?"

Aaron did most of the talking and Camille was happy to let him. He wisely left out several details, including Rosalia's kidnapping, along with the fact that they'd already killed three cartel members and were planning to take down the rest. He also failed to disclose that they were armed to the teeth.

Ana nodded frequently and asked a couple of questions, but was otherwise nonplussed. "So, you're both American law enforcement?"

"Yes," Aaron said.

"Have you contacted your work or your families yet?"

"Yes, on both accounts."

"I'm sure your families are anxious for your return. Perhaps you need a ride to the airport tonight?"

"Actually," Aaron hedged, "we're planning to stay in La Paz and gather intelligence on the cartel."

Ana covered Camille's hands with her own. "Remaining here would be very unsafe for you. The cartel—it is everywhere and it is merciless. If it finds you, you will die."

A tingle of fear crept over Camille's limbs, but she squelched it immediately. Her fear was nothing compared to what Rosalia must be experiencing. Besides, she and Aaron had already gone up against the cartel and survived. They could—and would—do so again, as many times as it took to secure Rosalia's freedom as well as their own.

"It's a risk we're prepared to take," she answered Ana. Aaron nodded his solidarity.

"Then I will help you as much as I can. You may stay with me as long as you need to."

"Thank you for the generous offer," Camille answered, "but one night is enough. Tomorrow the plan is for Aaron to find us a place to stay while I pick up supplies, then we'll be out of your way."

"Then tomorrow you may borrow my car to run errands. Sarah can drive me to work."

"But why would you put your safety at risk for us?" Camille added, sincerely baffled.

"You want to fight against the smugglers who bring guns into my country. It is an issue close to my heart. Let's leave it at that."

It was liberation time. While Aaron showered, Ana found a pair of scissors and a box of hair dye left over from the time she'd streaked her hair with red highlights. The chocolate-colored dye was a safety net in case she'd hated the highlights, which she hadn't.

"I've always wanted short hair," Ana whispered with conspiratorial enthusiasm. "Good for you."

Camille sat on a kitchen chair with a towel around her neck. "That page one color photo of me is reason enough for a change."

Ana picked up the scissors and made dramatic snipping motions in the air. Hopefully she'd be more prudent with the cut than her demonstration threatened. "Ready?"

"I've been ready for years." *Good riddance.*

"Stop! Oh my God. Are you crazy?" Aaron stomped from the bedroom with wet hair, clad in the same clothes he'd worn that day. He strode to Ana, snatched the scissors from her and chastised both women with furious eyes.

"Aaron, calm down. The cartel will be looking for a woman with long blond hair. It'd be stupid for me to leave it like that. And honestly, I can't wait to be rid of it. The only reason I kept it long was so I could put it in a bun for work. I think I'll look good as a short-haired brunette."

"Brunette?" He spit the word out as if it was a piece of gristle.

Camille pointed to the box of hair dye on the table.

Aaron's face twisted into a look of pure horror. He grabbed the box of dye, stuffed the scissors in his pocket and stomped to the front door. "Wear a hat."

He left, slamming the door behind him.

Camille shot a questioning look at Ana. "What was that about?"

"I think he likes your hair the way it is." Was that a hint of a smirk on Ana's face?

"What I do with my hair is none of his business. Do you have another pair of scissors we can use?"

Ana shook her head. "He took my only pair. You two are entertaining, you know that?" Oh, yeah, Ana was definitely smirking.

"I have no idea what you mean."

"I know, and that's why it's so amusing." Ana pulled the towel from around Camille's neck. "I have the perfect hat for you to borrow. Let's go look."

Adding scissors and hair dye to her mental grocery list for the next day, she allowed Ana to pull her by the arm to the bedroom closet.

The streets of La Paz bustled with activity now that the heat of the day had given way to a temperate evening. Aaron pulled his newly purchased ball cap low over his eyes and emerged from a corner market, his other purchases in hand. He ducked onto a quiet side street packed with towering, narrow houses and sat curbside in the shadow of a parked car.

He ripped the plastic covering from one of the two prepaid cell phones as he organized his thoughts. If he played this next conversation perfectly, he'd have ICE's considerable resources at his disposal for the duration of his and Camille's mission in Mexico. Play it wrong and not only would Thomas Dreyer likely demand their return to the U.S., as had been the original plan, but Aaron would jeopardize his future career.

At issue was Aaron's absolute certainty that Camille wouldn't leave Mexico without Rosalia Perez. And Aaron would never leave Camille to fight on her own. Short of being dragged away in a body bag, he'd have her back for as long as their mission took to complete—even if that meant disobeying a direct order from his superior.

He dialed Thomas Dreyer's personal number. He picked up on the second ring.

"Dreyer here."

"This is Montgomery."

"Did you and Fisher make it to La Paz?"

"We did, sir."

"Excellent. Arrangements have been confirmed for you two to hitch a ride to San Diego with a naval ship headed up the Pacific from South America."

Aaron screwed his mouth up. *Let the chess match begin.* "Fisher and I performed reconnaissance yesterday on the cartel compound where we were held. It had been vacated. We have no idea where Rosalia Perez was taken, sir."

Dreyer was silent for a beat. "Not surprising, given your escape. Not that the cartel is admitting to anything. They're demanding the prisoners' release in exchange for your freedom, and we've decided to let them go on believing they have the edge while we put the pieces in place for the girl's recovery. ICE received the San Diego Police Department's blessing to handle the case, but our hands are tied at this point because the girl's citizenship has been brought into question. Mexican officials are pushing to handle the rescue themselves."

"Sounds like a political stunt."

"Roger that. If diplomacy fails, we've got a black ops team on standby in Mexico City."

"Who's leading the unit?" Aaron asked.

"Diego Santero."

Damn. He'd never met the guy in person, but by all accounts, he was a surly jackass of the first degree. Too bad he was also the best ICE black ops field agent in the world.

When Aaron first set his sights on becoming a field agent, his motivation was to surpass the bar Santero had set.

He took a fortifying breath and hoped luck was on his side once more. Maybe he could turn his kidnapping into another golden ticket, one that led to his dream job with ICE. "If I can get a lead on Rosalia Perez's whereabouts, I want to be part of Santero's team for her extraction."

"Come again?"

"Officer Fisher and I are already in La Paz. We've had visual contact with Rosalia Perez and have a better chance than anyone of pinpointing where she's been taken. When I pass that intel on to ICE, I want to help with her rescue. I've trained for it—you know I have. I'm going to prove to you that I'm ICE agent material." He clamped his molars together, reeling at the note of desperation in his tone.

After a slow inhale, he tried again. "Think about it, sir. If Officer Fisher and I return to the States, we'll go into Witness Protection. We won't be doing anybody any good. If we stay in La Paz—where nobody, including the Mexican government, knows we are—we could make some real headway for ICE, not only with data on the cartel, but with a high-profile rescue. The intel I've already gathered about the cartel's smuggling operation alone will bump our unit to the best in the nation, guaranteed. This is our moment, sir. The opportunity our team's been waiting for." *That I've been waiting for.*

A long silence followed. "You're up for the challenge, Montgomery?"

"Absolutely."

"And Fisher, does she have the chops for this?"

"Fisher is former Special Forces. She was assigned to the Rosalia kidnapping case originally. With all due respect, sir, I don't think she'd leave Mexico without the girl if the President himself commanded her to."

Dreyer sighed and Aaron knew he'd won. "What do you need from me?"

"Time."

"Keep me in the loop, Montgomery. I'm putting my reputation on the line for you. Consider this your big audition. Don't screw it up."

"I won't, sir. Thank you."

After the call ended, Aaron sat for a long time, staring at his hands. The conversation had gone exactly as he'd hoped. Yet still, he couldn't shake the feeling that for the first time ever, his golden ticket hadn't presented him with a great opportunity, but with a hangman's noose.

Aaron returned over an hour later, acting as though nothing was amiss. Camille opened her mouth to press him for details about where he'd gone, but all that came out was a yawn.

"Let me show you your bed." Ana walked to the sofa and removed its cushions. "My first apartment was a loft without enough space for both a sofa and a bed, so my parents bought me this."

She tugged on a loop of material at the center of the sofa and out popped a collapsible mattress. The three of them made the bed with sheets and a blanket.

Camille stroked the pillow nearest her. "I'm tired just looking at it. I can't wait to sprawl."

Aaron raised an eyebrow. "On your side, of course."

"What? You and I aren't sharing a bed."

He looked at her as though she was crazy. "We escaped from a drug cartel and you're worried about sharing a bed with me?"

"Aaron, you're welcome to sleep with me," Ana purred. "My bed would accommodate both of us beautifully."

Camille huffed. "You're right, Aaron—I don't care what

the sleeping arrangements are. Sleep with Ana or sleep on the sofa bed. Whatever."

Ana had that annoying smirk on her face again. "I'm going to retire to my room. If you two need anything, let me know."

Camille watched the bedroom door close behind Ana, then crawled between the sheets.

Aaron stood on the opposite side with his arms crossed over his chest, watching her. It was damned disconcerting. Ana had loaned her pajamas, but under Aaron's gaze, she felt positively naked. She snapped the sheet over herself, a warning for him to mind his p's and q's.

As though he'd been waiting for Camille's undivided attention, he squared his body to the bed and tugged his shirt over his head. As if he wanted her to swoon over his rippling muscles and perfect physique.

Oh, please. What a jerk.

"I'm not sharing a bed with you if you're half-naked." She tried to modulate her voice, but still, it cracked once.

"We're going to be living in pretty close quarters for a while, so you'd better get used to the sight of me." Grinning broadly, he dropped his pants to the floor and stood with his hands on his hip bones in a pair of flimsy red cotton boxer-briefs.

Camille squeaked and scurried out of the bed. "Jesus, Aaron, put your pants back on."

"Worried I'm going to attack you while you sleep?"

"You already kissed me against my will. How should I know what you're capable of?"

"I can say with one hundred percent certainty that when we kissed, it was not against your will. Look, I told you it wouldn't happen again and I'm a man of my word. Any other promises you want me to make before we get in bed together?"

"Do you have to put it that way?"

"I think it has a nice ring to it."

"Promise you won't touch me."

He threw up his hands. "Oh, geez, Cam. I'm not a perv. I don't go around copping feels on frightened women."

"I'm not frightened." Especially not of some idiot who didn't have the decency to keep covered.

"Then why are you hiding behind that sheet?"

Camille looked to find her hands clutching the top sheet to her chest, nearly pulling it off the bed. She let go and straightened. She'd show him how not-frightened she was. "Say it."

Aaron yanked the sheets in his direction and fell into bed. The mattress groaned with the additional weight. "I promise not to grope you. Now stop yapping and get in bed."

With narrowed eyes, she lay back. She folded her hands over her stomach but found it uncomfortable, so she moved them to her sides. First above the covers, which was too chilly, and then below. She refluffed her pillow, flopped down and folded her hands across her chest. Aaron watched her with lazy eyes.

"How about I lie on my side and you can pretend I'm a wall?"

He turned his back to her and clicked off the floor lamp. Too much light streamed in from the streetlamp outside the window. Camille studied the taper of Aaron's wide shoulders to his trim waist. One thing was for sure—Aaron Montgomery could never be mistaken for a wall.

He knew Camille was tired. She'd gotten as little sleep as he had over the past few days. On the drive to La Paz, he'd seen the slump of her shoulders and the dark circles under her eyes. Yet Aaron felt those same eyes boring holes into his back long after he turned out the light.

After a while, Camille yawned quietly and shifted. Aaron

squelched the urge to command her to close her eyes. Instead, he tried a more diplomatic approach.

"Camille, I can't get my mind to stop thinking about kidnappings and guns and murder. Do you mind if we talk a little to help me unwind?"

"Talk about what?"

He scrambled for a neutral topic. "What's your favorite holiday?"

"Are you kidding?"

"No. It would be nice to think about something happy."

She was quiet for so long that he didn't think she'd answer. "Christmas," she blurted. "My favorite holiday is Christmas."

Aaron smiled, triumphant. "What makes it your favorite?"

"My sister and Jacob stay overnight at our parents' house. I don't get to see Juliana much now that she's married, so that's really nice. On Christmas morning, she does this big production of handing out silly gifts that make us laugh."

He heard the joy in Camille's words and wanted desperately to look at her but was afraid if he did, she'd clam up. "My mom makes this huge, elaborate meal and won't let us help. No matter what time she says dinner's at, it's always two hours late. Does your mom cook dinner?"

"We do it together. We make a turkey and a couple sides in the morning and nibble all day long. We never even sit at the dinner table. It's just…fun, relaxing. Next year'll be even better with little Alana for us to spoil."

Her voice drifted off. "Mmm," she added after a few quiet minutes.

It was a hum of contentment that rendered Aaron powerless to resist a peek. Careful not to shake the bed too much, he rolled over.

The light from the window slashed across the top of her head, illuminating her golden hair. She was asleep on her side facing him, with her hands on the pillow next to her cheek and a smile on her lips, totally peaceful.

Breathtaking.

He stared for a long time. She looked small, angelic. This warrior who was so strong and capable, so ready to battle the world when she was awake, was still a woman when she slept. A beautiful, complicated woman.

He raised the sheet to cover her shoulder. Her nose wrinkled and he was tempted to kiss it until he remembered his promise. Well, Camille hadn't said anything about invading her personal space. Satisfied to have found a loophole, he moved his pillow to abut hers and nestled in. He covered her hand with his, curling his fingers until they reached her palm. With the steady rhythm of her breath on his cheek, Aaron closed his eyes and fell asleep.

Camille woke after dawn in Ana's sofa bed. Ready to fight the bad guys. One problem—she couldn't move.

Aaron had her pinned. He was asleep on his side, with his face so close that she had to pull back to keep from brushing his nose, and his arm and leg slung over her body.

"Aaron?" She pushed against his chest. "Aaron."

His eyes opened. "Good morning, Blondie."

She considered calling him on the use of that god-awful nickname, but first things first. "Get off me."

"I'm too comfortable to move."

"You promised not to touch me."

"I promised not to grope you. This is different. This is snuggling." He closed his eyes again.

"My foot's asleep and I have to use the bathroom. Get off or I'll make you."

"Fine," he said melodramatically.

Once free, Camille was flustered to discover that she, too, had been quite comfortable tangled up in bed with Aaron. She'd have to make sure it never happened again.

Sarah arrived less than an hour later to pick Ana up for work. Aaron locked the door after ushering the teachers out, then pulled two disposable cell phones from a paper bag. "I bought these last night and programmed each with three numbers—each other, Ana and Thomas Dreyer, my boss. I touched base with him last night and he's offering us ICE's full support."

"That's fantastic." She held out her hand for the phone, but he stared at her as if something was bothering him. "What?"

"I've got a really bad feeling about splitting up today. Maybe we should scrap the plan and stick together. You could come with me to find a place for us to stay and some wheels, and I could shop for supplies with you tonight."

Camille snatched the phone from his hand and pocketed it along with Ana's car keys. "Nothing's going to happen. The supermarket and clothing shops are only a mile or so away. Don't worry so much. I'm a cop, remember? You have to stop treating me like a civilian. Besides, the faster we get everything we need, the sooner we can get on with finding Rosalia."

Aaron took hold of Camille's elbows and looked so seriously into her eyes, the skin on the back of her neck tingled.

"We meet here tonight at five o'clock," he said. "If something happens to me, if I don't come back, you call Dreyer. He'll get you out of Mexico by boat. The roads are too dangerous. There are armed checkpoints all along the highway to California. You don't want to get caught with a gun and you can't take the chance of coming across any crooked military types on the cartel's payroll. And don't try to be a hero by searching for Rosalia on your own. It's too risky. Promise me."

Rattled by his intensity, Camille whispered, "I promise."

"If something happens to you…if you're not back here

tonight, I'll find you." He closed his eyes and screwed up his mouth. "Just be here. That's an order."

"I will. You, too, okay?" She pulled away from his grip. "At least you know I'm not leaving this neighborhood. I don't know where you're going to end up today."

"I don't know either. How about I call you at noon to check in?"

"All right. I'll be waiting." She gave him her best reassuring smile.

After donning a blue crocheted hat, she slipped a 9 mm into her waistband, then shoveled a few stacks of money into one pocket of her borrowed jacket and a backup handgun into another. She slipped on a pair of dark glasses and followed Aaron out the door.

Chapter 8

By eleven-thirty, Camille was half done with her errands. While the clothes she'd chosen for herself and Aaron weren't the most expensive or fashionable, they were good enough. She threw in some hats, socks and—despite her mortification at the idea—underwear for them both. Around the corner from the shoe store, she'd chucked the nasty cartel sneakers in a Dumpster with so much exuberance that a few heads turned to stare at her. She was feeling so good about her new footwear that, on a whim, she popped into a pharmacy for a new box of hair dye.

Brunette, just to tick Aaron off.

Back at the apartment, she scribbled a grocery list before heading out once more. Gigante Market, the local grocery chain, was as sprawling as an American supermarket, and she practically worked up a limp walking from the car to the main entrance.

Starting at the produce section, she methodically walked each aisle, adding to her cart. Inspired by the aroma of baking bread wafting from behind the bakery counter, she waited her turn for a loaf of fresh sweet bread. With an appreciative sigh, she popped a chunk of the still-warm loaf in her mouth, then got back to business. Rounding the corner to the rice aisle, she saw three men loitering at the opposite end, closest to the exit.

The pock-cheeked man who'd tied Aaron's and Camille's legs to those rusty patio chairs stood next to the man with helmet-hard hair who'd skydived with her and a third man Camille didn't recognize. He looked to be in his late thirties, with the muscular build of a bulldog. If any of the three could claim to be a full-time hit man for the cartel, it would be this guy.

Not sure if she was spotted, Camille flipped a U-turn and walked around the corner. She abandoned the shopping cart on the next aisle, slipped her firearm from her waist and flipped off the safety. She peeked between the shelves, through the bottles of juice on her side and the bags of rice on the other, at where the three men had been but were no longer.

They appeared quietly, with smirking, destructive smiles, at the head of the juice aisle.

Adrenaline and panic flamed to life within her, making her breath shallow, her vision narrow. Her gun hand shook violently.

The men advanced.

She swept an arm across a shelf of bottles, and they crashed to the ground, embedding little bits of glass into her ankles. She sprinted three aisles over, praying the glass and liquid impeded her pursuers long enough for her to make it out the front entrance.

Three against one in an aisle-by-aisle chase were terrible odds, though. Halfway through the snack aisle, Helmet Hair appeared before her. She squeezed a round off that went wide and then she turned back the way she came, but

Hit Man and Pocked Face blocked her in. Their movement changing from running to stalking, they crowded in on her, drawing their guns.

She aimed her gun as best she could as it quaked in her hand and concentrated hard on her trigger finger, but it wouldn't move. Damn it.

On the edge of panic, she threw herself into a shelf, punching through the chips to the other side, and raced to the back of the store, scanning for a rear exit. What she came to first was the Mexican equivalent of an American deli section. She crashed into a refrigerated display case, then darted behind the counter and shoved past a shocked employee.

Dizzy with adrenaline and shock, she ducked behind a meat slicer and took in great gulps of air as blood surged with fiery purpose through her veins. Two sets of prowling feet appeared nearby. She tightened her grip on her gun as awareness dawned within her. She was going to have to kill them all if she wanted to make it out of the supermarket alive.

She rose into a squat beneath the table, waiting for the opportunity to strike.

Her cell phone rang.

She cursed and leaped from her hiding place. Helmet Hair, with his back to her, was the closest. Cringing with the effort of squeezing the trigger, she got a round off, hitting him in the shoulder. She kicked out at his midsection, knocking him face-first into the revolving vertical meat broiler. He shrieked in pain.

She twisted left and shot Pocked Face in the gut. He staggered and leveled his pistol at her.

Dodging right, she fired again, the bullet slicing a chunk from his neck. Blood gushed uncontrollably from both wounds. With a guttural cry, he shot at her at the same time Hit Man caught her left cheek with an upper jab.

The impact of the punch knocked her down. She rolled under the nearest stainless-steel table. Pocked Face fired in her direction and the table rocked on its legs as the bullet ricocheted and hit a display case, shattering glass in all directions. She braced for a second shot but none came. The only sound besides Helmet Hair's low moans of agony from the meat broiler was the soft clunk of Pocked Face's head hitting the floor.

Hit Man's booted feet moved toward her.

Gripping her gun hand hard with her left to minimize the quaking, she squeezed the trigger and got a shot off. It went wide.

She squeezed again.

The gun clicked benignly. Out of ammo.

She unzipped her jacket's inside pocket and reached for her backup weapon, but it snagged on the pocket liner.

Another spray of bullets rocked the table. Her time was running out. She fumbled with the jacket pocket but couldn't control her fingers enough to untangle the gun. Adrenaline and fear were making her clumsier with every passing second. With her pulse whooshing in her ears, she scrambled out the other end of the table.

Keeping low, she slipped back into the public area of the now-deserted store. The gunfire had done an effective job of clearing out shoppers. She dashed past the milk refrigerators toward the bakery, fumbling in her jacket pocket as she moved.

She veered behind the bakery display counter and hurled herself to the ground. Her hand shook so hard she couldn't close her fingers over the gun, much less unsnag it from the pocket lining and bring it out. She ground her teeth with rage against her stupid limitations that were about to get her killed. Taking a second deep breath, she focused on steadying her hand, but it was too late.

Hit Man dragged her up and punched her square in the

cheek he'd already pummeled. This time, Camille hit back. She put all her weight behind a right uppercut to his chin and when she retracted her fist, she backhanded the other side of his face.

He grabbed hold of her left wrist and torqued it until she screamed. She was millimeters away from having her arm broken and so she pivoted, desperate to straighten her arm. As soon as her back was to him, he released her wrist and locked his arm around her neck in a stranglehold.

She gasped for air that would not come. He tightened his grip and the edges of her vision went black. Struggling against an onslaught of shock, she shoved her quaking hand inside the pocket of her jacket, threaded the gun under her armpit and clamped down with her arm to steady her grip.

She fired twice.

Hit Man slumped over her. The unnatural warmth of spilled blood pooled across her back. Shouldering him off, she left the gun in her now-ragged jacket and ran out the screen door at the rear of the bakery, into an alley.

She paused and did a quick assessment of herself. Her side ached, probably from bullet shrapnel, she had a mean shiner on her cheek and she was covered in blood. It saturated her jacket, splattered into her hair and ran down her arms and legs.

Her cell phone rang again, a confusingly normal sound that blended with the wailing of multiple police sirens closing in. She wouldn't answer Aaron's call because no matter what she said, the fear and adrenaline in her voice would come through and she couldn't take the chance that he'd come for her. She'd rather die before dragging him into this new danger. Until she could guarantee Aaron's safety, she'd have to make due on her own.

She fished out the phone, turned the ringer off and ran.

She ran as fast and as long as her leg and its debilitating pain allowed. Then she kept going anyway, more slowly, but still making progress. Keeping to alleyways, trash heaps and abandoned buildings, she shrank into the shadows of the city and disappeared.

A tingling of dread niggled at Aaron when Camille didn't answer her phone. He called her at noon like he'd promised and again a few minutes later, but it rang and rang. After that, the phone was answered by a computerized message. Either her phone had been switched off or destroyed. Any way he looked at it, something was wrong.

His simmering dread devolved into full-fledged panic when, at three o'clock, he stopped by Ana's apartment and Camille was not there. Bags of new clothes had been piled on the sofa, but no Camille. He jogged to the supermarket where she'd planned to shop.

At the edge of the supermarket parking lot, he dropped to his knees at the sight of three covered bodies being loaded into ambulances. The parking lot was nearly empty of civilian vehicles and it didn't take any time at all to locate Ana's car.

Crazy with fear, he raced back to Ana's apartment to wait for her to come home from work so he could enlist her help. The market was crawling with cops and no way could Aaron take the chance of being recognized. If Camille was alive, what good would he be to her if he were taken into custody? Ana was already home when he arrived and agreed to go to the market to ask witnesses about the identities of the dead. Or, at least, if any of the bodies were an American female. *Dear God, let her be alive.*

Aaron kept vigil at the apartment, holding on to hope Camille would show up at five o'clock as they'd agreed. He cleaned and reloaded his guns twice, checked the strength of his phone service every minute or two and paced in circles around the kitchen table. He put in a call to Nicholas

Wells, his task-force buddy, but word of the market shoot-out hadn't trickled Stateside.

Five o'clock came and went.

Ana returned at five-thirty, frustrated by the lack of information she'd been able to elicit from onlookers. All she learned was that the market was a wreck, with blood and knives and bullets everywhere.

Together they waited thirty minutes more, until Aaron could no longer bear the idleness. After scribbling his cell phone number, he grabbed the bags of clothing and their stash of weapons, slung them around his body and loped to the dirt bike he'd purchased that morning. The heavy load was awkward and took a lot of concentration to balance, but he was grateful for the distraction to keep his mind from hurtling off the deep end.

After dropping the clothes and guns off at their new hideout, he sat on the bike on the side of the road, fingering his phone. If he didn't hear from her by midnight, he'd call Dreyer and enlist Santero's help. His terror at Camille's fate was palpable—like a second person standing too close, whispering, *I told you it was a bad idea to split up* over and over into his ear. Every five minutes, he redialed her number.

He decided not to search for her. It was a strange city, so large that the futility of a search was bound to destroy whatever hope he had left. And he might not hear her call over the high-pitched whine of the bike's engine.

At nine o'clock, after nine full hours of experiencing a level of panic he hadn't known was possible to survive from, his phone rang.

"Aaron?" Camille's voice was weak and breathy.

Aaron gritted his teeth against the emotion welling in his throat. She was alive.

"You scared me." His choked whisper sounded oddly similar to hers. "What took you so long to call?"

"I think I passed out."

Aaron closed his eyes. Now was not the time to lose the careful control he'd clung to all day. "Tell me where you are and I'll come get you."

She directed him to a partially constructed cinder-block structure in an alley off a major thoroughfare and asked him to bring her a change of clothes. She swore to him she'd keep her phone close at hand while she waited. Still, he hated the uncertainty that came with hanging up the call.

He flew through the streets in a daze and stopped next to a darkened cinder-block shell of a house, disbelieving that his Camille was inside such a cruel, filthy place. He'd never let a woman he knew walk through this alley, let alone linger after dark with only rats, roaches and stray dogs as company.

Camille sat in the far corner of the structure, propped against the wall. The bright lights of the thoroughfare streamed in through the empty spaces that would have been windows if the house had been finished. It was enough light to see Camille's swollen face and the dried brown blood that coated her like paint.

He ran to her and dropped to the ground.

"Where are you hurt?" He ripped the blood-drenched jacket and shirt over her head. "Where are you hurt, god-damn it?"

"It's not my blood."

He smoothed his fingers over her back, inspecting her skin, slick with blood and sweat, for the wound that was most certainly there. The jacket bore the irrefutable evidence of a bullet hole and a life-threatening wound.

"Where were you hit, Cam? Talk to me." His voice was frantic as his hands finished with her back and started on her front, roving over her stomach and sides and arms.

"It's not my blood."

"Like hell it's not. There's too much of it."

With a violent yank of material, her bloody, tattered pants

were off. His hands grazed the lengths of her legs. Bits of glass were embedded in her calves, but that wasn't what he was looking for.

"Aaron, stop. It's not my blood. I swear."

Finally, with no inch of her body left unchecked, he stood. His pulse was racing, his breath coming in ragged fits. Impossible that she could be covered in so much blood and not be injured. *Impossible.* But whatever her wounds were, he had to get a grip before he got them into more trouble.

He had to get Camille to safety. The urge to protect her was fierce. At that moment, there were fifty-fifty odds he'd call Dreyer to get them out of the country by morning. They might have to hide for the rest of their lives in WitSec, but she'd be safe and that was all that mattered.

He looked her way. Wearing nothing but panties and a bra, she sat utterly still, chanting quietly, looking more fragile than he knew her capable of being. That certainly got his attention.

Finally, he heard what she was chanting.

"It's not my blood."

Blinking rapidly, he nodded, processing. "It's not your blood."

"No."

"Whose?"

"Two men from the compound and another I didn't recognize."

"You killed them?"

"Yeah," she said wearily.

"You weren't shot?"

"No, just a little beat up."

Aaron looked around the ground for the change of clothes he'd brought, that he'd dropped in a fit of panic when he'd seen her. "Here, hurry. We need to leave."

She put her clothes on while sitting, even her pants. Aaron couldn't tear his eyes away from her, as if his sight held the power to keep her from evaporating into thin air. When she was done, he handed her a helmet.

"A motorcycle?"

"Dirt bike. With helmets on, there's no chance of being recognized."

Camille nodded. Aaron offered her a hand, which she accepted. She grimaced as she pushed to her feet, as though she was injured worse than the superficial wound on her ankle. But he had inspected every inch of her body.

"What's wrong?"

"Nothing," she replied thickly. "Get the bike started. I'll be out in a sec."

"No. You're not getting out of my sight again."

"I'm right behind you."

"What are you hiding from me, Camille?"

"I need a minute."

Then he noticed the way she stood—on her right foot. The pieces fell into place. The grocery store was at least six or seven miles away.

"You ran, didn't you? From the market?"

"I did what I had to do. Please, wait at the bike. I'll be there in a sec."

Aaron lifted her into his arms. Her bad leg had to be killing her, and she didn't want him to see her limp. Stubborn, stubborn woman.

"You promised—no pity."

"Right. No pity," he murmured absentmindedly as he walked.

"Then what do you call this?"

Taking care of you, my proud warrior. "Only trying to speed things along."

They barreled through the city. The feel of Camille, with her arms holding tight around his middle and her warmth pressed against his back, was a balm against the fear and regret that had consumed him. She was alive, relatively un-injured and safe.

Pulling into a private marina, Aaron cut the engine on the bike and used his feet to walk them down the ramp to the dock.

"You bought us a yacht?"

"Yeah." He helped her from the bike and over the railing of the boat. "Transportation-slash-housing all rolled into one."

Camille nodded. She looked exhausted.

He lifted the bike over the rail and onto the deck of the boat. Its lightness was one of the main reasons Aaron bought a dirt bike instead of a motorcycle. The other was its ability to traverse both streets and off-road trails, wherever their search for Rosalia Perez took them.

"The bathroom's by the bed," he said. "I'm going to get us offshore, then we'll talk."

"Okay." But she didn't move, just stood on her right leg, probably waiting for him to turn away so he wouldn't see her limp. Stubborn woman. Though he wanted to carry her, her safety was more important. Every moment on land kept Camille in danger.

Aaron untied the ropes that anchored them to the dock and climbed the ladder to the bridge. With a turn of a key, the boat rumbled to life. He pushed the throttle forward and the boat responded, racing them into the safety of the deep, black sea.

One hour later, with the boat anchored in a leeward cove of a tiny island off the coast, he sat on the bed and waited for Camille to finish showering, holding a pair of scissors and a box of hair dye he'd found amid her purchases. He worshipped her hair but valued her life even more. Maybe if she'd disguised her appearance sooner, before Aaron stopped her, the shoot-out could've been avoided. He wouldn't make such a careless mistake again.

She emerged from the bathroom dressed in sweatpants and a white T-shirt. The bruises on her cheek looked even worse in the light. Her left eye was almost completely swollen shut, but she zeroed in on the items in his hands and nodded.

She took a step and sniffed. Gathering her in his arms, he ignored her weak protestations and deposited her on the toilet lid.

Without a word, she turned, offering him access to her hair. He gathered it in his hand, gave it one final caress.

"I'm so sorry," he whispered. Then he made the first cut.

Before long, blond locks littered the floor. Camille remained still and silent as Aaron snipped her hair to chin length. When he'd finished, he opened the box of dye.

"I don't know how…" he started.

She turned toward him and set her hand over his. "I'll help you."

Her fingers were cold, shaky. He dropped to his knees and brought her hand to his lips. He felt a welling of sorrow and anger stir within him, threatening his careful composure, and cleared his throat. "We'll save enough dye for my hair, too. We're in this together."

She nodded and took the box of dye. Bent over the instructions together, they got to work.

An hour later, they were brunettes. Aaron dabbed her hair one final time with a towel, then lifted her into his arms. She complied without complaint as he carried her to the bed.

Rolling to her side, she stared at the wall with stormy intensity.

After turning off the lights, Aaron stripped to his boxers and slid beneath the covers, all the way over to her. She didn't acknowledge his nearness, but she didn't protest either. He rested the entire length of his body along her back, spooning her tightly. His fingers locked with hers.

He spent nine hours that day thinking she'd died in a vicious gun battle. Though he knew better now, he felt damaged by the experience. Tonight, he needed to hold her as much for his own healing as for hers.

Tonight, she let him.

Chapter 9

Camille woke with Aaron's nose touching her cheek and his arm draped across the underside of her breasts. She should get up. They had so much to do. Every moment they wasted kept their families and Rosalia in danger. But his body felt heavy and good and she dreaded moving her throbbing left leg.

She worked her fingers through the tips of Aaron's thick hair and felt the ends where it curled around his ear. He looked as handsome as ever with brown hair. Her fingers glided over his earlobe and around the strong angle of his jaw. When she did not dare explore him further, she rested the palm of her hand against his neck and concentrated on the beat of his pulse.

It would be worse now for her. If they survived this mission, it would be painful in a way she wanted to deny but couldn't—not if she was being honest with herself. She'd invested years of her energy hating Aaron, on actively trying not to think about what she wanted from him. That would be impossible now. The man she held for this brief moment in time beneath the palm of her hand would exist forever on the fringe of her life, unattainable and heartbreaking. She should have tried harder to hate him.

When the tickle of blinking eyelashes brushed her cheek, her hand flew from Aaron's neck. Silently, he levered himself onto an elbow. She met his fathomless brown eyes, felt his arms slide along her shoulders, caging her beneath him, his fingers tangling in her hair. He lowered his mouth. Through no conscious will of her own, Camille's lips parted. Hovering only centimeters above her, he closed his eyes, his breathing strained, shallow.

A lock of his hair fell forward, skimming her forehead. She closed her eyes, the effort to stay still, to not pull his head down that final bit, sapping her already negligible strength.

He sucked in a deep, tremulous gulp of air, rolled off the bed and staggered to the bathroom. Camille let go of the sheet she was twisting and pushed to a seated position at the edge of the bed. Her whole body hurt, as if the pain of her leg had seeped into her bloodstream and spread while she slept.

Good. Anything to keep her mind from dwelling on what just happened.

When Aaron emerged from the bathroom, neither spoke as he carried her up the three stairs to the sofa. She let him because, frankly, she couldn't think of a damn thing to say.

"This is the living area," he said without meeting her eyes. "There's a deck out back with a ladder that leads to the bridge. The boat's only thirty-three feet long, which is tiny, I know, but it was the best I could do."

In addition to the sofa on which Camille sat, the main cabin housed a dining table and a kitchenette complete with a sink, mini-fridge and microwave. "Actually, it's not much smaller than my apartment. How much did you pay?"

"A hundred grand, which would be steep for a legitimate

sale of a yacht this size, but on the black market, it seemed a reasonable price, especially since the guy selling it didn't care who I was and why I had so much cash. He got the boat as a gift for his wife last year and now she's hinting about a bigger one. Must be nice."

"This is perfect. Really great thinking." She tried to smile, but the action brought too much pain to her swollen cheek. "I didn't know you had experience with boats."

He shrugged. "Yeah. I've done my share of water-skiing and speedboating over the years. Never captained a yacht, but I'm getting the hang of it."

"How far offshore are we?"

He emptied a can of soup into a coffee mug. "Twenty miles. About an hour's drive."

"Great. I'll heat up the soup. You fire up the boat. We can start with surveillance. Make a few passes by the Gigante Market, see if any other cartel operators are lurking nearby who might lead us to Rosalia."

He set the mug in the microwave. "We're going to shore this afternoon, but only to meet Ana at the marina. She called last night while you were showering to check on you and offered to drop off some groceries. I asked her to pick up the package from Jacob and some materials one of my coworkers overnighted to me, too. You'll be staying in the cabin, out of sight. You're not getting off this boat for a few more days."

Anger tightened her throat. "Who the hell are you to issue a command like that? If I say I'm all right—" She pushed to standing, swallowing a gasp as waves of pain radiated from her leg.

Aaron was in her face before she could recover enough to speak, stabbing the air between them with his finger. His eyes were wild, furious. "Sit down. Right now. Never once in my life have I forced a woman to do anything she didn't want to, but so help me, Camille, you're going to stay off that leg if I have to tie you to the bed."

Camille bit back the challenge hanging on the tip of her tongue. *I'd like to see you try.* Because what if he seized on her words? What if he touched her again?

Still, she was far too stubborn to capitulate. Balancing on her good leg, she held her ground. "How dare you, you chauvinistic jackass. You'd never talk to one of your ICE unit members like that. If I say I'm all right, then I am. The fact that I'm a woman is immaterial."

Yet how could she ignore that truth when he stood so close? When she could smell soap on his skin and watch the throb of a vein in his forehead? She'd never been more aware that she was a woman than when she was near Aaron Montgomery. And for that alone, she wished she could hate him.

"You're a terrible patient."

"And you're an insufferable pig."

She jumped a little when she felt his hand on her hip. Trapped between his broad, solid body and the sofa, her only move was to scramble onto the cushions, but she was too confused to move. She sought out an answer in his eyes and found them narrowed with resolve.

"You're right. Your gender doesn't matter to me one bit. Never has, never will." His voice had turned a soothing, patronizing tone. His hand, rough and sure, slid along her thigh and she caught herself pressing into his touch as her body stirred to life. "In fact, I barely notice you're a woman at all." His other hand closed around her waist as his fingers skimmed her knee.

Her breathing grew shallow. She stared at his chest, unwilling to meet his gaze.

"But if we got in a jam while doing surveillance, you couldn't run fast enough to escape." He dug his fingertips into the sensitive hollow behind her knee and her standing leg buckled. Her arms flailed as she dropped to the sofa.

"And if you were caught, what good would you be to Rosalia?"

He was right, damn him.

She stared out the window at the rolling gray swells, her hands fisted to keep herself from rubbing the skin he'd seared with his touch. She could think of nothing to say, no clever retort or convincing threat. No argument to match his foolproof logic. She had to let him win this one. For Rosalia. For their families.

He banged the mug of soup down on the side table. She lifted it to her lips and drank deeply. Through her silence, she conceded defeat.

For the rest of the day, the yacht bobbed in the Sea of Cortez, so far from the mainland it looked like a layer of brown smog across the western horizon. Outside of using the bathroom, Aaron let Camille do nothing for herself—not walk, get a drink of water or brush her hair. He hovered, like the world's most handsome private nurse, over her every waking moment.

At four o'clock, the yacht rumbled to life and they made their way through the long, narrow Bay of La Paz. When they reached their slip in the marina, Aaron ducked his head into the cabin with a warning for Camille to stay out of sight. She responded with a huff of protest. After resting her knee for a full night and day, she was anxious to measure her recovery.

She waited for the sound of Aaron's heavy footfalls on the dock, listening to men calling out to each other in Spanish, car horns honking in the distance and the cries of seagulls, then eased onto her feet.

"Ugh, that smarts," she muttered under her breath as her every nerve ending protested the move. Using the cabin wall as a crutch, she limped toward the door and into the sunlight.

Ana was waiting for them outside the locked security

gate at the top of the ramp with four grocery bags, watching Aaron with a seductive grin as he approached. When she noticed Camille, she waved and her smile turned cheerful. Aaron glanced over his shoulder, then unlocked the gate for Ana. After grabbing the grocery bags, he stalked back down the ramp.

"What do you think you're doing?"

Camille clamored over the boat railing and onto the dock, schooling a grimace of discomfort away from her features. Standing on one leg as she was, she looked like a flamingo, but she refused to play into Aaron's argument by leaning on the boat for support. "Saying hello to Ana. You got a problem with that?"

"It's not safe out here. What if someone recognizes you?"

"What if someone recognizes *you?*"

His face reddened with fury. "I'm not the one—"

"Camille, I've been so worried!" Ana skirted Aaron to kiss Camille's cheek and pet her head. "Your hair looks beautiful in this shade. How are you?"

Camille leveled a defiant glare on Aaron before turning her attention to Ana.

"I'm fine. All I needed was a bit of rest."

Aaron scoffed.

Ana squeezed Camille's hand. "The rumor has always been that the cartel's control was limited to the commercial port near the ferry landing. If I had any idea the grocery store would be dangerous, I never would have suggested you shop there."

Aaron moved next to Camille and took her elbow in his hand. She tugged out of his grip. He draped an arm around her rib cage and pulled her tightly against his side. "Hopefully, with the intelligence Camille and I gather, we can help end the cartel's stronghold on your city. Getting back to something you mentioned—the rumor is that the cartel controls the commercial port?"

"That's what I've heard."

Aaron rubbed his jaw. "That might be useful."

"Whatever I can do to help."

"You've already helped," Camille said. "Thank you for bringing us food. I've never been so hungry in my life."

Aaron released her to rummage through the bags. He handed her a banana, the peel already started. As if she couldn't have done that herself. The man needed to chill out before she strangled him.

"Sorry for the brief visit, but we need to shove off. Too risky to linger." He stowed the grocery bags on deck, then took Ana's arm and speared a finger in Camille's direction. "I'm walking Ana up the dock. You don't move. I'll help you in the boat when I get back. No argument."

Yeah, right.

She hobbled along the side of the boat and took her first good look at it. It appeared smaller from the outside and practically brand-new. The metal shone, the windows were clean, the white hull was free of blemishes.

Then she noticed the boat's name. Raising her eyebrows, she stared in disbelief at the hot pink lettering. She read the words silently, then aloud, then silently again. Her laughter erupted first as a chortle deep in her lungs and rapidly devolved into waves of giggles with a touch of crazy thrown in—the kind of laughter she rarely, if ever, indulged in.

She couldn't help it.

Tears pooled in the corners of her eyes and her nose started to run. She laughed so hard that it soon made no sound, taking the form of silent full-body shudders that made her stomach muscles ache. She doubled over, bracing a hand on her good leg. She laughed so hard, she nearly forgot about her pain.

Aaron jogged into view. "What's wrong?"

He sounded worried, so she waved dismissively at him.

He set his hands on her shoulders. "Camille, are you laughing or crying?"

The concern in his voice made her laugh harder. She pointed a shaky finger at the boat.

"Oh, that." Aaron was smiling now, too. "Perfect name, isn't it? Kind of sums up our whole experience."

It took a few throat clearings before Camille could speak. "I have never, ever seen something so inappropriately named…and in hot pink to boot. It's like a floating joke. Who names their boat *that?*"

"An optimist?"

Well, that was about the funniest thing Aaron could have said. Camille's face contorted as she fell into another onslaught of unfettered giggles. Aaron pulled her into an easy embrace and she was too distracted by her giddiness to push him away. They rested their foreheads on each other's shoulders and let laughter overtake them.

When they were all laughed out, they broke apart and mopped their faces. Camille watched Aaron untie the boat from the dock. Then he lifted her into his arms and carried her on board the *Happily Ever After*.

Aaron pulled the boat away from the private marina slip that the previous owner had prepaid a year's rent for. It was a load off his mind to have a secure place to dock. Now he only had to worry about the minor detail of Camille's safety, he thought with halfhearted sarcasm, knowing how oppressively it weighed on his conscience.

As he rounded the jetty separating the marina from the rest of the bay, an expensive-looking powerboat cut in front of the yacht. The four men on board didn't fit. They neither looked wealthy, nor out for a pleasure cruise of the bay. As he considered them, all men on board except the captain drew guns.

Cursing, he wrenched the steering wheel to the left and

maxed the throttle. With a great rumbling, the yacht accelerated, but it was not a craft built for speed or tight maneuverability. Though he pushed their lumbering floating house to its max speed in the glassy water, the powerboat easily caught up.

"What're you doing?" Camille called behind him.

"They found us. Get your gun."

Side by side, the boats flew toward the mouth of the bay, dodging sailboats and fishing boats, buoys and kayaks.

Camille appeared again, armed with a rifle. She held up a grenade. "Get us in a position to use it."

While Aaron negotiated the bay, she crouched along the side wall of the bridge and shot a dozen or so rounds at the powerboat. She ducked as their weapons fired in response, then peered back over the edge.

"They're trying to board our boat," she yelled, squeezing off another volley of rounds. Bits of fiberglass rained on Aaron as the men returned fire.

Outrunning the powerboat was impossible. If they were going to survive, Aaron had to be smarter than the men trying to overtake them. In the distance, a beastly freighter laden with huge red-and-yellow shipping containers surged through the water.

"Keep them off our boat," he called to Camille. "I have a plan."

"Got it." She tipped her rifle over the railing and fired.

Aaron angled the yacht straight at the freighter's bow in a deadly game of chicken. As he knew it would, the powerboat corrected its angle to match the yacht. Neck and neck, they careened toward the freighter with alarming speed.

When they were within a few hundred yards of the container ship, he shouted, "Get ready to throw that grenade."

One at a time, Aaron wiped his sweaty palms on his jeans. He was an inexperienced boat captain and this next move would be a feat of boating expertise if he pulled it off.

If he didn't, he and Camille were about to smash headfirst into a shipping barge.

"Ready, Cam?"

"Ready."

Fifty feet to impact. Forty. The barge's horn blasted a warning.

Thirty feet. Fifteen.

"Now! Now!"

He couldn't look to see if Camille threw the grenade, or if it reached its target. The powerboat peeled off to the left side of the freighter as Aaron wrenched the wheel to the right, close enough to the ship to see the gray-green barnacles on its hull.

The yacht lurched and bucked in the wake of the freighter as a loud explosion boomed all around them. Black smoke curled into the sky from the other side of the ship. Camille hit her mark. As he raced for the open ocean, Aaron glanced over his shoulder at the skeleton of the speedboat, spewing fire and sinking into the bay.

Fury uncoiled in his gut. Every move they made, someone got the jump on them. Well, no more. Aaron's tolerance for playing defense had reached its threshold. How could they rescue a child when they could barely survive a grocery run to shore? How would they ever be free with a faceless enemy anticipating their every move and making the first strike?

Camille flopped into the cocaptain's chair. "It's like they were waiting for me at the Gigante Market. And now this. It can't be a coincidence." She sat a little straighter. "Ana…"

"Maybe. For all we know, the guy who sold me the boat tipped off the cartel about his slip in the marina. Or there's a rat on the task force leaking information. Anything's possible. From now on, we don't trust anyone—not ICE, not the SDPD, not Ana. We've got each other, Cam, and that's it."

After anchoring the yacht in the lee of one of the numerous uninhabited islands offshore, Aaron opened the package from Nicholas Wells. At the dining table, he and Camille leafed through a gray binder outlining the top operatives of the Cortez Cartel's weapon-smuggling unit, complete with names, aliases and photos.

Now that they'd decided not to trust Ana, Aaron was prepared to disregard her tip about the cartel's operations in La Paz's commercial port, but Wells seconded the intel in a handwritten note he'd included in the package. He and Camille would need to watch their backs and go in heavily armed, but the lead was too significant to ignore.

He watched Camille study the folder, her sharp gaze taking in the data with the practiced eye of a cop and a keen intelligence that never ceased to awe him, her slender fingers skimming the photographs. Her thick, brown hair fell like a curtain between them. It would be so easy to rake his fingers through it and tip her head back to expose the delicate length of her throat. He would taste her. He would drink his fill. And maybe those fingers would wrap around his shoulders and cling to him.

He wanted her to cling to him. And not just with those perfect fingers, but with her whole self. Someday soon, he vowed. He would have her in his arms, in their bed, for as long as he wanted, without the pressure of survival hanging over them. He shook his head, floored by the direction of his thoughts. Never in a million years would he have imagined he'd wish for more time with Camille Fisher, of all people.

All he knew was that sometime since they'd been taken to Mexico, his feelings for her had shifted in a catastrophic way. What he planned to do about it, he had no idea. For now, his only plan was keeping them alive and finding Rosalia Perez. He'd worry about the rest later.

"This guy, Eduardo Vasillo," she said, tapping a photograph. "He's one of the men who attacked me in the market."

He forced his mind to stay focused on the photograph—not Camille's fingers or hair.

"Sal de Largo," she went on, pointing to another picture on the page. "He was one of my attackers, too."

Aaron slipped the photographs from their pockets and crumpled them up. "We don't have to worry about them anymore. Let's see if anyone else looks familiar."

She turned the page. With how fast everything had happened in the past few days, the details of their captors' appearances were fuzzy in their memories. Every face, that was, except El Ocho, Rodrigo Perez, whose image Aaron recognized from the photograph Dreyer shared at his last task-force meeting. Perez wasn't the cartel boss, that was Alejandro Milán, but trapping Milán was virtually impossible, as the man was a ghost. If it could have been done, then either the Mexican government would have arrested him or a rival cartel would have killed him already.

The wheels were turning in Aaron's head. Sick of playing defense, he was hungry for battle. He was going to personally rescue Rosalia and take down Rodrigo Perez. And once Perez's minions were good and confused, they would scatter, and Aaron and Camille would be free.

Chapter 10

Three days later, Aaron woke before dawn. His erection was painful this time, throbbing with awareness of the woman sleeping mere inches away. He palmed it. It was hard as steel beneath his fingers. He could slip away to the bathroom for some temporary relief, but any cure he administered would be fleeting at best. After all, when he was done, he'd return to bed and it would start all over again. He let go and propped his hands behind his head.

Time to embrace the pain.

He wanted her badly. Every day, every night. It wasn't only her strength or her mouthwatering body that drew him to her, but every single damn thing about her, good and bad, pleasant and unpleasant. Everything.

The prosaic hours of her recovery had left Aaron with nothing to do but concentrate on her. Even his dreams wouldn't grant him a reprieve. Tonight's dream had been achingly vivid. Truth was, he was starting to hate the bed they shared. Because every night, she was there—close enough to touch, yet with such a wall of ice around her heart that breaching it seemed impossible.

The worst part was he felt possessive of her in a primitive way—which was royally disturbing for a modern, pro-feminist guy like he thought he was. The feeling had built to the point that he caught himself thinking he *owned* her body, proudly assessing and cataloging her attributes in his mind. From the mole on the top of her right foot to her slender fingers to the baby-fine hair at her neck, with each new detail he discovered, he simply thought, *that's mine.*

Her fleeting moments of vulnerability especially belonged to him. He'd seen her scared and sleepy, nervous and in pain, both furious and in the throes of uncontrollable giggles. These glimpses of her soul filled him with the kind of puffed-up machismo that declared *no other man knows her this way, only me.* And wasn't that a disquieting thought?

Holding her while they slept had devolved into yet another primordial demonstration of his ownership—as if, as a holdover of some ancient instinct passed down through thousands of years of male genes, he was protecting what was his. She was turning him into a caveman.

And she couldn't be more indifferent to him. She was impervious to flattery, chivalry, humor and all other types of flirting. He had to find a way to break the ice wall because his tolerance for her disinterest had reached its threshold. With the way they were risking their lives, he'd be damned if he spent many more nights trapped in another kind of torture. She was his and it was time she figured it out.

He just needed a better strategy.

Camille's bottom rustled against his thigh, the feel of which was both torturous and, though he fought hard to deny it, as necessary as breathing. Letting out a frustrated snort, he pulled her more snugly against him and stroked the fabric of her pajamas absentmindedly.

Maybe he'd been too subtle. Whenever she was nervous

or scared, he backed off to a safe distance. In retrospect, that was probably the worst thing he could have done. He'd given her too much space to deny what she felt, too much leeway to ignore their mutual attraction. It was time to drop the metaphorical hammer on her head.

He plodded from the room and climbed to the bridge, inhaling the crisp ocean air. Four days had passed since the Gigante Market shoot-out. Despite his dread at the notion, he could no longer justify bobbing in the lee of an uninhabited island for the sake of Camille's recovery. She no longer walked with a limp and the bruise on her cheek had subsided to a faint discoloration. It was time to return to shore and to the mission that threatened their lives at every turn.

After raising the anchor, he brought the boat to life and started the tedious drive through the bay to scope out a new marina slip to rent, paid for in cash under an alias. All the while, his mind remained fixed on the woman sleeping a few feet beneath him, plotting the details of her seduction.

La Paz had a large selection of private marinas for Aaron and Camille to choose from. They settled on one far enough from the commercial port to offer them a buffer should the cartel run periodic security sweeps around the vicinity of the port, but near enough to the main road that they could dock and set off on dirt bike if they caught a new lead.

Once docked, they zipped into town on their bike to pick up a can of white paint from a small hardware store. The flamboyant yacht name had given them a good laugh, but hot pink lettering and covert ops didn't jibe together. If Aaron and Camille wanted to stay alive and conduct a rescue, they needed to be as invisible as they could.

That accomplished, Camille sat on the bridge with Aaron as he braved the open water of the bay to reposition them as near to the commercial port as possible without arousing the suspicion of the police boats cruising the harbor or the machine gun-toting guards lining the dock terminal.

Maybe such tight security was standard, but Camille doubted it. "Guess the local law enforcement noticed our boat chase. We'll have to be even more careful not to get spotted. Going to Mexican jail would cramp my style."

"That makes two of us. I'll keep our boat inconspicuous. You get in the cabin and start looking for familiar faces or anything suspicious on the dock. The sooner we figure out if the cartel is operating out of the port, the sooner we can get the hell out of the line of fire."

Pichilingue, the so-named location of the commercial port and ferry landing, was really a short strip of land that jutted, hooklike, into the bay, creating a small, vegetation-free cove polluted with litter and oily water, overburdened with tall cranes and concrete piers. Presently command-ing the focus of the dock workers and cranes was a huge ferry with peeling white paint and faded red lettering on the side reading *Puerto Azul*. The back end of the ferry had been lowered to form a ramp for the waiting semitrucks, car freighters and civilian vehicles to drive on board.

Camille sat in the cabin with the gray binder on her lap and a pair of binoculars in hand, but even after two hours of looking, the stakeout hadn't yielded any results. Aaron had tucked the boat into the shadow of an anchored sport-fishing boat, which seemed to be keeping their profile low enough to escape notice.

Rapidly running out of patience, she repositioned to the rear of the cabin and shifted her focus away from the port, to the buildings beyond the dock fence line.

Bingo.

Within the jumble of warehouse buildings, at an angle that hadn't been visible before, two men in dark gray blaz-ers and black jeans paced between a shiny black sedan and a heavily graffitied building lined with roll-up metal doors.

Clearly, they were either waiting for something to happen or trying to make sure nothing did. Though neither displayed an obvious weapon, their stiff postures and shifty gazes spoke loud and clear of their capacity for menace.

She flipped through the folder from the ICE task force, comparing the men at the warehouse to the photos of the known cartel members.

She struck gold.

"Hello there, Carlos 'Two Down' Reyes," she muttered. Why he went by Two Down was an answer she hoped to never learn.

Tossing the binder aside, she pushed open the cabin door and opened her mouth to holler at Aaron about her discovery. But before she could speak, the yacht rumbled to life and started to move. Camille braced a hand on the bridge ladder as the boat picked up speed and flipped a U-turn.

"Hey, Aaron, what's happening?"

"Think we've been made by the harbor police."

Camille whirled around. Sure enough, a police vessel trailed them along the row of anchored ships. The captain lifted a radio to his mouth.

A loud curse reverberated from the bridge. The yacht engine roared and tipped as Aaron darted behind a barge. "We've got trouble in front of us, too."

Camille couldn't see any danger from the rear of the boat and hustled to the stateroom to look out the forward windows above the bed. Facing them head-on was a speedboat, as slick and tricked-out as the one they'd eluded three days earlier. Men with automatic rifles perched near the bow.

With her fist, Camille thumped the panel covering the secret cubby behind the headboard Aaron had punched out in case the police ever caught up to them and drew out an M16. She locked a magazine in place, loaded the chamber and shoved it into a pillowcase. No sense waving a high-powered automatic rifle at the police trailing them. Covered rifle in hand, she ran full-speed to the back of the boat and up to the bridge. Aaron wrenched the yacht into another sharp U-turn, tipping it perilously to one side as he tried to put some space between them and the other boat.

But no sooner had they made a one-eighty turn than the police vessel appeared in front of them.

Behind them, a quick succession of shots fired out. The men aboard the police vessel drew their firearms and aimed in their direction.

"Damn it," Aaron barked. "We're caught in the cross fire."

Camille looked from the men with guns behind them to the police with guns before them. "What do you say we introduce our friends here to each other and get the hell out of the way?"

"You got it." He pushed the throttle to max velocity. Camille glanced behind them to see the speedboat hot on their tail. A hundred feet from the police vessel, Aaron wrenched the steering wheel in a sharp turn and threaded the yacht between two fishing boats.

Gunfire and shouting exploded behind them. Aaron dropped the yacht to an inconspicuous speed, aimed it in the direction of their new marina slip and let out a long, slow exhale.

Burdened by the crazy urge to throw her arms around him, she plunged her hands in her pockets and nudged Aaron's leg with her foot. "Nice work, Captain."

"Yeah, well, I wish I didn't have a reason to show off my boating skills." He offered her a weary half smile and raked his fingers through his hair. Funny, Camille wanted to do the same. Her gaze dropped to his mouth. The kiss they shared on the ridge above the desert compound seemed a lifetime ago.

Maybe he noticed her looking because he glanced her way and set his hand on her thigh. Her breath catching, she slipped from beneath his grasp before his warmth had the chance to penetrate her jeans. Her bum leg ached again after so much running around, so she leaned against the rail. "I identified a cartel member, back at the warehouses near the port."

"Seriously?"

"Yeah. I was coming to tell you when the police showed up."

"We need to check that out right away. Let's dock the boat and double back on the bike."

They sped along the waterfront by bike. After chaining it to a fence several blocks from the warehouse, they crept the rest of the way by foot, winding through the maze of buildings in the glow of the fading sun.

Camille's leg was killing her. Normally, she could walk for ten minutes before pain set in. To her mortification, her stride began to hitch with a limp. Aaron shot her a concerned look, but pressed on without a word until the black sedan became visible the next building over. He led the way into a truck bed, then atop the cab, hoisting himself another four feet onto the flat roof of the building. Camille glared at the hand he offered.

"Stubborn woman. Give me your hand."

"Get out of my way. If you can't treat me like an equal, this isn't going to work."

"Fine, Camille. You win this round. Why accept help when you can struggle to do something yourself." He kept up a string of grumbling as he moved away from the edge on his hands and knees.

Camille pulled herself up without a problem, like she knew she could. They crawled the length of the building until they had a perfect line of sight to the sedan, the men and the roll-up door behind them.

"The roll-up door's opening," Aaron whispered.

A run-down, boxy white delivery truck lumbered out.

Camille huffed in frustration. "Crap. We can't get back to the bike in time to follow it." She stared at its rear bumper, memorizing the license plate number.

"Look where it's headed," Aaron said.

Sure enough, the truck drove through the entrance gate of the ferry terminal, waved in by the passive guard. It coasted past the line of waiting vehicles and up the ramp into the bowels of the ferry.

The two guards still stood outside the now-empty garage. Two Down looked restless, glancing at his watch every minute or so as the ferry engine came to life. The ramp closed. Another few minutes passed, then the ferry engines grew louder as it backed slowly away from the port.

Aaron tipped his head in the ship's direction. "Where do you suppose it's headed?"

"Wait—I remember reading this." She squinted up toward the sky, sifting through her memory of the La Paz map she'd studied while laid up with her bum knee. "Across the Sea of Cortez, to Mazatlán."

Before the ferry had cleared the mouth of the bay, a man strolled out from the shadows of the open garage.

"Good God," Camille muttered. "Rodrigo Perez." Her breath froze in her lungs and her eyes refused to blink. She inched toward the roof's edge, praying for a sign of Rosalia—a little girl's tinkling laugh, a flash of pink fabric, a toy, anything. Aaron clamped a hand on her arm, in either support or warning, she couldn't tell.

Perez was a short man with a broad, muscled build. He impatiently flicked a cigarette between the fingers of his black leather glove as Two Down opened the sedan's door for him.

Aaron tipped his head toward Camille so his lips brushed her earlobe as he whispered, "I'm going to go out on a limb and guess this is the distribution part of the cartel's weapons-smuggling operation."

Tiny bumps raised on the skin of Camille's arms and the back of her neck at the contact. She shifted, putting some necessary space between them, then did a quick scan for security cameras, finding none. "This is a conspicuous location for illegal activity. If you're right and this is the distribution point for weapons or drugs, then they're relying on some pretty flimsy security."

Two Down closed the warehouse unit and locked it with a chain and padlock.

"We could have that padlock off without breaking a sweat using a bolt cutter," she added.

"Maybe there's an alarm system."

"Or nothing of value inside. Makes me wonder where Perez relocated all those crates of weapons to after abandoning the desert compound. I don't think this is the spot."

"Maybe this is only a pick-up point, not long-term storage," Aaron said.

Camille kept her eyes on Perez. "I bet you anything their new storage facility is wherever that black sedan's headed. And I bet Rosalia's there, too."

Two Down climbed behind the wheel of the car and put it in gear. Camille scrambled away from the edge and crawled back the way they'd come as fast as her arms and legs would go. "Let's move. We can't lose this lead. Not when we're so close."

The sedan rolled toward the warehouse's east exit. Aaron and Camille hustled along the building, peeking over the edge for the truck they'd made use of before, but the road was empty. Nothing except blacktop at the end of a twelve-foot drop.

Aaron snagged Camille's elbow and whirled her to face him. "This is how it's going to be and you're not going to argue with me. I'm going to drop first and catch you. Got it?"

"You don't need—"

"Zip it. I get to win this one."

Before she could protest further, he backed over the edge on his stomach and dropped. Camille repeated the shimmy over the side into a dangle.

"Okay," Aaron said, "one…two…three."

She let go, hating the feel of the free fall. Then her arms were around Aaron's neck and his hands were on her butt. He flashed a white-toothed smile and gave her a squeeze.

"Remember your no-groping promise." She cringed at the hint of hysteria in her tone.

Aaron scoffed and set her on her feet. "That wasn't a grope. That was a catch." He took off in a flat run to the bike, calling over his shoulder, "Besides, that promise expired."

Camille trotted after him, teeth clenched against the pain. "Promises don't expire."

He doubled back for her on the bike. She reached for the helmet, but he pulled it away.

"Camille, that promise expired."

She lunged for the helmet and jerked it away from him. They'd have to argue about it later because they finally had a lead to run down. She vaulted onto the back of the bike and it took off with a spine-rattling whine.

And just like that, the hunt was on.

Chapter 11

As far as drinking establishments went, the bar Camille and Aaron had stared at for three hours was as hospitable as a crematorium. There were windows, or rather, pieces of glass framed in the graffitied wall that weren't clean enough to see through. A small sign named the place Casa del Perro Negro—House of the Black Dog—words even Camille could translate. Next to the sign was a crudely painted silhouette of what Camille assumed was a black dog, but looked more like a goat, its stubby tail up and its mouth open.

The black sedan had entered a garage on the side of the two-story building that housed the bar and otherwise appeared vacant. The oddity of the building, with its uniformly closed curtains, dusty front stoop and lack of activity, sent up a red flag in Camille's mind. Something about this place was *wrong*.

Before settling at the taquería, they'd circled the block on the bike. A dead-end alley cut through one side of the building, guarded by a single, large Latino man neither Camille nor Aaron recognized. They continued around to the taquería, purchased warm bottles of cola and settled at a window table. Their main focus was on two equally huge men, probably bouncers, who perched on stools on either side of the bar's entrance.

As darkness settled over the city and the bouncers crossed their arms over their chests and hunkered down like birds preparing to sleep, Camille and Aaron grew restless. In their three-hour surveillance, not a single person had come or gone from the place.

"Perez and his crew have been inside for hours," Aaron said quietly. "That's a long time to sit in a bar."

"Makes me wonder if it's really a bar."

Aaron rubbed his chin. "Next time Perez and his men leave, I'd like to check it out."

"Me, too. I hate this. Rosalia could be in there, only a couple hundred feet away from us. I've got an idea, but we'll need to go shopping first. We can come back tomorrow, fully armed."

"Sounds like a date."

As they walked to the bike they'd chained in an alley several blocks away, Aaron draped his arm loosely around Camille's shoulders and kissed her temple. He was probably attempting to blend in with other couples they'd seen out for strolls, enjoying the crisp, clear evening. Even still, he ought not to confuse her heart that way, with casual tenderness that meant nothing to him.

When he kissed her a second time, she ground to a halt, twisting free of his arm. "Is this about what you said earlier? That your promises to me expired?"

"They have."

Camille's stomach tightened uncomfortably. It took her a good thirty seconds to wind her anger up. When it did, she grabbed his jacket by the collar and dragged him into the shadows of the nearest alley. Wagging a finger like a knife in front of his face, she let it rip.

"Allow me to send a message straight to your bloated ego, Aaron. You don't get to do whatever you want. When a woman says no, you back off. Rules don't expire because you think they should, you entitled jerk. I told you once and I'm telling you again now—no kissing, no groping. In fact, no touching at all."

He brushed her lips with his thumb. "You sure that's what you want?"

"Goddamn it," she shrieked, sweeping her leg across his to trip him. He let out a surprised howl and hit the ground on his knees.

Then her foot was on his back, pushing him to his stomach. She ground her knee into his ribs while twisting his right arm behind him at an awkward angle, pinning him.

"I hope I've got your attention, because it's the last time I'm going to say this. Stop. Touching. Me. From now on, you'll show me the respect I deserve. Got it?"

"You've made your point."

"Good."

"But I have a question. How will you be punishing me if I touch you again?"

"Damn it, Aaron, you're in no position to be condescending." She tugged on his twisted arm to illustrate her point.

"Okay, okay. Ouch."

She released him and stood. She hadn't meant to lose her cool and was sorry she'd hurt him, but he was hurting her more than he knew, his every touch and look a torturous reminder of what she could never have.

Aaron gingerly got to his feet, brushed gravel from his knees and shook out his arm. With an apologetic smile, he offered his hand to shake, which she accepted. Then he crushed her to the wall.

Camille gasped.

He held both her hands in one of his above her head and spanned his other hand along her collarbone. With his knees, he pried her legs apart and with his hips, he pinned her waist to the wall. Breathless with shock, Camille struggled to twist away from his grip, but he increased the pressure of his knees, hips and hands until she was helplessly immobile.

Helplessly aroused.

She shifted her hips to cradle his erection more comfortably and he reacted by pressing against her more adamantly. Squeezing her eyes shut, she rolled her head to the side, fighting a moan of pleasure as wet heat gathered between her thighs.

"It's your turn to listen now." He buried his nose in the hair behind her ear, making her toes curl. "Did it ever occur to you that I antagonize you on purpose, for the pleasure of seeing you all riled up? Hmm? Ever think of that?"

She couldn't look at him, much less speak, she was so angry with him for making her vulnerable, for exposing the depth of her attraction to him.

Well, *attraction* was a gross simplification. She wanted to taste every inch of his perfect body, to slip those flimsy boxers off his hips and discover exactly where the trail of hair under his navel led. She wanted Aaron so badly, she felt an emptiness that hurt worse than the memory of her accident, worse than her leg after running for hours from the Gigante Market.

He delicately brushed his closed lips over hers. It took all her strength not to open her mouth in offering.

"You see, when you're angry, you get a tiny crease between your eyebrows and the pulse on your neck is visible." He slid his fingers from her collarbone and found her pounding heartbeat at the base of her jaw.

"And when you're really, really angry like you are now, you flush the most fascinating shade of pink from your ears all the way to the skin between your breasts." He touched the tip of his tongue to her earlobe. When she shivered, he growled, "Every little bit of you is mine, Camille."

She kept her eyes closed, fighting hard to ignore the feel of his hands and mouth.

He pushed away from the wall. "You want me to quit riling you up? Stop looking so damned tempting every time you're mad."

He strode from the alley.

Camille sagged against the wall. Her body hummed with residual sensation, as though his tongue still lingered on her ear and the hard length of him still pressed against her. The urge to touch herself in the places that still tingled was overwhelming. She resisted, flattening her palms against the rough stucco behind her.

After a few more gulps of air, she pushed away from the wall and jogged to catch up with him, careful to keep a car's length of space between them until the moment she had no choice but to mount the bike behind him and secure her arms around his warm, hard body for the drive to the store for supplies for the morning's operation.

Camille was working way too hard, that was for sure. Ignoring someone on a thirty-three foot yacht with one bathroom and only a handful of places to sit was exhausting. She devoted all her energy for the rest of the night toward that end. When Aaron sat at the dining table, she relocated to the bridge. When he climbed to the bridge, smiling his million-watt dimpled smile, she returned to the cabin.

Infinitely relieved when he turned off the stateroom light and climbed into bed, Camille opted for the sofa. As she lay there, trying desperately to get comfortable on the narrow cushions, she had plenty of time to think. Aaron had, in essence, propositioned her, which she decided was the culmination of two things. One, she didn't fall all over him like the rest of the female population, which he undoubtedly considered a challenge. And two, this was probably the longest he'd gone without sex and Camille was the closest warm body. Sure, she let him hold her while they slept, but that was different. That was… Well, she wasn't sure why she'd let him get away with that, but she certainly wasn't going to let it happen again.

No matter the reason behind Aaron's behavior, Camille needed to be more diligent in her effort to keep her distance from him. It wasn't about holding a grudge or hoping for an apology, it was about preserving the last shreds of her heart from the man she'd wanted beyond reason from the moment she met him, the man who disliked her for two straight years until he was trapped with her in Mexico.

She couldn't stand the idea of becoming his temporary, forgettable relief—not even if it meant the end of her long-maligned and embarrassing virginity.

She'd saved her virginity like a jewel in high school. In college, when it no longer meant so much to her, she feared her inexperience would make her look the fool. Then the accident took away years of her life. Time and opportunities slipped by her until the potential embarrassment of revealing her inexperience trumped her curiosity and desire for sex. As if any men were waiting in line for the privilege.

Well, a man was waiting in line now.

But she cared too much about him to give herself freely, not when she meant nothing to him in return. Hugging herself, she stared at the night sky through the window above the sofa. *Rosalia, I'm going to find you. I swear. And then I'm going to get as far away from Aaron Montgomery as I can. Before my heart shatters any more than it already has.*

After two hours of tossing and turning and agonizing over things she could never have, Aaron appeared above her.

"I'm ignoring you."

"I noticed."

"Go away and let me sleep."

"You're not getting any more sleep than I am, Camille." He worked his hands underneath her and lifted her into his arms. She considered fighting him but knew she'd only be fooling herself to deny that she'd let him do whatever he wanted.

"What are you doing?" she asked.

"Putting you back where you belong so we can get some rest."

"Oh." He only wanted to sleep. She was relieved...wasn't she?

He laid her on the bed and, instead of walking around to his side, had the audacity to climb over her—but only partially. His left leg and arm never made it over, but remained draped across her as if she was the world's first living, breathing full-body pillow.

"Mmm...that's better," he hummed softly, burrowing his face in her hair.

Camille stifled her own contented sigh.

Maybe she was approaching her needs all wrong. All her self-protection and fear of failure wasn't getting her very far in life. As she lay there in Aaron's embrace, on the precipice of sleep, she felt a shift in her perspective, as if the right sequence of numbers had finally been entered into the combination lock of a vault and it sat, ready to be opened. Perhaps it was time to set aside her fear. Perhaps it was time to change her life for the better.

Camille hated birthday celebrations. She hated the singling out, the special designation of a person not on the basis of merit, but simply because that person had survived another year. This distaste extended to other people's birthdays, but her own was the worst.

As a child, she begged her parents yearly to forgo her party. They compromised, agreeing to never mention her birthday to anyone outside the family so long as she accepted the fact that every February 20, she would endure cake and presents and singing and specialness, if only at their kitchen table.

It never occurred to her to tell Aaron today was her birthday. Not that she took turning thirty lightly. That she had survived to see this day was a milestone more significant than any other in her life. She just planned to mark the occasion privately.

As her gift, she had decided to reboot her mess of a life—assuming she made it out of Mexico alive. First off, she was going to quit her job. The police force had nothing left to offer her. She had enough money, both in savings and her portion of stolen cartel cash, that she could do anything she wanted, go anywhere she pleased.

She refused to live in fear anymore. If she survived Mexico, she wouldn't waste the rest of her life stubbornly clinging to her pride at the forfeit of her happiness. Aaron had been right, it was time she figured out how to be happy. No more laps in a pool, no more thankless job, no more lonely apartment. Maybe she'd take up scuba diving. Maybe she'd visit all seven continents. She definitely wanted to try skydiving again.

She rubbed the sleep from her eyes and sat up in bed. There was little point in dreaming of the future with a full day of cartel-hunting, child-rescuing danger ahead of her.

Today they were stealing inside the House of the Black Dog.

"Cam?" Aaron ducked his head through the stateroom door. "I'm docking the boat."

"I'll be ready."

Like the day she acted as police spokesperson for Rosalia's kidnapping, today she'd be costuming up again. She fished through the bag of items they bought the night before at Walmart. Grabbing the bikini, she headed to the bathroom.

An hour later, Camille and Aaron stood across the street from the bar at a bus stop, trying to look inconspicuous.

Aaron frowned. "Hmph. I don't think I like you wearing makeup. I mean, you're still beautiful, you always are, but it's not…you."

Camille, covered in a long coat, scowled as she balanced precariously in the cheaply made, strappy black heels that were digging into her feet. Walmart was a great source for many things, but a mecca for shoes it was not.

"I'd rather you didn't critique my appearance." She winced at the hostility in her voice, but the shoes were making her grumpy.

Looking serenely at her, Aaron slid an arm around her waist and leaned closer.

"Camille." His whisper was as soft as a caress. "You are the most beautiful woman I've ever seen."

This wasn't how she wanted it to be between them. She didn't want him to lavish her with sweet words that were little lies. It hurt too much.

"Don't do that. Please." She squirmed in a halfhearted effort to break free of his grip, but she didn't want to draw attention from passersby.

"You don't want to hear it, I know. We haven't always gotten along, but…" His lips grazed her temple and nipped at her ear.

Camille's mouth went dry. She may have stopped breathing but it was hard to tell with the way her pulse started racing and her insides grew heavy, as if all her blood was relocating to the sensitive juncture of her thighs. What had she been about to say? She couldn't remember.

"I'm trying to be patient," Aaron murmured, "so I'm going to give you a little more time to think about what you want."

"What I want?" This was not going according to plan. She was supposed to be fending off his advances. While she was grateful that she retained the ability to speak, she couldn't get her brain past the urge to tear his clothes off.

"The clock's ticking, Camille."

"What?" Did she miss something? What clock?

"What I'm saying is, you've got a little more time to think about what you want before I haul you onto our bed and give you what I know you need."

Her knees wobbled. She was saved from having to form coherent thoughts by the opening of the garage door on the side of the building and the emergence of a familiar sedan.

Aaron released his hold on her waist. "Showtime."

Camille tried to snap her body out of its trance, but it had frozen.

"Camille? Let's go."

"Just a sec." She blinked, trying to clear the fuzz from her mind.

The sedan drove southeast, toward Pichilingue. As soon as it disappeared, Aaron patiently removed her hand from his shirt collar, one finger at a time.

Aaron watched Camille walk south in order to approach the alley from the opposite direction. Once she was out of view, he walked the dirt bike around the north side and propped it against the wall a few feet from the alley entrance.

He gripped his gun, concealing it inside his jacket. Then he waited anxiously for Camille to reappear. She'd call him a chauvinistic jackass again for entertaining such a thought, but he hated to have her out of his sight for even a minute. As his anxiety mounted, she rounded the corner, walking toward him. The entrance of the alley gaped between them like a chasm. Setting her voluminous orange beach bag on the ground, she removed her coat.

Aaron's mouth went dry. He'd seen the red swimsuit she purchased, but he hadn't thought much about how it would actually look painted on her creamy-skinned, curvaceous body. Oblivious to his dismay, she gave him a determined nod and stumbled purposefully, spilling the contents of the bag. Hair spray, lipsticks and other womanly goodies rolled, exactly as planned, into the alley. Camille chased after the scattering contents, bridging the distance to the guard.

Sure enough, as soon as he caught sight of her, the man rose from his stool and sauntered her way, lecherously appraising her body. Thank God Camille didn't understand Spanish. Aaron, on the other hand, understood every single filthy word. While her bikini had been an unwelcome surprise, he was even less prepared for the rage that surged through him as he listened to the guard demean her.

The plan was for Aaron to hold his shot until the guard was standing near the Dumpsters in the middle of the alley. Aaron stood with his finger on the trigger of his gun and tried to be patient. But when the guard unzipped his pants and told Camille to get on her knees like the whore she was, Aaron pivoted into view and put two bullets through his chest.

Camille looked questioningly at Aaron but said nothing. They dragged the body between the Dumpsters, out of view from the street. While Aaron repositioned the bike in the alley for a getaway vehicle, Camille changed into sneakers, a T-shirt and shorts from her bag. She dropped the heels in the Dumpster, slung her rifle over her shoulder and got out a handgun with silencer—going from eye candy to warrior in seconds flat.

With Camille in the lead, they skulked into the bar

Chapter 12

The bar was empty.

No people, no tables or chairs, no alcohol. Exchanging a worried look with Camille, Aaron checked the solitary bathroom—empty. They took positions against the wall next to the front door. He pushed it open a few inches to get the bouncers' attention and stepped back into the shadows, hoping the men were curious sorts.

They were.

The bouncers advanced into the room with their guns drawn. Aaron aimed, as did Camille, only her gun hand shook so badly he couldn't see how she'd hit her target. Damn. He forgot about that complication. Without waiting to see if she got control of her aim, he shot both guards in the back. Camille fired, but her bullet lodged in the wall behind the bar.

She closed her eyes. When she reopened them, she nodded to Aaron with a look of cool determination. He squeezed her shoulder in a show of encouragement and motioned to the interior door on the far side of the room.

He tested the knob. Unlocked. Widening his stance, he put his finger on the trigger of his gun and gestured for Camille to open the door.

It only took a second to realize what a mistake they'd made.

At least a half dozen sets of eyes fixed on them from inside the room, which had been made up to look like a living room with sofas and a television. A little girl was seated on the floor.

At the first crack of gunfire from the room, Camille cursed and took off in a dead run for the alley, with Aaron outpacing her through the bar and onto the bike. Their helmets lay abandoned in the alley as they peeled away.

In no time, two Jeeps pulled into view, tailing Aaron and Camille and gaining ground fast. Aaron gunned it, but the Jeeps kept up with the punishing pace.

They flew through the city, negotiating the cars and people, ignoring stoplights and signs. Aaron shot west through the outlying neighborhoods of town where the roads were wider and less crowded. He took every possible shortcut through dirt lots and alleys but could not lose the Jeeps.

They sped past the airport, then the highway that marked the last vestiges of civilization, into the open desert. The landscape of Baja was denser than the California desert, but Aaron was banking on his experience with all-terrain vehicles as a Park Ranger to gain the advantage.

The butt of Camille's rifle poked him in the ribs. Aaron tried to keep the bike steady while she sprayed a quick staccato of shots. A loud screech and clattering sounded behind them.

"What's happening?" he yelled.

"One Jeep down, one to go."

The men in the remaining Jeep fired back. It sounded as though they only had handguns, but a bullet was a bullet.

Camille and Aaron's best hope of survival was to stay unpredictable. With that in mind, Aaron took each foothill fast, jumping dried riverbeds and weaving around the shrubs and rocks while Camille continued to fire.

"How many men?" he asked.

"Three—the driver and two shooters." They were fired at twice and Camille responded with another cluster of shots. "Check that, one shooter now."

Aaron swerved around a boulder the size of a shack and realized too late they were approaching a huge fissure in the earth too wide to jump and too near to stop or turn. Putting on the brakes, he pushed Camille off the bike and attempted a controlled crash. The momentum was too great. He and the downed bike skidded into the fissure.

Camille crawled to the edge. "Aaron!"

He clung to a tiny outcropping on the inner wall, his shoes pedaling against the side.

The rumble of an engine warned them of the Jeep's approach.

"Stay there," she whispered, scrambling out of view. Her rifle discharged a dozen more rounds. Aaron prayed she was hidden behind a boulder as the men's return fire echoed through the fissure.

The Jeep's engine cut out and a man shouted in English at Camille to freeze. A shuffle of feet on the sandy ground made Aaron brace for discovery, but no one peeked over the edge. Maybe they didn't realize he was there.

A sharp smack of flesh hitting flesh reverberated in the quiet, and Camille grunted softly.

They were hitting her. The men were hitting his Camille.

Aaron dug deep, finding a strength he didn't know he

had. He pulled up on the ledge and got a toe on it, then a knee. He pocketed a handful of sand, then got out his gun.

Smack. A man's laughter.

"Is that all you got?" Camille sneered in a hoarse voice.

In a state of focused fury, Aaron surrendered to the most ancient, savage part of his being. He vaulted out of the fissure with gun drawn.

Only one man was hurting Camille. A body lay slumped over the Jeep's passenger door as blood pooled on the dirt below.

Aaron took aim at the short, mustachioed, middle-aged Mexican who had Camille by the hair, jamming her own rifle into her shoulder as she knelt on the ground. The man's eyes were wide, as if Aaron had surprised him. Good.

"Aaron, you idiot. You should have saved yourself. Now we'll both die."

Aaron ignored her. He sized up her captor and plotted his next move.

"Drop your gun or I kill her," the man shouted in heavily accented English. He sounded nervous, as if he was in way over his head. Aaron knew exactly how to play this guy. He took a few steps forward.

"Forget about me. Kill him."

Unable to resist the impulse, he snorted. "You're killin' me with your whole martyr thing, Cam." He put his hand in his pocket as casually as possible, gathering sand.

"Drop the gun...now," the man hollered.

Aaron raised his arms in surrender, then took a few more steps forward and placed his gun on the ground too near to Camille for her captor to let it stay there. When the man let go of her hair and reached for the gun, Aaron flung the sand into his eyes, blinding him. Grabbing the rifle's nose, he deflected it into the sand as it fired.

The man doubled over with his hands covering his face, shrieking in pain. Aaron gripped the handle of the spare gun he'd stashed in a makeshift holder between his shoulder blades. He killed the bastard with a single shot, right through his ear.

Camille, under the light of the full moon, glowed an ethereal shade of blue. She sat in the cocaptain's chair, clad in loose-fitting white pants and a white T-shirt, hugging herself and gazing at the distant sea, exactly as Aaron left her when he went to wash the sand and blood spatter from his hair and skin.

After driving the cartel's Jeep to the outskirts of town, they'd snagged a taxi ride to the marina. The whole time, Aaron's nerves were a jumble of live wires. He never took his hand off the gun hidden beneath his shirt, nor his eyes off their surroundings, anticipating ambush at every turn. Even on the boat, after he'd anchored in the cove of an uninhabited island two hours from the mouth of the bay, he still didn't feel safe.

He wasn't sure if he'd ever feel safe again.

They'd survived the day but in infiltrating the cartel's hideout and killing more of its operatives, the targets on their backs were bigger than ever.

When Aaron cleared his throat to alert Camille of his presence, she looked at him and shivered. He removed the black flannel shirt he'd donned over his T-shirt and held it out in offering. She shook her head.

"Don't argue with me. Not tonight."

After a moment's hesitation, she accepted the shirt. He helped her on with it, then settled in the captain's chair. The sight of Camille wearing his clothes was unexpectedly erotic. The collar pressed against her cheeks, accentuating the ivory glow of her skin and her slender fingers peeking out from the cuffs. Their eyes met and she shivered again.

Aaron felt the air surrounding them charge, crackling

with electric current. He swallowed, then gestured to her bare feet. "I'll bring you some socks."

Mechanically, he walked through the cabin and found a pair of her socks. Camille watched his approach with eyes as black as the flannel shirt, as deep as the night around her. He sat and swiveled her chair to face his.

With a racing pulse, he brought her feet to his lap and inched his fingers up the lengths of her calves inside her pants. He'd never touched her here, not like this.

"Aaron, stop." Her voice was breathy, aroused. He stopped but didn't release his hold on her leg. "I don't...I don't want..."

"Don't try to tell me you don't want me, Camille. I know you better than that."

He captured her right foot in his hands. It was velvet against his calloused palms.

"You don't know me at all."

What a load of crap she was feeding herself. He'd spent every moment of the past week memorizing her—from her body to the cadence of her speech, every sigh and every look. He'd lain awake each night listening to her breathe, drenching his senses with the feel and scent of her hair, her skin. He knew Camille Fisher as well as he knew himself, better perhaps. "What have you convinced yourself of? What's going on in that sharp mind of yours?"

"I..."

As she searched for words, he cradled her foot, warming it.

"I don't want this between us."

He tipped her chin up until she looked into his eyes. "Baby, it's already between us."

The torment in her expression spoke of a battle raging within her. She knew he was right.

"If you tell me to stop again, I will. But you know as well

as I do there's no changing the truth. Even if we never act on the way we feel, this will always be here between us."

She stiffened and, for a moment, Aaron thought he'd ruined his chance. His fingers froze on her foot. He sucked in a frustrated breath.

Her right hand twisted the flannel as she seemed to consider his words.

She met his gaze, her green eyes piercing, as if testing his merit, weighing his honor. *Trust me, Camille. Let me show you how we could be together.*

With a nod, she slipped low in the chair and her knees fell open. It was sexy as hell.

Releasing the breath he'd been holding, he slid both thumbs along the arch. Her breath stuttered. Suppressing a smile, he concentrated on her foot, kneading and exploring, rolling each toe and sliding his index finger between them. She squirmed and purred softly, a response that ignited within Aaron something wholly atavistic. Before this night was over, every secret little place on her, previously ignored, was going to be branded by him.

He brought her leg to his mouth and kissed the inside of her ankle, tasting it with his tongue. She slouched further in the chair and her legs gaped apart. Aaron froze, not trusting himself to move one millimeter until he overcame the urge to take her right then and there.

Once he regained mastery over himself, he scooted forward and guided her feet up the lengths of his thighs until her toes touched the crease of his hips. He lifted his eyes to gauge her demeanor again. A corner of her lips turned up in a lazy smile. It was all he needed to see.

He pulled her onto his lap so she was straddling him.

Their bodies and mouths united like water hitting hot oil, the power of two opposing forces colliding. They kissed violently, openmouthed, tongues pushing and testing, nostrils flared with the strain of breathing, each taking and consuming the other. Demanding more. Camille's hands were in Aaron's hair and around his neck, clinging to him.

This time, he couldn't stop his mouth from curling into a hard smile, or his eyes from reflecting the possessiveness radiating through him. He tugged on the collar of her shirt, exposing her shoulder, and feasted on her sweet skin, only half aware of her own exploration of him. Her mouth sucked at his neck and earlobe. Her fingers remained threaded through his hair except for every so often, when she framed his face with her hands and forced his mouth back to hers.

The ferocity of her passion was what he'd been waiting for night after torturous night. He wanted her to hunger the way he hungered. To need like he needed. He licked a trail from her collarbone to the skin between her breasts. She moaned and tipped her chin up, arching to him.

It had been worth the wait.

When he was ready to do away with her clothes, he lifted her off him, back into her own chair. Crossing her arms, she gazed at the horizon in a show of prideful restraint—as though she thought he was done with her. The crease between her eyebrows appeared and, even in the shadows, the hard clench of her jaw was apparent.

So strong, yet so fragile, she would never beg him for more. If he walked away at that moment, she'd never breathe a word about their kiss, never let the shield guarding her vulnerability crack. What happened to her that made her demand so little of others, so much of herself? It was a question for another time. Tonight, he had far more important discoveries to make.

He stroked her cheek and turned her face up to his.

"I'm going to take you to our bed and make love to you now."

It was harder than Camille expected to give herself over to passion from a safe emotional distance.

She'd sat on the bridge, replaying Aaron's words outside the bar that morning in her head, confused and aroused. Terrified. As far as birthday resolutions went, hers was off to a dismal start. As a gift to herself, she'd vowed to let go of the stilted, fearful woman she'd become. To experience life to the fullest. To discover happiness. And yet, she'd lingered on the bridge that night, too scared to face Aaron within the confines of the cabin, praying he'd leave her alone so she could ignore the desire that was eating her from the inside out.

Pathetic.

And then he was on the bridge, looming over her, his eyes dark with desire. She didn't want to accept his flannel shirt, knowing it would smell of him—and it had. Rich and masculine, clean. *Aaron.* The fabric was damp and hinted at the shampoo he'd used. She'd turned up the collar and inhaled.

His skilled hands had touched her in a way no man had before, but it was his words that tipped her over the edge.

There's no changing the truth. This will always be here between us.

He was right. No matter how desperately she fought against her feelings for him, they would never change. Never burn out. Never leave her at peace. She had only one way to combat the fear that held her back—to bulldoze straight through it. To strike it down as it had stricken her for too many years.

So what if her desire for Aaron terrified her? So what if she was one more in a long line of conquests? He'd made her an offer and she'd be a hypocrite not to take him up on it.

The minute their clothes came off, her lack of experience would be obvious. She only hoped she wouldn't have to admit how inexperienced she actually was. But if he figured it out, if her hymen was miraculously still intact…there might be no getting around the truth. But she was no longer willing to let fear and pride hold her back.

Happy birthday, girl.

Aaron wasn't making it easy on her, though. She'd banked on his goofy sense of humor to emerge, for him to infuse the experience with playful banter and teasing smiles, but tonight he was dead serious. Did he dive into all his conquests' skins as if he was having them for dinner?

Did he always call it *making love?*

To counter her rising anxiety, she resolved to do the opposite of her fearful instincts for the rest of the night. So after her shirt was dispatched to the cabin floor by Aaron with lightning-quick efficiency and her instincts demanded she call the whole thing off, she grabbed fistfuls of his shirt and ripped it over his head. Then she did what she'd longed to for two long years. She caressed every single muscle of his rippling abs.

They shuffled past the sofa while kissing. Aaron reached around her and punched on a light in the kitchenette.

"Turn around and put your hands on the table."

It was a command spoken softly, but a command nonetheless.

Despite the screaming protests of her instincts, she faced the table and set her palms on it, surprised at the pulse of pleasure it gave her to give up control to him. If she were keeping score, pleasure would be leading instinct two to nothing.

With his thumbs hooked in her waistband, Aaron shoved her pants to the ground. Pinning her to the table with his lower body, he dived into the skin of her neck, which was about the most delicious feeling Camille had ever experienced. She arched into his touch and when his teeth bit gently into the skin of her shoulder, she whimpered helplessly.

He unsnapped her bra and threw it on the table.

She twisted around, but he pushed her shoulder back and

gently, but firmly, took her wrist and replaced her hands on the table, adding a squeeze of admonition.

He knelt and ran a finger along the side hem of her panties, beneath her buttocks and around to the front, until only thin, damp fabric separated his finger from where she really wanted it. His tongue followed his finger. Hunching into her arms, Camille put her head down, dizzy with sensation.

His teeth nipped at her inner thigh. His nose brushed against the panties. She widened her stance, wanting desperately for him to bury his finger or tongue in her. But instead of lingering, his lips skimmed across her panties and he continued the trek around her other thigh.

Finally, he slid her panties down and stood. Setting his hands over hers, he lifted their entwined fingers and straightened so that they were looking at their reflection in the window. She didn't recognize the woman she saw, half-naked and flushed with passion. Her breasts hung in the forefront, her nipples hardened with arousal. He moved their hands as one to cup her breasts, so that, really, she was the one doing the holding and he was the puppet-master. They felt foreign in her hands, plump and sensual.

She looked past her reflection to Aaron and gasped in shock. His eyes were fierce, and the muscles of his arms twitched like they did when he was agitated. That threw her off. He was enjoying it, too, wasn't he? Where was the Aaron she knew, the one with the dimples and the joyous laugh? Was she doing something wrong?

"Aaron..."

"Hmm?"

"I... Are you—"

Words failed her as he moved their joined right hands between her thighs. He manipulated his hold so both their index fingers swirled over the swollen pearl of nerve endings made slick with honeyed wetness. She writhed, straining to increase the pressure on this most sensitive part of her. He worked their fingers expertly until the world around Camille disappeared. All that existed was her raw need and the tips of their fingers.

Release swept like a strike of lightning through her body. She threw her head against his shoulder with a cry, the ferocity of her climax rocking them both where they stood locked together.

"You're mine," he rumbled into her ear.

The intensity of his tone made her eyes snap open. She studied his reflection and saw his first smile of the night—a savage grin that left her wondering how dimples could look so wicked.

Overcome with self-awareness, her urge to put some distance between them was a powerful one. But her instincts hadn't done her a lick of good, so now was hardly the time to let fear take over. Scared as hell but too stubborn to quit, she sunk to her knees and unfastened his jeans. It was time to even the playing field.

The jeans were the easy part—button off, zipper down and a tug. It was the boxers underneath that gave her pause. She had no idea what to do with Aaron's erection. Or rather, she had a general idea, but not many specific details and zero experience. She braced herself for the big reveal of her naïveté, then dropped the boxers to the floor and drew a sharp breath.

She'd seen a few male appendages in her day, but she'd never seen anything like this. All the jokes she'd made over the years about his tricked-out sports car compensating for something now seemed ridiculously inappropriate.

Aaron was huge. Monster.

She hesitantly grazed the shaft with her finger and watched it bob in response. Emboldened, she moved to the tip, slid the foreskin back and closed her mouth over the head. His body dipped and he staggered back, slamming into the kitchen counter. The muscles of her core pulsed

with impatience, even as she grinned at the discovery that
she had the power to do that to him. Oh, this could easily
become her obsession, this piece of Aaron's anatomy.

Happy birthday, girl. Here's a bonus gift....

Before her exploration had barely begun, he pushed her
away. "You're going to have to torment me on your own
time." His voice was husky. "I've got other plans for you
tonight."

He led her down the stairs. The light from the kitchenette filtered onto the bed like a spotlight into which she was
tossed with alarming ease. Crawling up the length of her
body, he kicked her legs apart with his knees. Then, beginning with her breasts, he proceeded to drive her into a
frenzy with his tongue.

Moments before her second orgasm shattered her last
threads of control, two random thoughts floated across her
mind. The first was that if practice made perfect then maybe
she should thank Aaron for being such a male slut. And
the second was that she was an idiot for waiting so long to
have sex.

With an echoing scream, she clamped her thighs around
his head. He kept his tongue on her, riding her waves of
pleasure until they subsided, then kissed his way back up
her body. Breathing hard, he positioned himself on his knees
between her legs. She thought briefly about using protection
but dismissed the idea. They were fifty miles from shore,
fighting for their lives in a foreign country. They couldn't
simply dash to a store for supplies. The universe would just
have to forgive her this one indiscretion on her birthday, because short of the fires of hell rising up around them, she
wouldn't have stopped Aaron for anything.

He positioned himself at her entrance, then swirled his
fingertips through her moisture. With his thumb caressing
her tender flesh, he dipped his fingers inside her.

"You're so tight."

That was the understatement of the century.

His massive girth was bound to make this part a bit of a challenge. She tried to relax, determined to lose her virginity to Aaron no matter how long it took her body to accommodate him.

She wrapped her legs around his waist. "Is that a problem?" she teased.

The shadow of a smile crossed his face. He pressed forward gently, and she felt him hit a wall. Two sets of eyes flew open.

Chapter 13

"Is that...? Are you...?"

"Yes, I think it is. I'm a virgin." She screwed up her mouth in a wince. "Damn it. I have the worst luck in the world."

Thoughts swirled so furiously in Aaron's head that his brain seemed near the verge of exploding. He made to rock back on his heels, but the grip of Camille's legs around his hips proved unyielding. How could a woman as beautiful as Camille, surrounded by men on the job every day as she was, not once give herself over to passion? Or not even passion, but a down and dirty screw? Leave it to Little Miss Martyr to deny herself such a fundamental human need.

Still reeling, he met her brilliant green eyes and recognized a familiar determination in them.

"But I turned thirty today, so don't you think it's time I did something about it?"

That knocked the wind from his sails. And here he

thought they were making progress on the intimacy front. "Today's your birthday? Weren't you going to tell me?"

"I didn't see a reason to."

Ah, baby. What a way to live, inside herself, alone.

But no more.

She wouldn't be lonely again. Because she had him, and he knew on an elemental level that he would never let her go. He had no idea where the knowledge came from, or what it meant for their future, but it burned inside him as fiercely as his desire. And, oh, did he burn with desire for her. He looked down, drinking in her juicy curves, amazing breasts and full lips. Her tight, wet body ready to be claimed by him. She was a virgin. She was his to take.

Battling that caveman part of him urging him forward, he kissed her temple. His hands trembled and his muscles strained, holding back his body's demand. "Are you sure this is what you want?"

Cupping his cheeks, she searched his face. "More than anything."

At her answer, a feeling like a howl swept through him and he let go of his restraint. Thrusting deeply, he took her virginity.

She nuzzled her face against his shoulder. He held motionless but for the heavy rise and fall of his lungs. The significance of the moment crushed the last vestiges of the restless, spoiled boy he'd been before the kidnapping that changed everything, before he fell in love with Camille. "A part of you belongs to me now," he rasped, aware of his possessive tone but unable to prevent it.

"I know," she whispered softly, stroking his dampened hair away from his temple.

He took her mouth in a kiss laced with only the slightest suggestion of tenderness. Then he began to move, determined to coax Camille's body toward ecstasy for the third time that night.

* * *

The longer Camille lay in Aaron's arms, listening to his even breathing, the worse she felt. She should have known better than to give her body to a man she cared about, not when it was just another roll in the hay for him. What a mess she'd created.

It turned out her greatest naïveté wasn't that of sexual inexperience, but of the way she'd believed she could separate her physical needs from her emotional ones. On the verge of a panic attack, she slid out of the room and found her clothes on the dark cabin floor.

The kitchen light turned on.

"Come back to bed," Aaron said quietly.

Camille glanced up and then away. She couldn't look at his perfect, nude body—such a painful reminder of how far out of her league he was. "Look, you don't need to pretend, not with me."

"What do you mean?"

"I'm not stupid. I knew I'd be another notch on your bedpost and I thought that would be okay. I didn't expect to feel so cheap afterward." She swallowed a lump in her throat.

Aaron tugged on her wrist, dragging her against him. "I won't let you belittle what happened here tonight. Look at me, Camille."

She could not. Never in her life had she felt so weak. And over what—a man?

He waited silently until she decided to get the inevitable battle over with and met his eyes.

"You don't think you mean anything to me, is that it?"

"Yeah, that's it."

He huffed. "Every single time I've had to make a choice, I've chosen you. Think about that. I've been with you every step you've taken and I've given you everything I have to give—my trust, my support, whatever is left of my life."

"That's your pride talking, Aaron. You can't stand that

I'm not falling all over myself with gratitude for the privilege of being bedded by you." A noise akin to thunder rolled through him. Camille felt the vibrations through her fists. Her resolve wavered, but it was too late to turn back. She'd dug her own grave and it was time to get in it. "Don't get me wrong, I'm relieved to be rid of my virginity, but that's all tonight was about. Nothing more."

Aaron's eyes were hard as stone. "Let me get this straight. You were using me?"

"Right." Oh, the lies she told.

"You don't need anyone, is that it?"

"I don't need anyone, especially you."

He pressed his forehead against her temple, his lips close to her ear. "Liar."

The word rippled through her like a puff of acrid smoke. She pushed against him. "Let me go." She had to get out of the situation before she broke down and begged him to forgive her.

His grip on her intensified before he abruptly released her. She stumbled back.

Aaron's features had taken on a sheen of anger, his eyes narrow, his muscles rigid. "I'm not going to beg you to be with me." His voice was tight with control. "But this conversation is far from over. Consider yourself warned."

He walked into the stateroom and shut the door.

Camille let out the breath she'd been holding and closed her eyes. Like everything else in her life, her thirtieth birthday had gone horribly wrong. Sure, she was no longer a virgin, but the price to her heart had been too steep.

According to the *Los Angeles Times,* Camille and Aaron were dead.

Three days after Camille's birthday, Aaron read the headline at a marina newsstand after picking up a package from Dreyer at a shipping store. Doing his best to play it cool, he piled a stack of local and international newspapers into his arms and handed a large bill to the cashier before hurrying back on board.

They'd laid low in the waters north of La Paz without daring to venture near the city until they'd formulated a new plan. It had taken them a day of brainstorming, but they had one now and it was worth breaking their own rule of trusting no one to contact Dreyer. Aaron didn't actually think Dreyer was the one who'd ratted their location out to the cartel, but since they'd cut off communications with the outside world, the ambushes had stopped. There was no arguing with results like that. Still, their plan required technological equipment neither of them were savvy enough to create from scratch.

Dreyer supported their idea, which was why a small cardboard box now sat on the kitchen counter. But before dealing with that, Aaron was itching to read what the newspapers had to say about him.

At the dining table, he pored over the papers. On the front page of the *L.A. Times,* a color photo of Rosalia's mother clutching a picture of her daughter at a candlelight vigil accompanied an article on the stalled negotiations between the Mexican and American governments on the girl's recovery. Aaron's heart clenched at the sobering reminder of what he and Camille were fighting for.

He turned the page and blinked back, caught off guard by a black-and-white still picture from a grainy video of a crowd of masked, armed men watching two bodies burn on a pyre. "Hey, Camille, according to the *Times,* the Cortez Cartel released a video of our deaths."

"Is that so?" She angled for a better view. "Looks like the paper's convinced the bodies are us. That's pretty shoddy journalism."

"The journalist tacks on a disclaimer that no indisputable proof of the bodies' identities has emerged, but—the journalist asks—why would the cartel lie about the murder of two Americans instead of continuing to use their captives as leverage?"

"I'm guessing it's because they don't want to show weakness by admitting their prisoners escaped."

Aaron skimmed a Mexican paper. "Get this—according to this paper, the only logical explanation for escalating violence in La Paz is that a rival cartel has moved in. Only no cartel—including the powerful La Mérida Cartel—had claimed responsibility for the violence. So the papers are making the leap of logic that an unknown cartel had entered the fray. The Ghost Cartel."

Camille broke out in laughter so genuine that Aaron stopped reading to watch the way her face lit up. God, she was beautiful. "I can't believe we've earned a nickname. That's terrible."

Aaron forced his gaze back to the paper before she had a chance to notice him gawking. "Listen to this. Mexican authorities' latest grisly discovery of three bodies in a Dumpster behind what appeared to be an abandoned hideout disguised as a bar brings the body count of dead Cortez operatives to nine in fourteen days. The city of La Paz is on the verge of a lockdown, with the mayor threatening curfews and stoppages of airline flights should the bloodshed continue."

"You need to call Dreyer, make sure our families know we're alive and well."

"When we spoke yesterday, he assured me our families have been warned that ICE is going to keep our escape on the down low. Hopefully they don't believe everything they read."

With an incredulous shake of his head, Aaron set the newspapers aside. Reading about his own death was bizarre, but not the only extraordinary thing to happen to Aaron while in Mexico. He didn't believe in fate and he definitely didn't believe in luck, but he'd always believed in his ability to create success by keeping his eyes open for unexpected opportunities. It was a fine theory and had led to many wonderful experiences in his life…right up until he realized that for two full years, he'd been blind to the fact that the woman he'd convinced himself to hate was actually his soul mate.

The tricky part was waiting for her to admit they belonged together. He could tell that on some level she'd figured it out…and was scared witless about it.

He wasn't sure how to alleviate her fears, wasn't even sure what she was afraid of and couldn't decide how to start a conversation about it. Would professing his love help the situation or scare her more? Until he figured it out, he'd decided to give her a lot of space, which was pretty much torture given how small the yacht was. He didn't touch her, tried not to watch her and didn't hassle her about her choice to spend nights on the sofa, though he suffered from absolute sleeplessness and knew she did the same.

Feigning indifference to her bordered on intolerable, so instead Aaron gave all his energy over to rescuing Rosalia Perez and digging up enough intel on the Cortez Cartel to shut down the cartel's weapons-smuggling operation and put Rodrigo Perez behind bars for life.

With that goal in mind, he opened the package from Dreyer and poured a state-of-the-art tracking device and GPS locator onto the table. "Looks good. Now we have to figure out how to get close enough to the cartel delivery truck to put this on."

Camille lifted the device, studying it. "The next ferry departure will be Tuesday. If the delivery truck's on it, it'll be locked up for the eighteen-hour trip. That's our window. That's when we plant the device."

"I like the way you think."

"Only problem is getting on board the ferry without ID."

"Very few people are above accepting a bribe if it's big enough. Hopefully that includes the ferry staff. I'm willing to risk it if you are."

"I am, absolutely."

"We can hire a private charter to Mazatlán. I've seen plenty of them around. Then we only need to bribe our way onto the ferry for the return trip."

Camille powered up the GPS locator. "I used a device like this on the job once upon a time. Unlike this model, that one had a self-destruct feature. Jacob and I used the explosion as a diversion while we breached a security fence. I might not have been able to build a tracking device, but I could definitely manage a bomb. What do you think?"

"Have you ever built a bomb?" Aaron asked.

"No, but I took a seminar on bomb defusing during Special Forces training, so I have a basic knowledge. I say we buy a cheap laptop and tap into an unsecured Wi-Fi signal, let the internet teach us the rest. I can handle—"

He glanced up to see Camille's gaze fixed on the window. He followed her line of sight to their reflection and straightened. The air surrounding them crackled with the tension of too many things left unsaid.

The last time they stood before this table, he'd brought her to orgasm with his finger. He'd watched her glorious, supple body writhe and shudder with pleasure in his arms. She'd whispered his name when she came. Every time she came that night. Under her breath, like a prayer or a curse. He wondered if she was conscious of doing that, wondered if she'd say his name again right now if he lifted her to the table and sunk his tongue into her sweet flesh.

Closing his eyes, he swallowed hard as the searing need to possess her ignited within him. He harnessed it, but barely, and opened them again to find her watching him through the reflection, her expression anxious and her skin flushed pink.

"I see you, Camille."

She stopped breathing. Her eyes grew wider.

"You're trying to hide from me, but you can't. I see you."

Her fingers shot out to tinker nervously with the tracking device. He settled his hand over hers and she stilled.

It was her turn to close her eyes. She shifted her body weight to lean against him as her head tilted back to rest on his shoulder, exposing the slender length of her neck. He grazed her skin with closed lips, wanting to stake his claim on her body with his teeth. Holding himself in check.

She sucked in a ragged breath and tensed. Twisting her hand from under his, she broke free of his hold, walked from the table and picked up her bike helmet. "Let's get out of here." Her voice was hoarse and trembling. "We have a bomb to build and we're wasting time."

It took several hours of research and shopping to come up with a blueprint and materials, but it was disturbingly easy how two people—foreigners, at that—could make up their minds to build a bomb and, within the same day, gather everything they needed.

Because their dirt bike was lying in a ravine in the desert, they took a taxi to a used motorbike lot and bought a new one. They then bought a cheap laptop and tapped into an internet signal at a downtown coffeehouse. Without much searching, they found easy-to-follow instructions for creating an explosive with a remote detonator. Walmart and two different hardware stores supplied almost everything else, except dynamite.

For that, they waited until midnight to cruise by the numerous construction sites that dotted the landscape between La Paz and Pichilingue. At a partially erected resort being carved into a cliff along the bay, they found what they were looking for behind a short chain-link fence, next to a portable office trailer. Camille's flashlight zeroed in on a non-descript metal supply shed secured by a chain and padlock.

With newly purchased bolt cutters, Aaron clipped a hole in the fence and they slipped in. The debris-strewn construction zone showed no signs of life, no security teams or guard dogs, only silent excavators and bulldozers that lay like sleeping giants amid innumerable pallets of pavers and Dumpsters.

The supply shed was a cinch to open with the cutters. The crate of dynamite was clearly marked with bright red lettering. *¡Cuidad! ¡Explosivos!* Aaron carefully plucked five sticks from the shredded-paper packing filler and nestled them into a backpack.

They were back on board the *Happily Ever After* before the moon hit the mountain ridges to the west of the city. After anchoring the boat on the leeward coast of a tiny island, Aaron joined Camille at the kitchen table, poring over the directions and sorting through their purchases.

"This is going to take some time. I don't want to make a mistake and blow us up."

"Gotta say, I'm happy to hear that. Anyhow, you have two days until Tuesday's ferry departure. If you need even more time, the delivery truck usually skips Thursday's ferry and goes out again on Saturday. Do what you have to do to get it right because if we screw up this chance, Perez and his men will go so deep underground, we might never find Rosalia."

Saturday afternoon, six days after Camille began building the bomb, both the *Puerto Azul* and the suddenly cash-flush cocaptains of *Sea Dreamin',* a private yacht charter, embarked on the eighteen-hour journey across the Sea of Cortez, the former transporting an unmarked delivery truck most likely filled with weapons and the latter transporting a pair of American newlyweds to the next destination of their honeymoon...or so Aaron and Camille's story went.

The bomb had been ready for the Tuesday ferry, but the cartel delivery truck had been nowhere in sight. Terrified that this, their only lead, had dried up, on Saturday they waited on the bike near the ferry terminal with frayed nerves until they caught a first glimpse of the delivery truck. They watched it drive up the ferry ramp on Saturday at noon, then took off toward the cluster of yacht charters vying for tourist dollars near the public marina.

Once at sea, Camille and Aaron settled onto a bench on the back deck of the *Sea Dreamin'*. As the sun set over the Baja peninsula and the water faded from cerulean to onyx as the sky darkened, the air turned cool and crisp. Camille tensed her muscles against a shiver, then glanced at Aaron to gauge if he'd noticed, but he was staring at her hand clutching the seat cushion. With a twitch of movement, he reached for it.

Inhaling sharply, she leaped to her feet. "Dibs on first shower," she said lamely.

Curving his fingers into a tight fist, he rolled his knuckles against his thigh. When he opened his mouth to speak, Camille darted through the cabin door before he had the chance. Better to feel the hollow ache of cowardliness than face another painful argument about an affair that never should've happened in the first place.

Lighter and smaller than the ferry, the *Sea Dreamin'* beat the *Puerto Azul* to Mazatlán by several hours, arriving at the public dock around seven in the morning. Camille watched the yacht dock from the porthole above the chair she'd slept in. Aaron sat cross-legged on the bed, fully dressed, staring at the wall.

"Ready?" Camille asked.

He glanced sideways at her and gave a curt nod. "Let's get to work."

Like the ferry terminal in La Paz, the landing in Mazatlán boasted the repugnant stench of fishiness and gasoline, but as Mazatlán was a major tourist destination, the landing was at least double the size of La Paz and opened onto a pedestrian-friendly boardwalk that boasted an endless string of trinket shops, restaurants and motels.

Not knowing if the truck would be greeted by a cartel welcoming committee, they tucked into a narrow alley fifty yards from the still-empty ferry terminal and scanned the surrounding area for anything suspicious.

"Two men sitting in a parked car on the north end of the boardwalk," Aaron said under his breath.

Camille followed his gaze. The car in question was angled toward the ferry terminal. The men inside didn't speak to each other. Both wore blazers despite the heat. Maybe to hide their firearms, would be Camille's guess. No doubt about it, she and Aaron couldn't discount the possibility of the Cortez Cartel's presence. There could be any number of men whose job it was to escort the delivery truck to its destination. They could be watching from windows or disguised as vendors.

"We can't get any closer without revealing ourselves," she whispered.

Aaron slid the pack from her shoulder and dropped it to the ground between her legs. "Then we try to look inconspicuous while we wait for the ferry to arrive." Before she could protest, he snaked an arm around her waist and rolled to pin her against the alley wall with his body, dipping his face close to hers. "No one will pay us any mind if we seem otherwise occupied, and once the truck disappears into the city, all the eyes watching it will follow. Then we'll find a hotel room for the night."

It was a solid plan, even if Aaron's nearness aroused in her a dizzying, if unwanted, desire. As they waited, Camille fought to think of anything except Aaron, the solid heat of his body radiating against hers, the perspiration gathering between them, the rise and fall of their chests in time with each other.

Just when Camille feared she might combust if he touched her a moment longer, the ferry appeared on the horizon. Once it had docked, the cartel truck was among the first vehicles to exit. It made a right turn onto the frontage road lining the boardwalk. The suspicious car pulled away from its parking spot and followed.

They held their position until the ferry had emptied of cars and people and traffic died down, then Aaron pushed from the wall and smoothed a hand over his sweat-drenched shirt. Camille took her first deep breath in over an hour and slung the backpack on her shoulder. After a final scan for danger, they slipped onto the sunny boardwalk and sought refuge in the nearest motel.

The desk clerk at the Hacienda del Playa Sur was happy to furnish them with a harbor-view room for only twenty more dollars a night than one looking out on the city. After weeks of sleeping in boats, room thirty-two seemed enormous.

While Aaron freshened up in the bathroom, she tucked the backpack with the tracking device into the deepest dresser drawer along with the guns and gazed solemnly at the comfortable-looking queen-size bed. She hadn't slept in a bed since the night before her birthday in her continuing effort to keep her distance from Aaron. But, man, did this bed beckon to her today.

With a bracing sigh, she wrenched her gaze from the bed and settled near the window with binoculars to scope out the area, painfully aware that she and Aaron had nothing left to do but wait in the room together until the following afternoon's ferry departure.

By that evening, the room that had seemed so enormous on first arrival had shrunk to a shoebox. Restless with nerves, they went over the strategy for the following day and checked the weapons. Aaron called his ICE team, then Camille phoned her boss with an update. After that, they were back to square one.

When they bumped into each other the second time while prowling aimlessly around the room, Aaron laughed. "That's enough. I'm ordering dinner."

Aaron conversed in Spanish with someone on the hotel's phone. Camille slipped into the bathroom, ready for a long, hot shower to give her a needed break from being too close to Aaron.

When she emerged, her skin pink from the hot water, her hair damp, Aaron had two place settings arranged on the room's small round table. The mouthwatering smell of garlic and peppers tempted her nose. With a boyishly anxious expression, he presented the setup with a wave of his hand.

"This is the closest I can get to taking you out on a proper date."

Camille froze in the bathroom doorway. *Oh, no...*

"Wine?" he asked, gesturing to a bottle on the table.

"Aaron, no. I—"

He shrugged and pulled out a chair. "Save it, Camille. Have a seat."

The food did smell amazing. And she could really use a drink to settle her nerves. Besides, what was her alternative plan? To hide in the bathroom until Aaron went to sleep? Even she wasn't that big of a coward. Tentatively, she settled into the chair. Aaron pushed a plastic cup toward her and kept his eyes on her while she drank deeply.

On such an empty stomach as she had, she felt the relaxing effects of the alcohol in no time flat. Before she knew it, she was laughing at Aaron's jokes and digging into her hearty plate of chicken, beans and a sweet-corn tamale.

Over a second round of wine, they talked about their lives growing up. Camille felt compelled to share stories with him she'd never revealed to anyone else, even her sister. And she'd laughed more than she had in years.

When their plates and the wine bottle were empty, Aaron stood and flicked on the clock radio. A slow guitar song floated through the air. Aaron offered her his hand. "Shall we dance?"

Camille's gut clenched. "No, thank you. I'm awful. Really, it's not my thing."

"But it's mine." He bent until his nose brushed her cheek and whispered, "Let me dance with you, Camille. There's no one here but us."

She knew the wine was to blame, but nevertheless, she found herself taking his hand. "Just one dance."

He pulled her near and kept her there with a hand pressed to the small of her back. To her surprise, relaxing into his lead came naturally to her. For the first time in her life, she enjoyed dancing. She nestled into his neck, relishing the way his stubble grazed her cheek. She inhaled and was overcome by his intoxicating scent. It was a bitter memory that she once thought he smelled of clean laundry—pristine and simple, full of sunshine and golden happiness. Now she knew better.

This was the scent of the man who carried her when she could barely move for the pain in her leg, the scent that wrapped around her each night with the promise of safekeeping until dawn. This scent was her partner, matching her every movement throughout each dangerous step of their mission. It was the heady blend of sweat, soap and maleness swirled with the spice of him that she tasted when he kissed her.

She had never needed anything or anyone as much as she needed this man.

And, in her fear, she was wasting what precious time they had left together. What a fool she was not to savor every second she had with Aaron before she lost him to the world. She stroked his jaw and ran the pad of her thumb across his lower lip.

Aaron's arms tightened around her. He angled his head to study her face, his expression guarded. She couldn't blame him for that. She'd done an ace job of pushing him away.

She poured her need into a hungry look. "Kiss me. Please."

His hands crept to either side of her face, locking her in place as his lips descended. He froze an inch away. "If I kiss you, we're taking it all the way." His voice verged on angry. "Tomorrow morning, I wake up with you in my arms. No regrets, no picking a fight this time. You get in bed with me tonight, you're staying there."

She studied the severity of his features, marveling at the way intimacy brought out the darkest aspects of his personality. Determined to lighten the mood, she quirked an eyebrow at him and nodded toward the bed. "Think we'll make it all the way to the bed?"

His smile was ruthless. "Eventually."

Chapter 14

Camille allowed Aaron to back her into the wall with a blazing kiss. He loved the way she wrapped a leg around his waist, cradling his hardness between her thighs. He pressed into her, and she answered by rotating her hips, stroking him—a move he felt all the way to his toes.

With a groan of blissful agony, he broke from her mouth to kiss a trail down her throat, pausing with his lips over her pulse point, feeling the pounding of her heart. "Oh, baby. What I want to do to you…"

"What *you* want to do to me?" she teased, reaching between them to unsnap the top button of his jeans. "What about what *I* want to do to you?"

He rose and looked into her vivid green eyes, brushing her lower lip with his thumb. She really didn't get it yet, did she? The depth of his love for her. "You've already done it, Camille."

Inhaling sharply, she tucked her chin, averting her gaze. One day soon, he'd push the issue of their future, but for tonight, making love to her was enough. After brushing a kiss across her temple, he dropped his hands from her face and pushed her pants and panties down, then divested her of her shirt and bra.

He slid a hand behind the small of her back, arching her chest up as though in offering to him, and captured a nipple between his lips. He teased it into a taut point, then suckled it between his teeth. Camille moaned and wound her leg around him.

"I love the way your skin tastes," he murmured. "I need more."

He swept her off her feet and set her atop the dresser. Beginning at her ankles, he kissed the inside of her leg all the way up. She braced her hands in his hair with the first stroke of his tongue on her folds. His name rolled from her lips, over and over, a plea and a prayer. The most exquisite sound he'd ever heard, raw and real and full of the love she was so scared to admit. He reached up her side and twined his fingers with hers as she tipped over the edge with the sharp cry of release.

He stood, licking the wetness from his lips, the need to be inside her stringing him as tight as a rubber band stretched beyond its limits. Out of habit, he reached for the wallet in his back pocket, trembling with the need to get a condom on and surge into Camille's body, but his hand only found the cheap, canvas wallet he'd bought at the corner store their first night in La Paz.

Then it hit him. The box of condoms he'd purchased on the sly the day after he decided to seduce her was tucked in the yacht's dresser—unopened. The night he and Camille made love, using protection hadn't once crossed his mind. He'd never forgotten before, not in the seventeen years since losing his virginity. Then again, he'd never felt as crazy in love or as crazy with need as he had that night on the boat.

All he'd wanted was to make her his in a permanent, tangible way. Well, mission accomplished.

For all either of them knew, Camille could be pregnant.

He stared in wide-eyed wonder at her gorgeous body, open and wet—ready for him. And maybe, miraculously, carrying his child. He braced his hands against the dresser on either side of her thighs. "Camille, the first time...we didn't use protection."

The calm strength on her face sent a fresh wave of surprise through his body. This wasn't news to her.

"I know," she whispered, dragging a finger along his tensed jaw. "It's okay."

"I don't have a condom tonight either." Impossibly hard and trembling with barely leashed control, he waited for her response to his unspoken question, not trusting himself to even brush her leg before she granted him permission to proceed. If she told him to stop, to wait until a different night when they were more prepared—God help him—he'd bow to her wishes. They had a lifetime to explore each other's bodies, and that knowledge might have to be enough to sustain him tonight.

Hurt flashed in her eyes. Nodding, she sat back, folding her arms over her breasts. "You want to stop. All right."

Slipping his fingers into her clenched fists, he tugged her arms away from her body and held her hands in his. "Oh, baby, it's not like that. I'm all in. This is your choice."

Gradually, her fingers relaxed in his grip and the worry lines on her forehead eased. She met his gaze, her expression no longer hurt, but stubborn. "I'm not scared of the future anymore, not like I once was." She reached a hand between them, her fingernails rasping against his stomach, and grasped his erection, stroking it to full hardness. "I want this. I want you."

Seizing hold of her hips, he pulled her toward him until the tip of his hardness nestled at the entrance of her body.

"You have me, Camille." His voice, low and raw, surprised him. He sounded as desperate as he felt.

With his hands under her hips, he surged into her. She met his challenging pace, demanding it as hard as he was willing to give. When she opened her mouth in a moan, he claimed it with his tongue, wondering if she tasted the lingering spice of her arousal on his lips, as he did.

The moment he felt his release building, he slowed the rhythm of his thrusts and reached a hand between them. As his fingers worked, he dived into the skin of her neck with his teeth and lips until she tensed and stopped breathing. Then she shattered with violent intensity around him. He moved his hand to her hips and thrust deeply into her pulsing core. With a guttural sound, he spilled himself into her.

Wrapping her tightly in his arms, he lowered his head to her shoulder, breathing hard, reveling in the feel of their bodies joined together. She clung to him, locking her ankles around his waist, squeezing his still-pulsing erection inside her. He knew, unequivocally, that he'd never let her go.

By midday on Monday, they were in final stages of preparation to board the four o'clock ferry. Once they confirmed that the cartel truck had embarked, Aaron walked to the terminal to purchase tickets. Camille stayed behind to prep their weapons and perform a final check of the tracking device and explosives.

As she strapped on her ankle holster, Aaron walked through the hotel room door. "I love it when you go into warrior mode." He smacked her backside. "It's sexy as hell. Maybe you can wear that to bed sometime."

She smiled indulgently, relieved that his playful side had returned in full force. Anything but the intense, dead-serious man he became during sex. "Do you have our tickets?"

"Yep. Had to double the bribe I wanted to pay to the ticket guy, but it's done."

Camille hoisted her backpack onto her shoulder. "Let's get to work."

Camille and Aaron boarded the ferry with at least fifty other people. They each wore hats and black shirts they'd picked up that morning, all with tourist slogans, and sunglasses. Camille carried the backpack with the tracking device wrapped in a change of clothes, should she need a fresh disguise. Aaron had a backpack, too, with a change of clothes, a flashlight and duct tape, among other items.

Another bribe gained them entry without passports to validate the names on their tickets. Once past the ticket taker, they descended the stairs to the auto level and slipped to a section packed tightly with vehicles whose drivers had already left for the upper decks. The cartel delivery truck sat sandwiched between an RV and a minivan near the center of the boat.

The smell, a heady blend of gasoline and car exhaust, was nauseating. Camille breathed through her mouth but was supremely annoyed by the distracting urge to throw up.

Aaron tested each door they passed until he found one unlocked. They hustled into the backseat of a tiny, rusted gray car in case the ferry personnel did a final check that the level was cleared of people before locking it for the journey. Aaron lay on the floor of the car and Camille dropped on top of him. There they waited, embracing tightly, two bundles of white-hot nerves.

They heard their entombment one sound at a time, each echoing through the cavernous chamber with unmistakable clarity—the gears grinding as the ramp lifted, the clunk of the light switch turning off followed by the receding hum of the fluorescent bulbs into silence, the stairwell door sealing with a dull thud and, finally, the turn of the lock.

The rumble of the ferry motor rose to a roar. Low haunting moans and creaks told them the ship had started its trip across the sea.

Camille rose, blinking and looking around, waiting for her eyes to adjust. It was disorienting to realize there would be no adjustment—there wasn't even the barest hint of light for her eyes to filter. She grabbed her backpack, opened the door and stepped into the darkness.

Aaron emerged behind her and shut the door. Camille cringed as the sound reverberated around them, even though she knew there was no logical reason to be stealthy. They were alone.

Not far away, a second car door shut. Aaron's arms stiffened around Camille. A man cleared his throat. The faint light of a cell phone reflected off car windows two aisles over. They stood frozen, listening as the man, in heavily accented English, spoke the words running through Camille's head.

"Someone else is here."

It was probably a stowaway, someone too cheap to pay the price of a ferry ticket, someone like them who had hidden until the coast was clear. Just because Camille and Aaron lived in constant awareness of danger didn't mean the rest of the world operated that way, too.

Hard-soled boots tapped a steady, unhurried pace along the floor, growing louder and closer. A flashlight flipped on, scanning over the cars like a floodlight at a prison sweeps the exercise yard at night. Camille and Aaron ducked, hunching next to the car door. This was no stowaway.

Maybe the ferry company kept a security officer with the autos to guard against vandalism. If that were the case, the risk to Camille and Aaron was potentially more substantial than being trapped overnight with a half dozen cartel thugs. They were in the country illegally and each was packing multiple weapons...including enough dynamite to sink the ferry.

Whether they were dealing with ferry security or the Cortez Cartel was immaterial at the moment, though. At the unmistakable *chink-chink* of a pump action shotgun cocking, Aaron dug his fingers into Camille's arm and pulled her under the car.

Camille lay rigidly next to Aaron, listening to the blood pounding under her skin in syncopated rhythm with the boots clicking toward them along the metal floor.

She tucked the pack with the tracking device against the inside of the car's rear tire, either hiding the evidence or keeping it safe for later—however the next critical minutes played out. When the light of the flashlight was bright enough for her to see Aaron's silhouette on the floor next to her, she nudged him, then scooted out the other side of the car into the aisle. Aaron followed.

They crouched in the shadows, their guns pointed at the ground, their eyes fixated on the flashlight as it swung left and right, searching. Though it threatened to expose them, the flashlight gave Aaron and Camille the upper hand. They knew precisely where their opponent was, his direction and speed, whereas he could have no idea how many people he was dealing with or where they were.

Because the vehicles were laid out in a grid of even rows, Camille and Aaron's options were limited to either moving in the same direction as their pursuer—beating him to the rear wall of the auto level and potentially cornering themselves—or the opposite, which meant they had to walk right past the person searching for them.

Keeping low, Aaron stepped toward the light. It was the same choice Camille would have made. He kept the pace slow and steady. Camille moved lightly on the balls of her feet in a crouched position under the level of the car windows they passed.

When the light swept over the car they were behind, they molded themselves against the tires until the beam passed over the tops of their heads. They continued moving until they stood on the opposite side of a small pickup truck from the person searching for them.

Peering through the truck windows, they were finally able to size up their opponent—a single man, tall and bulky. It was impossible to tell if he wore a security uniform or if he was a cartel operative, but he was indeed carrying a shotgun that he steadied by tucking under his arm. It was an odd choice of weapon because it required two hands to steady and fire. He would have to either drop the flashlight or hold it in his mouth to shoot accurately.

Camille's confidence blossomed. They could get this guy. Piece of cake.

After the man walked away from them, Aaron rose and jogged to the end of the aisle, Camille trailing him closely. When Aaron stopped, the rubber sole of his sneaker squeaked. They dropped to their stomachs next to the bumper of the first car on the row. Aaron cursed under his breath.

The flashlight beam grew erratic, waving wildly, then bobbing as the man trotted in their direction. Aaron unzipped his pack. Camille's eyes had adjusted enough to the dimness that she could make out the roll of tape and shirt he removed.

In the barest whisper, they hashed out the details of Aaron's plan. He shoved the shirt into his pocket, wore the tape like a bracelet and picked up his gun. "Let's move."

They sprinted across the aisle the man was running on and ducked behind the nearest car. There were several feet of space between that car and the motor home behind it. Camille crept behind Aaron into the shadow between the two vehicles, completely concealed behind the height of the motor home, and concentrated on the beam of light as it grew brighter. The *clip-clop* of the man's shoes grew louder, closer.

She withdrew a D-volt battery from her pocket, one of two she'd grabbed in case the flashlight ran out of juice.

She threw it. It landed with a clink several cars in front of them. The beam of light swerved toward the noise as the man jogged nearer.

They waited until he passed them. Then they burst forth and slammed into him, crushing him against a car hood. Camille pressed her gun to his temple. There was no need to speak. He got her message loud and clear and raised his arms in surrender.

Aaron disarmed him and took the flashlight and cell phone. Their captive twisted around, trying to see who had accosted him, but Aaron was smart enough not to reveal their identities and shone the flashlight into the man's face. He jolted and closed his eyes against the brightness.

Aaron and Camille shared a questioning look. She didn't recognize the man. Could be a cartel operative, could be ferry security. Aaron tore a strip of tape and affixed it over the man's mouth. The T-shirt went over his head. He crossed the man's wrists behind him and secured them with tape.

They marched their captive to the old, gray beater they'd hidden in initially. Aaron shoved him into the front passenger seat and taped his still-blindfolded head and torso to the seatback, rendering him immobile from the waist up.

As an extra precaution, Camille snapped both the interior doorknobs off. Even if the guy managed to wiggle a hand free, he wouldn't be able to escape. The owner of the car would be in for a shock the next morning, but Camille and Aaron planned on being long gone by then—before whoever the man called on his cell phone had a chance to spot them.

She retrieved the pack from under the car and they worked their way to the delivery truck. They scooted along the ground on their backs until they were staring at the truck's filthy undercarriage. Aaron assumed flashlight duty while Camille searched for the perfect nook in the space between the frame and the floor of the truck bed, finding one such spot near the front wheel axle.

The explosives that had seemed unassuming as they sat in the pack felt volatile and deadly as she rested them on her chest. The dynamite sticks were bundled together with tape, then strapped to a 6-volt battery and topped with a cell-phone detonator and the tracking device. Once they'd secured Rosalia's safety, all Camille would need to do was dial that phone's number using the cell phone in her pocket and…*boom.*

Her hands, sweating and shaky with nerves, fumbled the duct tape Aaron handed her as she picked at its tacky edge, trying to get it started. Twice, she dropped it.

Aaron took the tape and pulled out a length. "We've got all night. Try to relax."

"There's dynamite sitting on my heart. I'm not going to relax."

"All right, then, let's get it over with."

Camille glanced sideways at him, then tucked the bomb above the axle. She wound the duct tape around the bomb and the frame over and over again until she was satisfied that no matter how many potholes the truck was bound to hit between the ferry terminal and the warehouse, the device wouldn't move or fall off.

Aaron jostled the device a bit to double-check her handiwork. "That's good enough. Let's find someplace to crash for the rest of the night."

He helped Camille up and used the flashlight to check on their captive, who had remained silent and unmoving in the car. He led the way to a pickup truck that gave them a clear view of the man should they point a beam of light his direction. Camille stepped over various tools and ropes in the truck bed and sat against the cab. Aaron settled next to her and slung an arm around her shoulders.

In less time than she would have liked, the flashlight flickered and dimmed, then went out. In the darkness, Camille and Aaron instinctively pulled closer together.

"I don't think we should use our other flashlight, especially since we don't have enough backup batteries anymore," he said. "It's going to be a long night and who knows why we might need them later."

"You're right. Good call."

Camille had never feared darkness. But here, in the guts of a rusty ship amid cars lined up like metal caskets, with the stomach-turning stench of car exhaust and the ghostly creaking of the ship joints, it took her only a few minutes to realize how terrible this journey would have been without Aaron. The weight of his arm around her, his fingers entwined with hers, gave her the strength to keep the shadows at bay.

He pushed his watch light on and checked the time. "Only fifteen hours to go. Wanna make out?" He planted a kiss on her nose. "Oops, missed your mouth. Let me try again."

He groped her face with his fingers, pretending he couldn't find her lips. When he poked her in the ear, Camille smiled in spite of herself.

"Aha," he exclaimed, pretending to find her mouth. She felt the smile on his lips when he kissed her, as though he found himself highly amusing.

"You're a silly man."

"Yes, but you secretly love that about me."

She started to chuckle, but panic, sudden and violent, hit her like a sucker punch to her gut. She struggled for composure, but her brain was spinning so fast out of control that she feared she might pass out.

"Camille, are you all right?"

"I'm fine. Just tired."

But she wasn't fine, and the pain had only just begun. Planting a tracking device and staging a dangerous rescue was a piece of cake compared to this. Oh, God, she really did have the worst luck in the world. Her whole damn life was one big cautionary tale.

At some point, and she wasn't sure when because she hadn't been paying close enough attention, she'd let her guard down. She knew better than to get emotional about her affair with a man who treated casual sex like a hobby, yet she'd done it anyway.

She'd fallen madly, eternally, head over heels in love with Aaron Montgomery.

She drew a silent gasp, desperate for air as an involuntary shiver rattled her spine.

Before he'd shone his bright light into her life, she lived as if alone on a distant, dark planet. When they first met, she found his good humor threatening, as though levity were a sign of weakness. It took two years and being taken hostage by a drug cartel, but Camille finally realized the immeasurable value of Aaron's optimism. She had no idea how she would survive without him.

When they took down Rodrigo Perez and their mission was over, her plan was to go on a grand adventure. She was supposed to figure out what made her happy. What if she knew what made her happy, but he wasn't hers to keep?

Registering her agitation, Aaron hauled her onto his lap. "You're shaking like a leaf. Are you sure you're okay?"

She huffed. "I guess I have to be."

"Do you think you could sleep? I'll watch over you." He pressed her head to his chest and stroked her hair.

His touch hurt. His ever-present chivalry hurt. She squeezed her eyes shut. She should push him away, start weaning herself from her dependence on him. Impossible. The weakling that she was, she'd cling to the brightest light in her life until she was forced back into the darkness.

That he would leave her was a given. She had nothing to hold him to her, no argument that could convince him to give her a chance. What was she supposed to say? *I'm broken and pessimistic and awkward, but love me anyway. I have no career, no prospects, nothing to offer you but my sorry self...but I need you. You're the only thing in this world that makes me happy. Maybe you would be happy with me, too.*

Yeah, right.

Yet even though they would go separate ways after their mission, their connections to Juliana and Jacob would link them forever. Aaron would always be in her life, at barbecues and birthday parties, weddings and funerals. She would have to endure the sight of him flirting and dancing. It had been painful enough watching him with other women before she realized she loved him.

Someday, maybe she'd be able to watch him with detached fondness, remembering the adventure they shared in Mexico.

Someday, maybe.

For now, though, it was time to figuratively smack some sense into herself. Once she rescued Rosalia, she'd have a lifetime to feel the heartache that came with loving the wrong person and watching him walk away. Until then, she had work to do.

She reached into her pocket and fingered the cell phone that was the key to finding Rosalia. To drown out the sounds and odor of the ferry, she tucked her face under Aaron's chin. She drank in his fresh, familiar scent and let his heartbeat lull her to sleep.

Aaron woke Camille as soon as the heavy metal door to the auto level opened. Grabbing their packs, they slunk over the side of the pickup and behind a motor home, where they stood until car owners filed in around them.

Camille's heart pounded against her ribs and her hands shook with adrenaline and stress as she thought about the next few critical minutes. They had to make it past the commercial port's armed guards and into a taxi. Not to mention the fact that the man they'd captured had tipped someone off over the phone about the presence of people in the auto level. She just prayed that whoever it was wasn't waiting to ambush them the minute they stepped off the boat.

Aaron rummaged through his backpack with a concerned look on his face, muttering about how he couldn't find his cell phone. Under the pretense that he left it in their cabin, they pushed through the throng of people pouring onto the auto level and up two flights of stairs to the pedestrian exit ramp.

They kept their heads down, walking fast. Camille could see a line of waiting taxis on the other side of the chain-link fence surrounding the port, past two armed security guards. Fifty yards to relative safety.

She scanned the crowd on the dock. No black sedans in sight, no Perez. No thug-looking cartel types at all, only families and businessmen, truckers and vacationers. They had this. They skirted a slow-moving family on the ramp and tucked behind a tall, overweight man.

The exit ramp gave way to solid ground. Camille and Aaron stayed with the crowd moving toward the exit. Only twenty yards to the taxis.

Holding her breath, she kept her face on her feet as she crossed paths with the guards. No one stopped her or Aaron. Aiming at a tiny, white hatchback taxi, she hastened her steps. Aaron outpaced her and piled into the backseat first to give directions to the driver in Spanish. Camille tugged her door, but something kept it from closing.

She looked up to see the barrel of a pistol in her face.

Carlos "Two Down" Reyes sat beside her, sneering as he shoved the gun against Camille's throat. A second man dropped into the front passenger seat, a gun trained on the driver, who put the car in gear and started down the road in the opposite direction from La Paz. Camille clutched Aaron's hand.

Two Down gave a wheezy laugh and ground the gun into

her skin. "Let me guess, *señorita*. You're the brains and he's the brawn of your little operation?"

"Wrong, dimwit," Aaron answered. "She's the brains and the brawn. I'm just the arm candy."

She glanced sideways at him and saw that his door hadn't latched and he held it steady with his other hand. A plan took root in her mind. It wasn't perfectly thought out, but it might be their only hope.

She waited until Two Down started chattering in Spanish to the man in the front passenger seat. Slowly she reached into her pocket for the cell-phone detonator and the scrap of paper with the code and transferred them to Aaron's hand.

His eyes grew questioning as he tucked the items into his jacket pocket.

"I know you'll come for me," she said in the barest whisper.

"What?"

The taxi slowed to maneuver over a speed bump.

"This is the only way," she said. She lunged at Two Down, deflecting his gun as she pushed Aaron out of the car with her feet. "Drive," she shouted at the driver. He stepped on the gas. Camille pulled Aaron's door shut as Two Down's gun connected with the top of her skull. She fought against unconsciousness, but a second blow landed on her head and she was out.

Chapter 15

Aaron inspected the bloody road rash on his arm in the yacht's bathroom mirror. "Dreyer? Montgomery."

"Did something go wrong when you planted the tracking device?"

"Device is in place, but Fisher's been taken." What he didn't bother to mention was that Camille finally managed to martyr herself. Stubborn, stubborn woman. If those men laid a hand on her, he'd blow the entire Baja Peninsula out of the water. "Patch me through to Santero. We're going in tonight."

"Fisher was kidnapped again by the Cortez Cartel? Are you sure?"

Aaron picked a bit of blacktop out of his skin and slammed it into the sink. "Do I sound confused?" He bit back the rest of the rant on the tip of his tongue, remembering too late that he was speaking to his superior.

"No, you don't. Take a breath, Montgomery. Flying off the handle isn't going to save her."

He scrubbed a hand over his mouth. "I know that, sir. But going after her as soon as humanly possible will."

"Roger that. I'll contact Santero and green-light his team."

"I want to be a part of her rescue."

"That's not a good idea," Dreyer said. "You're too emotionally invested for a matter this delicate."

Aaron sucked in a breath through gritted teeth. "She threw herself at the cartel so I could escape." *And she's the love of my life.* "I need to help get her back. Please."

Dreyer was silent for a beat. "We can't take a chance of this line being tapped or you being followed, so I'll have someone pick you up in four hours and bring you to ICE's secure location within the city."

"Thank you, sir."

He rattled off the first location that came to mind for a rendezvous point, then ended the call and looked at the bed he'd shared with Camille and the bathroom where he'd cut her hair. This would be the last time he saw the *Happily Ever After*. No matter what happened tonight with the rescue, he wouldn't be back.

He grabbed a backpack and tossed in the binder of ICE intel and the rest of the cash and weapons. He dumped the contents of the dresser drawers on the bed, checking for anything he might need or any incriminating evidence of their time there. Out tumbled the box of condoms.

With a huff, he picked it up and sat on the bed.

Funny how life was. In the past few weeks, he'd done and experienced terrible things. And yet, in Camille's arms, he'd found his life's purpose—to be accountable to and cherished by a woman. This one particular woman. All his years in pursuit of amusement—years of fast women, fast cars and fast sports—had been ineffective attempts to stave off the emptiness that came with a lack of purpose. Camille had given his life substance. She made him invincible.

And she was gone.

He set the box aside. The possibility of having a baby with the woman he loved was wonderful and terrifying, but hardly pertinent. Camille's life was in danger, if she wasn't dead already.

Please, God, don't let her be dead.

He flipped on the tracking device locator and watched a red blip on the map a good ten miles or more southeast of La Paz. The delivery truck had reached its destination. The only question was, had Camille been taken to the same place? Only one way to find out.

He slung the backpack over his shoulder and strode from the room. Knowing he'd go insane if he stayed stationary until the rendezvous, he decided to perform some preliminary surveillance.

Following the GPS coordinates from the tracking device along the road southeast of La Paz, he drove past the ferry terminal. The dirt roads became crude, the homes more dilapidated and sparse until there were no homes at all but endless miles of shrub and cacti-covered foothills.

Over a half hour southeast of the city, twenty estates rose up from the desolation and lined the mouth of the bay. Thick, barbed wire-topped walls of brick and plaster standing ten feet tall separated the properties from each other and the road. In case the cartel stronghold was located here, Aaron kept his distance. No need to tip off any guards to his presence.

The tracking device transmitted from within the fourth property to the right. Set far back from the gate was a massive two-story mansion. He doubted Rodrigo Perez could afford such luxury. This place had to belong to Alejandro Milán.

The entrance gate was a solid sheet of dark iron topped by as much barbed wire as the fence line. At least from the front and sides, the estate was impenetrable. Hopefully Milán wasn't as meticulous about the security of his backyard.

In a text to Dreyer, he entered the GPS coordinates and requested satellite photos. After using the phone to snap pictures of the entrance gate, he watched for signs of activity until the rendezvous time approached, but all was quiet. As he waited and watched, his thoughts slid to his last moments with Camille and the expression of courage and resolve on her face as she shoved him from the cab.

She was incomparable to any person he'd ever known—and he'd destroy any man who hurt her.

With a final glare at Milán's entrance gate, he retraced his route to the city, through the cobblestone side streets of downtown and up a steep grade into a suburban neighborhood, past the Gigante Market. A glance at his watch told him he had thirty minutes to spare. On a whim, he made a right turn on to Ana's street.

Her car was parked curbside. He idled the bike half a block down and observed the quiet street. He might be connecting dots that weren't there, but his instincts kept niggling at him that somehow Ana was involved with the cartel. He and Camille had too many run-ins with them while in contact with her. On the other hand, if she had an allegiance to Alejandro Milán or Rodrigo Perez, she could have killed them the night they stayed at her house.

A hand touched his shoulder. Drawing his 9 mm, he twisted toward it.

Ana stood next to him, flanked by three huge men holding firearms inside the flaps of their jackets.

"Aaron, what a wonderful surprise." She sounded pleasant and not at all rattled to be standing at gunpoint.

Aaron held his aim. "Who are they?"

"This is my brother, Ramón." She gestured to the most sharply dressed man of the three who looked to be in his early forties. "And these are a couple of our…friends. They are in town on business."

He tried to play it cool, but the proliferation of firepower made it a tough sell. "Nice to meet you all. How have you been, Ana?"

She indulged in a throaty chuckle, but she was only a facsimile of the sexy teacher who had sheltered them for a night. The inhumanity exuding from her now made Aaron's mouth go dry. It was either divine intervention or blind luck she hadn't murdered them when she had the chance. "I'm well. How is Camille?"

Something about the way she asked set Aaron's teeth on edge. Maybe it was the slight quirk of a smug grin on her lips or the blade-sharp glint in her eyes. But he was certain she knew Camille had been recaptured.

"She's fine."

Ana's eyes narrowed the tiniest bit. "I'm sure she is. What are you doing outside my apartment, waving a gun in my face?"

He held the gun steady. "I was in the neighborhood."

"How convenient for me. Shall we go inside before we're all arrested for carrying illegal firearms?"

"Sweet of you to offer, but I'm late for a meeting. I'll see you around."

Her brother and the other men pulled their guns out of their jackets and aimed at Aaron's chest. Aaron thought about the arsenal stashed in his backpack, but he'd never have time to even pull the pin on a grenade before the three men shot him.

"I wasn't offering you a choice," she said.

One of the men plucked Aaron's gun from his hand. The other dragged him off the bike and frisked him. Ramón relieved him of the backpack. He was pushed along behind Ana up the stairs to her apartment, with Ramón and the others pulling up the rear of the procession.

"Tell me," Aaron said as they walked. "Do you work for Rodrigo Perez?"

"Oh, God, no. Ramón works for my father, Antonio Vega."

Nothing Ana could've said would have surprised Aaron more. They reached the apartment and he gaped at her as the hulking men shoved him inside. Ramón entered last and closed the door.

"You're related to Gael Vega?" Aaron whispered in disbelief. "You're with the La Mérida Cartel?"

She perched on the arm of the sofa and gestured for Aaron to sit in a chair. "Very good. Gael is my uncle. Since he was arrested, there has been quite a jostling for control. If my brother and I can deliver La Paz to our father, he will gain my uncle's approval as his replacement and we will become the most powerful family in Mexico."

"I assumed you were behind the Cortez Cartel's ambush of Camille at the supermarket. But you're part of the La Mérida Cartel," Aaron said.

"La Paz is about to become La Mérida's most important territory. Why dirty our hands ridding it of nosy American law enforcement when Perez wants you dead, too? I tipped off his men anonymously."

Aaron pulled his face in surprise. "Why kill us? We were doing all the dirty work for you."

"Yes. It is true that Milán's stronghold in La Paz made it too risky for our family to move in. But you and Camille have been extremely helpful. As soon as I realized that, I sat back and enjoyed the show."

The mention of the reclusive cartel boss threw Aaron for another loop. "Is Milán here, in La Paz?"

Ramón laughed. "Not for long."

Ana ignored her brother. "With so many of his men murdered in the past few weeks, Milán's not happy with Rodrigo Perez. He flew in yesterday to handle the mess and has recalled Perez and his men to his estate, making this the perfect opportunity for us to relieve them all of their power."

Aaron swallowed hard. The only way he understood cartels to oust each other from power was through vicious, indiscriminate bloodshed. "His estate is southeast of La Paz?"

"Yes. At least until we blow it up tonight."

Oh, no. "Wait," he croaked. "I have a counteroffer."

Ana looked amused. "That's sweet, Aaron. But like Milán, you have outlived your usefulness."

Ramón shoved the butt of his gun in Aaron's ribs and hoisted him onto his feet.

No. He couldn't die now, not when he was so close to saving Camille, not when his death would destroy her chance of rescue tonight by the ICE unit. Pulling his arm from Ramón's grip, he squared his shoulders. "I disagree. Why not let me finish the job by taking down Milán and Perez? It's no risk to your family to let me try. If the Cortez Cartel kills me in the process, your hands are still clean."

"I'm not sure I see how that would be worthwhile for me and my family."

"Look, if you blow up Milán's estate tonight, you'll kill Camille—a decorated law enforcement officer—and Rodrigo Perez's kidnapped daughter who's an American citizen. I've already notified my bosses about Camille's recapture at Milán's property. And I've already notified them about you, Ana. If you kill me, Camille and Perez's daughter, you'll bring the wrath of the entire Unites States law enforcement down on the La Mérida Cartel. You know I'm right. Do you think your uncle will allow your father to lead the family after that?"

Judging by the clench of her jaw and the white of her knuckles, she heard his message loud and clear.

She placed a hand on Ramón's wrist and he lowered his weapon. Crossing her arms over her chest, she studied Aaron. "How long do you need?"

Aaron's heart pounded as his hope blossomed. "One day, that's all. Give me one day and I'll hand you the keys to the city."

With a nod, she opened her front door and held his backpack out to him. "One day. And if you fail, you and your precious Camille won't live to see day two." She ran her tongue over her lower lip. "Get out of here before I change my mind."

Chapter 16

Aaron did a quick roll call with the three firearms he'd concealed on his person for his meeting with Santero. No doubt about it, he trusted the guy, but stalking through the alleyways of La Paz at dusk carried its own inherent risks. And the confrontation with Ana had rattled him to the core. He would not be caught off guard again.

Unlike the last time he'd come to this abandoned, half-constructed building, tonight he wheeled the dirt bike inside and propped it along the wall, out of sight from the road. Santero hadn't arrived, which gave Aaron too much time to think. Too much time to remember. But, then, what had he expected, choosing this building as a rendezvous point?

He crouched along the far wall and smoothed a hand over the smear of dry blood. First time he'd ever stripped Camille of her clothes had been in this very spot, when he'd thought the blood saturating her jacket and shirt had been hers.

"Jesus Christ," came a harsh whisper from the alley. Aaron whirled, drawing his gun. "You better be in there,

Montgomery, because a rat the size of a freakin' dog just ran over my foot."

"I'm here."

Through the doorway walked a lean-muscled, scowling Latino man about Aaron's age.

"Diego Santero?" Aaron asked.

"In the flesh. You gonna shoot me?"

Aaron tucked the gun in his waistband. "Sorry. I'm a little on edge."

"Maybe it's this creepy place you picked for a meeting. Is that blood on the wall?"

"You said to choose somewhere quiet, and I know first-hand a person could spend hours here without drawing notice."

Santero held his hands up in mock surrender. "I'm just saying. The ambience sucks."

"My partner's been kidnapped, so excuse me if I don't give a damn about ambience."

Santero sniffed and stalked to the window, sinking his weight into his arms on the ledge as he stared at the alley outside. "Here's the deal. When those federal stiffs asked me to share my operation with Mr. Desert ICE himself, I nearly peed my pants laughing. I never share control of my jobs. You got that?" He pushed from the window and glared at Aaron.

"Absolutely." He got it, all right, but was having trouble syncing the image he'd formed in his head about a Latin-American agent named Diego Santero and the hostile, Jersey-accent-sporting jerk who'd shown up. "By federal stiffs, you mean Dreyer?"

"Freakin' Dreyer. He has the personality of drywall. The man talks like he's got his butt cheeks clenched all the time. What a piece of work."

"He's your boss." Probably the wrong thing to say because Santero got up in his face real quick.

"You got a problem with my opinion already, Montgomery? You want to get into it right here in the middle of this rathole?"

Yikes. Aaron flexed his fingers, squelching the urge to punch Santero in the jaw. "Nope."

"This is my extraction job," Santero continued, backing off. "I call the shots. You want to play like you're a real ICE agent, fine. But you'd better keep a cool head because if your bleeding heart interferes with me doing my job, you're out. Understood?"

Aaron wasn't the one blowing his top at the moment, but he wasn't going to point that out. "I'm good. Let's roll."

As if he had his mood on some sort of switch, Santero's face softened. He slapped Aaron on the back. Maybe the anger had been an act to test Aaron's ability to keep his emotions in check. "We'll ditch your bike, take my van."

Aaron nodded and started for the door.

"One more thing, Montgomery." He waited for Aaron to stop and look at him "We're going to get her back. That's my job. And I'm really, really good at it."

Diego pulled into the garage of a ramshackle house on the western edge of the city. The place didn't look much like a covert ops war room, but while in Mexico, Aaron had learned the hard way that nothing—and no one, for that matter—could be taken at face value.

They entered the house through a door in the garage. The front room was full of dusty furniture, the curtain wide open to the street out front. Behind the wall separating the front room from the kitchen, out of view from the exposed window, Thomas Dreyer stood in front of a room full of high-tech computer equipment.

Aaron recovered from the shock of seeing his boss and shook Dreyer's hand. "Didn't realize you were going to be here, sir."

Dreyer afforded him a terse nod. "ICE agents always have

each other's backs. That's the first rule you'll need to know now that you're on the job, Agent Montgomery."

Wait...did that mean... "You're bringing me on to the ICE unit?"

"Welcome to the Department of Homeland Security. Glad to have you aboard."

Santero coughed. "I think I threw up a little in my mouth, watching you two kiss each other's butts. Real freakin' heartwarming. How about we get on with the mission?" He stalked down a hallway.

Aaron followed. He'd suddenly been hired for his dream job, something he'd worked himself to the bone for the past year to achieve, and he felt nothing. Job titles, Santero's belligerence—none of it mattered until Camille was safe in his arms again. Then maybe, just maybe, he'd sock Santero in the jaw like he wanted to and celebrate his new career.

In the middle of the back bedroom, four men and a woman leaned over a table covered in satellite photographs. A familiar face popped up, smiling. "Aaron!" Nicholas Wells strode over and shook his hand. "Good to see you alive and well, man."

"That would be thanks to Camille. She saved my hide more than once down here."

"Sounds like it's time to turn the tables and do a little saving of our own."

"Got that right. How'd you and Dreyer get down here so fast?"

Wells shrugged. "ICE sprung for the private jet, seeing as how we're going to bring down two cartel kingpins and rescue a missing child and a kidnapped police officer."

"Yeah, they're good like that."

Santero commanded the attention of the room. "Montgomery, you already know Wells. Here's the rest of my crew— Ryan Reitano, John Witter, Rory Alderman and Alicia Troy. We've got two choppers standing by on a Navy vessel on the Pacific side of Baja. You've already been to the target property, but check out these satellite images we pulled about an hour ago. Sorriest security system I've ever seen."

From an aerial view, the Milán estate wasn't so much a fortress as an opulent mansion set close to the water and padded with thick tropical landscape. With its multiple balconies, brickwork and innumerable windows, the house would be simple enough to breach once they got past the gates and the guards. The backyard boasted a white sand beach and a private dock with three impressive boats tied to it—a yacht larger than the *Happily Ever After,* a motorboat built for speed and a midsize fishing boat.

Troy tapped her finger on the photograph near the image of a huge, turquoise swimming pool. "Two armed guards are all we can pick out in the back. Two more in the front."

The white delivery truck sat in the circular driveway on the property's west side. "There's enough space on the front driveway to chopper down," Aaron said.

Santero shook off the idea. "Not the right call for a hostage situation. If the tangos get wind of us, they could slit the hostages' throats before we cross the property line."

He tossed a photograph on top of the pile, the image zoomed back to encompass the landscape and water for a good ten miles in either direction, and pointed to the water edging the first property on the north side, four estates from their target. "We'll swim in from here. Once we've breached the shore, we'll follow the fence line of Milán's property to the foliage under the south-side balcony. From there, subduing the tangos will be as easy as plinking cows with a BB gun. To get in that position, though, we'll need a diversion for the guards."

Aaron took Camille's cell-phone detonator out of his pocket and set it on the table. "That, I can handle."

Camille woke in darkness. Lying prone on the hard ground, she rolled to her side with a wince. Her head was killing her.

The layer of crust on her lips tasted like blood. Not surprising.

She squirmed her way to a seated position with her back resting against the wall to take stock of the situation.

Damn. Once again she was a cartel hostage, imprisoned in an empty, cell-like room. This time, her hands had been bound in front of her with zip ties. This time, she was without Aaron or a rusty chair or even a window.

She was clothed, which was a bonus, because the air was cold and pungent with the smell of dirt. As if maybe she was in a basement...or a dungeon. She looked at the bare ceiling, made visible by the thin strip of light streaming under the door, and hissed through the pain when the back of her head hit the wall.

She'd done the right thing, pushing Aaron from the taxi. If they'd both been captured, they'd both be trapped in this room with little hope of rescuing either themselves or Rosalia. If they'd both jumped from the car, the chance of one of them getting shot would've been too great. But with Aaron free, he could get help from the ICE unit standing by to rescue Rosalia, which was all that mattered to Camille. They could follow the tracking device to the cartel's stronghold, save the little girl and shut down the cartel.

Whether or not that's where Camille had been taken remained to be seen. Either way, sitting around waiting for help wasn't in her blood.

She tested the zip tie around her wrists. Made of heavy-duty nylon cable, it had been tightened to a snug fit that cut into her skin.

No problem.

She crawled to the thick metal door and listened for a sound of approach but heard none. Satisfied that she had at least a couple of minutes to work, she tucked her knee up close to her body and untied a shoelace.

One of the first lessons she'd learned as a Special Forces

cop was of the innumerable benefits of paracord, the super-strong nylon rope used for parachutes and a million other tactical applications. Jacob taught her that the simplest way to guarantee a ready supply was to use it as shoelaces. Military-grade paracord wasn't sold at every corner store, especially in Mexico. But Walmart carried the next best thing, a braided polyester utility cord. She'd swapped both her and Aaron's regular laces for it—and thank goodness she had because it was about to break her out of prison.

Once she'd cleared the lace from the shoe, she tied simple loop knots at either end and secured one loop around her shoe. She threaded the cord through the zip tie, then slipped the second loop over her other shoe. Voilà. She had herself a genuine friction saw.

Rocking back to balance on her butt, she pedaled her feet in the air, moving the cable fast over the zip tie like a saw. It snapped within seconds.

With her ear to the door again, she listened. No sound. Excellent.

She made quick work of lacing her shoe and stood, turning in a slow circle. Now for the hard part. How the hell was she going to break free from a square cinder-block room with a solid metal door? She looked at the broken zip tie in her hand and had her answer.

Five minutes later, she'd finessed the lock open and eased into a dark, quiet hallway.

Voices filtered through the ceiling, adding evidence to her theory that she'd been locked in a basement. It'd be helpful to know for certain, but what she needed, more than anything, was a lethal weapon. At the moment, all she had at her disposal was the broken zip tie. While it had made a great lock pick, and would probably work well as a shiv, unless she was within striking distance of someone's artery or eye, she'd need to come up with something that packed a bigger punch.

Somewhere nearby, she heard a faint sneeze. A child's sneeze.

Step by quiet, deliberate step, she approached the nearest door and put her ear to it.

Minutes ticked by. The talking continued upstairs, but Camille was starting to wonder if perhaps it was a television.

She moved to the second door and listened. After a minute, something inside the room rustled. Then, with the voice of a little girl, the person in the room began to sing "Twinkle, Twinkle, Little Star."

Camille sagged with relief against the door. Rosalia. And she was alive and within her reach. She put her ear to the metal again to double-check that the girl was alone. The worst that could happen would be for her to walk in on Rosalia sitting with her father.

When she was certain Rosalia was alone, she turned the knob and pushed the door open.

Rosalia sat in the middle of a small bed covered in a faded yellow quilt. She had a doll in her hands and seemed to be making it dance to the song she sang. When she saw Camille, she startled.

"It's okay, Rosalia. I'm a friend of your mom."

Rosalia blinked up at her, considering. Camille closed the door and looked around. This room had no window either and was as cold as Camille's holding cell had been. A pile of clothes sat in one corner and a few toys lined the wall. A bucket sat near the door and one whiff told Camille it had been used as a toilet. At least the bastards had provided Rosalia with a bed.

"I remember you," Rosalia finally said. "From my papa's other house. Your hair's different now. It's brown like mine."

Camille sat on the bed. It wiggled as though the frame was barely holding together. "Yeah. My friend helped me with it."

"It's pretty."

She took the girl's hand and smiled. "Oh, Rosalia. I am so happy to see you. What do you say we find a way out of this place so I can get you back to your mommy?"

"Yes, please."

"Stand over by your clothes for a minute. I need to get something from under your bed."

With Rosalia out of the way, Camille wiggled a metal bar of the bed frame until it snapped off. Still not as effective as a gun, but a hundred times better than a zip tie. Despite that, she tucked the tie into her pocket. One never knew when a shiv might come in handy.

Fifty yards from shore, water slapped at Aaron's face as he treaded water in the Sea of Cortez alongside the rest of the ICE unit. The wet suit offered some protection, but even in Mexico's tropical climate, the winter sea was frigid and choppy. Hopefully he wouldn't need to fire his gun anytime soon because he was losing the fine motor functioning of his fingers.

They'd stopped one property over from their target to assess the situation.

Milán's backyard was decoratively lit, with each palm tree and flowering bush individually illuminated by spotlights on the ground. The windows of the house were dark with drawn drapes, save for one on the first floor, which glowed with the light of a television behind sheer white curtains.

The swimming pool threw its artificial blue-green light around the patio and lit the two guards from the bottom up, highlighting their legs, weapons and necks as they stood between the pool and the house, facing toward the sea. Their hands rested on rifles that hung at gut level in front of them.

Aaron's objective was to position himself along the dock between the yacht and the speedboat. Then he'd blow up the delivery truck.

When Santero gave the go-ahead signal, Aaron inhaled deeply and swam as fast as he could toward the boats. Though his lungs burned, he pushed himself to remain underwater until his arm hit the yacht. After another big breath, he submerged again and traced his way to the right, along the curve of the hull, until he hit the slimy underbelly of the dock between the two boats.

Santero had matched him stroke for stroke in the water. As they'd agreed on, Dreyer, Wells and the rest of the team were farther back, behind the yacht.

Aaron slung the waterproof pack he'd carried onto the dock, but his fingers fumbled with the tiny zipper. Santero *tsk*ed impatiently. After a few clumsy attempts, Aaron shoved his fingers in his mouth to warm them. As soon as the painful sting of life returned to them, he tried again and this time, he succeeded.

He powered up the cell phone and dialed the numbers he'd memorized.

A deafening boom resounded all around them as a fire-ball belched into the sky, momentarily transforming night to day. Splinters of wood and debris rained over the house.

In sync with Santero, Aaron plunged underwater, swam under the dock and kept going all the way to the far edge of the property. He was aware of the rest of the team doing the same but kept his focus on moving through the water as fast as humanly possible.

A quick scan told him the guards had gone to investigate and the backyard was empty. On Santero's command, they swam ashore and sprinted into the shadows of the fence that ran along the side of the house. The air on land felt down-right balmy against Aaron's face and hands compared to the water, and his limbs rapidly regained full functionality. They divided into two groups, with one team scaling the balcony on the south side and the other on the north. Aaron had been paired with Santero, Alderman and Dreyer.

Distant shouting and the footfalls of men running inside the house spoke to the effectiveness of Aaron's diversion, but he didn't stop until he reached the side yard, out of view of the backyard and the flames peeking over the rooftop from the burning truck. If he had to guess, he'd say the explosion had set the front of the house on fire, too. It had taken her days of meticulous engineering, but Camille had built a top-notch bomb.

He hoped she heard it and knew he'd come for her.

Camille stood over a semiconscious Two Down, whom she'd trussed with the curtain cord. Not that he'd be getting up anytime soon with the whack to the head she'd doled out. Staring down the barrel of Two Down's gun, she allowed herself a small grin of triumph until, over the blare of the television, she heard Rosalia whimper from behind the sofa.

Sadness swept through Camille as she thought of all the violent acts the little girl had witnessed. By incapacitating Two Down in front of Rosalia, she'd added to her terrible memories. But Camille couldn't think of any alternative ways to get them out of the house safely.

A rumble like a powerful earthquake shook the house. The air grew thick with smoke, as though the house was on fire. Bits of drywall crumbled from the wall. Books tumbled from shelves. Camille dived over Rosalia, shielding the little girl's trembling body with her own. "It's okay, sweetie. I've got you."

She held tight to Rosalia, and though it seemed improbable, a tendril of hope flared to life. Could it be that Aaron had come for them?

Men's voices hollered from the second floor along with the sounds of people running, reacting, assessing the damage. Camille pressed into the back of the sofa as two men darted through the room, shouting in Spanish.

"What were those men saying?" Camille asked in a whisper.

Rosalia looked at her with frightened eyes. "I don't know. Something about a Mérida cartel. Something bad. I want my mommy."

La Mérida Cartel? Camille blinked, wrapping her mind around a new possibility. Maybe Aaron and his ICE unit weren't responsible for the explosion and the house was under attack from a whole new enemy. Maybe Rosalia and Camille had landed in the middle of a war between two rival crime families.

"Time to go, sweetie. Give me your hand."

Rosalia shook her head but otherwise didn't budge.

Camille grabbed a lamp and ran to the window. Beyond the yard, three boats sat tied to a dock. Maybe one of them had keys in its ignition.

She heaved the lamp through the window, then swept Rosalia into her arms and ran.

Aaron, Dreyer, Alderman and Santero shot grappling hooks onto the balcony and yanked the scaling ropes to set the hooks against the wrought-iron rail. Given his experience as a rock climber, Aaron reached the balcony ledge first. The sliding glass door was closed, and the room beyond was dark and curtained. He ungracefully threw himself over the rail and onto the floor. The others followed.

They pulled their rifles around from their backs. These weren't M16s like Aaron had used before, but M4 Carbine semiautomatics designed not to choke up after an ocean swim. He loved the way the instrument felt in his hands, solid and precise and deadly.

Santero unhooked a stun grenade from his utility belt. Aaron had protested the plan to use a stun grenade until Dreyer assured him they were used all the time in combat when civilians were present. The flash and bang temporarily disoriented people inside the blasting range but didn't cause any pain or permanent damage. While Aaron hated the idea of Camille and Rosalia being within a blasting range of any kind, to get them out of Milán and Perez's grasp safely, he'd agreed to the grenade use.

Dreyer shattered the glass from the door with the butt of his rifle.

"Hooyah," Santero shouted. He plucked the pin out and shoved the grenade through the hole.

An earsplitting bang and bright flash lit up the room beyond. Aaron heard a similar boom from the balcony on the north side. Both teams breached the house simultaneously.

A man wearing blue pinstriped pajamas staggered toward the hallway door on the opposite side of the room.

"Freeze," Santero boomed.

Dreyer and Alderman rushed the guy and slammed him to the wall. Aaron held position at the hall door and heard the snap of cuffs being applied.

"Look familiar?" Santero asked.

"Milán," Dreyer answered.

Well, well. The big man himself.

Grabbing hold of Milán's shirt, Dreyer shook him hard. "Where are they, the woman and the girl you kidnapped?"

"Screw you."

Santero edged toward the door. "We don't have time for this. Alderman, lock him to the bathroom plumbing while we clear the building and search for Fisher—"

He stopped talking at the sound of footsteps in the hallway. Aaron aimed his M4 at the door as it opened.

Rodrigo Perez stood in the hall, barefoot and shirtless. Black tattoos wrapped around his neck and down his torso and arms like a spreading fungus. A single scar sliced through the cleft of his chin. His bloodshot eyes zeroed in on Aaron. "You," he growled.

Aaron squeezed the trigger.

Like a frightened rabbit, Perez turned tail and took off.

Aaron squeezed off another round, then sprinted after him.

The world around him fell away. His breathing was even, his mind calm. No way was this rabbit going to disappear down a hole and escape. Perez had a head start and knowledge of the house's layout, but there was infinite power in being the man in pursuit instead of the one running for his life.

With each footfall through the hallway, then down a spiral staircase, Aaron felt his control of the situation hardening like steel in his spine. He tasted vengeance on his tongue, tasted his anticipation of the moment he overpowered Perez. Every horror Aaron and Camille had gone through in Mexico traced back to this man. The hurt, the fear, the constant struggle for survival—all because of Perez.

At the bottom of the stairs, Perez veered right across a living room with a blaring television and through a swinging door. Aaron trailed, shouldering through the door and into the kitchen. Perez skidded to a stop in front of a knife block on the far side of a rectangular island.

Aaron hit the island, leaned into it and fired. The shot pierced Perez's shoulder. With a grunt, Perez swung around and threw a knife in Aaron's direction.

Aaron ducked.

Adrenaline must have numbed Perez's pain because he seized the opportunity to bolt from the kitchen, a long-handled knife in his hand.

Aaron fired a round in his direction. He pushed through the door and ran across the living room in time to see Perez disappear out the back of the house through a broken window, the knife flashing in his hand. What an odd weapon of choice. Surely the man had an arsenal of firepower at his disposal, so why a knife?

Santero and Dreyer caught up with him. "Wells and his team secured the basement. No sign of Fisher and the girl, but they found evidence that they might be on the property. They're searching the rest of the house."

Aaron gritted his teeth. *Come on, Camille. Where are you?*

One thing at a time. For now, he had a rabbit to catch. He snapped a fresh magazine into his gun. "Perez jumped out the window. But he's not going to get very far."

"We've got your back," Dreyer said, running behind him.

They leaped from the house to see Perez had made it as far as the dock.

"The bastard better not have a key to one of those boats," Santero muttered, squeezing off a handful of rounds.

Perez leaped onto the deck of the yacht and disappeared from view.

"Cover me," Aaron said, running.

The yacht's cabin door opened. Perez must've been crawling because Aaron couldn't see anybody. He cleared the rail of the boat and nosed his gun around the doorframe. "Nowhere to go from here, Perez. Come out with your hands above your head."

"Think again," said Perez from inside the cabin.

Santero and Dreyer moved into position on either side of the door. Santero pulled another stun grenade from his belt and handed it to Aaron. With a signal, Santero kicked the door open and Aaron tossed the grenade in.

Flash. Boom.

Aaron rushed in. Dreyer flicked on the light.

Perez stood amid the smoke near the stateroom door, his eyes watery and blinking, a sneer on his lips. His knife rested across Camille's throat.

Chapter 17

Aaron held himself in check but his entire body quivered with fury and dread. He visualized capping Perez in the forehead, but he couldn't take the chance of hitting Camille or Rosalia, who huddled under the table. Three assault rifles against one knife were great odds, except that Perez had to already know he was going down, so threatening his life with their guns was useless. Unless another variable entered the equation, their strategy boiled down to reaction time and opportunity.

Like the day they were kidnapped, Aaron met Camille's gaze with a look of fear that she countered with one of iron-willed determination. She gave him an almost imperceptible nod of warning.

"Aaron, I'm okay. He threatened Rosalia. I had to do something. Get her out of here."

Santero slid into line with Aaron, his rifle trained on Perez, too. "Dreyer, that's all you. Take the girl to the chopper."

Perez rattled the knife against Camille's throat. A trickle of blood dripped onto her shirt. "Rosalia belongs with me, her father. I can give her more than her *puta* of a mother, living in a roach-infested apartment. With me, she's part of Mexico's royalty, with the money and privilege that comes with my power."

Aaron forced his gaze from Camille to Perez's knife hand. It was suddenly clear why Perez wore gloves and why a knife was his weapon of choice.

El Ocho. What a fitting moniker. Rodrigo Perez had no thumbs.

Dreyer waited for Perez to finish his tirade, then crouched. "Come on, Rosalia. I'm going to take you back to California. Your mom's waiting for you there. She misses you."

"Get behind me, *mija*," Perez bit out. "Don't listen to these strangers. Listen to your papa."

Rosalia covered her ears and wailed louder. "I'm scared."

"I know you're scared, sweetie," Camille said. "But remember what I told you? I'm going to take you to your mama. You have to trust me. Go with Agent Dreyer."

"No, *mija*. They're lying to you. All of them."

After a long, soulful look at her father, Rosalia crawled into Dreyer's arms. "I want my mommy."

Cooing words of comfort, Dreyer whisked her from the room.

Fearing Perez's fury at his daughter's choice, Aaron took a step nearer, training his sights on Perez's elbow. "Stop moving that knife, Perez, or I'm going to move it for you."

Camille's hand flexed, catching Aaron's attention. Then her thumb retracted, as if she was counting down from five.

Whatever plan she's cooking up, she'd better not get herself killed.

Next to Aaron, Santero adjusted the grip on his rifle, his gaze on Camille's hand same as Aaron's was.

Three...two...one...

In a blur of movement, she grabbed the wrist of Perez's knife hand and locked her other hand around his elbow, seizing control of his arm and knife. She ducked under the elbow she held and pivoted, thrusting his wrist at his gut, stabbing him. As Aaron and Santero rushed forward, Perez released the knife with a howl of pain.

Camille twisted it farther in, then kicked him in the groin. He staggered, pulling the knife from his body.

Shouting a warning, Aaron lunged for her. She ducked and the knife sailed over her head.

Santero squeezed a round off and hit Perez between the eyes. He stumbled backward through the stateroom door and crumpled to the ground.

Aaron fell as the knife connected with his chest. Pain blossomed from his torso to his limbs. He fought to keep his eyes focused and his breathing even.

"Aaron!" Camille knelt next to him. She ripped the wet-suit material from the wound site.

"Hurts. Is it deep?"

"No. Looks like the wet suit stopped it."

He angled his head and saw she was right. The knife had penetrated only about a half inch into his skin, hindered by the thick material and the zipper. He gnashed his teeth together and yanked it out with a grunt. Camille pressed a towel to his chest to staunch the blood flow.

"Camille," he said. "I have to tell you something."

"What is it?"

He took her hand. "I am sick and tired of people trying to kill you. It's getting on my nerves."

She let out a half laugh, half cry. "You're not the only one. How about we don't let it happen again?"

"Deal."

Santero wandered over from his inspection of Perez's body. He toed Aaron's foot. "Hey, you sure this broad needed us to rescue her? She seemed to be doing a bang-up job on her own."

Aaron smiled through the pain. "Knowing Camille, she would've been just fine without us."

"You know that's not true," she said quietly.

He winked.

Santero cleared his throat. "So, Fisher—Camille—those were quite the moves you put to that scumbag. Impressive. And totally hot. I've got to stay in Mexico to take care of this Vega cartel family Montgomery gave us a lead on, but how about next time I'm in the States I take you to dinner?"

Nice try, pal. Cringing in discomfort, Aaron pushed himself up and stood nose-to-nose with Santero.

"What?" Santero said. "I don't see you staking a claim on her."

"Staking a claim on me?" Camille spluttered.

"I got this, babe." Aaron wound back and slammed his fist into Santero's jaw...and it was as sweet as he'd imagined. "You're a chauvinistic jackass, Santero. No woman likes to be treated like a piece of meat. You ought to learn some respect."

Santero rubbed his chin and regarded Aaron with a look of grudging admiration. "Guess that settles that." He nodded toward the door. "Choppers are out front. Let's roll."

The morning after their chopper flight to a Navy vessel in the international waters of the Pacific, Aaron found Camille sitting on deck, staring at the line of the horizon over the ocean with stormy eyes. His favorite worry wrinkle slashed a deep line between her eyebrows and her fidgety fingers twisted the bottom hem of her shirt.

He'd come to talk with her about their future, to help her realize that she loved him as much as he loved her, but clearly she already had some heavy stuff on her mind.

She spared Aaron only a glance as he sat beside her.

"I'm going to quit my job on the police force."

He cradled her hand in his. "Good."

"I'm not sure what my next career will be, but I wasn't meant to be cooped up behind a desk."

"No, you weren't."

"I'm going to take your advice and start over, build a new life for myself. A happy life. I want to get my passport and see the world."

Sounded great to him. He didn't think Dreyer would have any qualms about granting Aaron a nice, long vacation before he started his new position as an ICE agent. "Where do you want to travel first?"

She shrugged. "Maybe I'll just pick a direction and go."

Aaron pulled his face back. He was missing something. "You mean *we.*"

"Excuse me?"

"*We'll* pick a direction and go."

"Oh, Aaron, no." Her voice was heavy with sadness. "You don't have to act like you want something more from me. I knew all along it was temporary."

What the hell was she trying to say? "What, exactly, do you think is going to happen between us once we get to San Diego?"

She looked distraught. "You know what'll happen. You'll get on with your life and I'll get on with mine." She hesitated, then pressed on. "If you're insinuating that you'd like to keep the option open for an occasional fling, then I'm sorry. I don't think I have it in me to be friends with benefits, or whatever it's called these days."

"Friends with benefits?" Now he was insulted. He pulled his face back. "You think I want us to be friends with benefits?"

"You're right. Of course you don't." Her eyes brimmed with moisture she tried to hide by turning her back to him.

The tears were like a slap to Aaron's face. His anger

evaporated. "This whole time, you thought I was going to leave you the first chance I got?"

"You will. Monogamy's not your gig, remember? And anyway, I'd never pressure you. You have to know that. Even if it turns out I'm pregnant, you don't have to worry. I won't ask you for anything."

"What?"

Her outrageous assessment of the situation took his breath away. If he didn't know her so well, he'd be insulted. But know her, he did. He should have guessed that instead of trying to convince her she was in love with him, it was going to be the other way around for Little Miss Martyr.

He took her head in his hands and forced her to meet his eyes. "Camille, I could no more walk away from you than I could walk away from myself."

The twisting of her shirt grew more agitated.

"Talk to me."

Tears spilled over her cheeks. "You are a wonderful man, the best I've ever met. You shouldn't settle for someone less than perfect—someone who's broken."

"Broken?"

"My leg…"

Aaron shook his head at her flimsy logic. "I think I can work around a five-year-old gunshot wound."

"Post-traumatic stress disorder. My hand shakes."

"Unless you're worried you won't be able to shoot me should you get it in your mind to, I hardly see how that matters." He grinned in an effort to coax her to do the same, but she wasn't having any of it.

"You could have any woman you want."

"Damn right I can. I do, right here. What's the real problem, Camille?"

She screwed her lips up. "I can't make you happy. If you settled for me because you were trying to do the right thing, you'd grow to resent me."

"Don't I get to decide what makes me happy?"

"Yes, but—"

"So if I say the idea of spending the rest of my life with you makes me happy, are you going to tell me I'm wrong?"

"But—"

He put a finger to her lips. "Hear me out, okay? You and me, we belong together. All that eternal bachelor stuff I used to think I wanted? I was so stupid. I had no idea how perfect and wonderful it felt to really love someone the way I love you."

"You love me?"

Stubborn woman. "More than I ever thought it was possible to love another human being."

"You love me?" Camille sat as though frozen, her eyes glazed over, weighing this new information. "Why didn't you tell me so sooner?"

Aaron chuckled, relieved she believed him, and hauled her onto his lap. "I didn't want to scare you away. Please say you'll let me take care of you for the rest of your life. Please tell me you can love me back."

She smiled and stroked his jaw. Good. They were getting somewhere.

"These past two years, I wrote off my feelings for you as physical attraction," she said. "But that night in the ferry, after we planted the bomb, I couldn't deny it anymore. I realized I loved you, but I thought it would take a miracle for you to have feelings for me."

He scoffed. "It wasn't a miracle. It was inevitable. The first time I saw you kicking some serious cartel ass, I was a goner."

"Aaron, are you sure about this? I don't think I'd survive if you changed your mind."

He'd never been more sure of anything in his life. "Don't be so afraid, my proud warrior. I'm not going to hurt you." He poured his love into a tender kiss.

* * *

Four days later, the water of the San Diego bay glittered in the afternoon sun as the Navy vessel docked. The journey home had been uneventful. Two days into their trip, word came from ICE headquarters that Santero and his team had delivered five members of the Vega family to Mexican authorities, including Ana and Ramón. They faced a laundry list of charges in their own country, as well as extradition to the United States.

While a piece of Aaron halfheartedly wished he could've assisted in the Vega family's capture, all he really wanted to do for the time being was lay low with Camille—and maybe, if luck was on his side, the baby they'd created.

After a first emotional night, Rosalia had settled into the idea that she was returning home. Camille's own mothering instincts had taken over and she had doted on her new charge with calm self-assurance. On the phone with her boss, she'd lobbied hard for a discreet reunion between Rosalia and her mother, but Aaron had a feeling that was impossible. Rosalia's kidnapping and rescue was far too sensational a story to be ignored by the ravenous American press.

After much debate, Aaron and Camille alerted Jacob and Juliana to their arrival, but not their parents. Camille, who especially hated being the center of attention, wanted only to hand Rosalia off to her mother, meet Jacob and Juliana's new baby and drop off the grid for a while. They owed ICE and the police innumerable hours of debriefing, but certainly they were entitled to some downtime after spending weeks on the run.

Two unmarked police cars, an ambulance and at least a dozen people met them at the marina. A woman with auburn hair and a stout build pushed through the crowd and reached the boat first.

"Mama!" Rosalia shouted with glee.

Camille lifted her over the edge. They watched as mother and daughter cried and embraced.

Aaron scanned the crowd for Jacob and found him standing in the shade with the petite brunette who had captured his heart. Juliana was clutching a pink bundle in her arms.

Jacob looked content, if not a little worn-out, standing with his wife and child. Juliana looked very little like Camille, who had at least three inches on her younger sibling and was far more voluptuous. Both shared the same nose and green eyes, but it was easy to see how Camille had settled into the role of the protective, take-charge big sister.

He squeezed Camille's hand. "Ready?"

"Ready." She took a breath, squared her shoulders and marched from the dock.

Aaron followed, marveling at her. She radiated self-efficiency and unflagging strength, but he knew better. He was keenly aware of the privilege it was to be the only man allowed to see her at her most vulnerable and he loved her all the more for it.

Camille and Juliana reached each other first, embracing and cooing over the baby. Aaron and Jacob hugged and slapped each other's backs. Then the teasing began.

"Is that a perm you've got, bro?" Jacob asked. "And brown, too? I've never seen your hair that dark and shaggy before."

"Hell, I thought it was Halloween with those dark circles you've got under your eyes. You put makeup on to get them that way or did you give up on sleeping?"

Jacob wiped a hand over his face. "I tell you what, this parenting stuff really knocks it out of you. Just you wait. Someday you'll know what I mean."

Aaron smiled. They'd need a pregnancy test to confirm it, but in the past few days, the signs all pointed to the possibility that a new life had taken root the first time he and Camille made love.

Camille eased the little pink bundle from Juliana's arms into her own and stole away to a bench. "Hello, Alana Rose. I'm your aunt Camille."

Aaron watched her with a wistful smile. "Did you bring it?" he whispered to Jacob.

Jacob rummaged in his jacket and handed Aaron his car keys. "Brought your car, like you wanted, but something tells me this is what you're really asking about." He slipped a small black velvet box into Aaron's hand.

"That's what I meant. Thank you."

Jacob eyed him curiously. "Your mom was pretty suspicious when I asked for your grandmother's wedding ring. She made me promise to tell you to use it wisely."

Aaron grinned even wider. "No worries there."

"Are you sure about this? Last I heard, you two hated each other."

"Yeah, that was way too much work. This —" Aaron rattled the box "—is much easier than pretending to hate her ever was."

"I bet it is. Your mom would have liked to see you today, you know. She and your dad have been worried."

"We wanted as little fanfare as possible. And I was afraid once my mom got a hold of me, she might never let go. Pass it on to them that we'll be back soon. This is just something we have to do for a while."

At that moment, Juliana rushed by. "Camille, are you crying?"

Aaron's head snapped up to see Camille holding the baby with fat tears streaming down her cheeks. Jacob snagged Juliana's arm. "Let Aaron take care of her."

Juliana responded, but Aaron didn't hear what she said. He strode to Camille, scooped both her and the baby into his arms and sat on the bench. He spared a glance and a wink at a stunned Juliana, who stood frozen, gawking at them openmouthed.

Between sniffles, Camille said dejectedly, "I'm crying, Aaron. I can't stop."

"It's okay to cry, babe."

"Not for me."

Aaron chuckled and tucked some stray hairs behind her ear. He'd loved her blond hair, but he'd take her any way she came. And the chocolate-brown was starting to grow on him. "It's been one heck of a ride." Then he whispered for her ears only, "Not to mention that your hormones are all out of whack."

Despite her tears, she deviously arched a brow at him. "My sister will strangle us for not telling her right away."

"She and my mom will have to fight each other for the honor. But you and I deserve a little time to enjoy the news privately. We've earned that much, I think."

"Yes, we have." She swiped at the wetness on her cheeks.

"Glad I found you both." It was one of the officers who'd escorted Rosalia's mom to the boat. "Sit tight because reporters are on the way. You're national heroes now. Your faces are going to be all over the news."

Aaron cringed. "Thanks for the warning." After the officer walked away, he kissed Camille's cheek. "I don't know about you, but being a national hero isn't on my agenda today."

"Uh, no."

"Then that's our cue to leave. Let me hold my goddaughter once before we go." He placed Camille on her feet and took the baby. "Hey, Alana, your aunt Camille and I are going to take off, so don't do anything interesting until we get back, okay? Take good care of your mommy and daddy for us."

With a kiss to her chubby, soft cheek, he handed her to Juliana, whose mouth still hung wide open. He kissed the top of Juliana's head and punched Jacob on the shoulder.

Then he offered Camille his hand. "Will you come with me, Camille?"

She crossed her arms and smiled indulgently at him. "Where to?"

He twirled his car keys. "Thought we'd just pick a direction and go."

That garnered a laugh from her as she entwined her fingers with his. Making her laugh was probably his favorite thing in the world. He planned to spend a lot of time in the future perfecting the art.

"How about north," she suggested. "I'm sure they've got great doctors in San Francisco."

"Doctors?" Juliana asked. "Why do you need a doctor? Are you hurt?"

Camille answered with a dismissive wave of her hand. "Don't worry about it."

Aaron caught a suspicious look from Jacob. He ignored it. "North it is."

Jacob shook his head, chuckling. "Have fun, you two."

Camille gave Juliana a one-armed hug. Juliana stammered and gestured at Aaron and Camille's joined hands. "When did you and Aaron...um... You look happy, Cam. You're glowing."

"I'll tell you about it soon, but we need to hit the road before the news vans show up."

Aaron smiled at her. "Ready to ride off into the sunset, babe?"

"Ready." Camille gave Jacob a quick hug, then walked with Aaron toward the parking lot.

"Not sure how you'd feel about the idea, but I've got the sudden urge to buy a boat."

Camille laughed. "Funny you should mention it. Me, too."

"You know, *Blondie* would make a terrific boat name."

She shook her head. "It would, but I think we should name it after the boat we fell in love on. What did you say before—it pretty much sums up our whole experience in Mexico?"

"At the time, I was being sarcastic."

"True, but *Happily Ever After* isn't such a big joke to me anymore. In fact, I'd say it's just about perfect."

* * * * *

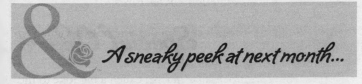

A sneaky peek at next month...

INTRIGUE...

BREATHTAKING ROMANTIC SUSPENSE

My wish list for next month's titles...

In stores from 15th March 2013:

☐ Soldier Under Siege – Elle Kennedy

& Hostage Midwife – Cassie Miles

☐ Deadly Sight – Cindy Dees

& The Awakening – Jana DeLeon

☐ A Widow's Guilty Secret – Marie Ferrarella

& Colton Showdown – Marie Ferrarella

☐ Beyond Valour – Lindsay McKenna

Available at WHSmith, Tesco, Asda, Eason, Amazon and Apple

Just can't wait?

Visit us Online

You can buy our books online a month before they hit the shops! **www.millsandboon.co.uk**

0313/46

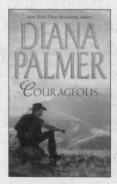